BY VAISHNAVI PATEL

Kaikeyi
Goddess of the River
Ten Incarnations of Rebellion

TEN
INCARNATIONS
OF
REBELLION

TEN INCARNATIONS OF REBELLION

a novel

VAISHNAVI PATEL

BALLANTINE BOOKS

NEW YORK

Ballantine Books
An imprint of Random House
A division of Penguin Random House LLC
1745 Broadway, New York, NY 10019
randomhousebooks.com
penguinrandomhouse.com

Copyright © 2025 by Vaishnavi Patel
Map copyright © 2025 by David Lindroth Inc.

Hardback ISBN 978-0-593-87476-9
Ebook ISBN 978-0-593-87477-6

Printed in the United States of America on acid-free paper

1st Printing

FIRST EDITION

Book design by Mary A. Wirth

The authorized representative in the EU for product safety and compliance is
Penguin Random House Ireland, Morrison Chambers, 32 Nassau Street,
Dublin D02 YH68, Ireland. https://eu-contact.penguin.ie

To the freedom fighters

PREFACE

Ten Incarnations of Rebellion is an alternate history, imagining an independence movement that might have been had the British Empire's freedom-suppressing tactics been more successfully employed in India. The book departs from history in the 1910s, and many of our timeline's foremost Indian freedom fighters are murdered in the next decades. The novel takes place in a still-colonized 1960s version of Mumbai, rife with militarized restrictions and cultural repression, that has been renamed Kingston and bears only a passing resemblance to the city of today. The events of this book are not history; for those interested in exploring India's freedom movement, I have included a list of further reading at the end of this book.

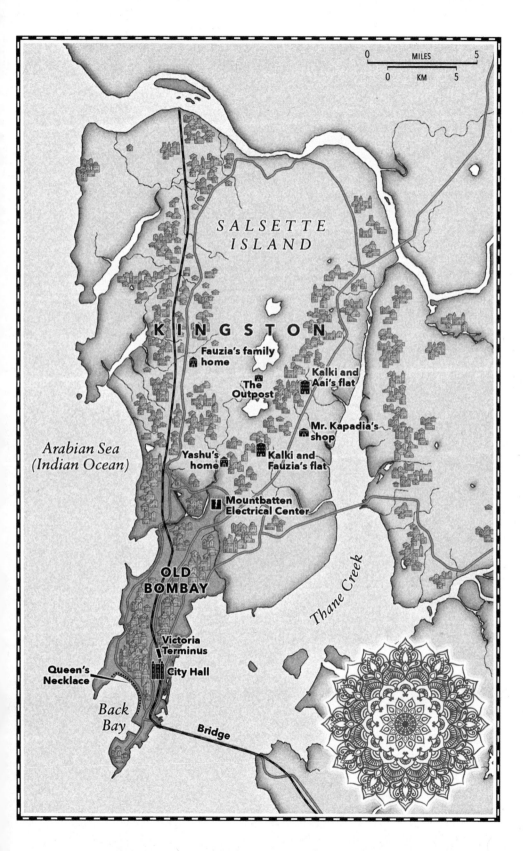

TEN
INCARNATIONS
OF
REBELLION

1

MATSYA, FISH

I learned how to hope at nineteen.

It started with a song. I did not, could not, know what was to come—the blood that would stain the streets, the fire that would fill the skies, the scars that would carve our souls—but even if I had, still I would have chosen it. Still I would have set myself on the path of rebellion.

On a windy March day in 1962, I pulled on my best and newest frock, a long navy-blue gown that Aai and I had commissioned from the local tailor. The high-waisted bust loosened into draped pleats, embroidered with silver sequins, and the sleeves went down to my elbows, pretty and modest. British styles often took some years to come to India, so the trend here had probably already gone out of fashion on their island. But I could not wear anything else, for saris or lehengas were not considered formal enough for British events.

The pointed heels were my least favorite part of the outfit, as they looked painful and felt worse. But Aai had insisted on buying them for my "promising career," and so I reluctantly slipped on the heels and staggered out of the flat. No matter what the British had done to my Baba, Aai was proud that I had been selected as one of the token students attending the chancellor's annual education night, a glittery affair meant to help philanthropists and educators feel better about the British project in India.

I had not told her my plan for the night. She would not have approved.

The headmaster had given me fare for a rickshaw, so I flagged one down and directed the driver to go to City Hall. He looked surprised but did not question it. After all, it was over an hour's ride from our neighborhood in Kingston, the Indian section covering the north of Salsette Island, to Old Bombay, the British peninsula of Salsette that had once been the southern tip of the Seven Islands. He would earn a good fare.

As we traveled toward southern Kingston, the homes became progressively nicer, the streets cleaner, the shops pricier. Here, the richest Indians could own their land—or at least rent it in ninety-nine-year terms from the British, who were the true owners of the isle. I passed by my school, which was twenty minutes by rickshaw but over an hour by the chain of buses and walking I usually undertook. Without fanfare, we crossed the invisible dividing line into Bombay. It was the first time in my memory I had left Kingston. The fare to Bombay was out of the question, and there was no reason to go anyway. I was almost disappointed, at first, for the homes here looked worse than the homes in Kingston. They were small, crowded, dilapidated.

But the deeper we traveled into Bombay, the nicer things got, and I realized—just as the richest Indians lived next to the British, the poorest British lived next to the Indians. As the buildings became more ornate, the clothes changed too; suddenly it appeared that every man was wearing a suit. People were out and about, not preparing for a curfew that discouraged leaving home after work for fear of getting caught outside after hours. I leaned my head out of the window to observe, glad that it was still March, before the muggy heat enveloped the city and melted even the tar on the roads. So this was how the British lived. The raucous colors of Kingston were nowhere to be seen, replaced by an unrelenting gray dullness.

As we approached downtown, the rickshawala asked, "Madam, can you spare ten more minutes?"

"Why? Is there a disturbance up ahead?"

"Nothing like that. I want to take an alternate route," he said. "No extra charge."

I had left early, so I figured it didn't matter much. "Yes, whatever way you think is best."

"This is best," he assured me. We drove for a little while longer, rounded the curve, and—

"Queen's Necklace," the rickshawala declared proudly.

I gasped before I could stop myself. We stood at one end of Back Bay, the southernmost bay of Salsette. In the setting sun, an arc of streetlights connected us to the other side of the bay in an unbroken chain of golden pearls, more striking than I had ever imagined. The Old Bombay skyline stretched ahead of us, and with it, the promise of this city.

He drove us down Marine Drive. For a moment we too were a part of the Queen's Necklace, the blurred, ever-moving lights that formed the string connecting each pearl. My lips stretched into a smile, but my shoulders tensed. The contradiction of it all—the British lights creating true splendor—made my head hurt.

Finally, we reached my destination. City Hall was beautiful. Far more beautiful than I had expected, and far more beautiful than it deserved to be. A century ago, just after the Sepoy Mutiny, Indian laborers built this palace out of marble, with columns of white and gray adorning the outside. The steps leading up to the doors were nearly pristine, despite the fact that the city never was. It appeared as though every light in the building was on. I supposed electricity rations wouldn't apply to those doing the rationing.

For the first time, I doubted my plan.

I had wanted to refuse the headmaster's invitation. What kind of daughter was I, to kiss the boots of those who drove my Baba from my home? It had been over a decade since I last saw him, and my memories of him were fraying at the edges. But when I told my mother, she said, "Of course you will go!" Then she hugged me tight and whispered, "Do you think they don't still watch us? Do you think they do not monitor us for odd behavior? I did not raise an idiot, Kalki. We must not do anything to raise their suspicions. You cannot refuse their invitation." She made a good point, and I hated it.

That night I tossed and turned, not knowing what I should do. I tried to remember Baba, his favorite song. I could hear his voice in the back of my mind, singing, but the words were lost. *Vande mataram* . . . and then nothing. What would he want me to do? That was when it hit me. The songs my Baba sang were long banned, the public's copies collected and burned. Nobody alive would dare sing them, if they remembered them at all. But City Hall would have them, I was sure, because the British loved their paperwork.

Now, looking up at the soaring white columns and marble doors, I wondered how I would possibly search their files. How would I even know where to look? If they had the power to build this place, then they certainly could prevent me from ever reaching my target. But it was too late to turn back.

I squared my shoulders and climbed the steps slowly, hitching my dress up so I wouldn't fall. A guard at the door checked off my name and gestured me into a lobby even more breathtaking than the outside. Above me, a tapered dome curved gracefully, adorned with glittering stones and brightly colored paint. Busts of men lined the edges of the room, and a banner reading "1962 Kingston Education Summit" hung above a small stage. The people in the great hall were equally gorgeous. For a moment, I felt awe toward them; the women's dresses utterly eclipsed mine, and I had never seen men's suits as crisp or dark. I felt vastly underdressed, the embroidery on my dress faded and plain in comparison.

Of course, most of the people in the room were British. I spotted a few Indians scattered among them, but they were obviously there for the same reason I was, to be the chancellor of Kingston's tokens. Servers, all of them Indian, ducked in and out of the crowd. I did not spot Yashu, my good friend who was supposed to be in attendance with me.

As I took all this in, a British woman approached me. "What is your name?" she asked.

"Kalki Divekar, madam," I said, wondering why she was talking to me.

"And which school are you from?"

"I'm from the Clarke Young Women's Academy, madam."

"That's a great school for your people," she told me, as if I didn't already know. "The Clarke family is so esteemed. You must be proud to go to a school bearing their name."

"Thank you," I forced out.

"We are so glad you could be here tonight. Please, get some food and mingle. Many of the people here will want to speak with you. Your perspective is so important for the work we do. The chancellor will start his remarks in an hour or so."

I tried to hide my total shock. But she seemed sincere, as if she really did believe my perspective was *important*. I suppressed a wild urge to laugh.

The woman put her hands on my shoulders and gave me a little push forward, as if I were a bullock cart that just needed to get started. I stumbled into the crowd. True to what she had said, people began turning to talk to me.

"So, what do your parents do?" a mustachioed man asked me.

"My mother is an assistant to a doctor, sir," I replied, omitting the fact that her "assisting" work consisted of sorting files, sanitizing supplies, and organizing rooms more than providing medical care. "My father—isn't with us anymore."

"Did he die?" the man asked thoughtlessly. In a way, in this moment, he owned me. Disobedience and disrespect were punishable offenses. Numbness crept into my heart.

"No, sir, he left us," I said quietly.

The man clicked his tongue and said to his friend, "These Indians. If they want better for themselves, then why do they abandon their families?" My cheeks darkened in instinctual shame, but either they couldn't tell or they didn't care. To me, he said, "Don't you agree? I am sure you wish your father had stayed with you, poor dear."

"So how does your mom afford the academy?" his friend asked before I could answer.

"I receive a scholarship," I replied.

"You must be so grateful." The man's mustache wiggled when he spoke, and I focused on it to distract myself from my rising ire.

"I am, sir."

"Well, good, good. You are a fine young woman. What will you do when you finish?"

I wondered for a moment what to say, then decided honesty was easiest. "I am hoping to go to junior college. I am trying to save money, but it is quite expensive."

"Nonsense! Junior college is made to be affordable for people like you."

"Tuition is a bit high for my mother alone," I clarified, hoping for an end to the conversation. I resisted the urge to walk away, knowing no good came of blatant disrespect.

"Perhaps you should get a job," he suggested.

"I have a job, sir," I said. "I work with my mother, but I can only work on the weekends. I am a student."

He turned away with a disapproving sound, and I took my chance to escape, darting toward the entrance in the hope of finding Yashu. I should have known, though, that Yashu would find me.

Even when we first met some six years ago, she had been the one to approach me as I sat with my only friend in the world, Fauzia, on a wooden bench in the schoolyard. Yashu's posture was ramrod straight, like something out of a manual, and she ate with a fork and knife rather than her hands. For almost a week, Fauzia and I thought a popular girl had deigned to sit with us and make stilted conversation, until we learned from whispers that she had just joined another classroom in our grade and nobody would speak to her because they thought her caste made her "dirty." We would never have guessed that she had faced such trials from the way she invited herself in, and knowing it only made us like her more.

I felt a tap on the shoulder and spun around to find Yashu, flushed and beaming. Her maroon dress was as plain as mine, but she looked radiant. Her hair shone in a thick braid, and her dark skin glowed in the light of the room.

"This is amazing," she said, grabbing my arm. "I can't believe we got invited." She tilted her head. "You're doing that face. The one you do when you're unhappy because you just lost a debate but you're trying to hide it."

I pulled her toward a dark corner. "These people are insufferable." Now, in the safety of Yashu's company, I was starting to feel some indignation over the conversation I had just muddled through.

"These people are the best of them," she whispered, eyes darting around to make sure we were not overheard. "Being petulant will only hurt us."

"Their opinions are fixed," I said. "What's the point of us being here? We're just performing. I don't understand how you can enjoy it."

"Look in the mirror before accusing them of fixed opinions," Yashu snapped. "I'm the first in my family to be in school past ten years of age, and now I am eighteen and graduating from Clarke Academy! I don't have to love the goray, but I'm not so self-centered as to spurn them for some stupid pettiness. They're better than what we had before." She stepped away from me, pasting a smile on her lips as she spun toward the crowd, leaving me to gape at the fact that she had used a Marathi word in the middle of City Hall. Yashu had never given any indication she was disobedient. She was always the first to fall in line. But how well did I really know her, and how much of her was an act?

I stood in the corner for a few minutes, awkwardly twisting my hands in my dress, until I was saved by the start of the program. The ushers passed out little booklets that laid out the order of speeches. The program was two hours in length, and I saw one Indian name in the whole program, a woman who worked at a school in Old Bombay teaching Indian geography. *See?* I could imagine the British saying. *If they work hard, they're rewarded, treated as equals.*

I scanned the crowd for Yashu, intending to push my way through the throng to find her and apologize. Instead, I found myself crushed by bodies trying to get closer to the stage and the speakers. I was suddenly claustrophobic, almost gasping for air. I needed to get out. Now was the time to make my move.

I slowly moved back toward the edge of the crowd, nervous that someone would notice me, but nobody cared. At one end of the room shone a brightly lit hallway. I spotted Yashu nearby, but I didn't want to drag her into this. I tugged off my heels so I could move silently and went down the hallway, then turned a corner into another, longer hallway. Each room was clearly labeled in the British fashion: "Office of the Census"; "Mr. S. Ratkins, Chief of Bombay Census"; "Office of Civil Supplies."

I had no idea how I would find my way back as I got farther into the maze of City Hall, but some instinct pulled me onward through the twists and turns. Finally, I reached a room with a sign proclaiming "Office of Media." Through the door's small window, huge floor-to-ceiling file cabinets, black with silver handles, gleamed in the low light. I felt certain in my soul that I had reached my destination.

From the end of the corridor, I heard footsteps. I tried to push open the door, but the doorknob wouldn't budge. Aai had left me a safety pin under my collar "in case of emergency," and I drew it with shaking fingers. As the steps got louder, I inserted the pin in the lock and wiggled it desperately, like Baba had taught me long ago, until the lock clicked and I fell through into the filing room. As quickly as I dared, I closed the door and hid in the nearest corner. My pulse thundered in my ears.

The footsteps passed me without incident, and only when I could no longer hear them did I turn toward the cabinets. I knew I did not have long. I wrenched open the closest cabinet and squinted at the machine-printed label on the box inside. "*The Times,* London, 1958–1959." Was this storage of British propaganda? My heart sank. That would be useless to me.

Methodically, I opened drawer after drawer, until I came to one that was a bit harder to wriggle free. Inside was a large label proclaiming the files to be "Contraband—Music" and then smaller folders each labeled with a letter of the alphabet. Though I knew I was looking for *v*, I was too nervous to look directly at it. As I paged through song after song, it became more obvious that the attempt to keep contraband from us had been very successful. Most of these songs were benign, too—about love for the country, or the pride and strength of our people—yet I had never heard them.

At last, I got to *v*, my heartbeat roaring in my ears. I needn't have worried. The first file was labeled "Vande Mataram." I lifted the pages out of the folder, fingers trembling, and read the lyrics. Somewhere clear in my memory, the song began to play.

I WAS CREEPING into the Kingston night for the very first time on my Baba's shoulders, clinging to him like a monkey. I was a small child at all of five, and he was strong despite being older than most other fathers I knew. He inched his way down the risers outside our modest flat, feet silent against the metal. My mind was bursting with questions, but I held my tongue, because even at five years old, I knew the severity of curfew.

A full moon hung low and ripe in the sky, lighting our way. Baba slipped down alleyways, hugging the shadowed walls, weaving in and out of streets as though he had a map that connected our building and the water. The roar of the ocean, once a distant sound, grew louder and louder, like a rakshasa in one of my storybooks, hungry for little girls.

Somehow, we encountered no patrols and no other people. I did not think it odd at the time, but I learned many years later that Baba had bribed a friend who made tea for a police station to reveal the exact patrol routes for the full moon. Soon, we had arrived at a small forest. Baba walked a path I could not see, humming to himself, until we rounded a corner and suddenly, through a gap between two trees, I could see it. The ocean.

To my eye, it went on forever. The crash of the waves against the sand filled my ears. I understood why all the other gods feared Varuna, god of the sea. Of course, this wasn't the true unexposed ocean at the other side of our island, but the inlet of Thane Creek, the bridge that connected us to the mainland invisible against the dark sky. But I did not know this then; the geography of Kingston had not yet imprinted on my heart.

I couldn't see Baba's face, but my fingertips clung to his cheeks, so I knew when his lips pulled into a smile. He pried my hands off of him and gently let me down, holding my hand and walking with me toward the waves.

"Baba!" I wailed. "Baba, don't go in!"

"Shh," he whispered. "Do not be afraid."

I let go of him as he waded into the water, jumping back as a wave tried to lick my feet. He turned back. "Come, beti."

I shook my head, covering my ears. "I want Aai!"

"I'm here," Baba said softly. "There's nothing to be afraid of. Everyone has to learn how to swim. We're safe here."

There was nothing safe about this monster. I took another step back, and Baba gave a tired sigh. I relaxed, thinking he was giving up. Then he lunged forward, scooping me up in his arms and walking me into the ocean as I shrieked and flailed. I could feel him start to loosen his hold on me and my limbs became leaden as he lowered me into the water.

Then my Baba was singing. He hummed the familiar tune around the house often, but now he sang it outright. I could barely hear him as a wave splashed over my face. I gasped for breath, then gagged on brackish water. In time, the familiarity of the tune calmed me slightly, and I became more malleable against him.

"Shasya shyamalam." His voice lilted upward as he tugged at my arms, which were clenched tightly around his waist. "Mataram," he crooned as he cradled me. "Vande mataram."

My Baba, I realized, was standing only waist-deep in the water, firm and solid as ever. He started to move my body in a rocking motion with the waves, his arms hooked around me as I relaxed, feeling the rhythm of the ocean. The sea pushed me up, lifting my body to the surface. In that moment, the water turned from a rakshasa into my Aai, loving and gentle.

I squinted up at Baba through stinging eyes, and he gently tapped one of my feet, then the other, alternating back and forth until I understood his meaning. I kicked one foot half-heartedly, surprised when that slight movement propelled me forward. Experimentally, I kicked my other leg much harder, and Baba moved with me.

"Keep going, Kalki," my Baba whispered. "I'm here. I have you." He held me up in the warm water as I kicked and kicked, continuing to murmur to me. "When I was younger than you, my Baba brought me here. We used to be able to swim and fish and watch the flamingos, until the British decided to block off this area. But this place is yours, and you must not forget it."

I wanted to listen to him, to keep playing in these waters, but already I could feel myself getting tired. With the exhaustion came a renewed fear of submergence, even though my Baba's hands were holding me up. Fortunately, my Baba understood, and lifted me out of the water and back onto his shoulders, wading through the shallows. "That's enough for today," he said. "We will come back. I promise."

I shivered slightly. "In the morning?"

"We cannot come in the morning. Maybe . . ." He trailed off, although his words were already beyond my understanding. "You will learn to love the nighttime," he said at last. "It is when the best work happens."

Then, from farther down the beach, pinpricks of light crested a sandy hill. Baba made a harsh noise under his breath and darted forward to the nearby line of trees we had come from. It took him three quick steps to make it under the cover. He tried to push forward into the thicket, but stopped suddenly when a branch cracked beneath his foot. Something brushed against my back, and I whimpered. Baba flinched at the noises.

"Kalki, I need you to be very, very quiet," he said, his voice barely a whisper. "I'm going to hold you in my arms now," he continued as he shifted us around to hold me against his chest. "Be very still. If . . . if we are found, you must pretend to be asleep. You must pretend you don't know how we got here. Nod if you understand."

I nodded. My heart was racing. Baba slowly, carefully crouched down, peering between the branches. I did the same. The lights were getting closer, but Baba was looking straight ahead as if petrified. I followed his gaze and saw our footprints in the sand.

It came to me in a flash of understanding. We weren't supposed to be here. If they followed the footprints toward us, we would be found breaking the law. And even a five-year-old knew that we could not break the law.

Baba clutched me to him, his grip uncomfortably tight. The lights were now mere meters away from the path. Wind whipped through the trees, and I managed not to cry out. And then something miraculous happened. A wave roared forward over the placid waters, splashing onto our footprints, the spray hitting us in the trees.

The lights flashed over smooth sand. "I don't see anything," came a crisply accented voice.

The wind picked up again, and the trees bent in it, branches swaying in front of us. "This patch of forest is impassable," another voice said.

"Must have been a trick of the light," said the first.

"Better to be safe. You know how these people are about their full moons."

The branches relented, lifting in time for us to see two British officers walking away, backs to us, leaving firm prints on the sand. Baba was shaking, holding me tight, but in his arms, surrounded by warmth, I knew I was safe.

When the officers had been out of sight for many minutes, Baba at last rose to his feet. He was humming once more.

I TOUCHED MY face in that chilly British filing room and my fingers came away wet. My heart beat in time to the music, in time to the memory, as I remembered my Baba's singing. How had I ever forgotten? I folded the pages carefully, then slipped them into my coin purse, which I pushed to the bottom of my bag while peeking out the window of the door. The way looked clear.

After a few wrong turns that led to dead ends, I heard faint applause and followed the sound until a glimmer of the bright party lights shone around the corner. I put my heels back on and rounded the turn, right into a solid body. A hand caught my elbow to steady me, and I leaned into the support for a moment, looking down to regain my footing before blinking up.

For a brief instant, I was confused, as though my brain were refusing to process what was happening. The man dropped my elbow and only then did I recognize him.

Samuel Clarke. The chancellor's son. Revulsion roiled in my stomach, but I tried to force a smile onto my face. I honestly did not know if I succeeded.

He looked me up and down. "What are you doing?" he asked.

I looked over his shoulder, unable to meet his eyes. "I was just, uh, using the water closet," I said, before hastily tacking on a "sir."

He relaxed slightly at my words, realizing I was just a lost native girl. "There's a closer one. You should not be back there. What is your name?"

You don't know me, but I know you, I wanted to say. I could not lose myself to the memory of our first meeting years ago. Given what had happened then, I knew he was a dangerous man to be alone with. I needed to get away. I opened my mouth to respond, but I could not bear to give him my name.

"Kalki! There you are!" Yashu's voice rang out, and I gave Samuel Clarke what I hoped was a sheepish smile.

"So sorry, sir. I must not keep you." I dashed off toward Yashu, who grabbed my arm in a bruising grip.

"Are you okay?" she whispered. I nodded, grateful. "Come, let's get food."

I glanced over my shoulder, but Samuel Clarke had turned away to something else. We found a tray of samosas and took identical bites, then choked at the same time. The inside of the samosa was bone-dry, the potatoes and peas mashed into a pulp. If there was spice in there, I certainly couldn't taste it. Yashu and I shared a look, then as one stuffed the remainder into our mouths.

I could hardly concentrate on the chancellor's speech, knowing what I had in my purse, but the remarks angered me all the same. "Our greatest prime minister, Winston Churchill, once said, 'Indians are not fit to rule; they are fit to be ruled.' When he was speaking, at a time of great upheaval on the verge of the Re-establishment, he was right. The empire has borne that great burden of ruling for decades. But it is my fervent hope that perhaps, twenty or thirty years from now, that reality will have changed, because we will have educated all the young men and women of this country in British customs, traditions, and deportment."

It was the same drivel that I had heard since birth. I stood close enough to see the sweat beading on his brow, and I had a momentary fantasy of jumping onto the stage and punching him.

"What happened?" Yashu whispered, and the moment was gone. "You disappeared, and I couldn't find you. I was scared you had been taken away, then I saw you talking to a British man down the hallway."

The words came out of her in a rush, unusual for someone as obsessed with being well spoken as Yashu. Even after we had just fought, Yashu had worried about me. Come looking for me. I leaned over to give her a quick one-armed hug. "We barely talked."

"I thought the worst," she said. "I'm so sorry I left you—"

"I was being stupid," I said quickly. "My feelings aren't everyone's feelings."

"No," she said slowly. "But I hope you know we still have some of the same feelings. I too would like . . . better. I can still be grateful, though, to have what I have. There are so many others who have less."

It was something I couldn't understand, this kind of gratitude to not be worse off. Why would I be grateful to be ruled, just because I also had a roof over my head? Still, I nodded and pretended to agree, because Yashu had been a far better friend to me tonight than I'd been to her. "I'm sorry," I said again. "Thank you for looking for me. It was very brave, and I don't know what I would have done without you."

In my purse, the song burned.

I WALKED OVER to Mr. Kapadia's store after school the next day. He had been my Baba's best friend, long ago, and owned a small shop that sold books, school supplies, and stationery. He had to sell this variety to stay in business, but everyone knew that he only had this shop to sell books. Although he sold the classics, and the popular British tomes, I knew he did a side trade in banned works for a select, trusted clientele. My Baba had once told me that what Mr. Kapadia didn't know about our history wasn't worth knowing. In another world, I might have called him Uncle. He had a new mimeograph in the back, which he had shown me a few weeks ago, but the existence of it was not widely known. Otherwise, people would be coming to him to make free prints for all their needs, and he did not have the time or money for that.

"Kalki, what a wonderful surprise!" he said, coming around from behind the counter to hug me. "What can I do for you?"

Wordlessly, I handed him the document I had stolen. He carefully unfolded the paper and read it. His hands shook, and he ran one finger down each line, mouthing the words. I watched as he reached the end of the song and then reread it. This time, as his finger traveled down the page, he hummed the melody.

"Where did you get this?" he asked.

I faltered. "I—"

"No, do not tell me," he interrupted. "I should not have asked. Foolish question."

We stood there in silence, facing each other awkwardly. He gripped the paper tightly, and I wondered if he would agree to part with it.

"What do you want me to do with this?" he asked finally.

"I thought . . ." Suddenly the foolishness of the plan hit me. I would print them, and then what? Under the cover of darkness, I would post the lyrics around the neighborhood. And after that? I would be caught, sent to jail, or worse.

"Kalki, whatever you want me to do . . . I will do it. This is truly a gift. Your father—" He glanced around, then said, "Your Baba, he would be so proud of you for this. Once, there was a time when everybody knew this song, but now it is too dangerous to remember."

My resolve returned. "I hoped we could make some prints."

Mr. Kapadia's eyes widened slightly. "And what will you do with them?"

"Put them up. So that everyone can—you know . . ." I couldn't say the words out loud, because they felt so foolish in the harshness of reality. But Mr. Kapadia knew what I meant.

"You can't do that," Mr. Kapadia said. I was opening my mouth to protest when he added, "Alone. You cannot do that alone. I will help you. You put up the posters around your area, from your flat going up north, and I will put them up to the south."

My mouth snapped shut and for a moment I could not reply. "What?" I managed.

Mr. Kapadia gave me a smile. "Your Baba and I were very good friends," he told me. "The only difference between us is that he got caught."

He went into the back room, and I followed him, trying to reconcile the image of Mr. Kapadia, kind shop owner, with Mr. Kapadia, crafty rebel. Then again, my Baba had worked at the rail depot—rebels still needed to support themselves. Mr. Kapadia sat down in front of a typewriter and lifted the ribbon from it before typing the lyrics onto a special paper stencil. I busied myself removing the mimeograph from its hiding place underneath a box of old schoolbooks. He let me crank the handle, and I watched in awe as the machine began churning out copy after copy of the lyrics until we had a few hundred pages stacked before us. With brisk efficiency, Mr. Kapadia burned the stencil with a match before handing me half the stack.

"Be careful," he warned, rummaging around in a drawer and tossing me a tube of glue. "If you hear any noises, hide. You can ditch the papers and run if needed. Do not risk yourself."

"Yes, Mr. Kapadia," I said.

"Listen to me, Kalki. You can do so much more than just this. You must not get caught up in the romance of rebellion and gamble with your life." He looked almost sad, and I promised again not to take too many risks. If I met my Baba's fate, it would devastate Mr. Kapadia, and it would destroy Aai. Even young and hopeful, I knew better than to chance that.

MY AAI KNEW I planned to go out, some tingling of that third eye mothers always have. She didn't seek to dissuade me, just as I never heard her dissuade my Baba when I was young. I was glad she didn't try. Instead, she came into my room after curfew had begun and helped me wrap a black scarf around my face until only my eyes peeked out from beneath the cloth.

"Come home, Kalki," she whispered to me. "Just come home afterward."

I didn't say anything. I couldn't—a painful lump had formed in my throat. I hugged her instead, and she kissed the top of my head. Then I slipped out of our building and onto the deserted streets. In the middle of Kingston, everyone lived in flats with basic amenities and safety. Though vast gulfs of religion divided our neighborhoods, we all had in common the ability to put food on the table, so long as no misfortune befell us. North of us were the slums, alternately towering and sprawling, and the factories, and beyond them the farms that kept Salsette Island as self-sustaining as possible, so that most of us would never have reason to protest our inability to leave the watery bounds of our city. I decided to start as far north as I dared. Once I reached an area that was primarily shops, I pulled out the tube. For a moment, I contemplated heading back to the flat. What if someone caught me?

Before I could think too much, I squeezed out some glue and pressed the paper to the wall of a store. In the blanket of dark, the paper blended in with the advertisements. Hopefully no patrols would notice it until morning. My breath came heavily inside the scarf, nearly suffocating me. I resisted the urge to rip the scarf off and instead pressed myself against the wall of an alleyway, willing away the anxiety until my heart rate relaxed.

There were fewer patrols now. Even ten years ago, the city had been a hotbed of renewed resistance activity, which came in cycles that the government easily predicted. But now, while they had to prepare for big events—holidays, the announcement of war—the need for ordinary patrols had been greatly reduced, and besides, they were already stretched thin, the pace of new recruits from their homeland slowing in recent years. I reminded myself of this several times, and then pushed off the wall to go several stores down. I repeated the process over and over until there was a paper every hundred meters. My supply was dwindling now, and I made my way back toward the flat, stopping once every block to add a paper.

I heard the footsteps several seconds in advance, which was the only reason I could duck into an alleyway. The footsteps got closer, and I knew even flush against the wall they would see me. There were a few foul-smelling piles of trash in the alley, and nothing else. I gasped in some fresher air and leaped behind the refuse just as two policemen walked past. They briefly looked down the passage, then continued on, but even in that time my lungs were burning. As soon as I could, I released the breath and immediately gagged, trying not to make noise as I stumbled away. My shoes were steeped in some disgusting fermented liquid, or perhaps urine. A few blocks from our flat, I hastily put up the last few papers, threw the remaining glue into the gutter, and ran the rest of the way home.

Aai was sitting in the kitchen waiting for me. When she saw me in the doorway, her face briefly lit in a smile before she sobered and ushered me inside, recoiling at the smell. I knew she was relieved I had come back. We luckily had enough water left in our tank for her to draw me a bucket for bathing. While I scrubbed away the filth of the street, she soaked my shoes in some vinegary concoction to remove the evidence.

"Will I know what happened?" she asked as I headed for my bedroom.

"Pay attention when you leave tomorrow," I told her. "I don't think it will be available to see for long."

AAI WAS GONE before I even awoke, and imagining her seeing the lyrics made me happier than successfully making it home the night before. I met Fauzia outside my building, and we walked to school together. She immediately began telling me some story about her family. Grateful to not have to speak, I watched the smile take over her face and admired her easy beauty. Yashu was elegant, put together, but Fauzia was always something more. She knew she was beautiful and accepted it casually, twirling a strand of her curling hair around her finger. I watched the pattern of it, entranced, until I remembered the secret I was keeping from her.

By the time we made it to school, everyone knew what had happened.

"Did you hear?" Yashu asked.

"Hear what?" Fauzia replied. "Some new announcement from the chancellor?"

"About . . ." Yashu glanced around, as if everyone wasn't already gossiping about the news themselves. "About the papers that went up. Nobody knows who it was. They put up banned music."

Fauzia looked surprised. I tried to as well. Certainly, I was surprised that everyone already had such good information. "What did they post?" Fauzia asked.

" 'Vande Mataram,' " Yashu whispered. "The song."

"Did you see it?" I asked. Yashu stared intently at my face for a moment, and belatedly I realized I was smiling.

"No," she said. "Kalki. Tell me you—" I saw the moment where she finally pieced it together, and rage flashed across her features, even though she kept her voice pitched so low I could hardly hear her. "That's why you—that's how you ran into him! And to think I was worried when . . . we were together! You put me in danger too. How *could* you?"

"So that's what you care about?" I had risked so much for everyone to see the song, and she was mad about this? I took a step closer to her until we were almost forehead to forehead. "You were never at risk."

"Oh, I've seen how *careful* you are." Her voice made her disdain clear. "You're unbelievable. Do you think you're some revolutionary, come to save us? The revolutionaries are dead for a reason. All this will do is get us killed too. You don't know—"

"Wow, there's no need to get so worked up over an English paper!" Fauzia said loudly. Yashu and I both jerked upright to find a teacher approaching us. "You both always go too far. It's just a mark!"

The teacher kept walking, but the argument had passed. Already we were both calming down, at least enough to realize getting into this fight in the school courtyard was a bad idea.

"You can't change anything," Yashu muttered. "You have to accept what you have. Everyone else knows it, so why can't you just be normal?" She stalked off, but I knew in a few hours or days we would come back around to each other.

Fauzia was looking at me with a strange mix of emotions. "Why didn't you tell me?" she demanded.

"I didn't want to put you at risk."

"Isn't that something I should decide?" She crossed her arms, brows furrowed. "I could have helped you!"

"You . . . you would have helped?"

"Who do you think I am, Kalki?" We stared each other down for a moment, before she threw her arms around me. "What you did was amazing. But next time, I'm going to help."

I wrapped my arms around her, squeezing. "All right, I'll tell you . . . *if* there's a next time."

Fauzia drew away and rolled her eyes. "I know you. There will be a next time."

She put her arm in mine, and we made a loop of the grounds, which were filled with whispers. I heard snatches of the lyrics in various conversations and had to fight the temptation to smile, or laugh, or shout my victory from the rooftops.

Inside, the teachers buzzed with nervous energy, hanging

around the edges of every conversation and ending any discussion not focused on schoolwork. Forbidding it only made it more tempting, and by the end of the day, everyone had committed the lyrics to memory. I hadn't known what to expect when I put up the song, but this exceeded even my own most secret dreams. Not a single girl seemed upset at this breach of British authority—or if they were, they found their position too indefensible or unpopular to voice.

I WENT STRAIGHT home after school, too worried about guilt by association to try looking at my work in the light of day. The posters had probably been taken down anyway, and I already had the sheet completely memorized. Fauzia walked home beside me, our conversation short and stilted. At my building, I watched her leave, and once she rounded the corner out of my sight I spun around in a long, slow circle. A burning ember of hope lit even the tips of my being. And yet my world, the street on which I had grown up, had not changed in the slightest. I must have stood out there staring at the buildings around me for some time, because suddenly Aai was embracing me.

"Oh, Kalki," she said, and I wrapped my arms around her. She was shaking slightly, but when we pulled away, her eyes were dry.

We went into our flat, and she closed the door and pressed her back to it. "He would be proud," she whispered, and then louder, "he would be proud." She talked as though Baba was a long-gone ancestor. Though we assumed him dead, it hurt to hear him spoken of this way.

"Did you see it?"

"I did," she said, smiling. "I caught a glimpse on my way to work. It brought it all back. Your Baba used to sing that to me, when we were courting."

"You courted?" I asked, surprised. My Baba had left before I was old enough to learn about my parents' marriage, and after he left, we rarely talked about him.

Aai nodded. "We courted. Our families knew each other, but we weren't of the same community." I had known they weren't of the same caste and so the marriage had not been formally arranged, but I had never imagined something so romantic as Baba singing to Aai as they fell in love.

"So you knew he might be . . . when you married him?"

"Yes. Although, of course, I never thought it would happen to him. To us."

"I miss him," I said softly. Today especially, that decade-old wound in my heart throbbed painfully.

"Me too, Kalki." She pushed off of the door and went into the kitchen to begin dinner. "If you want to go to Mr. Kapadia's store, you should go now, before dinner."

"How did . . ." I trailed off, unsure how to end that question.

"He's a troublemaker, that one," Aai said, glancing over at me. "Of course I know. I know everything, remember?"

"Yes, Aai," I agreed, and ducked out the door.

I kept my head down, shoulders hunched, all the way to Mr. Kapadia's. There were a few people in the shop, so I pretended to browse the shelves until they left. When the last customer was gone, he came and found me staring at the book display, examining a paperback of *The Lion, the Witch and the Wardrobe*.

"Everything went all right?" he asked.

"Yes. I stayed safe, like you said."

"You did a good job."

I couldn't stop the grin from creeping across my face. "Thanks, Mr. Kapadia."

"But don't go thinking about what's next," Mr. Kapadia said, and my mental processes ground to a halt.

"Why? There is so much we can do, now that we know—"

"Know what?" Mr. Kapadia interrupted. "All these people who are excited now would turn you in without hesitation. This is a great victory, yes, but not everything will be a victory. Don't get cocky."

"Okay, okay, I get it. I'll be careful."

Mr. Kapadia turned to me and placed his hands on my shoulders. He waited until I met his gaze. "I'm not asking you to be careful. I am asking you to stop. Lie low for some time, until they have stopped looking for the culprit. You must have patience. Please, I cannot lose you too."

In that moment, Mr. Kapadia looked very old. I saw the weight of all the friends he had lost in the purges of rebels, and the terror he must have felt even now. I don't remember exactly what I said, but I solemnly promised to stop looking for trouble, at least until we were absolutely sure they had given up on finding the vandal.

At my sad expression, though, Mr. Kapadia softened. "Your Baba loved you very much. And he would be proud."

As I walked back home, I remembered that long ago night, cradled in my Baba's arms. After the police left, he had cautioned me to always stay hidden from the British. "I wish I could promise you will never have to think of such things. . . . Fate willing, the years will be kind."

At the time, it had sounded like gibberish. Baba liked to ramble, but I was too tired to even pretend to pay attention. "I want to go home."

"We're not far," Baba said. "I'll tell you a story, and by the time I'm finished, we will be home."

I nodded, my face still buried in his chest, and he began to whisper. I did not realize it then, but it was a call to believe, to have faith, to hope that a small action now would one day bring salvation, though that day might be distant or impossible to fathom.

"Once upon a time, there was a man named Manu. He went down to the river to drink some water, but as he raised his cupped hands to his face, he noticed a little fish, Matsya. The fish begged Manu to protect him from the bigger fish in the river and promised in return to aid Manu in his time of need.

"Manu was a kind man, and he brought the fish home with him and kept it in a small bowl. The fish rapidly grew bigger, so Manu dug a ditch outside his home and moved the fish into that makeshift pond. Matsya grew and grew until one day Manu returned him to the river. The fish thanked Manu for his help and told Manu that in one year a flood would envelop the world. Manu did not think that any flood could be so great, but he recognized that a talking, ever-growing fish was a sign beyond his reckoning. And so Manu hoped that if he listened to his heart and his instincts, he might save his family. He might help his people.

"In the year that followed, Manu began preparations. He built a boat and stocked provisions in case that flood did come, and on the appointed day, he pushed the boat onto the river with his loved ones aboard. Just as promised, Matsya appeared, ten times bigger now, and Manu tied his boat onto the fish's horn. At that moment, a wave of water came cresting over the hills, sweeping away men, animals, and houses. But Matsya was an incarnation of Vishnu, come to rescue humanity. Matsya pulled Manu to safety, and from Manu came the rest of humankind."

2

KURMA, TORTOISE

I learned how to lie at twenty.

After years of going to school with us, Yashu had not continued on with me and Fauzia to junior college. She had always worked in a clothing factory on the weekends, but now she worked all day and went to typing school by night. When we first met her, she had slowly opened up about those shifts where she and other children were forced to spin the cotton until their little fingers—better suited to the fast, detailed work—bled. She said she was happier now on the garment-cutting line, that it "wasn't so bad," but we still worried about her safety. People died there. Fauzia and I felt guilty for loving junior college when Yashu could not come at all. I had always listened to Yashu's tirades about the treatment of lower castes, and had come to agree with her, but I had not thought her predicament as important as the injustice of British rule. Now, leaving her behind, I understood why she always said that British or Indian rule made no difference.

The "Vande Mataram" incident had changed something between Fauzia and me, awakened the memory of how we had first bound ourselves to each other in an act of revolt. But there wasn't much we could do beyond venting our frustrations.

With my headmaster's assistance, I had won a scholarship that allowed me to enroll in junior college. Ever since I posted "Vande Mataram," I chased the buoyant feeling of defiance. Fauzia often helped. Sometimes we would write up basic Hindu myths, taken from the Mahabharata or the Ramayana, and post them. Sometimes we would do the same with passages from the Qur'an. Once or twice, we even painted over important British notices, but we never went further than that. I knew deep down it was not enough to cause change, and so it was not enough to bring a true investigation to our doors; the British had their hands full with other matters.

The war with China that had been building for years was finally beginning outright. There was little love lost between India and China, but even so none of us wanted combat. Every night, the British news anchors would talk about Assam, and oil reserves, and we would watch clips of people who looked quite different from us working diligently on tea plantations, contrasted with threatening speeches in some Chinese language that the British translated via captions and paired with shots of tanks. We were, of course, ignorant of the real situation in Assam. What did it matter when the British would defend their territory with all of our lives?

The night before the war was officially declared, the broadcasters announced that over two hundred Indians had died as a result of a Chinese incursion into the province and London was considering a formal declaration of war. Suddenly, the Assamese people felt like our people, because they were suffering at the hands of the foreigners. And the mood shifted, inexplicably, into a curfew violation. At first it was just younger people, whom I watched with jealousy from my window, Aai's fingers digging into my shoulder to prevent me from bolting. But then a few older adults entered the street, and I could tell by the general murmur that the discontent was spreading.

"What are those fools doing?" Aai hissed. After a moment of hesitation, she left the flat and I followed close behind her down the rickety stairs. "What are you doing?" she shouted again the moment we were in the open air. "Go inside before they see you!"

"Don't worry," someone responded. In the assemblage, I couldn't tell who. "We are going to walk peacefully toward the Outpost so they know we do not support this." Whether *this* was the killing of Indians or the declaration of war was unclear.

"Are you stupid?" Aai screeched. "They'll kill you."

But already the assembly was moving, and I snuck myself into it. I saw Aai's face, frantic, scanning the crowd before we turned the corner. Aai was overcautious, always trying to rein me in since her uncharacteristic allowance of the "Vande Mataram" postings, and I wanted to be part of a communal feeling for once. I could hardly understand where this energy was coming from, for many other unfavorable news reports had passed without incident. Yet it seemed half of Kingston was marching in the streets. I heard older men grumbling about their paychecks, students talking fearfully of a draft, young people crying at the deaths, and other murmurs about oil reserves and international politics I did not care to pay attention to. Even so, the mood was almost joyous as we stood in the darkness where we were never allowed.

Then I spotted the outline of the Outpost, lit bright against the night sky, and my feet stopped moving. I was struck with apprehension at the sight. Perhaps it was the memory of my Baba, his fascination with and aversion toward it, warring in me. He saved my life.

I couldn't see anything, crouched in the shadows against a building, but I could feel a sudden fear spread like a ripple through the crowd. My palms felt clammy with it. "Disperse!" came an order, resounding as though delivered by loudspeaker. The forces by the Outpost had mobilized quickly.

At that one word, the crowd turned quiet and began to back away as one, pushing away from the Outpost. The sight of the police had provided an unwelcome reminder of reality, and we knew disobedience would be punished.

A loud pop sounded in the air, and the mass of people flinched as one. A scream. Another pop, and this time I saw a cloud rising up. Belatedly, I recognized that they were firing gas into the crowd, and watched as the smudge of the police surged forward, batons raised.

Survival instincts took hold, and I began to weave in and out of the throng, my small stature useful for something. The amassed people were turning into a stampede, screams and pops and crunches. Around me people tripped, fell. They had told us to disperse and then fallen upon us immediately. Why had I left? Why hadn't I listened to Aai?

My lungs burned as the wind picked up the airborne agent of the British, something foul stinging my eyes. I remembered distantly a lesson from my Baba telling me what to do if I found myself caught in a mob, but I could recall little practical advice other than this: *Keep moving. Don't stop.* Behind me people were bleeding, bones were breaking, and if I fell it would be me in agony beside them. I put my head down and ran.

Someone fell onto me from behind, and I stumbled, my hands scraping the road. I pushed myself back up before the crowd could step on me, but I looked over my shoulder and saw a slumped, twitching body on the ground. I swallowed down bile and forged ahead. Perhaps they would survive the stampede to be caught by the British—either way, it was a fate worse than I wished to imagine.

I kept running, until the screams sounded distant and the people had thinned out. Where was everyone I had come with? Where were the men Aai had—

A hand grabbed me, and I screamed before I recognized the feel of it. I would have known her anywhere. "Aai!" I gasped out, looking up. We were on the corner of our street. She had waited here for me. My body started to shake, but Aai jerked my arm.

"Quick, inside!"

I followed her blindly, wordlessly, as she ran down the street and into our building. It was eerily silent.

"I—I don't—what—why—" I was shaking, stammering, unable to marshal my thoughts. We had just been walking in the streets. Nobody had been protesting or making demands or doing anything threatening at all. I couldn't understand. They had to have a reason to hurt us, to kill us, didn't they? They always claimed to have a reason.

Aai's hands pressed against my back, probing it. "Kalki, where is all this blood from? Were you hit? Does it hurt?"

"What blood?" I mumbled. In a disorienting flash, I remembered a crack of a hard object on bone, the force of someone falling onto me. "It's not mine," I said.

"Take it off," Aai ordered. When I didn't move, she pulled off my shirt in a violent motion and strode into the bathroom. I stood in the living room, shivering, until my mind caught up and I followed her. She was kneeling on the floor, scrubbing my shirt. "Nobody can know you were there," she said without looking up. "Wash your face and change. Wipe your shoes. When they come by, you say you were here all night. I don't know how you made it back—" Her voice caught. I had never told her about Baba's sporadic lessons—which included the best places to hide, how to pick locks, basic self-defense, and how to run from the British—because I knew she wouldn't approve. I could barely remember Baba's voice, but I held his teachings close.

Aai shook her head. "We don't question such gifts. You were here, doing your homework."

"Aai—"

"Don't speak to me," she snapped. "How could I have raised such a selfish daughter? Just shut up." She turned away from me, slamming the door to her bedroom and leaving me in silence.

THE SILENCE DID not last. I sat at the table, doing my homework, for I could not bear to lie alone in the darkness, and Aai did not emerge. I chose accounting, thinking that telecommunications or English would be too painful, but the numbers swam before my vision. All around me, the building was filled with the same unnatural stillness. The first knocks caused me to startle so hard that I snapped my pencil lead. Then the screaming started. I ran to find a knife and grabbed the doorknob before I stopped myself. There was nothing I could do.

I leaned my forehead against the door instead, listening and bearing witness as the screaming grew more and more distant. Someone had been dragged from the building, under protest. I wondered who it was. They sounded male. There was one elder, Mr. Lele, who lived on the first floor and I had glimpsed in the crowd. He would slip me Polo mints sometimes if we passed each other on our way out in the morning. I tried not to think about what might happen to him in the Outpost. People went in and never came out.

The knocking continued, a steady beat, and occasionally the sound of voices or screaming came through. As the knocks grew closer, I set the knife on the chair next to me and exchanged my accounting book for my English reader, flipping to *Henry V* and letting my eyes glance uselessly over the page. I could not cry. I could not give any indication that I knew what was going on, because that would give me away. I read the same line over and over: *Once more unto the breach, dear friends, once more; or close the wall up with our English dead!* Although I was usually quite skilled at understanding Shakespeare, it was like reading some foreign language. I wondered about Fauzia and Yashu, hoping there had not been any marches in their areas. Yashu was closer to the border, so she was probably safe from such sentiments, but Fauzia lived as near to the Outpost as we did, albeit in a different direction.

A rap came at our door. I hastened to open it, knowing that they would expect a prompt response, and Aai emerged silently from her room.

"We are investigating a disturbance that occurred earlier tonight," an officer said without warning, stepping into our flat. "Where were you this evening?"

"Studying, sir," I lied easily, gesturing to my open book on the table.

"And your mother?"

"I've been sleeping," Aai said. "We heard some noise on the street earlier, but I managed to fall asleep once it faded."

The officer bent down to look at our shoes by the door, lifting them to look at the soles. I had given mine a quick scrub to get out the still-wet blood in the grooves, but tried to leave the normal dirt caked in. He looked at them for so long I began preparing to lunge for a knife, or else to launch myself from the balcony, just to give myself some sense of control. But apparently he found them unremarkable, because at last he dropped them. "Where is your husband?"

"He's been gone for years, sir," Aai said. It had been nearly a decade since our household was last under suspicion—two women, a single mother and a daughter, weren't likely to carry on a man's revolutionary fervor. I searched his face, reading the anger and tension in the furrows of his brow. I remembered the knife hidden from view on the chair and wondered whether to grab it, but the officer only gave a sharp nod.

"Did you hear any of your neighbors go out?" the officer asked. "I assure you, there will be no trouble for them. We are only trying to understand what happened."

I opened my mouth to tell him no, hoping to prevent Aai from speaking, for I did not know if she would give up others to keep us safe. But she still answered before me. "No, I thought our building was quiet. The noise was all out on the road, as I said."

"Thank you for your time," the man said, stepping out of our flat and moving down to the next. I closed our door behind him, turning to speak to Aai, but she had already shut herself back in her room.

I still couldn't think of sleeping, so I sat instead in front of my book, trying in vain to read Henry V's speech. Tears began to fall, dripping onto the book. How many nameless would run into the breach of our bleeding land? I was not sure if there were enough to close that wound in the whole of India.

THE CITY REMAINED in lockdown for the weekend as war was declared. The chancellor himself came on the radio to condemn the actions of the native mobs and to announce that, in order to keep us safe, he would be mobilizing the full Kingston police force to investigate and stop the violence. His words sent chills down my spine, their true meaning plain.

Aai and I went downstairs to see Mrs. Lele and learned that her husband had indeed been dragged away screaming that night. The other neighbors kept their distance, but we knew that shame well and would not ignore her. Aai cooked for her, and I did my homework next to Mrs. Lele, who sat immobile on her couch, so she would not be alone.

When we emerged blinking into the school week, I had almost convinced myself I hadn't been at the march, almost managed not to feel guilt at escaping unscathed. I checked on Mr. Kapadia— who gripped my shoulder tightly when he saw me, speaking softly to himself in a prayer—and tried to study my friends to see if they carried any extra pain with them. I knew that all around our neighborhood, and in Mrs. Lele's empty flat, people were experiencing the same agonizing hurt we had felt when Baba had gone.

As the weeks passed, it began to feel like that night had just been a painful nightmare, nothing more. If we were never allowed to discuss it or remember it to one another, had it really happened? Even though she checked in on Mrs. Lele, Aai pretended that night had never existed, and the one time I brought it up to Fauzia, admitting I had gone out, she had reprimanded me.

"A few people from our streets went out too, but not my family. How could you be so foolish?"

"Don't you want to be a part of something bigger than yourself?" I asked, the words feeling heady on my tongue. "To make yourself known?"

"Not if it would endanger my family! And not if I knew it would be pointless! You know better, Kalki. How could you do this to your mother?"

My eyes prickled with tears, because the more I thought about it, the more I realized how monstrously awful I had been to Aai. And yet I did not regret it. I thought of what my Baba might say and found I could not be ashamed for marching. I felt shame only for having fled, for not having stood my ground, for not having anything to show for what had happened.

In wartime, I found new, smaller enemies to focus on. The electricity rationing became the object of my frustrations instead. We never knew when the electricity would go out, only that it would. There were candles strategically placed in every room, although they were a poor substitute for lightbulbs.

I had begun to collect contraband reading material, and I learned to love reading it by candlelight. Even though I could have turned on the light sometimes, the sense of mystery and deprivation felt right to me. When I lit the candle and squinted at the tiny words, some silent kinship connected me to rebels across the world, cursing rations and the British custom of always squeezing the native people first. It was the only kinship I could bring myself to act on now that I truly understood how any defiance was treated. In addition to the copy of Gandhi's autobiography Baba had hidden under the slate tiles of our floor, I had managed to acquire from Mr. Kapadia *The Wretched of the Earth* and *Anandamath*, which had a longer, original version of "Vande Mataram." He told me he dug them out of hiding because my Baba would have wanted me to have them, in a way that made me wonder if my Baba had given them to Mr. Kapadia for me. Or perhaps it was wishful thinking. I lost myself in the words, and most of all in the idea that there was something beyond the empire. That there were people and ideologies that disagreed with British rule, and they were important enough to print books about.

That people whose skins held the shades of the earth could have self-determination.

DESPITE THE WRONGS of the world, I focused on learning as much as I could in junior college. Fauzia and I made friends, reveling in the ability to take classes with men. A few of them didn't seem to like being in courses with women and openly scorned our presence, but for the most part they just wanted to do well and graduate. They weren't quite as competitive as me, so I tried to hide my aggressive side for the sake of making friends.

Early in my first semester, I established a rapport with a boy named Bhaskar, who sat next to me on the first day of telecommunications class. Though most men and women kept to themselves on different sides of the classroom, there had been only one seat available when he arrived that day and he continued to claim that seat every day thereafter. He offered me a besan laddoo once when my stomach grumbled, and then started leaning over to read my notes when he got distracted. I playfully swatted his arm, then realized I had gotten comfortable with him. Bhaskar was not yet a friend, but he was someone who liked me purely for my presence, knowing nothing else about me. And I liked that about him. So I introduced Bhaskar to Fauzia, thinking we could all study together. Then the trouble started.

"That boy is trying to date you," she hissed as soon as we passed out of earshot of Bhaskar. "Did you see the way he dresses?"

"You think he wants to date me because of how he dresses?" I asked, thinking she was joking.

"His pants were so loose. I'm sure it is because they are easier to take off," she told me seriously.

"Who would even think that?" Her expression was stormy. "Oh," I said, feeling foolish. "You're not just joking with me."

"No! This is not a joke. We are in junior college now. People are looking for eligible spouses. And you're a catch! Kind of. I mean, you look like you'd clean up nicely if you washed your hair and didn't dress like a blind woman."

"That's what I've always wanted to hear." By this time, we had reached the canteen.

, "And the way he talked! How did he even get into junior college?"

I found an empty table and began heading toward it. "You spoke to him for less than five minutes, and he was trying to be friendly. Did you expect him to speak in formal English?"

"Some amount of polish would have been nice," she huffed as we sat down. "I am just trying to protect you."

"Bhaskar is nice, if you would give him a chance instead of being so jealous. What, are you afraid someone will steal my affections? You never worried about Yashu. Am I only allowed to have friends you pick for me?" I watched her face get more and more annoyed and couldn't help but laugh.

"I'm not jealous," she insisted. "I just don't think he's up to your standards. You can find better friends than that."

I unpacked the tiffins Aai had prepared for both me and Fauzia, a tradition started years ago because Fauzia had a longer route to school and often forgot her meals. Aai always sent a few chapatis with a dash of ghee—as much as we could afford—and whatever bhaji we had the night before. Today it was okra, a particular favorite of mine, liberally spiced with garam masala. The moment I popped the lid, the smell made my mouth water. "I'm not proposing that we become the best of friends, but I thought it would be nice to expand our circle now that we're here."

"Hey, Kalki!" someone shouted above the din. I turned to find none other than Bhaskar, friend in tow, approaching us. I studied his appearance. He was clean-shaven, well dressed, with a medium build. I couldn't understand Fauzia's problem.

"Seriously?" Fauzia muttered.

"I know, he hasn't even tightened his belt," I shot back.

"Can we sit with you?" Bhaskar asked, reaching the table. "By the way, this is Omar. Omar, Fauzia and Kalki."

"Great to meet both of you," Omar said in a way that expressed his desire to be anywhere but here.

Fauzia gave me a look that said quite plainly, *See? Even his friends are low quality.*

"So, have you known each other for long?" I asked Omar, trying to break the strange tension.

"We've been friends for years," Bhaskar jumped in. "And we're roommates now."

"That's so great," I said. Fauzia snorted in an attempt not to laugh at my fake enthusiasm.

"It's fun," Bhaskar agreed. "One of the few good things about not having parents."

"You're *glad* your parents are dead?" Fauzia demanded, aghast. It was very unlike her to be so tactless, but perhaps she was trying to scare them off.

Bhaskar cleared his throat. "Omar was raised by his uncle until he was eighteen, but then his uncle was—he had to leave the island. And my aunt and uncle raised me, but then my uncle got special dispensation after my aunt died to leave and go back to his family's farm near Solapur. And it's basically impossible to get back into Kingston. So nobody can really tell us what to do. Orphans have more fun." He gave a sardonic smile.

"I understand," I said, desperate to break the tension. It wasn't totally true, but I at least knew the pain of losing a parent.

"Do you?" Omar asked, a hint of bitterness lacing his tone.

"Why wouldn't she?" Fauzia rebutted, almost daring him to disagree. A shot of warmth ran through me at her instant defense, even if she was only doing it to bother Omar, who sighed and pulled a beaten-up sandwich out of his bag.

We ate in an awkward silence for about ten minutes before Fauzia suddenly stood. "Kalki, we need to go to that place, remember?"

Mentally I reserved a few choice words for Fauzia, but I got up and left with her anyway. "They could be good friends," I told her. "Why don't you see it?"

"What sort of decent Muslim dresses that way?" she asked, talking right past me.

"It's the fashion. And since when do you care about religious dress?" I couldn't believe I was defending Omar already, but Fauzia's comment prompted a realization. "Don't you think it odd that they live together?"

"Well, clearly they don't respect their elders—" she continued.

"Fauzia. Think. They must be extraordinarily committed to each other to convince their building to allow the mixed-religion rental."

"The British have made it—"

"The British can say whatever they want, you *know* most landlords don't rent to other religions, even closer to Old Bombay. The Hindus rent to Hindus, the Muslims to Muslims, so for one of them to cross lines and convince a place to rent to them . . ."

"What are you trying to say?" Fauzia asked.

"Maybe they're . . . you know . . ."

She raised an eyebrow. "You think they're . . . *friends*?" Her emphasis on the word left no confusion.

"I mean, you never know. Wouldn't you like to find other people like . . . that?" I said in a hurried whisper.

Fauzia gave me a flat look. "I appreciate that you're always trying to look out for me, but you don't need to try to find me homosexual friends. You never do anything by halves, do you?"

"Come on," I said, almost whining. "Maybe we should give them a chance. And see if they might be worth being friends with."

"You're making so many assumptions."

"*Oh, Kalki, Bhaskar's so stupid and rude, don't be his friend!*" I made my voice high, reedy, and Fauzia whacked me on the arm. "Now you want to talk about making assumptions?"

"I knew something was off about them," she insisted. "It was a real concern, even if you want to mock me. So if you're right, that means I am also right."

I gave her a look. "That's so unfair, and you know it." But I let her giggle and get away with it, knowing I had won.

COURTING WAS NOT something either of us ever truly considered—it never seemed possible for us. Fauzia assumed that one day her family would find a man for her to marry, but she would never have interest in him, because she only liked women.

This was the other secret we had kept from Yashu: the day when we were fifteen and Fauzia brought me to her family's flat. It was an odd time, when our bodies and minds were changing, although I did not feel the same attractions then that others talked about. She invited me over while her family was gone, and we remained in her room in silence for several long minutes.

"Something's wrong with me," Fauzia whispered at last.

Whatever I had expected, it wasn't this. "Are you sick?" I whispered back. The thought was too painful to bear.

She swallowed, shook her head, and pushed on. "You know how all the girls from school talk about boys? I—I don't care for them."

"I don't either," I said, and she looked at me with hope in her eyes. "The girls who only want to talk about boys are so *boring*."

The light left Fauzia's face, and she made a frustrated sound. "That's not what I meant! I meant I don't like boys!" Her angry statement reverberated, and I blinked twice at her, shocked more at her ferocity than anything.

"All right," I said after a moment. "So what? Neither do I. Boys themselves are also boring." I laughed at that, but she didn't.

"Kalki, be serious," Fauzia snapped. "I'm trying to tell you something important and you're just—just mocking me."

I had been trying to return things to normal, but I was clearly making things worse. "I'm not mocking you," I said at last. I knew Fauzia hated that more than anything. "But you're not making any sense."

She stood there, breathing hard as though she had been exercising. "I like girls," she murmured at last. "I think they're—beautiful, and I want—" She turned away from me and toward the wall, and I understood then that she could not express exactly what she wanted.

"Do you like *me*?" I blurted out without thinking.

She did not face me, and from the hunching of her shoulders, I could tell I'd accidentally struck true. "I thought maybe . . . you might be like me?" Her voice was desperately small.

I wished that I could understand, wished more than I had wished for anything in years that whatever change had come over everyone else would hit me too and I could better *want*. I liked her, of course I did, would happily hold hands with her as some young men and women did when they were sure no adults were around. But whatever depth of feeling she was experiencing was, at that time, foreign to me.

"Well, say something," she said at last, still not facing me.

"I—I don't know what to say," I mumbled, but I could sense that was not what Fauzia needed. I loved her, and hated her pain, so I pushed myself to keep going. "I don't understand it when the girls at school talk about boys. I don't understand what you're saying either. I . . . you're my best friend. You're special. But I am not like you."

Fauzia sighed and turned to look at me. She looked calmer now. "Everything is so literal with you, Kalki. If you don't . . . then it's fine. It was stupid anyway. But . . . you're not angry?"

"Why would I be angry?"

She reached out a hand, and I took it in both of mine. She was shaking. I felt that same strange wave of her movement inside of me, incomprehensible. She did not look afraid, but I sensed her fear lurking just below the surface. We both were old enough to know that it was considered *wrong* to feel this way, that men who loved men were beaten and jailed, that women who loved women were forced into marriages and made to submit. It was the way of the world, especially with the British laws naming such pairings unnatural. But she did not need to fear me, would never need to fear me.

"Do you . . . like someone?" I asked after a bit, just to break the silence. Fauzia whacked me on the shoulder, releasing my hand. "Someone else?" I pushed, seeing that Fauzia needed some teasing. "Not Meghana!" I was referring to a girl that I knew Fauzia hated.

"Oh, yes, of course, how could I not love Meghana?" Fauzia said, and she came back into herself with each word. "There's something so beautiful about the way she picks her nose. Mmm."

For some reason this was the funniest thing to us, and within moments we were both on the ground, clutching our stomachs. It was not, in truth, all that funny. But we needed to laugh to release that tension, so there would be no more distance between us.

In the years that had followed, we rarely spoke of it. In time, I saw Fauzia's feelings for me pass. She never stared at me anymore, and she talked openly about others instead. I knew she struggled, falling for those who would never fall for her, and yet it never dimmed her belief that she would find her people if she tried hard enough. I did not know why it was so difficult when every bit of her, from the thick curve of her lashes to the graceful twists of her hands, was beautiful. But I imagined those who might love Fauzia back in that way were also afraid.

Still, the expectations of others were a powerful thing. The more time I spent with Bhaskar, the more others looked at us. Classmates asked what I liked about him, and when I told the truth, that he was kind and serious, they tittered and laughed. They asked me what I thought of his eyes—I did not even remember their color—and whether he minded my height—what was wrong with it?—and whether we had kissed—I had never even considered it. It was funny, for Fauzia and I were far closer and more intimate and not once did anyone ever think we might be together. Bhaskar and I, on the other hand, had a simple friend-ship. We could study together in companionable silence, share food. I would never dream of voicing my true thoughts to him.

Fauzia was the one to transform in her friendship with the boys. The next time we met up with Bhaskar and Omar, Fauzia put on her most winning persona, which I envied; both she and Yashu often teased me for failing to muster any charm at all. I was who I was through and through. This Fauzia wasn't fake, but it was as though her haughty and judgmental side had disap-peared, leaving only the smiling, funny, agreeable version of her. Even sullen and suspicious Omar came out of his shell.

I watched in awe as Fauzia drew them in with ever more var-ied questions, each answer raising yet more questions. "Do you have girlfriends?" she asked once.

"You're girls, and our friends," Bhaskar answered without looking up from his textbook.

Fauzia groaned. "You know what I mean."

"Why, are you interested?" Omar shot back. "Do you have a boyfriend?"

Fauzia seemed to take Omar's acerbic attitude as encourage-ment. "Do *you* have one?"

We watched closely for their reactions, but their faces re-mained impassive. Bhaskar looked up from his textbook and rolled his eyes. "If you two are going to bicker, maybe you should find a different table from me and Kalki, yes? Some people are trying to study." It made me oddly happy that he thought to in-clude me in his sniping.

"I'm simply making sure you're using your time in junior col-lege wisely, to meet your future wives," Fauzia said with a sunny smile.

Omar failed to suppress a snort. "Why, so we can be fathers before we finish school?"

"Getting married is for older people," Bhaskar agreed.

"It's tragic for men of your age to never have had a girlfriend," Fauzia said, hoping they would at least confirm that. We were all the same age and Fauzia and I had never dated, but then again, courting wasn't common for girls until college.

"What's going to be tragic is your exam marks," Bhaskar said, and with a groan Fauzia turned back to her papers.

We couldn't figure them out, because they showed no interest in girls and had such a perfect casualness with each other that it was hard to say if it was real or not. At first we thought we were wrong and they might unfortunately have interest in us, but our hands never touched theirs except by accident, and they never asked us alone to the movies or to the canteen. In trying to discover the truth, we grew closer as friends, while everyone else decided we were going out—Bhaskar with me, and Omar with Fauzia.

Gossip was at least a distraction from what felt like an impossible-to-win war, which had spread in just half a year to the entire border between British India and China. We did not have a strong grasp on what China wanted, or its motives, for day after day we received only British information—the threat of communism, how it would turn us all into beggars in the streets, and how Britain's ally the United States of America was waging a similar war in Vietnam. While of course we all knew that it wasn't the whole truth, even we couldn't tell how subtly we were being manipulated. In Kingston, which was majority Hindu, we began hearing how majority-Muslim Kashmir had decided to ally itself with China in open rebellion against British rule. When a draft was announced a few days later to support the new front in the north of the territory, it was obvious whom we were meant to blame . . . and we did.

I was hanging around in Fauzia's family's general store as she organized and cleaned on our day off when we heard the shouting and sounds of glass breaking from the street. The rest of her family, her parents and her much older brothers, maintained a sense of bemused remove toward me even after all these years—only Basma, her younger sister, ever made small talk with me—but today they had gone to visit an ailing relative across the city.

Religious tensions had been brewing for days, and they had picked a terrible time to boil over. Once the fighting started, no one would be safe on either side. "We have to go," Fauzia said. "Come on, let's sneak out the back."

"Where do we go?" I asked. "Back to my place?"

At that, she seemed to startle. "Are you crazy? There's no way I'm going to your neighborhood. How naïve are you?"

The shouting was getting closer.

"Omar's!" Fauzia said.

"What?" I asked, but she was already dragging me into the alley.

"They live in a mixed area, south of your place. It's a few kilometers through safer territory."

"We can't just show up at their flat!" I protested.

"What other choice do we have?" she asked. She was right. All our other options were firmly in Hindu or Muslim neighborhoods, and far too dangerous. So I let myself be led through the alleys until we emerged blinking onto a street that was almost jarringly normal. People looked wary, hurrying about, but there had been no destruction here yet.

"Wait, how do you know where they live?" I asked, my mind finally catching up.

"They've only mentioned they live here twenty times," Fauzia said. "Honestly, do you never listen?"

She strode confidently into the building—a three-story house where each floor had been split into two separate flats. "Do you know what floor?" I asked.

She gave me a dirty look. I had missed a lot.

When Bhaskar opened the door, he looked confused, but let us in. "Are you all right?" he said, looking us both over.

We slipped off our shoes. "They came for my store, but I wasn't hurt," Fauzia said.

"What's going on?" Omar's voice came from deeper in the flat.

Bhaskar winced, beckoning us into their small living room. "Kalki and Fauzia are here!"

There was a muffled sound, followed by some scrambling, and then Omar emerged from the sole bedroom, his shirt half-buttoned and his hair in total disarray. It was common enough for friends living alone to share a bedroom, but their expressions and Omar's midday undress told us all we needed to know.

Fauzia and I shared a glance, trying not to laugh.

"You already knew," Bhaskar said with a sigh, sinking down onto the couch.

"We guessed," I said. "Especially when you didn't end the rumors about us but didn't talk to us about them either."

"Well, it's . . ." Omar paused.

"Convenient?" Fauzia finished. "Agreed. Kalki here doesn't really care, but I'll keep your secret if you get me into one of those gatherings." Fauzia had told me about these before, how people like her held secret meetings to find one another and be fully themselves but she didn't know anybody who could give her an invitation.

"Are you trying to blackmail us?" Omar asked, his lips twitching.

Fauzia shrugged. "Yes, I suppose I am."

A MONTH LATER, and a week after Fauzia had gone to her first meetup and kissed her first girl—an experience I heard about in detail the next morning—she came to me, clearly wanting to talk. We sat in a quiet corner of the canteen, shoulder to shoulder. Fauzia fidgeted, reading the same line of her accounting textbook over and over until at last, not looking at me, she asked, "Would you ever want to be married?"

My heart sank. "Are your parents—"

"Nothing like that," Fauzia jumped in quickly. "No. I was just thinking . . ."

My stomach turned at the idea that Fauzia was thinking of someone else. If she found love, I knew she would not have time for me anymore, not in the same way. "I know you like that girl you met, but—"

"I'm not an idiot!" Fauzia snapped. She seemed determined not to let me finish a single sentence. "I meant marrying a man. Having children. Don't you want children?"

I was already shaking my head. I knew Fauzia had always wanted children, but that path was not for me, not now. "Definitely not."

"Why? You'd be a great mother. Strong and—"

"That's not the problem," I said. "I couldn't bring a child into this."

"Maybe things will change," Fauzia said, but she was very quiet.

I glanced around, but nobody was near enough to hear. "If things change, I intend to be a part of it. And that risk . . . I couldn't do it." Suddenly I was blinking back tears, hot and unexpected. I squeezed my eyes shut. "I couldn't leave behind a child the way my father did."

Cool thumbs touched my cheeks, brushing away the tears. "I understand," she said at last. "Truthfully, I asked you because I was thinking that perhaps Omar and I could marry. We could have an understanding, and so much more freedom if we were married. I could move about more freely, without answering questions, and he would be above suspicion with a wife. And if we wanted a child, we would have each other. And perhaps you and Bhaskar . . . it would give you independence."

My eyes flew open, but her face told me she wasn't joking. "Omar?" I asked, trying not to laugh. "You could do so much better."

She swatted my arm. "Now who's judgmental?" she asked. "Anyway, just think about it."

"You don't need my blessing," I said.

Fauzia gave me a look. "Yes, I do."

OUR DECISION WAS not left to time. The draft began a month later, a month spent deepening our friendship over games of cards and conversations extending perilously close to curfew at Bhaskar and Omar's flat, with no eyes on us but one another's. The war had worsened significantly in the past weeks, with the French seeming to ally with China, supplying its army with weapons in the hopes of gaining part of India for themselves. Proxy wars were being fought in sub-Saharan Africa and South America, and even Spain and Russia were involved. Across the country, young Indian men were being called up to fight in a war that they did not want to win.

When Fauzia and I sat to hear the draft in what had now become our second home, we all had something precious to lose. Worse still, Bhaskar and Omar had yet to be called up, making it all the more likely that one of their numbers would be called tonight. As much as we tried to ignore it, the tension in the air had become unbearable. Too nervous to listen, the boys were instead distracting themselves—loudly—in the bedroom.

The other day, Samuel Clarke, dressed in a sharp military uniform, had spoken on the television in our school canteen, claiming that "in this war, there is no skin color, no white or dark, no British or Indian, just soldiers united in making the ultimate sacrifice for our future." The high-minded words made my fists clench and my heart race with anger. The British men worked in "intelligence" and "supply"—they weren't the foot soldiers fueling the war. Samuel Clarke and his father constituted a dynasty of evil, perpetrators and inheritors of atrocity.

Fauzia and I fumed silently as the radio announcers continued in Clarke's spirit, droning on about what an honor it would be to serve the empire, delaying the announcement of the new draft birth dates while we waited on pins and needles. Fauzia held herself stiffly, her spine ramrod straight, but I could hardly hold myself up at all. I had my head on her shoulder, and my legs over her lap, the two of us so intertwined we could feel each other shaking.

At last, they began to call the numbers.

The second number called was Omar's, and a cold fear washed over me. Fauzia gasped and gripped my arm so hard it would have hurt if I was not completely numb.

Omar. Omar was leaving us.

Tears blurred my vision, and my throat was so tight I could barely swallow, but we couldn't yet end our vigil. And so we sat, adrenaline and fury coursing through our veins, as more numbers were called.

When Bhaskar's number was the final pick, the knife slid deeper.

Fauzia reached forward and groped at the radio to silence it. We both sat there, unmoving, incapable of words. Bhaskar and Omar must have heard the quiet, because a few moments later they padded out, clutching each other's hands and staring at our pale faces.

"Whose was it?" Bhaskar asked finally, his voice raspy as if he had already cried.

I opened my mouth to answer, but no sound came out. I shook my head as Fauzia said, "Both of yours. Omar, you will be reporting first, but may Allah help you, they called both your numbers."

Omar turned to Bhaskar, his eyes wild. "Maybe—maybe we'll be in the same company. And we'll be together. That's something, right?"

"Yes! Yes, we can request to be in the same unit. I'll even enlist earlier, so I can go with you." A feral sort of determination spread across Bhaskar's face.

"Don't be sad," Omar said to us. "We will keep each other safe. This is the best possible outcome."

They truly believed it, this foolishness. The sheer absurdity of it overwhelmed me, and I moved off of Fauzia to bury my face in my hands, finally allowing the tears of despair burning behind my eyes to escape. I didn't want them to see my expression and lose their glimmer of hope, but I couldn't control myself.

"Do you not understand?" Fauzia shouted, rising from the sofa. "Leave the country. *Please,* you can try to leave. Bhaskar, you at least have time. Get out, dodge their draft—that's the only way to survive!"

"You don't know what you're talking about," Omar snapped. "Don't say that!"

"It's the truth!" Fauzia's breath hitched in a sob. "Boys leave for the front and they don't return."

"No," Bhaskar said softly. I lifted my tearstained face out of my hands in time to see Bhaskar kiss Omar fiercely and freely. "If you are so sure Omar will die out there, then I will not leave him. We'll go together."

"How can you be so calm about this?" I asked him, rising to my feet.

Before he could answer, Omar interrupted. "Fauzia, can you get him out?" He turned to Bhaskar. "She's right. You should leave. Please. Go."

Bhaskar shook his head. "We go together, or not at all," he said.

Fauzia buried her face in my shoulder. Omar came up and embraced her from behind, and Bhaskar joined in a moment later. For those few moments, our hearts beat as one. After an eternity, or maybe a millisecond, we all pulled away, our eyes red and puffy.

"Who will take care of my uncle?" Bhaskar asked, looking haunted. "He lives off my wages from the school kitchens. And my new job as a government clerk—it would have paid for his cataract surgery."

"Can't he get your military wages?" I asked.

"He never adopted me," Bhaskar said. "They have a lot of rules. Wives, parents. Not even siblings, except as death beneficiaries."

My mind spun as I remembered Fauzia's idea a month ago. Bhaskar and Omar were leaving now, and we would lose our freedom without them. The privacy of their flat, the ability to move and socialize more easily, the protection of being connected to a man. And the boys needed someone at home—to guard their flat, look after their interests, and take home their wages. "Marry me."

He looked at me like I had grown a third head. "What?"

"Marry me. I'll get your wages and, God forbid, your pension. I won't use it—I'll send every rupee to your uncle."

Fauzia turned to Omar. "I'm also marriageable. We can keep the flat, so you have a place to come home to." Our families would approve. Quick weddings were a common practice these days, and outwardly they were good and devout boys.

"Okay," Bhaskar agreed. Omar nodded his assent.

We were engaged.

I RAN UP to our flat, taking the steps two at a time, and burst through the door. Aai stood in the kitchen, chopping green beans more deftly than I ever could. She looked up as I came in, and the sorrow in her eyes was palpable.

"Did he ask for your hand?" she asked.

"How did you—"

"I heard on the radio. It's what everyone does." Aai looked down at her vegetables, and studied her work intently before raising her eyes back to me. "Do you love him?"

"I like him," I said. "That has to be enough." Aai's mouth twisted, but she didn't say anything. Was she going to say no? "He respects me," I added.

She sighed, shaking her head at some thoughts I was not privy to. "Okay, Kalki. Then congratulations are in order."

"Not yet. He will come here and ask for your blessing." I didn't add that I had been the one to propose to him.

Aai smiled, but her eyes stayed tight. "He is a good boy," she said.

"Yes," I confirmed. "He is."

"You will have a small wedding. Just the families, and a few friends. Our guruji will do that for us, he understands the urgency."

For the first time since proposing the idea—since Fauzia had suggested it to me—the weight of our actions began to sink in. As if sensing my thoughts, Aai came to embrace me. "You will be fine, Kalki. It may not feel like it now, but you will be. Marriage . . . it is never what anyone expects, but there are blessings in it. You will find them, and you will survive his absence."

I could sense her thinking of Baba, and so I wrapped my arms around her and tried to stave off the high tide of grief rising in both of us.

I WENT TO invite Mr. Kapadia in person, since he was family. The door chimed as I entered, and I kicked around his store waiting for him to come speak to me, pausing in front of his display of books. Years ago, my Baba had stood in front of this very display, counted the third book from the back, and pulled out a Marathi book. "It's there if you know where to look," he said to me with a laugh, then shook his best friend's hand.

Now I counted through, but there was nothing, only a slim volume entitled *Night*.

"It's an excellent read. Heartbreaking, but excellent." Mr. Kapadia appeared behind me.

"I'll take it, then," I said, digging in my bag for money.

Mr. Kapadia studied my face. "You didn't come here for a book. What is it?"

"I have a question," I said. He gestured at me to go on. "Why aren't you married? You have a good job, you're kind . . ."

"Oh, Kalki." There was so much sadness in his voice, I immediately felt guilty. "Your Baba asked the same. But I'll tell you what I told him: I couldn't have a wife and a child and take on that risk, doing what we did. And even now, I still harbor a hope that prevents me from doing it. It scares me, the idea of bringing someone pain. I'm not as strong as him."

"That sounds strong to me. To deprive yourself, so you don't hurt anyone." I hadn't realized that I was angry at Baba until I said it.

"Your father gave the world a blessing by having you," Mr. Kapadia said. "But he could not stop fighting, despite the terror it caused him. Perhaps he was both brave and foolish."

His words were a blow to the chest. "I'm getting married," I said. "To a soldier, about to deploy."

If he was surprised, he did not say. "Are you happy?" he asked.

"I don't know."

"Even if you wish to fight, your happiness also matters," he said to me. "You cannot shut off all happiness, because then what future are you fighting for?"

I swallowed past a lump in my throat. "And you?"

"You bring me happiness. This store brings me happiness. My memories of my friends bring me happiness. You do not need a husband to be happy, but you must find joy. Do you understand?"

My throat was too tight to respond, but I nodded. I had happiness in Fauzia, and Aai, and Yashu, and Mr. Kapadia. Why did it not feel like enough?

My wedding passed in a haze. I was dressed in a yellow sari, the Marathi custom. Mehendi traced down my hands in intricate patterns, and every time I looked down, I thought my hands were bleeding. Bhaskar's name was hidden in the whorls, but I had not bothered to find it.

I had not thought I would feel anything at my wedding, knowing the truth of its circumstances, but now with yellow silk draped over my shoulder, I sensed the gravity of this undertaking. My eyes sought out my friends, but through the haze of the smoke I could find nobody, not even Fauzia. I could barely look Bhaskar in the eye as we gave offerings to the flames and Aai tied our scarves together. She looked old in that moment, and so very sad. She must have been thinking about my Baba. Theirs had been a love marriage.

The memories swirled around me, pressing close as I rose to take seven circles around the fire with Bhaskar.

The first circle was for nourishment.

We had not had much, but Aai and Baba had always nourished each other, and me. Baba would bring me comic books from Mr. Kapadia's back room and tell me to hide them under my mattress whenever I left the room, even if I thought nobody else could see them. The books intrigued me with their vivid illustrations, but I struggled to understand the words, for they were written in Marathi, a language that we could not speak in public or write. The official slogan pasted up in our schoolrooms went "English language for the English people."

Although Aai was not a rebel, she told me I needed to learn Marathi so I would never forget the people I came from. By candlelight, she would take an old black chalkboard and write the curved, beautiful letters, sounding out the characters, then erase them with a sweep of her hand. "*Uh, ah, i, ee, u, oo, ay, ai, o, ou, um, aha,*" we recited together. We progressed to words, and then sentences, pressing the chalk as lightly as possible to conserve it. When we finished our lesson, Aai would wash the board clean, then write out a grocery list or some other mundane items in perfect English.

The second circle was for strength.

I read my comic books fervently, sounding out the words with childlike precision, determined to reach perfection. My best memories of those summers were of reading these books in the quiet solitude of our flat after escaping Mrs. Lele's watchful eyes. There were comics of the Ramayana and the Mahabharata, my Baba's favorites. He called them "the great Indian epics" and would mutter to himself about the superiority and advancement they showed compared to English texts. I was too engrossed in the stories themselves to care—they weren't taught at school, even in translation. Aai preferred the stories about Krishna, the clever little boy who grew up into a king and a leader of mankind. But my favorites were the goddesses. Sarasvati, goddess of knowledge and music, Lakshmi, goddess of wealth and fortune, and Kali, goddess of war and triumph.

I often longed to close my books and take a cool bath, but most mornings our ration filled only a fifth of our water drum. If we wanted to drink water and clean our dishes, we could wash only our faces. I watched my parents bear every indignity with straight-backed strength, and I tried to follow them in all things.

The third circle was for prosperity.

The day my Baba left, I was reading about the god Ganesha, the remover of obstacles, who possessed an elephant head and whom Aai prayed to as Ganapati Bappa. He rode a mouse instead of a horse or elephant, the most interesting thing about an otherwise boring god. The knock on the door startled me so much that I actually fell off my bed, landing in a heap on the ground.

"One moment!" I shouted, straightening my dress and remembering just in time to shove the comic under the mattress before answering the door.

A white man stood on the flat's landing. My young mind registered all the signs of his significance—pressed ribbons, weighty medals, even gleaming shoes, protected from the street's dust and grime by a car. This was no ordinary policeman that walked down our street. This was a man who safeguarded the wealth of the empire.

The fourth circle was for family.

"What is your name?" the officer asked me.

His perfectly accented voice put me on edge. A pit formed in my stomach, pulling my soul down to my feet, and I felt my throat seize. "Kalki Divekar, sir."

My parents' warnings rang loudly in my ears. *The rules are the only thing that can keep you safe,* they had said. *Call British officers "sir" or "madam." Move slowly and speak in slow En-*

glish. Answer their questions promptly with "yes" or "no." Do not smile or cry or frown. Do not ask questions. Do not give more information than they ask for.

The officer's smile remained firmly in place, and I was very afraid. "Is your father Rajendra Divekar?" *Ra-jahn-duh-rah.* My teachers would swoon over his pronunciation, but he had butchered my Baba's name with his proper accent.

"Yes, sir." I tried to keep my voice steady, because I now knew two things. One, the British were looking for my Baba. And two, Baba was gone.

Early in the morning, well before dawn, he had woken me up and pressed a kiss to my forehead. "You must be good, okay? Be good for your Aai. I love you, beti." I had been too bewildered to respond, so I kissed him on the cheek and let sleep drag me under, oblivious to the furious whispers from the living room.

And now this British man stood on our doorstep. "Is he inside?" he asked.

"No, sir." I would not give him up.

The fifth circle was for togetherness.

The officer entered our house and went straight for my parents' room. He opened drawers methodically, rifling through clothes and tossing them on the floor like trash, then smashed a photo sitting on the dresser of my Aai and Baba on their wedding day as if searching for something else in the frame. Finding nothing, the man let the photo fall to the floor and stomped on my Baba's face on his way to the mattress. Again, he found nothing, and I could tell he was disappointed. I was proud. Baba would have known they were coming, the way he knew patrols by heart.

Without a word to me, the officer left to enter the adjacent room.

"This is my room, sir," I said quietly, trailing behind him. What did he need in my room?

"All the same," he said, and began giving my room the same treatment.

He approached the bed, where I had shoved my comic under my mattress only minutes before.

A sharp pain pierced my stomach. He would find it, and then they would take me to prison. But he raised the mattress a few inches and hardly looked beneath it before dropping it back into place. Wiping his forehead and muttering under his breath, he left my bedroom. I heard him turn on the sink and use our water ration to splash his face with cool water.

He turned to our living room and kitchen in much the same way. Distantly, I could tell he was damaging Baba's books and denting our steel dishes, but the only thing I cared about was survival.

At last, he turned to me, standing in my corner. "Where is your father?" His forced smile had slipped away, and his hard expression put me at ease more than his snakelike politeness.

"My father is at work, sir." The word *father* felt unfamiliar on my tongue, and it made the lie go down more easily. Baba needed to get away from this man, and I would not fail him.

The sixth circle was for health.

The man pivoted on his heel and left. His clean uniform contrasted so vividly with his surroundings that when I closed my eyes, I could still see a bright imprint of his figure against my eyelids. I stayed watching the stairwell for several minutes, afraid he would somehow come back to look under my mattress.

As I stepped back inside around the carnage left by the officer, I felt the apathy leave me, replaced by a dull rage. What right had he to throw our clothes on the floor and ruin our possessions? When I picked up the photograph, there was dirt patterned on my Baba's face, a clear imprint of the officer's shoe. With shaking hands, I wet the edge of my shift and gently wiped the photograph until my Baba's face was visible again, smudged and wrinkled.

I swept in a furious frenzy, strange fantasies running through my head of the British officer impaling his foot on the glass, fat drops of his red blood staining our floor. It gave me satisfaction, for the nauseating anger would not leave me. All I could think to do was undo everything the British man had done, working my way through the rooms until the flat looked like he hadn't been there. But he had irrevocably changed the dynamics in our home, and I knew that my Baba would not be coming back.

I could not heal what had been destroyed today.

The seventh circle was for devotion.

When Aai came home that night, she did not speak of Baba. That night, she set out only two plates. We didn't speak of him that whole summer; it was as though he had been cut out from our lives. But I spoke about him every week with the British officers who never failed to show up at our flat, to conduct some new search as though my Baba would have returned. I stopped watching them go about their work, knowing that when they had left I would have to put things back to rights. Knowing that I would find something irreparably broken. Knowing that slowly but surely they were diminishing our little life, and wondering if one day everything in this flat would be broken, if there would be nothing left for me to put back together.

I was breathing hard at the end of the seven circles, so wrapped up in the intensity of the memory that I had not heard a single word the guruji had said. Was it better that my marriage was a lie? That it was without love, that I would never go through the pain that Aai had, never put a child through what I had experienced?

Now, suddenly, I could see Fauzia sitting next to Omar near the front, her eyes bright with unshed tears. When she saw me, she smiled, and instead of remembering the past, I could for a moment imagine the future. Fauzia feeding me a barfi at my tiny reception, her fingertips still stained with the mehendi from her wedding two weeks before. Fauzia playing a game of cards with me tonight, her finger coiling a strand of thick hair as she thought. Fauzia and I living together, close enough that her smell might seep into my clothes.

I chanced a glance at Aai. She was crying, but she was smiling

too. Aai was better than me, sturdy and solid and able to bear
unimaginable pain without folding. The night that Baba fled, she
had tried to impart that strength to me too. When she asked if I
remembered Kurma, I shook my head, hungry for a story. Stories
were comfort in our family, and I desperately needed solace. Back
then, I only heard the words, the muted adventure of the story.
Only now, so many years later, did I see what she had truly meant
by it. That sometimes, it took time and patience and effort to
survive the demons. That hiding and trickery could be more effective than fighting. That lying—whether to officers, or even to
the world—could be an act of faith and goodness.

"Long ago, when the earth was still new, the gods were tricked
into becoming mortal. The gods knew that without their power,
they could not prevail in their struggle against the demons. So
they sought the nectar of immortality, which they knew was buried deep in the darkest part of the cosmic ocean.

"The gods made a pact with the demons to search through the
ocean together in order to find the nectar. Vishnu transformed
himself into the tortoise Kurma and dove into the water, lifting
the massive mountain Mandara on his shell so that it would not
sink into the ocean. He bore the burden patiently as the gods and
demons roped a great snake to the mountain and used the mountain as a staff. With this staff they churned the sea, as one churns
butter.

"Out of the cosmic ocean emerged many awesome things,
both great and terrible. The goddess Lakshmi came up from the
depths, as did the creation-destroying poison Halahala. Finally,
just as the gods and demons began to tire of their task, the heav-
enly nectar was found. The gods and demons immediately began
to fight over it, their truce ended. But Kurma was wise. He took
the form of a beautiful woman and convinced the gods and demons to line up to receive the precious gift. Blinded by her beauty,
the demons agreed, and lined up behind the gods."

At this, I remember squinting at her. "Lord Vishnu was going
to give it to the demons?"

Aai smiled. "The new form of Vishnu, Mohini, went down the line one by one, distributing the nectar to each god. By the time she reached the demons, no nectar remained in her urn. She had never intended to give it to them. She had lied to spare the universe. Furious, the demons attacked, but it was too late. The gods had become immortal once more."

3

VARAHA, BOAR

I learned how to fight at twenty-one.

It began quietly enough, on one of those rare Sundays when Yashu and I were both free. Fauzia and I could see Yashu more often now that we had a place to host her, and Yashu had secured a typist job at City Hall. Bhaskar and Omar wrote us every so often, describing their harsh training program and the tasteless, hard food and their fear of being attacked. Meanwhile, Fauzia and I were close to graduating from our two-year programs in junior college, a whole world away from their suffering.

Though Fauzia was helping out at her family shop as usual, Yashu had a rare weekend off from her second job at a factory. We hadn't seen each other in almost a month, and we met outside our flat to wander the streets. The heat was just barely tolerable, but there were so few tolerable days in May that we took advantage where we could.

Yashu's family was Dalit—a term Yashu had taught me and had chosen to wear with pride—and as a child I had been surprised to learn that although she lived in one of the bungalows near the border of Old Bombay, her family's lives were still hard and marked by prejudice. It had been our first argument, at the age of about thirteen, one I had lost, when I tried to tell her that her family had come out on top during the Colonial Reestablishment. She was furious, explaining how her family shared their broken-down bungalow with five other large families, how they had to travel by foot to reach their menial waste-disposal and factory jobs that formed the backbone of Kingston's economy, how their employers would give them only work they considered too backbreaking or disgusting for other Indians. "We're definitely on top!" she concluded sarcastically.

Things were cool between us for a few weeks. Then one day at lunch, an older girl came up to our table looking for Yashu. For months I had not known which girls were from collaborator families, which were simply wealthy, and which were scholarship students like us, until Fauzia had taught me whom to watch out for. I had learned the names of the most important families, and I could also make out the quality of their uniforms, the shine and sturdiness of their shoes, the gold in their earrings. I classified this girl as belonging to an independently successful family. Not a collaborator. The collaborator children usually behaved the worst—their families generally had held power before the British and had thrown in their lot with their colonizers for the promise of continued riches. They had been rewarded for the ultimate betrayal.

"Hey," she said to Yashu, not deigning to meet her eyes. "There was a spill on the third floor, and you're available. Come quickly."

Yashu stared fixedly at her food.

"Hey," the girl said again, more sharply this time. "What are you waiting for?"

"Excuse me?" Fauzia asked, her voice low. "Shouldn't you be cleaning it up?"

The girl turned to Fauzia. "My tuition money pays for people like her to come here. I've earned my place here, same as you. But her kind get in as charity—she should at least work for it."

"Leave it," Yashu muttered to Fauzia. She was hunched in on herself, cheeks bright red. "I'll finish my lunch and come."

The girl scowled. "I said—"

"I'm sorry, did you earn your place or did your father buy your seat?" I broke in, unable to stop myself. "It sounds like you got in with a bribe, while the three of us passed the entrance exams on our actual intelligence. But I guess because you don't have any brains you wouldn't know that there are no special seats for anybody . . . except rich girls, apparently."

The girl turned her cool gaze on me, seeming unaffected by my words, and opened her mouth to deliver a comeback, but nothing came out. She spun on her heel and flounced away, and I heaved a sigh of relief.

I turned to Fauzia, who was grinning, and Yashu, who was . . . shoveling food into her mouth. At my confused expression, she chewed quickly and swallowed before saying, "I'm not going to anger them by refusing."

I wanted to track down that girl and shake her until she apologized, but I could tell that was not what Yashu wanted. When Yashu rose, so did Fauzia and I. She looked at both of us, considered saying something, and then turned away abruptly. "Come on, then," she said, her voice thick. "We probably have a lot to do."

This memory was on my mind as we walked. Even now, I could not countenance her argument that British rule was at least good for condemning the caste system and forcing the Indian people to abandon their backward attitudes. They had been entirely and purposefully ineffectual, because they thrived on our infighting.

"That Indians are still backward about caste is not the fault of the British," Yashu was saying. "At least legally we're protected. That's more than we could say before." From the glint in Yashu's eye, I could tell that she was feeling the pleasure of giving voice to anger.

"And in how many instances have people brought these claims before the British?"

Yashu scoffed. "It does happen! The fact that the option exists means they're definitely better than the Marathas used to be."

We paused briefly to buy bhel puri from a food cart, and I savored the sweet and spicy tang of the chutneys. "Just because now you have more protections and a house—"

"I might complain, but it's better than the slums! Which, by the way, is where most of us still live!" Yashu's voice rose and I gestured for her to speak softly. "We still do the worst jobs, the most dangerous and disgusting."

"So the British haven't even fixed *that,* you admit it!" I jabbed a finger toward her and she swatted it away. "Anyone who disagrees with them disappears, and we know what really happens to them. How is that good?"

"Freedom for you would mean further oppression for me," Yashu declared. "I'd rather have the British than *Gandhi.*" She spoke the name with a disgust that would have made our teachers proud.

My Baba had loved Gandhi, had read to me from Gandhi's own writings, telling the story of a man who was kind and just. He wanted to end suffering for his people, *our* people. He believed that all Indians, regardless of birth, were intelligent enough to govern themselves, and that we should govern ourselves, without any British officers or schoolteachers or royalty.

This Gandhi reminded me a lot of Baba. They both loved the word *independence.* My Baba taught me that word, helped me pronounce it. A perfect word, a ringing bell, calling for our freedom.

We learned a very different story in our British schools, one I would have dismissed if not for the various documents our teachers showed us and Yashu's distaste for him. This Gandhi was a murderer responsible for the deaths of millions of Indians. He tried to fight the British so he could be king of all of India, for he wanted to reimpose a strict caste hierarchy with himself and his followers at the top. He promised riches to anyone who supported him. He stole and stockpiled India's salt to drive up the prices and grow his coffers. Other Indian natives, fearful of his behavior, warned the British of his plans, and the army moved to intercept him. At the seashore of Gujarat, they struck down Gandhi and his followers, saving India from his tyrannical rule.

The British realized, after Gandhi's rebellion, that the people of India had not yet learned the lessons of modern governance, that they could not be trusted. Our teachers always acted as though the people of India had squandered their opportunity, as though they had been given every chance to have their own political parties and newspapers and reforms, but even in school we learned that as early as World War I the "native rule" was suppressed because it was dangerous and violent, its leaders jailed and transported and worse. I could not see how we had ever received any chance at all. We were taught that it was Gandhi who finally convinced the British to unite India as a single British colony under a Western system of governance. The Colonial Reestablishment ended the practices of decentralized administration and the minor autonomous kingdoms and made the British Raj a permanent administrative state under the British Crown, which remained ever vigilant to prevent another Gandhi from attaining the same power.

"Forget Gandhi," I said, because even though I knew the British lied, I had seen the pictures of the bodies of Indian natives whom Gandhi had sent to die without reason. When we learned of things like the Sepoy Mutiny, where Indian rebels brutally raped and murdered every British civilian in sight before turning on one another, unable to govern, I felt shameful stirrings of sympathy for the British.

Still, it was nothing compared to what we had been through. I had spent the last year educating myself on the real history of

India. Fauzia had relatives across the empire, and even a few in the United States of America. Among these was a distant cousin who was Anglo-Indian but lived under a white name with his white wife at the border of Old Bombay. Though racial mixing was officially banned, the British still raped whomever they wished, and occasionally would take on bastard sons who were young and light-skinned enough to pass. Some of the bastard heirs were eager to repudiate where they came from, but many more were willing to undertake small acts of rebellion to ease their guilt. After Fauzia's cousin learned of her interest in history, he occasionally passed her short items that were allowed in British homes but banned in Indian ones.

Through these pamphlets, I learned that my Baba's stories only scratched the surface of Indian history. Indians, untold millions of them, had fought, been beaten back, and fought again for independence. They used everything they had—violence, protests, marches, speeches, negotiations—and in turn received every cruel and brutal punishment the British could muster—murder, rape, famine, forced migration, torture. From the place where I had locked it away, that awful night of the march sometimes came back to me in violent flashes—but now I knew that what we had seen was the least of what they were capable of. It made me so sick I spent an evening vomiting, thinking of these things happening to Baba. To Mr. Lele. To my neighbors, my friends. My family.

I had been told I had no relatives—my Aai was an only child, my Baba's younger brother was long gone, and their extended families lived across the water, a place I had never seen. My grandparents were dead, my Aai's parents lost in the blaze that gave birth to Kingston and my Baba's parents lost to illness before that. But sometimes I wondered if that was a story too, if my Baba had inherited his fervor from somewhere. If his family had suffered worse things than the horrifying fate of immolation. Had they rotted in prisons, been sent to camps to be starved and tortured, been shot and thrown into mass graves, their souls doomed? I knew Aai would never tell me, and my imagination ran rampant.

But my picture remained incomplete. I had read maybe twenty or thirty contraband documents out of tens of thousands. How I itched to get my hands on the British repositories, even for a few minutes. When I told Fauzia this, she suggested I get a government job. Then, she said, I could slowly access whatever I wanted, like her cousin. She tried to convince me it was a way to fight back, right under their noses. Like most of my friends, and like most Indians who did well in school, Fauzia planned on taking a government position, whether working for the actual administration or in a state-sponsored business. At first I found this idea impossible to stomach. But righteous rage alone could not save India, or we would have been free long ago. If loss or sacrifice or passion were enough to stop the British, the whole world would be rid of them. I needed to know my enemy, learn their tools and beliefs and weaknesses. And so, two years after I stole the song from the British, I would return to the scene of the crime as an employee.

Yashu was looking at me expectantly as the anger and shame mixed in me. My voice sounded weak as I argued, "Why should the British live in Old Bombay all comfortable and we be relegated here? Why—"

We finally entered the marketplace proper, a wall of sound and sight, and I cut myself off, for it was certainly too crowded to debate such ideas.

"Kalki, I know you mean well, but I've told you before—the British might be bad, but it's the kind of bad we have learned how to survive. We can't throw that away when native rule was just as terrible. We should try to improve what we can, but . . ."

Wasn't it worth risking it all for the chance at something better? For freedom? And yet I knew Yashu was right to be skeptical. There were too many people around, and I could not think of any way to voice my feelings in public.

"Time's up, and I think this counts as your defeat," Yashu said with a laugh. "Loser has to buy the mangoes."

I groaned, but truthfully I enjoyed having a few paise with which to treat my friends. I'd have more when I began working full time, though some part of me felt like I was joining the ranks of those girls we avoided in school, who always had money for treats and new clothes, money earned on the backs of everyone else.

Yashu dragged me toward a stall selling a huge variety of mangoes. The Alphonsos glimmered like bright orange jewels, while the other mangoes looked dull, green, and unripe. But who could afford to pay the extra twenty rupees?

Yashu and I picked through the wares, selecting two pairi mangoes.

"Only fifty paise!" the vendor exclaimed.

I rolled my eyes. "Fifty?" Everyone knew the rule of the market: the less desperate the haggler, the better the deal. "These are the first of the season. Ten, and no more."

"Ten? Sister, are you trying to bankrupt me? These are worth at least thirty."

I pretended to consider it. "Fifteen seems fair. I can spare an extra five out of the goodness of my heart."

"Twenty-five," he countered.

"Fifteen," I responded.

"No, sister, there's just no way."

I shrugged and deployed my final gambit: walking away. I made it three steps before he shouted at me, "Twenty! Sister, twenty paise, just for you."

I dumped the coins in his hand, and Yashu and I ran off before he could try to sell us anything more. I pulled a pocketknife out of my bag and began carefully skinning and dividing the mangoes. It wasn't technically legal to carry a pocketknife, but no one was looking.

We paused on the side of the road, and I sank my teeth into the firm flesh, juice exploding inside my mouth. Savoring the flavor, I watched the crowded street, bustling with life and activity, and a calm euphoria settled over me. In that moment, I wasn't a child with no father, or a likely widow, or a soon-to-be sellout. I was just a college student, eating a mango and enjoying the weather.

As I waited for Yashu to finish up, I wandered over to a stall selling small bracelets and necklaces. They were simply made, with white string and tiny colored beads, but had been assembled with great care and skill into beautiful geometric patterns, in the newest Indian style. Several women stood clustered around the stand, haggling with the shopkeeper.

A man stopped at the stall and lifted his eyes briefly, his gaze connecting with mine.

Electricity shot through my limbs. He was pleasing to the eyes, but that wasn't why; a small silver chain hung around his neck, its pendant a wheel that caught the sunlight. I openly stared, unable to believe that he would so blatantly flash that symbol.

Independent India. I had a bookmark at home, hidden in a book under my bed, with the same symbol on it. My Aai had given it to me for my tenth birthday, in the week after Baba left. He had painted it for me, a royal-blue wheel against a saffron background, and for months Aai had made me keep it with Mr. Kapadia, until the officers finally stopped returning.

And here this man wore the unmistakable symbol on his chest. *Independent India.* How did nobody else see this, nobody else care? Or did they just pretend to be oblivious, ignoring his foolishness in the hope it would not attach to them?

I took a small step closer to him, and then another. What was I doing, walking into danger in front of everyone? Yet I longed to be a part of his hopeful world, to taste it as I had that mango.

The man bought a bracelet at the stand, exchanging a few words with the stall keeper, and then moved onto the walkway where we stood. Now that he was closer, I saw how young he was, maybe only slightly older than me. He glanced at me again, and we moved toward each other. His hand gently brushed against mine, and I felt a rustle of paper. I clenched my hand into a fist, spinning around just as he turned the corner and disappeared out of sight.

It felt like I had crossed a chasm, but I had only moved a few meters from Yashu. "I have to go," I told her, hoping she couldn't see how my hands shook even as I clenched them. I could feel the May humidity pressing into every inch of me, making it hard to breathe. "I completely forgot I promised to run an errand for my Aai."

Yashu suspected nothing as she ate the remainder of her fruit, shaking her head. "You miscreant. Thanks for the mango. I'll swing by your place next Sunday, maybe? If we all aren't working?"

"Sounds good." My mouth felt uncomfortably dry.

Yashu patted me on the shoulder. "Don't worry too much. I'm sure she's not going to be *that* mad, married woman."

I forced a laugh at our running joke about how I of all people was married, and Yashu slipped out of the marketplace. I walked as quickly as I could to the opposite end of the market and finally uncrumpled the paper to read: *4 May 1964 14:00; phone booth Dominion Way.* Today, in an hour. My mind raced. Was I to meet someone at the location or make a call? Who was I meant to speak with? Why did they contact me? What did they want?

I made the journey to Dominion Way on slow, unsteady feet, keeping my eyes down as I trod the path to the short street in the heart of Kingston. Dominion Way was one block from the British Outpost, filled with restaurants and other shops to serve its substantial workforce. I could not help the chill that ran down my spine in the shadow of the Outpost. It was a great stone structure, cold and imposing, its broad windows made of bulletproof glass. Where once I might have thought of it as strong and protective, now its power seemed monstrous, for I knew what it was, what it did. Inside was the center of control of Kingston, not only local administrative functions that could be wielded as weapons, but also detention centers, torture chambers, and all the things the British needed to make their problems disappear. Though the government sat in Old Bombay, the Outpost allowed them to govern.

I watched a large, sturdy vehicle with far too many wheels roll up to the side of the Outpost. Two white men stepped out of the front dressed in camouflage and khakis, and a few others came out of the building to greet them. I stood on the other side of the street, rooted to the spot as they unlocked the back of the transport to reveal several Indian men chained together at the ankles and handcuffed. The chain was tugged too quickly, and the last one out stumbled, falling onto the man before him. Faster than I could track, a soldier yanked the last prisoner up by the back of his neck and struck him with a club.

The prisoner cried out and fell to his knees, a splash of red blotting his pale brown uniform. All around me people went about their business, unseeing or uncaring. But I couldn't look away as the prisoners in front of him marched forward into the Outpost, dragging him with them.

For a moment, I wondered whether my Baba had been caught and subjected to the same treatment in some faraway Outpost. He stood tall and proud in my memory, but he would be older now, and weak after running for so long, if he was still alive. Would he have fallen behind and been dragged away, his last moments robbed of dignity? Tears pricked at my eyes, and I blinked rapidly so they would not fall.

As the lunchtime crowds began to disperse—the British did not stop even for their holy Sunday—and I paced the streets around Dominion Way to avoid attention, I realized the genius of the location. It would be deserted at 14:00 because people would be inside to avoid the heat, but it was also so close to the Outpost that nobody would dare engage in treachery here. It avoided suspicion, even if every glimpse of the building made my heart pound. After all, the consequences for rebellion were banishment or execution.

In the bright light on Dominion Way, it was obvious nobody

else was out of place or here to meet me. I approached the phone booth, trying to look confident, a few paise in hand. As soon as I closed the booth door, shielding myself in the tinted glass, the phone rang.

I fumbled for the receiver, my hands shaking so badly that I whacked my face with the phone while lifting it to my ear.

"Hello?" I whispered.

"Beti," a voice on the other end said.

My legs gave out, and I pulled the phone and cord down with me to the floor, gasping for breath.

"Beti," my Baba said again, and my sob stuck in my throat, coming out as half a cough.

"Baba," I replied, voice barely above a whisper. "Baba, Baba, Baba." My mouth could not say anything other than that. All my love and pain and fear and grief flooded me, and all the rest— *where have you been why have you never contacted me before are you all right I love you I miss you please come back*—got stuck. I clutched the phone like a lifeline.

"Beti, I love you so much," he said. "I love you. Are you well?"

"Yes," I managed to get out. "Are you? Where are you?"

"I am well," he told me, and I knew instinctively he was lying. "I cannot tell you where I am, but I am safe. I miss you so much, beti. I love you. I am so very proud of you. I don't have much more time."

"Baba, no, please," I begged. I was a child again, with a child's tongue. I hoped he would know what I meant. *No, please, we only just started talking, you cannot leave me so quickly.*

"Beti, I called to tell you something. Your Aai wouldn't agree with me, but I know you will. It is time for a new generation to begin its work in Kingston. It is your time now." I could barely comprehend his words.

"Baba, what do you mean?"

"I'm sorry, beti, I have no time to explain. Follow your in-stincts. We will talk again. Tell your Aai—" He paused for a moment, trying to control the tremor in his voice. In the background of his call, I could hear a rising commotion. "Tell her I love her too."

The phone clicked, and I wailed. I held the receiver to my ear another minute longer, listening to the long tone, hoping he would return. But he was gone. I returned the phone to its cradle and rose to my feet in the cramped booth. My body went through motions my mind could not comprehend. I dried my tears, straightened my shirt, took deep breaths until my tremors calmed.

I stepped out of the booth as though I had placed a random call of no import and walked quickly—but not too quickly—out of Dominion Way until I escaped the shadow of the Outpost. Then I broke into a run, wild and frenzied, sprinting until I slammed through the door of Aai's small flat.

Aai sat at the table. Her hands were folded on the tabletop, and she watched me with an expression resembling hunger. "What did he say?" she asked.

The world tilted on its axis, reoriented, then turned red.

"You *knew*?" I ran up to her, violence building, and banged my palm against the top of her chair. I did not know how to express the deep rage inside of me, but I wanted to make her understand my pain. Aai just took it, calm as ever, but when I looked more closely at her face, dried tears streaked her skin. She had been crying.

"You knew," I whispered, sinking down to kneel at her feet. I could not fathom a reason why she would keep this from me.

"I knew," she said, voice choking. "I knew, and it was the hardest thing I ever did to keep it from you."

"Why?" I asked. No reason would satisfy me, but still I needed to know.

"Because your Baba asked me to. He didn't want to risk that you might let it slip when you were younger. That you might talk about him in the present tense instead of the past or hope for a reunion. We can talk to him, beti, but he is never coming back."

"I'm twenty-one. I'm married. You could have told me years

ago. Why would you keep it from me?" I was shouting, but I couldn't stop myself.

"Your Baba—he couldn't bear it. I convinced him last we spoke, months ago."

I began to cry. What had I expected? Alive, he was still a fugitive, and it would always be too risky for us to meet him again. But the past ten minutes had given me hope for the first time in a long time. Momentarily, an entire future had bloomed in front of me, a future where Baba would come back and we would be a happy family.

I had only had ten minutes of that fantasy, but I mourned for it in long keens, sobbing so intensely I thought I would vomit. This was far worse than when Baba left, because I was old enough to both see my future with him and understand the loss. In that moment, knowing he lived just out of reach seemed crueler than his death.

When I finally came to my senses, I realized Aai was crouched down on her knees beside me, holding my shaking body. Her hands rubbed my back in slow, soothing patterns, and she rocked us both back and forth. I trembled in her arms, but I couldn't control myself. My hearing returned, and I realized she was singing Baba's favorite song.

"Vande mataram, sujalam suphalam, malayajashitalam, shasya shyamalam, mataram." *Mother, I bow to you, rich with your hurrying streams, bright with your orchard gleams, cool with the winds of delight, dark fields waving, mother of might, mother free.*

I allowed my breathing to even out to the rhythm of the song. My shaking subsided into shivers. A hole throbbed now where part of my heart used to be. The pain of it felt good, confirmed that the events of the past half hour were real and that my Baba really lived somewhere out there, unable to ever return.

"Kalki, I am so sorry," Aai said. It was the first and only time she ever apologized to me for something she had done.

"Aai," I managed, before I started crying again.

She brushed out my hair and coaxed my body to lie down in her lap. "What did he say?"

"He said he loved me," I said.

"Well, of course he does," Aai responded. "How is he?"

"Wouldn't you know?" I asked angrily. "Why do you need me to tell you?"

"Kalki, how often do you think he can call? He must pass a note on to me, and then he must have the electricity and the anti-surveillance equipment to call. I last spoke with him over six months ago. I told him he must call you, that you were old enough and ready, and it took him six months to arrange it."

"Oh," I said, because what else could I say? "Baba said he was well. He wanted me to tell you he loves you." I remembered then what more Baba had said. *It is time for a new generation.* Aai would not approve, it was true, but I knew why he had finally revealed himself to me after all these years. "Is he with the Indian Liberation Movement?"

"I know he is with others, and you and I both know what he is doing with them. But I know no specifics. Let's not talk about it further." In my mind's eye, I saw it. Men like my Baba and Mr. Kapadia and others, all gathered around a small table in a dimly lit room, looking at maps and arguing about their next attack, or their most recent intelligence-gathering mission. It made me proud to know that Baba still fought, but already I was afraid for him. I knew that if he died, we would never learn of it. The British would burn his body or toss it into the pits they kept for their enemies, and we would sit by the phone and grow old waiting for him.

"Did he say anything else?" Her question brought me out of this vision. In that moment, even though she had betrayed me more deeply than I thought possible, I felt sorry for her. She waited months for a few seconds of conversation, and today, I had taken up that time. It could be another six months before she got a chance to talk to her husband.

But still I lied to her. "No."

WHAT DID AN independence movement do? In the old days, long before my Baba's time, it organized our people to fight back and become self-sufficient, published papers, held rallies, and fought for reform. But by the time World War I was over, Indian newspapers were banned and spinning wheels burned, bullets littering the ground of every meeting place. All the great potential of this country, the great Indians with voices strong enough to echo—Nehru and Jinnah and Bose and Ambedkar and Azad and on and on—were hanged or assassinated or exiled forever. I had heard my Baba's stories of the 1930s, of the killing of Gandhi and the brutal Colonial Reestablishment on the eve of World War II, of the burning of Kingston during the war when the city tried to rise up in resistance, every person willing to stand up and fight plucked like a leaf from the vine until the plant was barren. I wondered if there were another world where fate had been on our side and we had already gained independence. Perhaps I would have been born into a free India, would have traveled the country, would have had my family whole at my side. It was a ridiculous idea, unproductive to dwell on, and yet I could not help but dream of having my Baba back.

I thought back to what I knew of Baba's work. A few months before he disappeared, he had shown me an article about a firebomb that blew up part of Kingston's British Outpost. The black-and-white picture in the newspaper showed a smoking silhouette of the formerly impressive structure, with a few British men gathered around it. The headline read, "Organized Anarchists or Lone Actor?" Baba had taken me on a walk past the Outpost a few weeks before the bombing. I admired its magnificence as a child, for it looked so strong and clean, and Baba's grip had tightened on my hand until it was almost painful.

"There is nothing good about this place," he whispered to me. "You must remember this."

"Why?" I asked, and he turned to look at me with tears in his eyes. He picked me up, even though I was too large to be held comfortably, and began walking away.

"That place is like a parasite. It is strong and impressive only because it sucks the lifeblood from us."

I remembered enough of that outing that when I saw the article, I was afraid. Who could bring down the Outpost? "Will they come for us next?" I asked my Baba.

"No, beti. They are doing this for us, they would not hurt us."

"They broke the law. My teacher said that extremists will do anything to hurt anybody. Yesterday the Outpost, today our houses!"

"Some lawbreakers are heroes," he told me. "The British, they are—"

Fire raced up the paper. Aai was holding it to a lit match, dropping the page to the floor only when flames licked her fingertips. Ashes fell into Baba's lap, and she stamped out the remaining fire with her slipper. "You cannot win," she said. Her voice was colder than I had ever heard it.

"We did not win this time," Baba said, staring at me instead of looking at Aai. "But one day the Outpost will fall. It must."

"Do not fill her head with your stupidity!" Aai snapped, her voice like a whip. "She is barely nine. Do you have no shame?"

"The only shame for us is living beneath the heels of the British," my Baba hissed. "To resist is to be a hero."

Aai whirled around to face me, and I took a step back at her fury. "Kalki, you listen to me. We obey the law because it keeps us safe. Heroes end up dead, or worse. Do you understand?"

Scared, I nodded, but I felt a yearning deep in my stomach to be a hero, as my Baba had said. And I remembered that feeling now. Baba would want me to try to take down the Outpost again, right?

"What are you thinking?" Aai asked over dinner. My leg jittered under the table.

"Nothing," I got out.

"Kalki, I know this is hard. I know you're angry. But going

and doing something tonight is not a good idea. You could be put under suspicion and jeopardize your future. Think this through."

She didn't voice the most urgent concern of all: I could get caught and never come home. I picked at my food, unable to formulate a response. How had she read my mind?

"Are you listening to me?" she asked. "Please."

This last word shook me out of my reverie. "They destroyed our family. Aren't you mad?"

Aai ignored my question. "Kalki, please. What are you planning?"

"It's better you don't know, right?"

She reached across the table to hold my hand. "I cannot lose you too. Please, Kalki. Be safe. That's all I ever want for you. If something were to happen to you . . ."

Her voice cracked, and with it my resolve. I had no plan, no resources, and no way to protect Aai. If the old fighters had failed to win freedom with decades of experience, I could not do it now. Not without a plan.

I TOLD FAUZIA the next day. We told each other everything, shared every thought we had. When we first moved into the flat, our closeness deepening, I began to wonder whether Fauzia might still have feelings for me. I didn't know, really, what being together entailed, but I realized I wouldn't mind her soft, beautiful hands on me, noticed I thought more than I should about her perfectly shaped lips. I thought perhaps if she had not found anyone else, I might be better than nothing at all. . . . But when I asked her, in a sidelong, teasing, manner, if she still liked me, she scoffed. The reaction was too fast, and too decisive, to be anything but true. She was far too good for me anyway, and so I buried those thoughts as best I could. And if on occasion my eyes lingered on her, or I brushed against her by accident, I told myself that was the closeness of friends. Nothing more.

Now, though, as the story of my Baba's survival and wanting

to take down the Outpost spilled out of me, I found myself captivated by the spark in her eyes. My words seemed to awaken something in her, the same desire for freedom that blazed in me. "It will take more than just burning down the Outpost to liberate this city," she said. "I think he wants you to get others to join the cause. I think he wanted you to start a movement, Kalki. Did he say anything more?"

I shook my head. "No. He didn't have the time. We barely had the chance to talk and then he had to go." For the first time I thought of how Baba must have felt, sending me into danger with only the hope that his old, vague lessons might keep me safe. It wasn't fair, but he had no other choice. India had to be freed, no matter the cost. "I'm so angry, I have to do something. I have to hurt them."

"I know," Fauzia said. "I know. But your family already has a mark against them." I felt Fauzia's hand on my shoulder. "Kalki. We're going to do it, okay?" I looked up at her determined face, and it was like I was seeing her for the first time, transcendent. "We're going to beat them. To start, we should talk to Yashu."

"Yashu's not interested," I said immediately. "She doesn't think there's any point to change."

Fauzia clicked her tongue. "You don't know that. She likes antagonizing you, but—"

"No, she doesn't think there's any point, because she says liberation for India would not be liberation for her people. And she might be right. I don't want to put her in that position."

"You're getting ahead of yourself," Fauzia said with a small laugh. "Yashu is a brilliant woman who knows her own mind far better than you do. We can talk to her, and she can decide for herself, yes? And then we'll recruit other people we can trust."

"Fine," I agreed slowly, letting her vision bloom in front of me. "Yes. We're going to fight."

Fauzia continued planning, playing with her bracelet as she spoke. I was still reeling from the shattering of my world, but it grounded me to see the bracelet, which I had gotten her many years ago to replace the heirloom she had sold.

Early in our friendship, before we had met Yashu, Fauzia and I had been walking home when I saw a group of girls down the street. I wanted to impress them, despite Fauzia hissing at me to leave it alone. I practically swaggered down the street, begging the other girls to notice. They did.

"Hey, where are you headed?" one girl called out to us.

Fauzia looked over at me but didn't say anything. "Down to Mountbatten Road," I responded.

"Oh, we were just going that way," the other girl said. "Want to get a ride with us?"

I hadn't been expecting that kind offer, and by Fauzia's expression, neither had she. "Sure!" she agreed.

The girls bought some fruit from the stand and then flagged down a rickshaw. All five of us crammed into the tiny compartment, sitting knee to knee in the yellow box. I could tell from the way they smelled that their parents had money. That they had the water allocation to bathe daily and had perfumes to help mask the scent of the streets. That they washed their uniforms after every wear. I imagined their lives, with maids and servants, new clothes and jewelry, and all the English books they wanted. Even though they had been nice to us, ever-present anger smoldered inside of me that they reaped such rewards for disloyalty while the rest of us suffered. I wondered if they could smell the difference on Fauzia and me. If they could, they didn't comment on it in the rickshaw.

After about ten minutes, we arrived outside my complex. I climbed out quickly, not wanting to linger in front of the obviously decrepit building in which I lived.

Fauzia got out after me, and we were bidding the girls farewell when the girl who had originally invited us asked, "Aren't you going to pay the rickshaw driver?"

Behind me, I heard Fauzia's slight inhale, and knew what had happened. I dipped my hand into my schoolbag and pretended to fish around for some coins, even though I knew I would find none.

"I must have forgotten to take some rupees from my mother today," I told her. She tittered, and I realized my mistake—the upper-class Indians referred to our currency with the British terms *pound* and *shilling* even though we had a separate colonial currency. I soldiered on, knowing I would have to humiliate my-self. "Could you pay it for us?"

The girl turned back to look knowingly at her friends, then said, "My mother always taught me not to give charity to beg-gars." Her friends giggled behind her, and I felt my cheeks flame.

"I'm not a beggar!" I said. Then, more quietly, "I just forgot my money."

"Then you will pay me back tomorrow?" she asked. We both knew I could not.

"Yes, we will," Fauzia spoke up. She squeezed my hand.

The girl smiled at us, a tiger's grin, as my Aai would say. She instructed the rickshawala to move on, and they went off down the road.

As soon as they were out of earshot, I spun around to face Fauzia. "Where are you going to find money? You shouldn't have said that!" Tears pooled in my eyes, threatening to spill over, frustration and anger rapidly building to rage.

"I can get the money," Fauzia said calmly. "But I told you so. Don't yell at me when this is your fault. You wanted to impress *collaborators* of all people." A cool edge invaded her voice, and my heart sank. She was never going to speak to stupid, reckless Kalki again. Without saying goodbye, she turned on her heel and walked briskly down the road. I watched her go, too scared to say anything. Now I truly had a reason to be ashamed.

I made the trek to school the next day alone, the anvil of de-spair crushing me with every step. In less than a year, I would lose the only friend I had ever made. I wanted to run back home, but for all my failings, I was no coward. And when I approached the school, Fauzia stood outside, waiting for me, a slight smile on her face as if nothing had happened. "I paid them," she told me. "Trust me, they will not trouble us now."

Those girls never approached me again. Later I learned that Fauzia had sold her only gold bracelet, a gift from her grandmother that was inlaid with green glass and a single pearl. She had paid the girl back thrice our rickshaw fare and said, "We gave you charity by letting you ride with us. Generosity will be paid back many times over." The girl had been so surprised that she had no retort, and Fauzia had left with the last word.

Fauzia never said anything to me, and never showed any resentment, but I knew that she was upset about the loss. Almost a year after the rickshaw incident, when I finally saved enough to buy her a new one, I went to a shop and found a new golden bracelet, and two more bracelets made of blue-green glass.

"An excellent choice," said the old woman sitting behind the counter, who had named such a fair price I could not even bring myself to haggle.

"Thank you, grandmother," I said, ducking my head.

"Those glass ones," she continued, leaning forward, "they remind me of one of my favorite stories."

I wanted to run to Fauzia, but she had taught me how ridiculous my impulsiveness was. So I gave the old woman a smile and said, "What is your favorite story?"

"That of Varaha and the Earth." Her eyes had a faraway look to them. "When the Earth was just a young woman, a power-hungry demon kidnapped her. He wanted to make her his mistress, and when she refused, he threatened her and tortured her, and she cried out for aid. Angered by her disobedience and humiliated by her rejection, the demon dropped her into the cosmic ocean, where she began to sink.

"Vishnu heard her cry and ran to her rescue. But in his path stood the demon, who was determined to let no one rescue the Earth. Vishnu assumed the form of a tiny boar, Varaha, no bigger than your pinkie finger. Seeing this, the demon laughed and laughed, until he saw Varaha begin to grow before his very eyes. He grew to the size of a boar, then the size of a tree, then a hill, then a mountain. He grew until he was the height of the space between earth and sky, and the cosmos trembled at his single step. His body was black, his mighty tusks white, and his great mane orange with fearsome flame."

I saw in her words Fauzia, who looked so small and unassuming but had stood up for both of us. And now, in the depths of my mind, I saw my future, one woman bringing down an unbreakable building. It would happen. I knew it.

"The demon was afraid now, but still he stood to face Varaha on the field of battle. Varaha was strong and righteous, and though they fought bitterly, when the time came, he gored the demon with his tusks, turning them red with the blood of victory. Varaha tossed the demon aside and ran to the edge of the ocean, searching for any sign of the Earth. Finding none, Varaha plunged into the cosmic ocean. He swam down into its currents and found the Earth, still struggling to survive. He balanced her on his snout and carried her out of the depths. Gently, he placed her above the cosmic ocean, and balance was restored once more."

4

NARASIMHA, HALF LION, HALF MAN

I learned how to prepare at twenty-two.

I watched Kingston deteriorate around me as the British settled in for a long war with China. Bhaskar and Omar had been at the front for more than a year. Whenever I thought of them, my stomach churned with worry, followed by anger that I was powerless to help them. In Kingston, rations on food and water tightened every month, and the frustrated British lashed out at civilians. It had previously been very difficult and expensive to leave the island, and few ever could because the permits were so hard to obtain, but now it was impossible without prior written approval from the highest officials. All we knew was what news came to us, mostly from the British.

So I felt slightly guilty that my own fortunes seemed on the rise. My full-time position in the colonial administration earned me almost five hundred rupees a month. It was more than my Aai had ever made, and so I swallowed my pride and hatred and took the crowded bus into Old Bombay to report to the majestic City Hall, where we had plentiful water and electricity all day. I worked in the rations office, doing data entry. Although I sat in the open rows where all the Indian girls worked, I had the seat closest to the office of Mr. Jenkins, the head of the rations office. He had taken a "liking" to me on my first day, leering at me, brushing my bottom with his hand, and always picking me to deliver things to him in his small office, where I could feel his hot breath on me. But I knew women had suffered far worse under this regime.

Inside, I was itching with my Baba's message. Yashu had, to my surprise, not shot me down immediately. But both she and Fauzia had counseled me to wait, to finish the probationary period at my new job so I would no longer be under significant scrutiny. Now, half a year into the position, I could wait no longer. In late December there was a break from work for the Christian holidays, and the British emptied out of Kingston to see their families in their fatherland. Both Fauzia and Yashu, despite having good jobs in the administration that they could scarcely afford to lose, had agreed to help me arrange a meeting of like-minded individuals.

"I don't want you to be mad if I don't join up," Yashu had told me a few weeks earlier. "I am only doing this for you because you're my friend. But I'm still not sure your movement is my friend."

Her words hurt, but I understood her position. "I won't be mad," I said. "Well, I won't be that mad." Yashu laughed, and we left it at that. We saw a lot more of each other now because we both worked in City Hall. The legal department was so close to mine that we often sat together on our lunch breaks. It was a far cry from how we had once spent our lunch breaks, debating politics and history in hushed tones. Now we talked about my and Fauzia's flat, our parents, her female cousins. The men were off-limits—Bhaskar and Omar and Yashu's loved ones—because the men of Kingston had been stolen from us.

Three months earlier, Bhaskar had written that Omar was wounded in the leg by shrapnel. I had come to love them even more in their letters, opening each one with shaking hands, scanning for that holy word: *alive*. They described the horror of the front without hiding it, although sometimes lines would be blacked out by the censors. But the parts about the cold seeping into their bones, the frostbite and hunger, we were allowed to know. Now Bhaskar and Omar, who had grown up without cold, were adrift in the snow, and their pain bled into our hearts as we read their words. Although our boys did not mention their love, we read it between the lines. And now we watched Kingston's young men depart the moment they turned eighteen.

In my heart, I wondered whether it wasn't just the empire's need for fresh bodies on its many war fronts, but also because the history books taught that the last several rebellions had been fueled by younger men. With all the rest of us left behind struggling to keep the city functioning, how could we think about revolution?

I had raised the issue to Fauzia not long before, but she scoffed. "We are enough. I would not expect you of all people to think we need men."

I rolled my eyes. "Stop being dramatic, there's nobody around to appreciate it. I'm not saying we need men because they're better. We need men because they can do certain things without suspicion, things that we can't do."

"Like what?" Fauzia challenged.

"They can hold higher jobs in the administration. They can try to lie their way into befriending their superiors. Listen in."

"There are no young men left. And the old men aren't rebels. They had their chance, and either they were cowards or they're dead."

Watching Fauzia spit out the word *cowards* took me back to the last time we had ever seen Bhaskar. We were on the crowded train platform, with all the other young men about to ship out, trying hard not to cry.

"Write to us," Fauzia told him. "Tell us if you find Omar, and about the conditions."

"I doubt I will be able to tell you anything, but I will try."

"Don't be brave," I whispered, keeping my voice low even though I knew many mothers were right now telling their sons the same thing. "If you're in a dangerous situation, run. Get away. You don't need to be at the front of anything. Just survive."

"I'm not going to just abandon—"

"Do not finish that thought," Fauzia cut in. "You are not fighting for India. You are fighting for the British. They care nothing about you. They care nothing about this place. Better to be a living coward than a dead hero."

The final call for boarding sounded. Bhaskar gave Fauzia a quick hug and pulled me in a few seconds longer. He kissed my cheek. "Be good," he said softly, and then slipped away.

There was something different between the cowardice she spoke of then and now, but still I thought the past two years had changed her. She was harder, angrier. More like me, although she still retained an essential kindness that I lacked. And she was right.

I nodded. "We have to work with what we've got. We can do this just as well."

THE PLAN WAS meticulous. We paid some rowdy kids to set off fireworks—technically a crime, but by the time the police triangulated the location and converged, the children would be long gone. We supplied them with orange, green, and white firecrackers, the colors of the old movement. We didn't want to be too obvious—didn't want to approximate a wheel or a lion that might tip our hand—but still we had orange for the Hindu color of sacrifice, green for the Muslim color of paradise, and white for freedom.

When I got worried that this would all come to naught, I tried to imagine the colors, shining even through the haze of light and air pollution, and the impotent rage of the British police. The image calmed me. The Indians would know what it meant.

I spoke to Mr. Kapadia, who was the only rebel I knew. "It's time," I told him, and in response he took me to the back room, where I had been many times. There was a thick woven tapestry on one wall, and when he pushed it aside, there was an opening and a large, empty room.

"This has an entrance from the alley," he said. "It looks like a door to a house, but it's a passage that leads here. The police think it's to prevent theft, and I will fill it with inventory once more." He was not a coward, nor was he dead—he was a survivor, and ready to rebel once more.

I threw my arms around him. "Thank you, thank you, thank you!"

I could not tell Aai. If she knew I was standing in the same room where my Baba had once—no. Our lives had gradually separated after I moved out, and though she still worried about me, I thought it a blessing that she could not see what I was doing now.

Yashu and Fauzia came to help me clean the room, which was dusty and unused. As I bent low with the long-bristled broom, I wondered whether my Baba had ever done the same in preparation for a meeting of his comrades. It was the dirt stinging my eyes that drew tears, I told myself. My friends came beside me, placing their warm hands on my shoulders, and I turned to embrace them. "Thank you," I said. I knew they heard *I love you*.

My worry increased as the night approached. "They'll be here," Fauzia reassured me as I paced back and forth in the dimly lit back room. Mr. Kapadia kept rearranging chairs, even though they were perfectly aligned. Yashu had already left to collect the first group of people and guide them in.

I rubbed the hem of my dress, my fingers moving in frenetic pace with my heart. "What if they've tipped off the authorities?"

"They wouldn't. They're our closest friends—so we know too

much about them." Fauzia managed not to sound too annoyed, even though we had already had this conversation twice.

"Maybe they did it for immunity!" I burst out.

"The fireworks are their cue to come," said Fauzia. "Wait for those to go off before you start worrying."

I lay down on the ground and covered my eyes with my arm, making Fauzia laugh. The rough floor poked into my back through the thin material of my top, but I didn't care. I took some deep breaths, trying to calm my roiling stomach, but it did not help. I had hardly slept last night, worrying over all the things that could go wrong. Kingston's ILM chapter might get purged before it even began. I might lead my friends to their deaths.

Pops sounded outside, distant but clear. "That would be them," Fauzia said softly.

I pushed myself up onto my elbows. "We're sure the alleyway entrance is unlocked?"

"It's propped open a hair," Mr. Kapadia confirmed.

Fauzia offered me a hand and I let her pull me up. We stood staring at each other, hands clasped, until the first three women entered the store's back room. Fauzia gave them quick hugs. "Found everything all right?" I asked.

"Yes, it was all quite easy," Yashu confirmed. I swallowed past a lump in my throat, knowing she had risked herself just for me.

"This is exciting," Simran added. "Thank you." She was a friend from school whom Fauzia had always been close to, and Fauzia had vouched for her. Simi, as we called her, was Sikh, and her family had lost generations fighting for independence in the past. The three of them took seats right in the front row. A slow but steady stream of women trickled in after them, chattering quietly, until most of the seats were full.

"All right," Fauzia whispered in my ear. "Go ahead."

I looked out at the sea of faces, shadowy in the candlelight, and my throat went dry.

Fauzia glanced at me expectantly, then stepped to the front herself.

"I'm so glad all of you could make it tonight. Thank you for coming. High electricity usage in a shop after curfew could be suspicious, so please excuse the candlelight. Now please welcome Kalki!" Fauzia gave my arm a little tug and then walked briskly toward an empty seat in the back. Scattered applause broke out, disorienting me.

"Um, good to see you all." I looked for someone to come to my rescue, then plunged onward. "All of you have been involved, I think, in, um, expressing displeasure about the conditions we live in. I, personally, have put up leaflets, and launched fireworks. But, uh, as cathartic as that is, it's important to have a purpose with the stuff we do, beyond just mayhem."

Sweat beaded on my forehead, and I resisted the urge to wipe it away in a nervous motion. "We invited you here saying we would simply vent our dissatisfaction, but what I'm proposing is something more. I'm suggesting that we start our own chapter of the Indian Liberation Movement."

Silence. Then someone from the back asked, "The Indian Liberation Movement? Aren't they just a legend?"

"No, they're not a legend. My Baba was one of them, in Kingston, before he had to leave. They brought down the Outpost thirteen years ago. I'm sure some among you remember the 1951 bombing."

"Where are they now? Surely there's a chapter in Kingston already." That sounded distinctly like Yashu. She was feeding me an easy question, and still I struggled to answer.

"Most of the old members were killed, imprisoned, or transported out to the work camps in other colonies a long time ago. My Baba had to flee as well. But now we have a chance to try again."

"Won't it be dangerous?" someone else asked. It sounded like Simi, but I couldn't be sure.

"Coming here was dangerous, and you did it. Setting off fire-works, breaking curfew, all these things are dangerous," I said. "But now maybe we can do something more. Change things, make our own history. I want to try. I hope you do too."

"Hopefully they will never realize that these small, random acts are connected to the ILM," Fauzia added. "So long as all of us keep it a secret."

There was a hushed moment, and then the room exploded.

"What would we—"

"Is this some sort of official member—"

"Why just the people—"

Simi's voice cut through. "Why us?"

"Why you?" I echoed, heart racing. "Because we know and confide in one another. We've already had political discussions, expressed treasonous beliefs, so every person in this room is tied together by trust and friendship. As for the official-ness of it all, the Indian Liberation Movement is not official, but it is very real and very serious. If you don't think that's for you, then go now in peace."

Nobody moved.

"So what happens next?" someone called when it became clear everyone was staying.

All my ideas dissipated, and instead I saw myself as the others were seeing me. A young woman, younger than many of them, clad in a black dress crumpled from lying on the floor, her leggings torn at the knee from an earlier mishap, her short hair messy with sweat. How could I possibly think to lead them? I knew nothing. I was no one.

From the back, Fauzia said, "I have a job in the broadcast center. I've pretended to lose bulletins to inconvenience the British out of spite, but still I am one of the first people to learn of any news. I can pass along key information for us to act on, and I'll have insight into how they're interpreting it."

Then Asha spoke up. "I work on an investigations team at the Outpost. I'm just a stenographer, but I can occasionally alter my reports to keep them looking in the other direction. They won't know the difference. And I would know if we were in real danger of being found out." Asha was a friend of mine from junior college who had once made a rude gesture to the back of a police officer when we were walking.

Inspired, I pushed myself onward. "You see, the British have made a mistake. During the Reestablishment, they restructured their administration to make sure that Indians were relegated to jobs outside of functions of state. But now, with the war, they've been forced to let us back in. They think it won't matter, because they're bringing in harmless young women whom they've successfully brought to heel. But we know better, don't we?" The room stared back at me, and I felt their anticipation, their hope that I had an answer. Fauzia beamed at me from the back, and I took from her the strength to keep going. "Our way cannot be to fight them in the open, to blow up their buildings and lead great protests and assassinate their leaders, no matter how much they might deserve it. That will just bring the soldiers back, and we know now that we would be caught. Bravery and sacrifice alone is not enough to win—we have to fight another way.

"There was an older lady, Mrs. Lele, who used to live in my building," I continued. "She took care of me when I was young and my parents were working. Then her husband was dragged away for protesting, even though he had hardly done anything. She had no money, so she found a job at one of the mills doing winding. She would come home with her fingers bleeding, and nobody wanted to help her because of her husband's fate." I broke off, my blood heating, then said, "In last year's heat wave, the power went out around midday. As the building got hotter, she got confused. She . . . she wandered out of the house, thinking she needed to be at work. It was hours before anybody found her. By then, it was too late."

"My aunt died three years ago because she couldn't get treatment for her cancer," someone piped up.

"It is cruelly common," I said. "Because not only do the British let us die from disregard, they also make it nearly impossible for us to help each other in any way that matters. But we are going to change that. I don't know if we can find cancer treatments, but we can certainly help people get food and water and electricity, and perhaps get them into hospitals or other places. We will use the fact that it is mostly women like us who are employed in the empire's operations, and that we are not viewed as threats. When we use our positions to covertly aid others, they will assume we are mildly incompetent at our jobs—they won't suspect treason. I'm not saying it's without risk. But I think that we can slowly weaken the empire and drive them out. The revolution will come, but the revolt starts tonight."

From the back, Fauzia started to clap, and others joined in until I began worrying that the applause could be heard outside. As if we all had the same thought, the noise rapidly died down.

Then one of Fauzia's friends said, "I have a job in the Office of Imports. I'll know if a shortage is coming, or a tightening of standards. A couple decimal places of error may not mean much to them, but it could translate into hundreds more kilos of rice being sent over. That's something, right?" Her voice was calming, and I gave her a smile.

One by one, the other women shared. They had a job in one of the phone companies run by the British, or they worked in a state hospital and had access to medicines, or they worked in the home of a wealthy British family, and they could see clear ways to work toward this common cause.

In the back, Fauzia took rapid notes in the shorthand she had developed from her work in broadcast. I listened carefully and provided suggestions on how each person could contribute.

Finally, Yashu spoke up. "I know you're a good person, Kalki." She was right in the front, staring at me with determination. "And I trust your heart is in the right place. But there are people who won't fight for you, because people like you have never been on our side. And they shouldn't be vilified for it, or looked down on. The people in this room—you're not rich, but you're not poor either. You can't comprehend the lives of Dalits, relegated generation after generation to the worst, most dirty and dangerous work. We have value too, even if we don't have your privileges. I'm with you now, though I have the most to lose of anyone in this room, because I know you." Yashu lifted her chin high. "And I know you're going to win. But when you win, you have to promise me, we are never going back. That you will lay down your life for our freedom the same as you would for your own."

Everyone shifted to look at me, and I felt with all of my hubris that this was the moment that would change everything. I swore to myself that it would. That caste would not matter in this new world we were making. Yashu wanted me to say it out loud, to make a promise before witnesses and ensure everyone agreed. It was certainly arrogant to believe we could root out this decay when greater Indians than us had fought for reform, but I was not thinking about them.

"You have my word, and everyone's in this room," I said with a nod. "If anyone disagrees, you have no place here." No one moved. Yashu did not smile, but her sharp nod was enough. I would have to earn her trust for this project, as I had earned her trust for our friendship.

From there, we set goals about the information we wanted to collect. We planned the activities we wanted to disrupt. And, most importantly, our strategy for communication came together.

Mr. Kapadia guided us, explaining the procedures that had worked for the ILM of old. We would never again put anything in writing, physical or technological. Someone suggested that we destroy all materials, so Fauzia's notes were burned at the end of the night, when we had committed the relevant details to memory. The cell would pass along all information through direct conversations with me, Fauzia, or Mr. Kapadia, and then we would share relevant details back down the chain. We would meet like this only once every three months, the date of each meeting whispered through our chain of friends.

Caught up in the excitement of this moment, we even crafted a plan for expansion on that first night. Each person in this room would recruit others and run their own cell. Cell members would not mix and would be instructed to rebuff duplicate recruitment efforts without giving themselves away. We would be the founding members and the leaders, and other cell members could know at most two of us.

After everyone had left, Yashu and Fauzia stayed behind. "That went well," Fauzia said. "That was—"

"Exhilarating," Yashu said with a laugh.

I looked at her in shock. "I thought you were only here to keep us in line."

"Liberation," Yashu said, like she was tasting the word. "Who wouldn't want that? Of course I'm wary, but . . ." Her eyes were glittering. "What you said, I felt it. That future. I want freedom, and we're going to do this. Help our people."

Fauzia took my hand in hers. "Do you really think we can win where all others have failed?" she asked softly.

My heart clenched. "I don't think we're better. But we have new people, a new chance at luck. I believe that we can free our city."

"Or die trying," Fauzia murmured.

It was a chilling statement, and true. Who was I, outside of this rebellion, this need to see my people freed? Fauzia and Yashu had other goals, other lives. Fauzia wanted to find love, start a family; Yashu wanted to bring her family security, prove that someone from her community could succeed. I wanted nothing more than this. It felt in that moment that I was just a vessel for the work, and there was no room for anything else. I would live and breathe this until I won or died. Yashu and Fauzia were making the greater sacrifice, to set aside their other dreams for this one.

"Or die trying," I whispered.

"Or die trying," Yashu repeated, and my eyes filled with tears.

Our first week back at work after the holidays, Yashu and I were sitting and eating when I saw a familiar man walking toward us. Samuel Clarke, the chancellor's son.

"Shit," I whispered to her. "Is he coming for us?"

"What are you talking about?" she asked, before straightening and giving a smile. "Mr. Clarke! How can I help you, sir?"

Samuel Clarke stopped when he reached Yashu. "Miss Kamble, we have an urgent case. Be at your desk in five minutes."

My stomach turned. Yashu worked with Samuel Clarke? He spoke to her so comfortably. How could I protect her if something happened at work? Mr. Jenkins had never gone beyond occasional harassment, but Samuel Clarke would have no such qualms.

Yashu smiled. "Yes, sir."

"And you are . . ." He raised an eyebrow at me.

"Kalki Divekar, sir," I said stiffly. It had been three years since I had run into him at the annual education night. There was no recognition in his eyes, only a cool disregard.

"Good to meet you, Miss Divekar," he said. He looked right through me, the very picture of a classic British officer, before turning on his heel and walking away.

Yashu began shoveling the remaining bhaji from her tiffin into her mouth. Plain potatoes with turmeric and mustard seeds—too dry to swallow so fast. "Yashu," I snapped. She looked up at me in alarm.

"Are you okay?" she asked. "You look like you've seen a ghost."

"Your boss," I said, trying to pull myself together. "If he's making you do things . . ."

"That's the job of a boss," she said.

"I meant, he does terrible things to women," I said. "Are you—is he forcing you—"

"Oh." Yashu blinked at me, then shook her head. "I didn't

know he had that reputation. He's always treated me and the other women well. But I'll be careful, Kalki, don't worry."

She left, and I scrubbed a hand over my eyes. I could not stop seeing it, in slow replay, behind my lids.

It was a hot, sticky day at the start of the school year some ten years ago. I was walking home when I heard an odd noise that shuddered down my spine. It repelled me, made me want to run, but I forced myself to turn and walk back. In the back of an alleyway, among heaps of rotting food scraps and other filth, a girl from my school stood trembling. Two British boys towered over her, their backs to me.

Fat tears rolled down the girl's face, but no sound escaped her lips. I could see from her expression that she knew her situation and had resigned herself to her fate. While nobody spoke of these incidents, we all knew that they occurred. Nobody could accuse a white man of such a crime, and even if the police did respond, nobody would admit to being dirtied in that way. The boys knew they held all the power.

One of the boys reached toward her hair. She flinched, but the other boy grabbed on to her and held her steady.

The first boy yanked her dupatta off her chest. It was the sole "Indian" item we were allowed in our uniforms, and now the bright turquoise of the material lay in the dusty brown of the alleyway, beautiful and strange and entirely out of place. She cried out, and the second boy slapped her across the face. As the first boy turned his face toward his friend, I realized I knew him from the paper. He was the chancellor's son, Samuel Clarke.

The chancellor's son leaned in and grabbed her face, pulling her toward him, and nausea roiled up inside me. I was furious. In that moment, years of anger finally boiled over.

Before I could think twice, I slipped off my sandals, for they made a distinctive slap as they hit the ground, and I could not run in them. Taking my own solid black dupatta from my shoulders, I wrapped the material around my head, mirroring the motion I'd seen my Baba make so many times before. I knew he would never stand by and watch, and that knowledge gave me strength.

The second boy had lifted the girl's dress, and Samuel Clarke was embracing her. The girl had stopped struggling and gone limp, but when she saw me over his shoulder, she locked eyes with me and shook her head, warning me to stay away. I had always been too stubborn to listen.

The ground scalded my feet, and heat stifled me inside my scarf, but I did not care. There was a pounding in my ears, and I realized that it was the sound of my own heart, beating so hard that I could feel it in my skull.

The chancellor's son laughed, and whatever last ounce of hesitation or fear I had snapped.

I launched forward, strong and assured, feeling as though Vayu himself propelled me. Even though I had never fought anyone before, I remembered my Baba's lessons. *A man's most sensitive point is between his legs. Go for the groin, and then the neck or stomach to knock their breath out. Do you understand, Kalki?* I brought my knee up into the space between Samuel Clarke's legs and he went down, howling in pain. The second boy jerked around, naked fear spreading across his face, and behind my scarf I grinned. Before he could move, I elbowed him just below his heart, then stamped on his foot. He groaned, doubling over, wheezing for breath.

Now freed, the other girl kicked Samuel Clarke in the stomach where he lay on the ground. It was time to run. I grabbed her hand, my nails digging into her sweaty palm, and pulled her away.

We reentered the bright street, ducking and weaving through the crowded market, as I led us to the nearest safe space I knew: Mr. Kapadia's store. Mr. Kapadia looked up at us when the bell tinkled, and the tinny noise brought me back into my body. We looked a fright. My scarf had slipped off my face into a disheveled mess around my neck, and a few strands of the girl's hair had slipped out of her bun. We were both panting, our sweaty fingers still intertwined.

"Namaskar, Mr. Kapadia," I got out between breaths, my mind defaulting to the greeting that I used with him when I came to his shop with Aai. People were not jailed for such words, but I still shot an alarmed glance at the girl, for the last thing I needed was to be marked as backward. She didn't seem to have noticed, and as I came back to myself, I was distracted by something digging into my heel. I reached my hand down to see what had happened. My fingertips touched something hard and sharp, and when I brought them back up, they were glistening red. The girl gave a shriek of surprise at the sight of blood.

Mr. Kapadia's eyes combed over us, worried, but he did not ask any questions. He sat me down on a stool, and when he went to grab some supplies, I inspected my foot. A jagged piece of green glass jutted out from my heel.

"Thank you for helping me," the girl said, drawing my attention.

"What is your name? You're in my class, right?"

"Fauzia," she replied. "My name is Fauzia Naseer."

I BLINKED BACK tears from the memory and tried to force lunch into my churning belly.

That was when I noticed a fair-skinned girl hovering nearby. Catching my eye, she sat down next to me.

I looked the girl up and down. She was within a year or so of my age. "Smita Deshmukh," she said, offering me a hand to shake. I took it, reluctantly. This girl looked wealthy, and I wondered why she was working.

"Nice to meet you," I said.

"I work in public relations," she said. "How about you? Where do you work? What's your name?"

This was a lot of questions for a girl I had never seen before, though her name sounded familiar. Most people kept to themselves or to people they already knew. Was she from a collaborator family? In my distress at seeing Samuel Clarke, my memory was failing me. "My name is Kalki," I said. "I work in the rations department."

"Want some chocolate cake?" I shifted uncomfortably at the non sequitur.

"No, thank you, I'm all right."

Her face fell. "Am I doing something wrong?" she asked. "I know we've just met, but tell me truly. Why does everyone seem to hate me?"

"I just don't like cake," I told her honestly. I wondered whether I should say anything more. I knew what it felt like to be excluded, even if I had been excluded for being poor and she was just weird. "You're welcome to sit with me, though. How's . . . your job?"

Smita lit up like I had gifted her gold. "Thank you! My job is wonderful. I'm in the department where my father's friend works, so I know my supervisor very well. They have me posing for photos sometimes too! It's so nice to have something to do."

I nearly choked on my mouthful of rice. Now I was sure. This was the daughter of a collaborator, working in public relations to aid in pretending Kingston's native people supported the administration. I tried not to let disgust show on my face. "I see," I said. "That's nice."

She smiled again, although this time it was less intense. "It is, isn't it? I like keeping busy. Although . . ." She lowered her voice. "I wish my work was *different,* you know? Sometimes I think, what if we also gave out food with our flyer campaigns?"

I had often wondered, in my first few months on the job, whether anybody else lucky enough to get a job in the imperial administration felt this way, whether they felt any sympathy for the people of Kingston they had left behind. I felt a bit of warmth toward this odd girl. "That's kind of you," I said. "I wonder the same, in rations."

She blinked at me in shock. "You do?"

"I'm only human," I said.

"I see the poor, living on the streets, and I feel so bad for them," she said eagerly. "I know that they have had opportunities to improve their lives and haven't taken them, but I still feel bad that they starve."

The privilege dripping from her words was so obvious I almost burst out laughing. But how would she know any better? "That's admirable," I told her. "You have a kind heart."

Taking my encouragement as a sign, she started chattering my ear off. I did not pay much attention as she detailed how she wanted to continue her parents' charity, and instead tried to think. Was this an opportunity? Her family had gotten ahead by betraying their own people—but unlike Samuel Clarke, who had fully embraced the sins of his father, Smita seemed kind. If I could cultivate this girl's friendship, we could have access to resources on an unprecedented level. Money was one thing we didn't have.

When she stopped to take a breath, I said, "I have to go, but it was nice to meet you, Smita. You should sit with me again sometime."

The happiness radiating from her almost made me forget the disaster that had started my lunch hour.

"SAMUEL CLARKE IS Yashu's supervisor," I blurted out to Fauzia the moment I got home.

She dropped the chapati in her hand and it fell into the fire. When she pulled it out, it was badly burned.

"Is she . . ." Fauzia's voice shook. "Oh, God!"

"She said she's fine." I leaned against the kitchen counter.

Fauzia's hands were shaking too much to continue cooking. "Remember when we were students? Yashu will bear anything in silence. She would say she's fine even as a dog was biting off her foot! Can she get a transfer? Can she—"

A knock sounded at our door. "It's me," Yashu called. "Let me in."

I opened the door, and she swept in, taking in Fauzia's appearance. "I knew you two would be sitting here stewing," she said with a sigh. "I'm fine. I don't know what you've heard, but he's a good supervisor, and the job is an excellent source of information."

"Who cares about the rebellion?" Fauzia took Yashu's face in her hands as though inspecting her for damage. "Your safety is what matters."

"I am safe." Yashu tugged herself free. "You think I haven't dealt with a million lecherous men? Sure, he's powerful, but it's nothing I can't handle."

Fauzia looked to me, but I didn't know what to say. She turned back to Yashu. "If he ever even touches you—"

"I'll keep myself safe." Yashu tossed her head back and laughed. "You both are so predictable. We have other things to worry about!"

Fauzia went back to finish up cooking. I could tell she was still concerned, but Yashu was stubborn. She wasn't going to change her mind now. "I met a potential ally today," I said, to break the tension. "She works in public relations. Her name is Smita Deshmukh—"

"Deshmukh?" Fauzia asked. "Like the industrialist?"

"I worked in his garment factories as a child," Yashu said, wrinkling her nose. "He is no friend of ours."

The collaborator factories were well known for having the most dangerous, unsafe, horrifying conditions. Yashu had told us the stories: how the children would perch precariously over the looms, all day, every day, how they lost their fingers, or limbs, or lives, but nobody cared because they were just factory parts to the owners.

"His daughter seems different," I insisted. "Smita has compassion. I think we should at least try to get her to help us. Think of what she might know. The kind of money she might have . . ."

"You can try," Fauzia called from the kitchen. "But we should be sticking with our own. I've got a few friends together, and someone has access to an electric mimeograph. We're going to write up some statements about our Indian history and the flaws of the British and paper them, and I think Simi will be doing the same. That's a solid first step—start spreading the word through neighborhoods that someone out there is standing up, even if just in words."

"I'm just putting out feelers," Yashu said. "It's going to take some time to get the lowest-paid wage laborers on board, but we will need them to hit the British where it hurts."

It sounded so slow. It *was* slow. A rebellion built on waiting and testing each step. I was burning to get out there, to do something big like destroying the Outpost—but they would just rebuild it like they had thirteen years ago. Fauzia and Yashu were right; cautious and careful was the right way.

It reminded me of a story my Baba had always loved telling me. This one was special, for I could see in it now the story of the ILM, patiently preparing for the day of reckoning.

"Long ago there lived a demon king named Hiranyakashipu," he would say, drawing himself up and miming tusks. "Varaha had slain his brother many years ago, and so Hiranyakashipu hated Vishnu with all his might. But even a demon king could not defeat a god. He knew he needed more power to enact his revenge. After he had passed many years doing penance and living in austerity, the god Brahma offered him a boon—anything he wished. Hiranyakashipu asked for immortality, but not even a god could grant that gift, so instead he asked Brahma to bless him so he could not die by man or by beast or by any weapon, neither in the morning nor the night, neither outside nor inside.

"Empowered by this blessing, Hiranyakashipu began to persecute all followers of Vishnu. He ordered them to cease their worship or die. Hiranyakashipu's only son, Prahlada, was a devout follower of Vishnu, and when his father ordered him to stop, Prahlada refused. Enraged, the king ordered him killed. Prahlada prayed for help, and no help came. But he was patient; he knew his time would come.

"Hiranyakashipu's subjects tried to kill Prahlada in many ways. They poisoned him, and burned him, and attacked him. Although no god came to rescue him, every attempted murder was miraculously averted.

"Finally, one evening, Hiranyakashipu called Prahlada before him and ordered him to end his madness. Prahlada refused. 'If your Vishnu is all-powerful,' the king asked, 'why is he not here?' 'He is here,' Prahlada calmly responded. Hiranyakashipu laughed. 'Is Vishnu in this pillar?' he asked mockingly. 'He is in that pillar,' Prahlada said. 'He is everywhere.'

"The king swung his mace at the pillar, shattering it into a thousand pieces. A noise sounded, like the roaring of a thousand lions. When the dust settled, Narasimha stood amid the rubble, ready to protect his disciple. Narasimha had the head and body of a lion and the legs of a man. He dragged the king out onto the balcony in the light of the setting sun. Narasimha was neither man nor beast, it was neither morning nor night, and they were neither outside nor inside, and so he slashed his claws through Hiranyakashipu's belly and slew the king."

5

VAMANA, DWARF

I learned how to trick at twenty-three.

The British Empire was losing ground on the northern border as they fought a never-ending war with China, but that was the least of their worries. The streets of Kingston were quiet as soldiers deployed not just to Assam or Kashmir or the borderlands of Afghanistan to fight China, but also to Nigeria, Kenya, or places farther away, like the Americas, on clusters of tropical islands, to defend the empire on other fronts in other conflicts. We still heard from Bhaskar and Omar periodically. Omar had recovered from his injuries and they had both gone back out to fight, this time in Kashmir, but we knew little more than that. If Bhaskar and Omar were sending us any real information, it was all censored in paragraphs of black. We tried, sometimes, to hold the letters to the light or use a flame to see through the marks, but the censorship held fast.

It was clear in the ways they annotated their own letters that they were trying to prevent us from worrying. Bhaskar wrote, "We have been praying for hot rations for weeks now," and then, in cramped writing in the margins, added, "We have plenty of dry rations and are not starving the way they are in—" The rest was redacted. We wrote back, whispering into the night about what we should say—we could not allude to our activities in any way, but what could we do that would give them comfort or hope? Fauzia and I did not want to make them homesick or remind them of things they could not have. So we spoke of how grateful we were for their flat, how we used it to host friends, and how we could not wait until they returned. We hoped this told them that although we could not say it in words, we were doing something more.

Our "revolution" grew in fits and starts. Our first acts of rebellion were small and isolated—a diverted food shipment here, a whispered warning to a police suspect there. All our information gathering was useless, though, if we didn't do more. This was on my mind as we prepared for another meeting of our core group, this time in our flat for lunch.

I fried the puris carefully, dropping Fauzia's perfectly rounded circles into the oil and watching them inflate and redden. The mindlessness helped me focus as Fauzia placed a blanket on the floor of our living room and set out plates.

"I wish we had more time," Fauzia said, surveying her setup.

"We still have another hour," I reminded her.

"Why did we invite people over?" she asked.

"Because it's nice to have our friends over, it's easier than sneaking around, and we have the space," I said.

"We don't have the space! They're going to have to sit on the ground!"

"It's traditional." I let out an exaggerated sigh. "Things will be fine."

"You're getting crumbs all over the floor!" she exclaimed, diving toward the kitchen. "Kalki, it's like you're trying to be messy!"

I rolled my eyes as Fauzia retrieved the long-brush broom from a cabinet and began furiously sweeping around me. "Careful, or you're going to take the floor right off," I teased.

"It's not funny, Kalki. We can't invite people into a dirty home. And this home, right now, is a mess."

Within a month of living with her, I had discovered Fauzia Naseer's dark side: She was what the British would call fussy. She insisted on everything being in its proper place and everything being clean. Crumbs on the floor, dishes in the sink, books strewn about—these things stressed her out beyond measure.

"Fauzia, we're inviting people here to commit actual treason. Do you really think a little dirt from food that we cooked for them will put them off?"

"Cleanliness is next to godliness!" Fauzia shouted.

"Really? You're going to quote a British axiom at me? Now?"

Fauzia's face was flushed, her hair in disarray from the frenzied cleaning. "It's not just the British. Our cultures taught the importance of cleanliness long before them!"

I stifled a laugh. "Maybe you should . . . uh . . . take care of yourself, then. You're a little—" I gestured to her hair.

She reached up a hand to her now ruined bun and rushed off to the bedroom. When I followed her in, she was frantically searching her dresser for a hairpin.

"Let it down," I told her and tugged on her ribbon. Her hair tumbled out, and a small thrill shot through me. Her locks were beautiful, silky and smooth, and I couldn't help but tangle my fingers in them.

"Kalki!" She slapped my hand away and began brushing her hair back into a bun. "We don't have much time and I don't intend to look disheveled."

I made to reach for her hair again, but she pushed me out and kicked the door shut. Outside, I closed my eyes for a moment, reveling in the memory of stroking her hair. It reminded me of a dream I had had just a few days ago, a dream that had confused and excited me in equal measure. In it, Fauzia and I were sharing a bed, as we occasionally did when we stayed up too late and fell asleep together, and I opened my eyes to find her staring at me, her eyes bright despite the dark. Her fingers lightly stroked my arm, sending shivers down my skin, and a pleasant heat spread through my limbs. Then she leaned in toward me, her breath ghosting over my lips, and—

I had jolted awake.

The embarrassment of it caused me to shake out my arm now and push the sensation from my mind. I couldn't want this. She was my best friend. She had no interest in me, and it was wrong of me to think this way.

I turned back to the kitchen, burying myself in preparations. By the time Fauzia returned, the puris were almost arranged. "Only forty-five minutes until people start arriving! We have to be ready, Kalki."

I threw up my hands. "Do you want me to stop—" A knock at the door cut me off. Fauzia went on tiptoe to peer through the peephole before unlocking and unchaining the door.

"Yashu!" Fauzia exclaimed. "You're a bit, well . . ."

"Early?" Yashu finished. "I know. I wanted to talk to you before everyone else got here. How can I help?"

Fauzia clicked her tongue. "You're our guest! Please, come sit. What's going on?"

Yashu rolled her eyes and grabbed a cloth to start wiping our counter. "Don't insult me by calling me a guest." She scrubbed for a while, then said, "I think someone at work knows what I'm doing."

I dropped a puri on my foot and yelped at the burning oil.

"Why do you think that?" Fauzia asked calmly, ignoring me.

"Someone left this on my desk yesterday morning," Yashu said, pulling out a manila envelope from her purse and handing a few sheets of paper to Fauzia, who began rapidly scanning them.

"Is this true?" she asked at last. "Do you know if it's accurate?"

Yashu nodded. "At least the first page. That memo was borne

out yesterday afternoon. They had a small announcement about the task force."

"Was there a note or anything identifiable?"

"No. The names and addresses are all cut out."

My curiosity could wait no longer. "What are you talking about?"

"There are three memos here," Yashu said, coming over to me. "One recommends forming a task force immediately to hunt down the growing numbers of draft dodgers hiding in the city. The decision was announced a few hours after I received this. The next two list planned electricity outages for the next few weeks. And the last page has a note on it—*Your faithful servant, O'Brien.*"

"I knew they weren't random!" I exclaimed. In addition to our regular electricity rationing, seemingly random portions of the city would lose electricity for hours on end because of purported equipment malfunctions. We all thought the British were using it to siphon power for various pursuits: freezing their ice-skating rinks in the middle of summer, lighting up extravagant displays during state visits, or storing power for use in their buildings so they did not have to obey citywide rations. It wasn't lost on us that they had the gift of constant leisure while we died in the heat. But, of course, we never had any proof. The loss of spoiled food, illness from drinking unfiltered water, and deaths from heatstroke were all blamed on faulty equipment.

"Maybe somebody wants us to think they're not random because they're trying to trap us," Fauzia said.

"How would they trap us?" I asked.

"Get caught holding it?" Yashu offered. "Maybe this is a test."

Fauzia thought for a moment. "Here's what we'll do. We burn the papers now, so they can't be traced back to us. We wait and see if the second memo's prediction comes true. If it does, we can act on the third."

"Won't they expect that of us?" Yashu asked.

"I think they would expect us to act on the second document

because the first came true, if they're expecting anything at all," I mused. "And if nothing happens, well, then we know we have an ally."

I fired up the gas and slid the papers into the flame until the edges caught. I clung to the papers as they crumbled into ash on the floor, the flames nearing my fingertips. For a brief moment, I saw my Aai, lighting a newspaper on fire, the flame flickering toward her fingertips, and felt a pang of guilt. She had burned that newspaper to protect me, and now I stood here endangering myself and my friends. I had pulled away from her in the last year to protect her, and it hurt. When was the last time I had seen her, had a real conversation? Was she all right, all alone in her flat? The brush of a broom against my feet brought me back as Fauzia swept up the debris from the floor.

The others joined us soon after, and by some unspoken agreement, the three of us said nothing about what had just occurred.

THE FIRST OUTAGE happened. O'Brien, whoever they were, had been proved a faithful servant indeed. Yashu came pounding at our door on Saturday, already drenched in sweat. "The power in my building is out. It's out for blocks all around," she said, panting. "The power has been out since last night, and an official notice posted said it will be out for a few days. In this heat . . ." Fauzia grabbed a newspaper and started fanning her, ushering her under our ceiling fan, which was at maximum speed. It was indeed a very hot day.

"I almost wish we had acted," I said.

Yashu drained a glass of cool water. "We might have put people at risk by trying to warn them." She sighed then, staring down at the floor. "Every time this happens, I lose someone I know— the sick, the elderly, the very young. It's awful, but that's how it's always been. I can't wonder what might have happened if we'd acted. . . . The guilt would eat me alive."

Fauzia put her free arm around Yashu. "Put it from your

mind," she said. "We will tell everyone that you discovered evidence of another outage, and we will plan for next time. This will not happen again."

Yashu nodded. The redness had faded from her face, and she looked calm and collected once more. "Not our fault, I know that. What shall we do next time?"

As the plan took shape over the next week, it felt almost like a spy picture, if James Bond weren't an agent of the British.

First, I spoke to Smita Deshmukh, who attended Fauzia's cell meetings and was eager to help. I told her that we were looking to buy fans to help people if any further blackouts happened, and did she have any idea where we could buy them? We wanted to use fans because they would be cooling without being too suspicious—more useful items like generators were far too valuable to be stolen without notice. "There's a distribution center in Old Bombay," she said. "My father just got a shipment of fans a week ago. I don't know if they'd sell to you, but you could try. I know not everyone lives the way we do—I was so worried over the weekend that people might not survive the heat."

"That's what we're scared of too," I said. "We'll check the distribution center."

"Maybe I could contribute some of our fans?" she asked. "I'm sure my father's staff won't notice a few missing."

"I don't want to get the staff in trouble," I said quickly. "But thank you, you've been so helpful."

Maryam, one of Fauzia's friends from her street, worked as an inventory specialist in that very distribution center. On her break, she moved a box of battery-powered fans into a nook hidden from the omnipresent guards. Then Yashu came to walk home with Maryam, pulling a box on a cart, purportedly a package she had picked up from the post office. In the alcove, their actions shielded from view by their bodies, they swapped the boxes and then left. They did this for several days in a row, until they had stockpiled several boxes. Though they made it seem straightforward, I could see Maryam's hands shaking as she described it. We distributed the fans in the neighborhoods we knew would be affected.

The morning of May 16, 1966, dawned stifling hot. Sun baked the roads, and at ten a shimmering wave of heat already rose from the street. Few people were outside, and those who were seemed in a hurry to get out of the sun. Fauzia and I walked toward Yashu's flat, located on one of the targeted blocks—not a coincidence, I assumed, that one of the few places willing to rent to her was in a poorer, resource-starved area. Many of the battery-operated fans we had distributed last night had already been taken inside.

"I hope they weren't stolen," Fauzia whispered. "But thieves are probably too tired to leave the house."

"I regret leaving our place," I replied. My throat already felt dry, and the beginnings of a heat headache throbbed in my temples.

"Almost there," Fauzia said. A goddess, she seemed immune to the heat. She had wrapped her head in a light blue dupatta, which did a better job of keeping her cool than my pitch-black hair did for me. She usually covered her hair only when praying, but right now I envied her foresight. I had tied a ponytail, but I could feel a few loose strands sticking to the back of my neck.

A five-minute eternity later, Fauzia knocked on Yashu's door. I tried to continue holding myself upright. Yashu ushered us in quickly, and we found most of the others clustered under Yashu's ceiling fan.

"How's it going?" Fauzia asked as I gulped down the water Yashu handed me. I wanted to upend the glass over my hair but could not rationalize the waste. I offered the glass to Fauzia, who took a few dainty sips.

"I saw several people taking in the fans on this block. Today is a fiendish day for an outage."

"I just hope we did enough," Maryam said. She had taken such a risk to help us that we had let her into the rest of the operation.

"We did what we could. Now we—" Whatever Fauzia was going to say next got cut off by the low whine that signaled a power outage. The ceiling fan began slowing down as the lights in the room flickered once and gave up.

"Well, shit," Yashu breathed, going to the window. "It looks like the streetlight is out."

Fauzia squeezed my hand. Someone rapped against Yashu's door, and she went to open it.

"Yashu, are you all right in there?" a matronly voice asked. "We have some extra fans, do you need one?"

"A fan would be great," Yashu said, restricting the view into her flat slightly with her body. "Where did you get these?"

The woman didn't say anything, but Yashu laughed at some expression out of our view and said, "All right. Thank you, Parvana Aunty."

"Take care of yourself," the woman said. Yashu closed the door, and we distantly heard a knock on another door.

Yashu turned to show us the fan. "We did it!"

"In this building," Simi cautioned. "Let's go check the rest."

"Everyone know what street they're covering?" I asked, grabbing hand fans we had bought for this purpose. We confirmed our assignments and then left the building at staggered intervals, spreading out in all directions to visit people in the affected area, disguised as concerned citizens offering our ineffective fans. We hoped to get rejected.

Sweat dripped into my eyes, and I attempted to fan myself with little result. I cut through an alleyway, reveling in the brief moment of shade. When I exited onto the main street, the sun shone so bright into my eyes that for a moment I didn't realize I had company. Then my vision cleared enough to notice the two British officers climbing onto someone's front step mere feet away from me. I ducked back into the alleyway to listen, praying they hadn't seen me.

They knocked on the door, which opened after a brief pause. "Hello, madam, we're just walking through the block to inform people that there is a temporary outage occurring in this area. Power should be back any minute." I rolled my eyes.

"Thank you, sir," the woman said. "We appreciate it."

An awkward silence descended. Then he said, "That's a lovely fan you have. Looks brand-new in fact, like some of the ones we have in the station. Where did you get it?"

Without missing a beat, the woman replied, "Someone was out selling them a few weeks ago. Great prices. Most of us bought some, sir."

"Who was this man?"

"I don't know, sir. Average height. Black mustache. Unbeatable price."

"Thank you for your time," one of the officers said. They proceeded down the street, and I knew I couldn't canvass the block after them. I slowly made my way back to Yashu's place and let myself in with the key she hid under the mat. I lay on the floor fanning myself, ecstatic. People were defending us. Even without knowing whom they defended, or why, they would lie straight to the British just for the small kindness of a strong fan in a power outage.

I must have nodded off, because then I was opening my eyes to the sound of the door. I scrambled up off the floor, but Simi and Yashu had still seen me. "Wow, working hard, Kalki?" Simi teased. She lay down on the floor where I had been and declared in a mock high-class British accent, "Fan me!"

Although we had gone to school together, it was only in the last year that we had become close. Simi had a ridiculous sense of humor, pretending to be British nobility and doing impressions to make us laugh. I knelt next to her and jokingly fanned her face.

Yashu sat heavily on the ground next to us, and I told her what happened.

"Yours went well?" I asked.

"We gave out a couple of hand fans, but most of them already had the battery-powered ones. They were cool and relaxed, when normally people are frantically trying to cool themselves and look like they're melting."

"I'm melting," Simi added helpfully.

"Fan yourself," I said, passing the fan to her and then stretching myself out on the floor. "I can't believe it. I think it really worked!"

Someone knocked, and Yashu opened it to find Fauzia. "I need water," she panted.

Yashu poured Fauzia a glass out of the clay matka she had stored in the shade. "That's the coldest it's going to get."

Fauzia gulped down the water, leaning against the wall. The hair under her scarf looked a little disheveled and sweat tracks streaked her face. She spilled water down the front of her shirt and dabbed ineffectually at it with her hand. Somehow, she was still the most beautiful person in the room.

Asha entered moments later, followed by Maryam. They both looked just as sweaty and pleased as the rest of us, and soon everyone was excitedly chatting, despite the rising heat in the room. I was suddenly aware of how small and spare Yashu's flat was. She had a job similar to mine and Fauzia's, and although she lived alone, she still should have been able to afford better than this. She must have been giving her family every rupee she could spare. Sometimes, when I looked at Fauzia and Yashu, I was struck by their fundamental goodness. And now, together, we had pulled off a true act of insurgence.

I RODE THAT high as we planned other, similar projects. It wasn't the revolutions of history, and we acted in the dark, but it was *something*. In the days-long power outage, we had likely saved lives. I began to hold myself a little taller.

On the bus to work a few weeks later, a lean man with a black beard squeezed in next to me. His face was close to mine, and I tried to look at the ground to avoid any impropriety, until I saw it—the wheel pendant. It had been two years since the messenger had delivered the slip of paper from Baba to me, and I had cursed my past self for failing to ask him any questions. But now here he was again, the pendant unmistakable, his gaze familiar. He bent to my ear and whispered, "Rajendraji sent me." My body froze, which was a lucky thing, because reacting would have been suspicious. "I'll see you tonight?" he asked instead, still pitched low, breath warm against my neck. "He said you would know where."

My mind started working again. There was one place my Baba had always taken me, one place where I knew we would have some privacy. For the first time in over a decade, I would visit Thane Creek. I nodded in acknowledgment.

I wanted so badly to speak to him, to ask—did he live in Kingston? How did he know my Baba? How had he found me twice, and why? But this was certainly not the time or place to ask.

The entire workday, I was on edge, shaking. I made one error after another, scratching out my usually neat work, thinking only of the man, and my Baba, thoughts scrambling. What did he want? What would I say?

Time blurred, and before I knew it, I was taking the bus home. I didn't stop at my flat; I didn't know how to tell Fauzia what was happening. I ate some pani puri at a street cart and began walking. By the time darkness fell I was almost at the line of trees, and after observing the patrols from behind a trash bin for several minutes I felt confident enough to dart through. Nobody came after me. Then I was in the groves, clutching my bag with its tiny pocketknife and hoping I hadn't been idiotic enough to walk into a trap.

But the messenger stood alone in the last fully enclosed clearing before the beach, holding a flashlight pointed at the ground. "You came," he said. "I wasn't sure you would."

"Why wouldn't I?" I asked.

The man shrugged. "Your father sent me to figure out why you never started a Kingston branch of the movement."

"What?" I demanded, gathering my thoughts. What would Fauzia and Yashu tell me to do here? *Calm down, assess the situation.* "How do I know you're not a spy?"

"He says he left you a bookmark, with the wheel of self-reliance."

I hesitated. Only Aai and I knew that, and I had burned that bookmark last year, my most beloved possession destroyed for self-protection in case I was ever searched.

"And besides that," he continued, "you have seen me before."

"Yes, in the marketplace two years ago."

His eyes seemed to light with approval. "Good. You're observant, then."

"If you know my Baba, then you should know what my Baba knows. I started a chapter. We have at least a hundred recruits, across multiple cells. We've made significant progress."

"You have?" The man looked confused now.

"We've been helping the citizens of this city. Getting them food, fans, other supplies—"

"So you're a relief operation," the stranger said, and his voice was filled with disdain. "That's not a *rebellion*. That's a social group."

My first instinct was to be offended. But a worse, more shameful thought followed. *He's not wrong.* What had we done to break British control of this city? What were we planning to do? Nothing. "We're developing a network within the government," I told him, trying to sound confident. "We are placing people within their ranks and cultivating informants."

He scoffed. "So you're good little workers, taking home British salaries, and doing this to assuage your guilt. I didn't expect this of Rajendra Divekar's daughter, but . . ." He crossed his arms, the implication clear.

"It's not as though we were given instructions," I argued. "We have done the best we could! What would you have us do, when the movement has left us to work alone?"

"I would have you fight," he said. "As would everyone else who is actually fighting *for* you, while you parade around with the sole purpose of feeling better about yourself."

"That's—"

"Forget it." He turned away from me, peering into the darkness.

"Who do you think you are?" His manner and dismissal had hurt me, but I did not even know him. What right did he have to criticize? "What have you been doing, if you have so many opinions? I don't see you engaging the British in combat."

"My name is Adi Naik, and I am a lieutenant in the Indian Liberation Movement." He examined our surroundings instead of meeting my gaze. "I have been leading operations throughout the West Deccan. And yes, unlike your little group, I have been in combat with the British armies. Disrupted their troop movements. Educated people to fight for themselves, men and women, old and young. But you city people are so blinded to everything outside your limits—"

"How did you get in?" I snapped.

"The ILM has a few routes still available for sparing use."

"Ah, yes, you used a secret route that nobody has told us about, but you expect us to be, what? Helping you on the mainland? If you haven't noticed, the only people who can freely leave *are the British*." The British Raj had isolated Kingston from the presidencies of the rest of the subcontinent, forcing us to be an island unto ourselves. How could he possibly understand our position, living as he was in the Deccan Presidency with far more freedom than we could imagine? "We are trapped on an island with them. You can run, you can have bases, but we have this. We have adapted to our city, without any aid from you. We fight—"

"You do not fight!" he said, raising his voice for the first time. "You are no better than the Red Cross, and what do they care for independence? No. If Kingston were to truly fight against British rule, you could reduce the troops they send elsewhere. Free prisoners who are being transported. Give them another front so that independence becomes inevitable. But you do nothing, and I will return to my people to tell them Kingston can provide no aid."

His handsome face was stony, eyes glittering with righteous

anger. The wind rushed through the trees, and I shivered despite the heat. There was a dark, musty smell to this place that I had never noticed in all my years of being here. Was it new, or was it apparent only with the senses of adulthood? There was nothing I could say to his rejoinder. We had no true plan for liberation, only a desperation for freedom and friendship. That was worthless in the real world. I was worthless.

Adi seemed to take pity on me, his expression softening. "I came here as a favor to your father, who is with the movement in Jammu. I can smuggle you out to Pune, and from there you could be reunited with him. Your mother too."

My mind stopped. "I—what?" There was no way I had heard him correctly.

"You could help your father," he said. "It would do a lot more good than what you are doing here. I'm leaving tomorrow. You will have to decide by then."

I still could not comprehend what I was being offered. I fixated on the small things. Logistics. "And what will you be doing while I decide?"

"If you were a member, I might tell you." He was still staring out, and I followed the direction of his gaze until I saw the dim light of the bridge visible through the thicket.

"You can't possibly use the bridge!"

"The similarity between the things you couldn't imagine and the things we do every day would shock you," he said.

I couldn't help myself. In a quick, sharp movement, I stamped on his foot. He jerked in surprise but he made no sound of pain. "You're a terrible person," I told him. "I'm sure my father agrees. That's probably why you were sent, because he wanted to be rid of you. I'll give you my answer tomorrow, here, same time—"

"I will be leaving at this time, and possibly with you and your mother," he said, unfazed. "You will meet me by the Old Bombay rail depot at six P.M."

"You can't just—"

Adi gripped my arm, his strong, broad hand clamping me in place. My face flushed, but I met his eyes defiantly and saw his gaze burning back at me in the dark. "I can see that you have the same fire that we all do, but you don't know how to use it. Don't be angry at me. Be angry at them, and come fight."

And then he turned and walked away, before I could tell him all the ways that was an awful idea.

DESPITE CURFEW, I walked openly in the streets, reeling, and muscle memory alone bore me safely to Aai's flat. I wanted so badly to see Baba, to leap into his arms, even though I had not seen him in well over a decade. I knew there were those who longed to leave Kingston, but I never had.

I had asked Baba once if he had ever left. "When I was a child, I went to Pune, and Nashik, and even up into the Ghats," he said.

"What was it like?" I demanded, angling for a story.

My Baba's eyes had a faraway look. "When I was a child, the rest of the Bombay Presidency—that's what it was all called, before they carved out the Deccan Presidency and isolated the island of Kingston—felt like a wilderness. This was a time when it seemed that independence was so very close, that the British Raj would soon end. We would run around with our cousins through the streets. Climb trees and steal mangoes. Eat sugarcane raw, even if it would leave us with a stomachache." My father never directly spoke of his younger brother, who had been killed in a protest before the fire, but I heard it in the *we*. Mourned what I might have had—an uncle and cousins, all the potential of family consumed. It was on Baba's mind too. "It wasn't until after the fire that it became difficult to leave. That was the last time I left, when we stayed in refugee camps across the bay after the mandatory evacuation, and were ferried across to work and rebuild. Your Aai was pregnant with you. So you have left Kingston too."

I wrinkled my nose. That certainly did not count. "Do you think we'll leave?"

My Baba ruffled my hair, murmured a soft prayer. "Fate willing."

I remember at the time I had groaned, annoyed. I had meant the question practically, but here he was, dreaming. And then he had fled, not in the way he hoped fate would take him.

I snuck in via the balcony to Aai's room, since nosy neighbors could report me for breaking curfew. It had been too long since I had last been here, and yet nothing had changed. Aai began to shift when I crept through, trying to reach my old room. "Kalki?" She sounded alert, despite just waking from her slumber.

I knelt down next to her. "Aai." My voice cracked, and she sat upright.

"What is it, baccha?"

"Have you ever wanted to leave Kingston?" I whispered to her. I had hoped to speak in the morning, when I had organized my thoughts better. Now I could not even force myself to be honest. "Do you want to go out to the far fringes of the country, where Baba is? Where we would be free of all this?"

Aai drew me to her. "I miss him too," she said to me. It was a sentiment only spoken in the dark. "But we have to live in reality."

"If there was a way . . ." I pressed my face into her shoulder, breathing in the scent of the coconut oil she combed through her hair.

"My Ajji had a saying," she said, stroking my head. "Mrigajalachya maage dhavun aapli onjal riti rahate. Running toward a mirage leaves you empty-handed. Of course I want to see your Baba again. But that can never happen. Our life is here. In peace."

I had hoped Aai would give me an answer, but it only reminded me that if we left together, she would not let me fight. Was the joy of reuniting worth giving up everything else—my friends, my hopes for Kingston—permanently? I swallowed down the truth, that we had been offered an escape. I decided to be horrible, to be selfish, because I could not stomach the alternative. I stole the choice from Aai.

"You need to sleep, Kalki," Aai said when I didn't respond, and she pulled me down beside her. "Sleep here tonight. It's been too long since I saw you. You will feel better in the morning."

I hadn't slept next to Aai in years, since the nightmares from my Baba's departure had faded. I did not think it would be possible to sleep with the decision before me. But lying next to Aai, it was the easiest thing in the world.

THE MOMENT CURFEW lifted in the early morning, I made a dash for Fauzia. I needed to catch her before she left.

She was waiting for me, dark circles under her eyes. She reached for me with a gasp of joy, pulling me in for a hug, one hand cradling the back of my neck, then pushed me away. "I thought you were dead! Or caught! You didn't come home, your Aai hadn't seen you . . ."

"I met a member of the ILM from the mainland," I told her. "He had been sent to speak to me." I recited our argument verbatim, up until his offer. When I got there, the words stuck in my throat, as they had with Aai.

"What is it?" Fauzia asked. "What aren't you telling me?"

Fauzia knew me far too well. "He offered—he said—he . . ." I gathered my courage. "He's offered to smuggle me and Aai out of the city and help us get to my Baba. Tonight. I have to give him my answer at the train depot at six."

Fauzia's face went flat. "I see," she said.

"Are you angry?"

"I'll miss you." It didn't sound like she would miss me.

"I spoke to my Aai, and she didn't give me a real answer on what she wanted."

Fauzia turned away from me for a moment. I counted the seconds, five then ten then fifteen, until she passed a hand over her face. "What do you want?" she asked finally.

"I want to see my Baba again," I told her. Now that I was voicing them, my jumbled thoughts came pouring out. "But I don't want to leave my city. I don't want to leave you. You are my family—all of you are. And I know our ILM is useless right now, but we can do so much more. I want to see it become powerful. What would you do?"

She turned back to me. Her eyes were wet, and I realized with a start that the idea had hurt her. "I would not leave you," she said. She took my hand and squeezed it, and it sent a frisson of electricity through me. "I would not judge my worth by the words of a man I had never met, and I would not leave my city either."

It became clear, with every word Fauzia spoke, that I did not actually want to leave. But I dreaded saying no, rejecting what would likely be the only opportunity I would ever get to see Baba again. It was selfish of me to go, and selfish of me to stay, and selfish of me to not have told Aai the truth so that I could make the decision myself. But the only selfishness I would regret was leaving. And that was answer enough.

I was distracted all through work, but nobody seemed to care. At lunch, I found Yashu, and told her everything in hushed tones.

Yashu gaped at me for a moment, before shaking her head with contempt. "If you want to risk it all for some idiotic attempt at getting away, then go for it. Enjoy life on the run, eating rats on the frontier." Her voice increased in pitch as she spoke until I was shushing her.

This was the same reaction Fauzia had. "It's not my fault I was offered that," I told her.

"But it is your fault for abandoning us—abandoning everything. I put my life at risk for you because I never thought you were the type to just abandon your own."

"I'm not." Someone walked by our table and we both straightened slightly. I made my words vague. "I'm not leaving."

"Oh." Yashu pushed back some of her hair that had escaped her braid. "All right, then." She began gathering up her things to leave. "I'll talk to you later." She was gone before I could protest. Clearly, she thought I was selfish for considering leaving . . . but I would be selfish for staying too.

I headed back to the office, lost in my own thoughts, and bounced off of Mr. Jenkins, who took the opportunity to grab my shoulders, giving a genial laugh that crawled up my spine. "Couldn't stay away from me, eh, Kalki? Well . . ." He grabbed my arm and started maneuvering me into his office before I could understand what was happening. Had he finally decided to take what he wanted from me? Was he just trying to talk to me about work? Should I fight? My mind was so muddled that I did not feel the alarm I knew I should.

"Kalki!" A call pierced through the fog. "Kalki, I was looking for you—oh, apologies, sir, am I interrupting?"

Smita Deshmukh stared at Mr. Jenkins, waiting for an answer, until he dropped my arm and retreated into his office. He closed the door with a mutter I could not make out, and she looked at me with concern. "Are you all right?"

"Yes, I—" I stopped myself from saying anything more, in case others were listening. "I'm fine. You were looking for me?"

"I came to tell you that I heard something from my father you might want to know." Her voice dropped to a conspiratorial whisper.

At last my brain kicked into gear. "What is it?"

"Something is happening tonight that—"

I held up a hand. "If it's something like that, then the right person to tell is the leader of your group."

Her face fell. "I thought I could tell you."

"The rules exist for a reason," I said. We were both speaking in a whisper, using ambiguous words that could have just as easily applied to work. I gave her an encouraging smile. "We so appreciate you and how you're using your position. I wish I could talk to you about it, but we work in different divisions. What I talked to you about before, that was a personal matter. But for official business, we must follow official rules."

Fauzia and Yashu had said we ought to keep Smita at a distance, and though I didn't agree, I would listen to them.

She gave a tight smile. "Okay. I understand." On instinct, I gave her a brief, one-armed hug. I could feel her perking up like a watered plant. "Thanks, Kalki!"

The moment I was allowed to leave, I gathered my things and hastened with the crowd out of the building. The Old Bombay rail depot was an odd place I had first seen after starting my job. In Kingston proper, we had a rickety rail system that brought in goods and shipped out soldiers, but seeing a genuine train terminal was a novelty. The passenger station, Victoria Terminus, had been rebuilt after the fire into an opulent, high-vaulted station for the British to move off and on the island. It was a tourist attraction for those of us who could make it to Old Bombay, and even I was swept up in the grandeur of the pristine white marble, the gold-plated chandeliers, the pink stone sculptures. Of course, though the British tolerated our presence there, it was only because all the workers in the station and supply depot were Indian. I assumed Adi wanted to meet in the depot, where both men and women worked, and where two Indians talking would not be considered odd.

I found him helping lift crates into a car, and when he saw me, he walked over. To my irritation, I noticed that he was quite strong.

"Are you prepared to go?" he asked me with a cocky smile I wanted to slap off his face.

I had been practicing my words as I walked over here, and now they came smoothly. "I'm not leaving. You're right I have no idea how you fight. But you have no idea what it's like to be trapped, no exit or entry allowed, surveilled at every turn. We live in a city on an island, not a vast and sprawling countryside. If you're so confident that you know better, then you can stay. When the work is done, we can go to my father." He didn't speak. I thought of what Fauzia and Yashu had said to me, what we had resolved. "Not all of what you have said is useless. But how dare you stand here and judge without helping? I am going to stay, and I am going to fight to keep my people safe."

"Are you certain? After tonight, our route will not remain usable. This is your last chance."

"I am sure."

He shrugged. "If that's what you want."

I might not have been the smartest at recognizing motivations, but even I knew this was an odd response. "Didn't you come here to convince me to leave?"

"I—" His eyes fixed on something behind me, and he grabbed my arm hard enough to bruise. "Did you tell someone you were coming here?"

"What?" I used my free arm to brush my hair over my shoulder, discreetly looking, and saw—Fauzia and Yashu? "They're with me," I said, projecting a confidence I didn't feel. "Let go of me."

He dropped his hand as my friends arrived. "So, this is the mystery man," Fauzia said, looking him up and down with one eyebrow raised.

"He's here for the prisoner transport," Yashu added. Adi's expression morphed from shock to anger to fear before he composed himself, and Yashu grinned in triumph. "I'm sure he did mean whatever promises he made to you, but he was also going to bring you into some half-baked plan to free his friends."

"The West Deccan ILM recently suffered a catastrophic loss, isn't that right?" Fauzia asked, cocking her hip, assured and gorgeous in her superior knowledge. "But here he is to lecture us—"

"Because we tried!" Adi whisper-shouted. "We tried, and we gave as good as we got, and that's better than slow, plodding plans that don't even drive them away!"

It had taken me a moment to follow what was going on, but I had grasped it by now. Fauzia and Yashu must have discussed what I had told them, pieced together why an ILM operative would be here, and come to find me. And despite my giving them only scattered information, they had succeeded on every count. My heart swelled in my chest. They had come for me, and they were terrifying.

"How do you plan to free the prisoners?" I asked Adi.

Fauzia and Yashu flanked me. I wondered what any workers looking our way would think—that I was a woman confronting her deadbeat husband, perhaps, if they looked at all.

Sweat beaded on Adi's forehead as he weighed his options. At last, he ushered us to a secluded area behind a large stack of crates until we were completely hidden. "The transport comes in at ten, just after curfew begins. The main bridge has gates at either end, and the approaches are monitored. But the bridge itself is not, because only vehicles approved on approach can enter. At the changing of the guard, a person can slip through the bars into the main part of the bridge, and then exit the other end at will, because the guards are only looking for entrants."

From beyond the crates, someone shouted, "These boxes are wrong, who did this?"

Adi winced. I stared at him.

"You have no idea how this city works, do you?" I asked. "If you're trying to smuggle items onto a train, you need to swap out items using the same crate. If you know nothing about our processes, how do you think you're going to free a prison convoy by sneaking across the bridge?"

"I'll intercept the convoy while they're crossing," he said. Yashu snorted. "I have weapons, and I can take a transport."

"How would you get the transport out, if you were between the gates?" Fauzia asked, confused.

"We would go on foot," Adi said. "I'm only telling you in the hopes that you might learn something. We've done this kind of operation twice before, successfully. The British operate all their bridges the same way."

"Do you know how quickly they mobilize in the city?" Yashu asked. "You wouldn't be able to escape on foot."

I jumped in before he could say something else idiotic. "I know you don't believe us—"

"I do," he said. I blinked, shocked. He gave me a small smile, a peace offering, and I felt my shoulders drop. I remembered what he had said last night. *You have the same fire that we all do.* He closed his eyes, took a deep breath, and then nodded at us. "We got off on the wrong foot, but I hear you. You know this city, and I'm in your territory. So, tell me, what will free my men?"

I HAD NEVER been close to the bridge before. It was officially known as the Queen Elizabeth Bridge, but since Indian residents could not traffic it, we only called it the bridge. As I approached the main guard station on our side of the bridge, I realized that it was wide enough for three large lorries to pass abreast. The guard tower loomed, and I tugged at my skirt. Although I was still dressed in what I always wore to work—a black skirt hitting below the knees and a pressed blouse—I forwent my hose in an attempt to appear more vulnerable. I hated losing that layer of protection about as much as I hated that I had been given the role of damsel in distress.

Yashu's division had access to the light codes for the tower, and she had once nicked the translation key for long enough to copy it down. I watched the closer tower signal a guard change to the far tower. At that moment, Yashu and Adi were slipping over the edge of the bridge. They would both climb back up onto the top of the bridge during the distraction, use Adi's tools to wrench open the vehicle and knock out the soldiers, and then Adi would drive the vehicle away while Yashu ran back to our side. She had the harder job, and yet I was more nervous.

I waited, heart battering my ribs, until lights appeared at the far side of the bridge. This would be the prisoners, and it was also my cue. I took a deep breath and then ran across the highway, shouting, "Help! Help!"

Nobody came out of the guard post until I was almost upon it. The door swung open, light spilling out, and a young man stepped forward, gun cradled in one hand. One of three men staffing this guardhouse. "Help!" I shouted, waving to him.

"This is a military station, and it's past curfew," he said. "You cannot be here."

"I'm sorry, sir, you were the closest place I could think of," I panted. It wasn't an act; I really was out of breath. I pushed myself through the doorway into a room the size of my entire childhood flat, filled with luxuries half the homes in Kingston did not have: thick windows, a connected bathroom, and an electrical panel. All three men were staring at me. I could only hope that Yashu and Adi had heard my screaming and were taking the van. "My boss kept me late, you see, and I was walking home very late, I swear I'm usually not out this late—"

"Get to the point," barked the eldest man.

"Sorry, sorry, sir!" I pressed a hand to my chest and heaved in a breath. This was certainly over-the-top, but I had never been known for my subtlety. "I was walking home and I passed by Colville Square, where several men were discussing—they were discussing how to attack you!"

The older man drew his eyebrows together. For a moment, I thought I had failed, but then he leaned toward the panel and flicked some switches. I hoped to whatever gods were listening that he had hailed a pause signal to the prison van. "Attack the bridge, you mean?"

I nodded, playing dumb. "They were planning to set a fire, or perhaps an explosion. They were talking about freeing some friends. I confronted them, accused them of treason, and one of them started to chase me. This was the only place I could think of, sir—I was so scared!" I covered my face with my hands at this point and tried to sob.

Around me, there was a flurry of activity. A hand touched my shoulder, and I jumped. The older man was looking down at me, and I hastily pretended to wipe my eyes. "You have done very well," he said. "Peter, go take a—"

There was a rumble from across the highway, followed by sparks flying into the air—fireworks, I knew, courtesy of Fauzia and her cell. It was in fact Smita Deshmukh who had confirmed

Fauzia's suspicions about what Adi was here to do, and though Fauzia still seemed wary of Smita, she had let her get involved with their cell's job: causing a commotion, then disappearing by the time guards arrived. Hopefully it would be alarming enough that—

"Turn it around!" the older man barked. One man lunged for the control board and began flashing signals. The van, visible through a window, made a sharp turn. I had to fight to prevent myself from whooping. We had tricked the British into giving up the prisoners. Two of the guards ran out, leaving me with the older man to watch until the van disappeared out of sight beyond the bridge's gate.

"You did well, young lady," he said. "I appreciate your quick thinking. That was a convoy of dangerous prisoners being brought to the Outpost, and we wouldn't want to take any risks."

I put a hand over my mouth, feigning shock. "My goodness!"

He turned from me and scribbled something on official-looking paper. "Here is a note to get you home safely. If anyone stops you, show them this."

I left immediately and walked along the highway toward home. I was stopped twice, but the older man's signature got me waved along both times. It was only as I neared our flat, hoping to find Fauzia and Yashu already there, that I realized how unbelievably lucky we were that our trick had worked. It was a better plan than Adi's, to be sure, but it had still relied on good fortune. Despite pulling off such an operation and proving we were true rebels, I knew: We would not always be this lucky.

Still, the thrill of it sustained us as we started planning for disruption as well as aid. Now, finally, we knew we could.

A MONTH LATER, I received a letter without any identifying marks beyond my address. It had clearly already been opened and found harmless, for inside there was only a brief tale, written on a typewriter. There was no way to be sure, and yet I knew it was a message from Baba. Forgiveness, for not leaving. Praise, for what I had helped accomplish. Acknowledgment, that our tactics, though different, still had power.

Long ago a demon king grew in strength and power. At first, Bali seemed helpful, friendly even. So the peoples of the earth and the heavens assisted his rise. But slowly he became crueler in his conquest, greedier, until he held all existence under his tyrannical rule.

The gods knew they needed to restore cosmic balance, but he seemed too powerful to challenge. Then Bali announced he would designate a day to celebrate his conquests, and he would grant the wishes of all who came before him that day, in order to prove his generosity to his people. Vishnu took the form of Vamana, a dwarf, and went before the king. Seeing this small man before him, the king asked what he wanted. Bali offered jewels, animals, and other such riches. Vamana refused all of these. Instead, he asked for three paces' worth of land.

I was pleased that he had chosen this story about the way that cleverness might defeat great power. It was his tacit blessing for our ILM to run the way we thought best.

The king looked at the dwarf and laughed. "Only three paces? Surely you must want more." But Vamana insisted three paces would be enough for him. Bali agreed. Then Vamana began growing. The demon king looked on in horror as Vamana towered over his palace. He grew and grew until in one step, he eclipsed the earth. In another step, he circled the heavens. And on his third step, he placed his foot on the king's head and pushed him into the underworld.

6

PARASHURAMA, AXE WARRIOR

I learned how to destroy at twenty-four.

Turmoil enveloped the country as the British tightened their grasp. It had never been harder to hear news from outside Kingston, because the news had never been better—rebellion was igniting the land as Indians rose up in numbers too great to be contained. But Kingston was an administrative state unto itself, containing its own elite, its own laborers, its own farms. I wanted all of India to be free, the same way I wanted all colonies to be free, but I fought only for these six hundred square kilometers. I knew that Kingston could achieve freedom, and I was going to be the one to lead us there.

I had spoken to my Baba twice more since he had called the Dominion Way phone and breathed purpose into my life. During his most recent call, he had told me that Adi had spoken highly of me and our work—in the end, Adi had recognized the revolutionary fervor in us. In me.

"You have your soldiers ready, beti," Baba had said. "It's time for greater action now. It is noble to help our people, but now you must make the British too afraid to remain."

"But then they might learn of us," I whispered. It was my greatest fear, and I was ashamed, but I knew I could tell him. "And then . . ."

He was silent for a moment, but then he sighed. "I know, Kalki. I know. But you are smarter than me, and more careful. You will succeed where I did not."

"Baba . . ." I said, and then stopped. I wanted to ask for comfort or tell him I wasn't ready, but I wasn't just his daughter. We were both comrades in this fight, and I had to do my duty. I could not be selfish.

"We have plans," I reassured him instead. "We are working on it."

"Good, good." There was a brief pause, and I shifted from foot to foot. We loved each other, yet were almost strangers. "How is your Aai?"

"She's well. She doesn't have to work long hours anymore, because of my job, so she has more time. She's started helping some of the older women in the building, and visiting Mr. Kapadia so he's not as lonely. What should I tell her?"

"That I'm well, beti. Well and safe." We both knew he was lying. "Someday, we will all be together again."

Footsteps rounded the corner, growing louder, and I slammed the phone down before I could think twice. I exited the booth, trying my hardest not to cry, and found Samuel Clarke standing outside. My stomach dropped.

"H-hello," I stammered. "Sir."

His face was stoic. Although my instincts were screaming to run, I knew that would make me look suspicious. "What were you doing?" he asked, voice betraying nothing.

"I was—I was trying to reach my husband, sir. He's deployed. But I couldn't." His expression changed slightly, revealing the barest hint of empathy, and I commended myself on the quick lie. I had never actually tried to call Bhaskar, because our letters said everything they needed to, and placing calls to the border was a ridiculous proposition besides. But British officers could make calls, and so Samuel Clarke believed it.

"Very well," he said, already turning away. I was hardly worth his time.

And then I ran, probably a little faster than I should have, from the frying pan into the fire. My boss, Mr. Jenkins, had moved me into his office to better increase "collaboration," by which he meant that I was the youngest woman in our division and he enjoyed having me close. As his personal secretary, I remained the target of his advances, looks, and touches. It was a sacrifice of myself that I gladly made for the greater access that being in his office afforded me. I spent my days justifying water rations, earlier curfews, and population control measures like child taxes. Then I spent my nights calculating how much water we could steal from British cisterns without detection, sneaking people under suspicion to safe houses, and, following the new tax on families with more than two children, spiriting away newborns to homes that could afford them.

It was during one of my routine perusals of Mr. Jenkins's inbox that I discovered plans to expand the British-only power plant located on the outskirts of Old Bombay. The plant, the Mountbatten Electrical Center, provided electricity to City Hall and the entire British quarter, ensuring the lights were always on while the rest of us suffered through blackouts and rationing. If we had any doubts, Yashu's "friend" O'Brien delivered those same plans to her a week later. He—for Yashu was convinced he had a man's handwriting—had passed us intelligence of this sort before, and although we remained suspicious of his motives, we had stopped doubting his veracity. An expansion would give them more power to tighten their rule. Improved efficiency, more British work hours, and even better lighting in certain areas would pose a danger to our work.

Simi had been promoted to some type of low-level engineer and transferred to Mountbatten. She ran her own small cell now, the way Fauzia and Yashu and others did, using her ridiculous jokes to help her recruit—falling behind the veneer of "only joking" if things went awry. By commiserating with the humblest British workers, she learned that the expansion would likely be finished in mid-August.

Beginning in June, she slowly set up our task. Every day, she made tiny changes in the transformer room, carefully stripping key transmission wires bare so we could cut them when the opportunity came.

I planned to do the final deed, because I was always itching for action. To my surprise, Maryam—who had helped so much with the fans—volunteered as well. Although she had seemed nervous during that operation, she said she hadn't been able to stop thinking of it since. She wanted to get her hands dirty, which I respected. Smita volunteered from Fauzia's group, and Simi suggested her friend Abhaya as the fourth and final person, because she was also a Mountbatten worker and familiar with the place.

By then, our ILM chapter had grown experienced with running missions. Every other month a few of us undertook small sabotages of the British. In the meantime, we ran laps around our houses, practiced moving heavy objects, and escaped from one another's grips. I taught our group the eclectic mix of skills my Baba had given me so they could pass them on: how to pick a simple lock, basic self-defense tactics, ways to blend into a dark alley, and how to hide from patrols.

With our homegrown skills, we snuck into the night to steal police files, drain oil from transport trucks, damage railroads—whatever we could think of to stop the newest horrifying plans. We could not do these things too often without drawing suspicion, but we managed to stay under the radar by not accumulating a body count. It was unthinkable to the British that opposition beyond the occasional disgruntled youth could rise again here in insulated Kingston, when the various penal codes made rebellion punishable by a swift death.

But to us, a swift death was preferable to a slow one. Even a week of incapacitating British operations was worth the risk.

Our plan was simple. Simi would activate the power plant's emergency alarm, forcing workers to exit for a congregation point outside. She would leave the doors unlocked and we would sneak into the transformer room. Maryam and Smita would cut the wires to the newly installed security cameras, a challenging new technology the British had introduced to their most important institutions, while Abhaya and I went to the two main rooms to cut every power line we could find with special insulated tools Yashu had made for us—when I expressed surprise, she reminded me that most everyone she knew was a laborer, and so she had access to strong blades that only needed a rubber coating added. Replacing lines and fixing the power system could take months, and it would take at least a week to bring power back to the British neighborhoods.

At first, everything seemed to work. The alarm went off, and after sixty seconds, Maryam and I slipped inside. Smita and Abhaya were already on the other side of the plant as the first team to move. Smita had raced off with enthusiasm, and I felt proud that I had recruited her. Maryam and I would meet up again outside the plant, so I had to move as quickly as possible on my own. The target room mostly consisted of many, many wires emerging from a large, elevated box and plunging into the ground at the other end of the room.

Simi had warned me about how thick the wires were, but I had not expected them to be wider than my whole body. This was going to take longer than I had anticipated, and speed was of the essence, so I got straight to work rather than scoping out the room. When I carefully slid under the large box in the center, I saw that out of plain view the plastic and rubber protecting the wire had been stripped off by Simi's careful attentions. The serrated blade Yashu had given me was as long as my arm and had to be held at either end by the heavily insulated handle. "All you have to do is aim the sharp part into the wire and push," she had instructed me. "Even you can't mess it up." Sure enough, the tool slid easily through the wire cables, and sparks singed my clothes.

I was on the sixth wire when footsteps entered the room. I scrambled out to find myself face-to-face with a young, pimply engineer. He was pale, with yellow, wiry hair: plainly British.

For a moment he could not comprehend my presence. "Where is everyone? I was in the loo and now— What are you doing?"

I did the only thing I could think of: I punched him in the face. He stumbled back, and I punched him again, then elbowed him in his solar plexus. He fell to the ground, wheezing, and I stood over him, uncertain.

"You people are so dumb," he whispered from his position curled on the floor. "Your mask has slipped."

I raised a gloved hand to my mask to confirm. He knew what I looked like. He moved to pick himself up, and I kicked him in the gut, then slammed his head against the ground, hoping to knock him out. When he woke up, he wouldn't remember what he had seen, and I would be long gone. His skull cracked against the floor. He made an odd, strangled noise, and his expression went blank.

Fear jolted through me.

Panting, I pulled off a glove and checked for a pulse. Nothing. I scrabbled for his wrist. Still nothing.

The enormity of what I had done hadn't hit me yet, though I could feel a dull ache somewhere deep in my stomach that I tried to push away. I dragged his body toward the transformer and cut the last two wires in a haze before crawling out from the box and curling one of his hands around the tool. My gut churned, but I tried to breathe through it. Then I threw his other hand toward one of the sparking stubs coming from the transformer. I felt as though I were watching myself go through the motions from a distant position above. Even though he was dead, the man's body danced with electricity for a few seconds. Now it would look like an accidental electrocution or, better yet, an act of sabotage by one of their own. He might have gotten the head wound while falling. It sickened me, that I had thought of this idea so quickly.

Acid burned my throat as I exited the building and raced toward our meeting point. Maryam was waiting. "How did it go?"

"Completely fine," I lied. I did not mention the fact that my sloppiness had killed someone. How could I? He was a member of the evil machine, but it was not up to me to be the arbiter of his fate. And yet, violence was necessary to rebellion.

Except that I had not done it for any greater purpose, but to cover my own mistake. He was just a person, a man working a job. I had exchanged his life for my own, and the guilt and sorrow mingled with shame, for I knew that even with more time to consider the decision, I would have done the same thing. I would have chosen myself.

"You don't have your tool," Maryam observed, panic creeping into her voice. "Where did you leave it?"

I pretended to look at my hands as though in shock. They were shaking. I didn't know when that had started. My whole body was shaking; I had killed someone. And Maryam was expecting a response. "I must have left it. I can—"

"Shit," Maryam said. "No, no. They'll know someone cut them anyway. It's all right. We should get to safety."

And I followed her into the night.

I DID NOT tell Fauzia what I had done, couldn't bring myself to say it aloud. Couldn't bring myself to face her disgust and hatred when she learned I had become a killer.

Nobody came knocking at our door that night. The next morning was a Saturday, and after Fauzia left to help her parents, I turned on the radio and listened to the news. For the first half hour or so, I was alone with my thoughts, confused as to why they were not reporting on the outage at all.

In the warm morning light, the panic and guilt of the previous night threatened to overtake me. I had stopped shaking, but I could not stop seeing the man, his blank expression, the blood. I had done that. I was a killer.

I tried to think of what my Baba would say. He would have told me that all the heroes of our land had blood on their hands, that it was a necessary evil. Maharaja Shivaji Bhonsle had been a minor footnote in history books written by the British—he was a Shudra bandit, they said, whose life's work was destroyed by the Brahmins who could not accept his rise to power because he was not a true Kshatriya. It was a classic British tale of Indian history, showing both the founder of a strong Indian kingdom and those around him in a bad light, but it was also untrue. In the histories written by our people, I had learned how the British *fled* from him all those years ago. They fled him, and fled our island, returning only after his death. He had united many disparate groups, and most did not care that he came from low roots. They cared that he fought for them and made them powerful, prosperous. And Shivaji had cemented his status with an act of murder; Baba would tell me not to hate myself when the price of any progress was blood.

Still, though, I was agitated, uncomfortable inside my skin. I began cleaning the flat, trying to channel some of my energy in a way I knew Fauzia might appreciate, when a male reporter came on. "This is a rebroadcast of an earlier breaking news announcement," he said, sounding very calm. The possibility hadn't occurred to me that perhaps I had missed the news by sleeping in. "Late last night, Mountbatten Electrical Center reported a failure. Inspection showed a young local engineer from Kingston, Hakeem Mustafa, had cut through several wires. He was found electrocuted next to his handiwork."

What? No. That couldn't be right. He had been *white,* not just light-skinned. Right? Had I killed one of my own?

"Authorities are still investigating, but it appears as though he was angry he lost a promotion to a Hindu man and wanted to punish his supervisor. The rolling blackouts necessary to repair the plant may last for months throughout Kingston . . ."

I lunged for the light switch and flicked it. Nothing. Our radio was handheld, battery operated. The power had been out *all morning* and I hadn't even noticed. I let out a scream of pure frustration. "No, no, no!" My hand hit the stove so hard I drew blood. The walls of our flat closed in on me. They were dark, so dark, forcing me to my knees. How could this happen? Mountbatten served only the British.

Except, of course, the answer was obvious. They would divert power from our plants, and deprive us, and blame us, and it was all a lie, and it was—

Something crashed outside.

It was all an attempt to turn us against one another.

The British had invented Hakeem Mustafa so that this act of sabotage that they believed was committed by their own would instead shore up their own power. Who needed the truth, when lies could cause irreparable damage between Hindus and Muslims?

And that thought was chased by—

Fauzia. Her family's shop was always a target. I had no idea how long the power had been out, how long the news had been known, but it was long enough for the rioting to have already reached a frenzied pitch.

I ran outside. The streets were hot and crowded, thick with a kind of chaos that I didn't often see. The hatred was almost palpable in the air, and people were coming or going with bricks in their hands and blood on their shirts. Broken glass crunched under my shoes.

But Bhaskar and Omar's flat had been my home for years, and the quickest route to Fauzia's family's shop was not something I could forget. I kept my head down, my figure and loose clothing letting me pass for a young boy, and hurried past a small temple that was charred and smoking, ignoring men and women lying bloody in dark corners. I saw not one British officer. The Muslim mobs must have been proactive about their retaliation, striking out at Hindus because they knew already that the Hindu mobs were heading for their mosques and neighborhoods. They knew that the Hindus would blame them for the loss of power and all its subsequent privations. And they had probably burned the temple to prevent it from being a refuge during the riots, which was convenient when they also hated idol worship. Of course, the British didn't think any better of us—that was why they were all safe and secure on their side of the island as the violence unfolded.

Just get to Fauzia, I told myself over and over, until I approached the boundary line that sectioned off a Muslim-majority neighborhood. It was too dangerous to cross directly—that was just inviting a beating or worse. Instead, I ducked into an alley I knew connected via a circuitous route to Fauzia's family's store. There were more people than I had ever seen back here, mostly women trying to use these routes to travel. All our faces had the same grim set; we were ready to fight or run at the first sign of trouble.

The back door to the shop looked untouched, but that didn't mean anything. I unclasped the safety pin I always had on my dress to pick the lock. Their security had never been good, this lock old and easily broken, which only made me more nervous. I pushed the door, but it wouldn't budge. I strained against it until it opened just enough to admit me and saw that a shelf had toppled over onto it.

My breath caught.

The store had been *destroyed*. I remembered seeing Mr. Kapadia's store once, after a rampage by some British boys. His hands had shaken as he picked up broken glass and disposed of destroyed merchandise, and I had thought that was the worst that could happen to someone's livelihood. I had been a naïve child.

What had happened to Mr. Kapadia's store was nothing compared to this. The floor was wet and slick from smashed bottles of hair oil and shampoo, every window was broken, and the front door was hanging off its hinges. Where Mr. Kapadia's store had been ransacked as an act of terror, the mob here had destroyed everything in an act of total domination. There was nothing to be salvaged; everything would have to be rebuilt from scratch.

"Fauzia?" I shouted, panic gripping me. "Fauzia!" She wasn't here. I studied the floor and was relieved to find no blood. That didn't mean much, though. I hoped she had run, that she hadn't—

The floor thumped next to me, and I grabbed for a wooden board to defend myself just as Fauzia emerged from the cellar. She threw her arms around me and we clutched each other close for a blessed second, breathing each other in.

"You're such an idiot," she said, but she was smiling, talking quickly. "Don't worry, I'm fine. They came through fast, and I ran to the cellar and crouched behind a crate of biscuits. They didn't even think to look. But you really shouldn't have come, it's—" A bang in the distance cut her off.

"Dangerous?" I finished, smiling back despite the circumstances. She was here, close enough to touch. Alive. "I heard on the radio, and I had to come find you."

"Were you going to rescue me with your wooden board? Then we'd both have been in for it."

"I didn't think it through," I said. The shouting was getting louder. "Where's your family?"

"Visiting my aunt up north. Basma is meeting a potential suitor." Fauzia glanced around the shop, all mirth gone. "We're ruined," she whispered. "What are we going to do?"

At that moment the door flew off its already broken hinges, and a man came hurtling through. There was nowhere for us to run or hide. I threw myself in front of Fauzia.

The older man was holding a wooden board with nails hammered into one end. There was a prominent tilak on his head. I noticed with a roiling of my stomach that there was blood smeared all over one of his hands, up to his arm.

"Jai Shri Rama!" I called out. *Hindu, I'm Hindu!*

He lowered his board slightly. "Who are you?" he snapped. "What are you doing here?"

"My name is Kalki, and this is my friend Fa—Falguni," I stammered. "We were out shopping when there was a rush of people. We ran in here for shelter. We've been too scared to leave."

"How do I know you're telling the truth?" he demanded. "You could be Muslim spies and stab me in the back."

I decided not to point out that that made no sense, since we were hiding in an abandoned, looted shop and had no idea who he was, but I bit my tongue. "Please, sir. We just want to get home."

He reached out with his bloody hand. I flinched back. "This is pig's blood," he said. "If you are telling the truth, you will take my hand." I grabbed it without hesitation, hoping he would not demand the same of Fauzia, whom I did not want to let suffer though I knew she would do it to survive. But then my hand was slick with blood and he was turning from me, and we were safe. "Follow me," he said.

Fauzia kept her head down, saying nothing, as he led us back onto the street. I gave him Aai's address, because her solidly Hindu neighborhood bolstered our story. The riots, it seemed, had lulled, revealing the true destruction. I saw a bloody form sprawled outside of a butcher shop a few doors down, and I could see smoke up the way where I knew Fauzia's mosque stood. As we crossed into the Hindu area, we passed a small temple where the statues' faces had been smashed to bits. A man was huddled over one of the shards, rocking back and forth. One side of his head was covered in blood. Fauzia took my clean hand in hers for a moment, squeezing it.

Had she put the pieces together and figured out that I had done this? I had left a dead man behind and dared the British to create a story. And our people had immediately believed the blatant manipulations, proving themselves to be exactly what the British said we were.

No. It was so easy to repeat those words, but the British visited the same violence on us without provocation. They starved us and stole our friends and—my stomach churned as I saw a woman lying face down on the footpath, sobbing. I could tell she was Muslim, but her dupatta was askew, her dress ripped, and it was obvious what had happened. How could I tell myself the British were the problem? I knew they were, I knew it, and still it was hard to remember at this minute, when we hurt ourselves as badly as any foreigner.

The power was still out.

FAUZIA DECIDED TO nap in my room as Aai and I listened to the news on the battery-operated radio. Clipped British voices discussed the outbreak of violence in the native quarters of Kingston.

"It is clear that the sheer savagery of retaliation we have seen from the native Hindu population is a sign of deeper problems in the community," a high-ranking police captain explained.

"Yes, of course," said one of the radio hosts. "The population has high unemployment, which certainly doesn't help. But they haven't yet learned that violence is not the answer. Hurting others won't turn the power back on, but working harder could."

"I understand their frustrations," the captain responded. "After all, they live cheek by jowl with the Muslim population, who are responding to the Hindus' frustration with acts of violence, as is typical of their religion. Neither party is behaving well." The captain was clearly trying to appear analytical, but to me he seemed almost gleeful.

Then the host announced that they had on, as a guest, a representative of City Hall and a reserve member of the military—Samuel Clarke. He thanked them for having him before explaining he was going to read a statement written by the chancellor. "The British and the Indians are united in creating this bountiful land," he began. "But the British have the grave responsibility of building a modern, civilized world here. Often, we take pride in the progress of these native people, but today we see a step back—"

I slammed the radio off, unable to hear another word out of his pathetic, conniving mouth.

"They had it coming," Aai said without warning. "Those Muslims have always had it better than us, and now their people caused an outage for us just because for once they weren't favored."

"But they're affected too," I argued, because I knew that this wasn't a Muslim's fault—it was mine. "Besides, sharing a religion doesn't make them guilty of any crime. You don't hate Indian Christians for what British Christians do. Most of the whites who hurt us are Christian."

"You don't understand." Aai looked out the window, as though she could see something beyond the buildings I could not. "All you know is Kingston, and what the British tell you. But you must have learned in school how the Muslims conquered us before the British ever did. They practically handed us over to them!"

I was fairly sure that wasn't true, because we had learned about the ineptitudes of the Hindu-majority Maratha Empire that had held the region before British rule, and I knew the history of Muslims in India could not be boiled down to simple conquest, but I didn't know how to refute her. She seemed so certain. Even though I had long since accepted that Aai and I would never see eye to eye on some things, I still struggled to reconcile what I had personally observed with the stories she told me about the people of our city. "Fauzia's family is ruined. If I hadn't been there, she might have been raped, or murdered."

"Fauzia's one of the good ones," Aai said. And though I thought that was a ridiculous statement, I did not want to argue more with Fauzia sleeping in the next room. So I swallowed my argument and sat there in the quiet dark.

We waited at Aai's for much of the day until there was a brief burst of electricity, which we used to immediately call Yashu. She picked up on the first ring—she had been trying to contact us.

"We're fine up here," she whispered into the phone. "Too close to the border for it to get bad. I was worried about you two. I called your flat."

"We found each other and came to my mother's place. It was closer. We'll head over now in case you need to reach us—the riots seem to have died down."

I could hear the frown in Yashu's voice. "That seems risky."

"What's life without a little risk?" I asked her, and the ridiculousness of asking that question pulled a laugh out of her and Fauzia, who was listening in.

But we followed Yashu's warning and waited to head back until the evening, when the city had calmed. We thought the worst was over.

Then Simi came pounding at our door, just a few minutes before curfew. She was wearing a dark cloak over trousers, her face ruddy in the low light of our candles as though she had been running. "What is it?" Fauzia asked, bustling Simi into a chair. "What happened? Your family?"

Simi shook her head. She seemed, for a moment, beyond words. "They took Abhaya," she whispered.

I was already headed for the door. "Where were you when they took her? Which way did they go? Fauzia, maybe you should come with me—"

"The police took her!" Simi shouted. I froze, my hand on the door. "I had gone to see her—she lives down the street from me, and since we live in a mixed Sikh and Hindu neighborhood, it hasn't been too bad there. Then the police came knocking, and I went out the window, and heard them arrest her. For being involved with the power plant. Because she works there too, and they must have figured it out somehow, and—" Here Simi abruptly cut herself off and ran for our bathroom. Fauzia and I listened as she retched, staring at each other.

"How—"

"I don't know, I wasn't with her," I said. Abhaya was going to die. And, selfishly, I had another thought. Was Abhaya going to give us up? Were we all going to die?

Simi came back, pale and shaking. "We have to find her," she said. "We have to free her. We can't let her die!"

I stood there, my jaw clenching until it hurt and my fingernails digging into my palms. It was Fauzia who moved forward and found the words, folding Simi in her arms. "We don't know what's happening. Tomorrow, we will ask Yashu to see if she can get any information and go from there. I'm so sorry, Simi. I'm glad you're safe."

"Do you know anything about the dead man they've been talking about?" Simi asked me. "You were there. I can't think what it could be."

I opened my mouth, but Fauzia got there first. "They must be making it up because they don't know how we got in or did it. It was obvious sabotage, since we cut through the wires."

"Or the first engineer on the scene was stupid enough to touch the wires," Simi mused. "But now Abhaya's paying the price."

"She knew the risks," Fauzia said. I could tell she was upset, but she maintained an outward calm, lending dignity to her words. "She knew she might give her life, and she agreed to pay that price. We will do what we can, but . . ."

There was nothing more to be said. The thought of it settled in my chest like a knife.

"TRANSPORTATION," YASHU TOLD me the next day, the moment we were alone on our lunch break. She did not have to say who. The word had spread among our cell, and we couldn't risk being overheard. I wondered who else in the lunchroom was one of us—Smita had been transferred to a better job, so there was nobody I knew here.

"When?" I asked.

"It's already happened. She probably won't make it to her destination." Yashu shook her head. I could tell she was upset from the scrunching of her eyes, but otherwise she looked like she was discussing the weather. We were all perhaps too good at burying our emotions.

"Are you sure?"

"I work in the legal department, and even if I didn't, *he* left me a note with his sympathies." O'Brien, then. How did he always predict exactly what we wanted to know? "What a disaster. How's Fauzia?"

I accepted the change of topic. What more was there to say? At least we could pretend that Abhaya would survive in whatever African colony she was being shipped to, even though we knew traitors were never heard from again. There would be time for us to decide how to compensate her family without telling them, to determine whether she had given us away, to mourn and remember. But for now we were all trying to make sense of the chaos we had caused. It had been our decision to shut down the plant, and now our people would suffer and die under the blackouts, learning to hate one another more.

"It's my fault," I admitted, slumping forward to rest my head on my hands. This was not suspicious, since every Indian worker here looked miserable. Several were missing—I hoped they were not gone forever. That would be my fault, too.

Yashu patted the top of my head in an awkward motion. "It's their fault," she said. "Don't be ridiculous."

"You know the man on the news?" I asked, tilting my head to look up at her. "Hakeem?" Yashu nodded. I didn't say anything further, but the pained look on my face told all. *Please understand*, I begged, and Yashu froze.

"No."

"Yes."

We looked at each other for several long seconds. "Self-defense?" she asked.

"Yes."

Yashu gave me a sharp nod. "Okay, then." She reached out again and placed her hand on mine. "Still their fault."

I spotted Samuel Clarke walking toward us and stiffened, blinking away the tears. "Ms. Kamble!" he called out.

"Yes, sir—how can I help?" Yashu said, turning to him.

"Has everyone in our division reported in?" The last syllable lingered, as though he wanted to say something more.

"There are no absences from our division today, sir. I can come down—"

"No need." He glanced around the lunchroom, as if confirming for himself, and then left without saying goodbye.

"What was that?" I whispered to Yashu.

Yashu pressed her lips together, as if considering her words. At last, she offered, "People make mistakes, horrible mistakes, but that's not all they are."

I did not know if she was referring to Samuel Clarke or myself—or both. But I did not want to know what she meant, either, for fear of what she might say. We finished our lunch in silence.

WHEN I GOT home, Fauzia was pacing our small living room.

"Transportation. Already done," I reported.

She looked up at the ceiling, blinking rapidly. We didn't know Abhaya well—she was Simi's friend first—but that didn't dull the blow. Finally, she asked, "You did it, didn't you?"

I averted my eyes, unable to look at her. "I'm so sorry. It was self-defense."

She stalked into our shared bedroom, removed her prayer rug from under her bed, and rolled it out, facing west.

"What are you doing?" I asked, lingering in the doorway between the living room and bedroom.

"What do you think I'm doing?" she snapped. "I'm praying. It's Maghrib, and I'm praying."

"But you don't normally—"

"You don't get a say in when I pray, Kalki." She slammed the door in my face.

Even though I couldn't see her, I knew exactly what she was doing. Fauzia normally prayed twice a day, as the British government almost never granted religious dispensations to take prayer breaks. Occasionally, during Ramzan, Muslim employees would get a chance to stop and pray during the workday, but never year-round. We had this in common, Hindus and Muslims, that we did not fit into the Britishers' preferred religion—not that it mattered anymore.

At least here, at home, we could pray in relative peace. I had a small shrine set up in my corner of our room, and Fauzia had her rug. The prayer rug was beautiful, a wedding gift from her aunt. A very talented seamstress had embroidered the deep red fabric with gold and blue interlocking designs, so intricate they appeared almost three-dimensional. Fauzia loved that rug more than any gift, except perhaps my bracelet.

Right about now she would be pressing her forehead to the top strip of maroon, and then, in another moment, stretching her whole body up toward the heavens. Belatedly, I realized she had not even paused to complete the ritual ablutions beforehand—or maybe she was just performing them out of sight. Even through the door I could sense how upset she was at me.

I waited for the normal ten minutes and expected Fauzia to emerge. She did not. Another ten minutes passed, and then ten further. Just as I rose from the sofa to check on her, the door opened, and she stepped out quietly.

"That took some time," I observed, trying to engage her before she could slip away again.

"Yes, it did," she agreed, sitting beside me on the sofa. She paused for a moment, weighing whether to say more, before adding, "I had to ask forgiveness."

"On my behalf? You don't have to do that."

"No." Fauzia looked at me, and I saw stone in her eyes. "I asked for forgiveness for myself. For loving a killer, even after she confessed."

I stared at her with growing anger. The love between us, though deep and true, remained largely unspoken, as it did between all friends. And yet she would hurl it in my face in this moment just to hurt me? "Excuse me?" I demanded. "You don't even know how it happened. What grounds do you have to judge me?"

"People lost their lives. People with families and children." Her gaze pierced through me, sharp and brittle.

"They chose to kill their own people, to riot—"

"I did not say they were blameless, just that they were not evil. You do not have the right to choose who lives—you are not Him."

"I don't believe in Allah," I said, feeling that I had somehow lost ground and attempting to regain my footing.

Fauzia rolled her eyes. "You're not Shiva either. I'm not going to debate religion with you, Kalki."

"I'm not sorry I killed him," I said, because I could not lie to her.

"I know. That's why I had to ask forgiveness." She shook her head slowly. "You committed a crime."

"Against the British!"

"Kalki," she began, her hands clenched into tight fists, "do you think murder will be legal in your new India? Do you think acts of violence, however well intentioned, will be welcomed?"

"Free expression—"

"This wasn't free expression!" she shouted, rising to her feet. "Did you even take full precautions, or is this whole situation your fault? Self-defense is one thing, but you should not have needed it if you had followed the plan. You're so passionate about hating the British, but you have no idea what sort of India you want to replace them with."

I had never seen her so angry at me. Some deep part of me felt wounded that she was this mad, worried that she wouldn't love me anymore. But more than that, I was indignant at her anger, because I cared about the rebellion more than anything, and she was attacking my part in it. "You're right, I made a mistake. But the British were the ones who spun it, destroyed *everything*. They're the ones at fault. We have to fight. For Kingston."

"You may not believe, but my religion teaches that we must fight those who war against us without transgressing ourselves. I know Hinduism must do the same. You can't fight one way and then magically change to a different system when you win. The fight for Indian independence has long used nonviolence, and—"

"And where did it get us?" I interrupted her. "Yes, Gandhi tried nonviolence, he used diplomacy and politics and protest. What did that get him and his followers? A place in the killings! Or did you forget that?" Now rage was heating my blood, and I continued, "Did you forget that Jawaharlal Nehru and Muhammad Ali Jinnah were hanged for their crimes against the Crown? Some of their followers didn't die, but they might as well have, and you know it. Sent away to Kenya, or Australia, or other British territories to work, separated from their families and made to labor until their dying days. The British effectively wiped out a whole generation of the independence movement. Nonviolence is *useless*. All we have is death."

I thought, bizarrely, of Adi, who had sent me an unsigned note to thank me for the assistance in saving the prisoners and remind me that we were part of a bigger struggle. *Never forget your fighting spirit,* he had written, which is how I recognized him. And then, scratched out in a line at the bottom, *Perhaps, in another life*—but how many revolutionaries had ever succeeded in getting to that other life? Adi had sneered at us and our inaction, and he had been right that pure nonviolence had gotten us no-where.

"You know that's not what I am saying," Fauzia said, break-ing my reverie. "That is not an indictment of the nonviolent movement, it's a mark of the horror of British rule. Your argu-ment is flawed, and we're not even—"

"Is it?" I asked. Suddenly, I wasn't regretful at all. Fauzia was mad I had killed the British? The ones who had just taken Ab-haya? How *dare* she. "Because the nonviolent movement tried again. But they were too slow, because nonviolence is too slow for people as depraved and violently efficient as our enemy. They were slaughtered. My Aai could have died because my Baba de-cided to march and protest the British. I didn't exist, but if I had, the British would have sent me to an orphanage—"

"Kalki! Shut up, shut up, *shut up*! I know all of this, you ar-rogant, selfish idiot! I don't care what everyone else did. The problem is that you are not *sorry* for what you did. You were wrong, you were sloppy, and someone died."

"I was defending myself! And our friends!"

"We have *responsibilities* now. But you still have the same reckless streak. The British aren't even human lives to you, are they?"

"The British don't think of *us* as human lives!"

Fauzia slumped, as though weights were pressing on her shoulders. "Never mind. Let's just move on."

I wasn't ready to, not now that she had gotten me so riled up. "Yashu could forgive me my mistake without inane lecturing. But I guess you see yourself as above us, since we're just infidels, and better off dead—"

Fauzia slapped me across the face. She did not put her full weight behind it, and I did not cry out. But even though the slap was not hard enough to hurt, the action jarred my soul. I lifted a trembling hand to touch my cheek, tears springing to my eyes. Fauzia had struck me. My best friend had raised her hand against me.

Fauzia held her trembling hand, observing it for a moment before looking back at me. "I cannot believe you would even imply . . ." She shook her head.

I relented. Her willingness to resort to physical violence and her obvious despair had finally moved me. I recalled how Aai would occasionally slap me as a child, just to startle me out of my idiocy. Now, as then, the fight left me. "I shouldn't have said that. I didn't mean to hurt you. I was just so angry. I didn't mean to kill the man. I wanted to knock him out—I wasn't expecting death," I babbled. "I promise you."

She considered this for a moment. "It does make me feel a bit better. That you weren't actually trying to kill him. But that doesn't change the outcome." The edge slowly seeped out of her voice with each word. "I'm sorry. I should not have slapped you. I treated you like Basma, like a child, but you're not. You already know everything I have said. I—I shouldn't resort to violence either."

Her face was flushed, her lips tinted with color, and for some reason she reminded me of the way she had looked at her wedding. She was so very beautiful, the most perfect person I had ever seen, and it made me angry that the British occupation had changed her so much since that day.

Fauzia had worn a beautiful white sharara, the borders elaborately embroidered with sequins and stones. The delicate lace sleeves drew attention to her beautiful hands. I could see the traditional green glass bangles that all Marathi brides wore for prosperity peeking out from the lace, and I thought I spied my gift to her nestled among them. Her hands were exquisitely patterned with mehendi that had stained deep red, flowers and ribbons running up her fingers into her palms in a fluid design. Someone had pulled her hair up into a tight bun, much neater than her customary work. A scarf adorned her head, embroidered in that same gold pattern, and she wore a tikka that lay like a bright jewel against her forehead.

One of the fasteners of her kurta came out just minutes before she was meant to enter the main area of the mosque, and I grabbed a box of safety pins and made my way down her back, trying my best to hide each pin. My hands shook, brushing lightly against her skin in small jolts.

When I finished with the dress, Fauzia grinned at me. "How do I look?" She did a little twirl and the edges of her kurta lifted, revealing the matching flared pants beneath. With her whole outfit and jewelry and makeup, she resembled a dancer I had seen in one of my Baba's books about India. Although I had never had an interest in dance, and most forms of Indian dance were considered dirty and sexual, I had stared at the picture for hours. I couldn't believe that the effortlessly spinning dancer in the illustration could be real. Now I understood.

"Incredible," I said softly. "You're beautiful." I could hardly breathe, basked in her light. Fauzia reached out one beautifully mehendied hand and cupped my chin. I could smell the earthy scent of the coloring, and under that, Fauzia. Without thinking, I turned my head and kissed her hand, and she laughed.

"I wish . . ." She did not continue the thought, instead leaning in to hug me, turning her face carefully away so the makeup wouldn't smear onto my dress. I held her for a moment, her solid warmth comforting and assured.

If not for the circumstances, I would have enjoyed watching the wedding ceremony, for I had never seen a nikah before. Instead I sat stiffly between Aai and Yashu, who had slipped in not a moment too soon. Omar and Fauzia skipped the traditional entrance and any other festivities, standing at the front with a dupatta held between them. Celebrations of love and joy had no place in the desperation-filled marriages forced upon us.

Then came the official ceremony. After reciting verses from the Qur'an that I could not understand, the imam asked Fauzia thrice if she wanted to marry Omar, and thrice Fauzia said yes. Thrice, Omar too said yes. When the dupatta was lowered, they both had shy smiles on their faces, the look of young newlyweds. Even though they were not in love, not getting married in the way everyone thought, they were entitled to some small happiness at getting this chance to have a wedding in front of their families. They signed the contract, and it was done. Afterward, Fauzia's family held a small reception, and then she and Omar set off for their new home, Omar's old flat, together. Bhaskar and I bade them farewell as they went off in their rickshaw.

"Omar leaves in a week," I said to him.

Bhaskar's hands shook ever so slightly, but his voice held steady. "I'll go back in another couple of hours."

I placed my hands on his own and held them for a moment. To all others, it probably seemed a tender moment between a young couple who would be parted too soon. I willed strength and resolve into his hands, and sent a silent prayer to whatever gods watched over me. Vishnu, the protector, or Ganapati Bappa, remover of obstacles. *Please bring them both home safely. Please.*

Now, four years later, they were not home, and I was what felt like an entirely different woman. Harsher, more dangerous. But Fauzia, despite her newfound anger and hardness, still saw the good in the world and tried to preserve it. I loved Fauzia so much; I did not want to hurt her with my callousness. I wished so desperately in this moment to be different. Less selfish, more worthy. More like her. But I was who I was. "You know, my Aai once told me the same thing, in a way. A few days after I reconnected with my Baba, she reminded me of the story of Parashurama. A story I heard many times as a child. He too killed people in anger, and later repented in shame."

"Tell me the story," Fauzia said softly. I could tell it was an olive branch, and I grabbed it eagerly.

"Once upon a time the warrior kings of India got too lazy and too greedy," I began, trying to remember the way Aai told it. "They got used to having whatever they wanted. One day, one of these kings happened upon an old Brahmin. The king coveted the old man's cow, but the man refused to give it up. 'This cow is sacred,' he said, 'brought forth from the ocean of milk. I am sworn to care for it.' Humiliated, the king murdered the old man.

When Parashurama, the old man's son, discovered what had happened, he went mad with grief. Although Parashurama was also a Brahmin, and sworn to a nonviolent life, he challenged the king to a duel and killed him with a single blow from his axe.

"When the other warrior kings and nobility heard this, they all challenged Parashurama to combat in order to avenge their fallen brother. Parashurama faced down every one of them. Fueled by rage, he defeated all of his challengers with his axe. The corrupt warriors fell one by one, until none were left and Parashurama stood triumphant."

It had felt good to overpower the worker in the moment; in Parashurama's victory I saw myself before I realized what I had done. I hung my head, looking at the floor as I finished the story.

"But after his victory, he was visited by the spirit of his father. Rather than being proud of his son's exploits, the father was horrified at what his son had wrought. The kings may have committed great violence and atrocities, but Parashurama had committed the greatest sin of all. He had become blinded and controlled by anger. Upon hearing his father's denouncement, Parashurama cast aside his axe and retreated into the mountains. He spent the remainder of his days living as an ascetic, repenting for all that he had done."

7

RAMA, KING

I learned how to lead at twenty-five.

The world was up in arms. Our backs bent under the weight of curfews and rations, of loss and sacrifice. But we stood up straight in back rooms as we whispered the word *revolution*.

The British had given up the pretense that the war with China was their priority, or that China was interested in wounding anything but their pride. Instead, on India's borders, the guerrilla warfare of the Indian Liberation Movement and other freedom fighters picked off both armies, considering them equally opposed to independence. The ILM was careful not to target Indian soldiers, but our people got caught in the crossfire occasionally. In response, the British took further emergency measures. They acknowledged now that they were contending with "anarchist, separatist movements" in the borderlands, and in response, they partitioned the territories where they claimed the violence was the worst. Assam, they said, was too volatile and full of unfaithful traitors, and in order to better break the spirit of the territory—

this part was not said out loud—the Assam Presidency would be split into two parts, drawing a line through the Hindu and Muslim populations, so that half of each would be in each part, weakened and under military rule.

Meanwhile, because the violence and riots were spilling into neighboring Bengal, the British were reimposing a religious partition there. I had heard much about Bengal because growing up our teachers had portrayed it as the ideal state, in contrast to Kingston. Their writers produced great works of art in English, the Hindu and Muslim populations lived together in peace, and the British had even been persuaded by the local population using peaceable means to undo a religious partition in 1911. Our teachers said this showed that if the native populations could learn self-improvement, they would be rewarded. But now Bengal had been repartitioned into the East Bengal Presidency for the Muslims and the West Bengal Presidency for the Hindus, and the state was tearing itself apart—which, we assumed, was the point. In quiet conversations we swapped knowledge and determined that if Bengal had fully risen up in rebellion, the British might have lost the entire front in East India, and so they made the population fight one another instead. In quieter conversations, we wondered if it was working, or if perhaps the people remembered who their true enemy was.

And then came the letters. Two missives, arriving at our flat on the same day in April but postmarked two months earlier, February 1968. Official letters. Fauzia was the first to arrive home. For two hours I blithely continued on with my day, chatting with Yashu as we walked to the bus stop after work, visiting my Aai to pick up some modak she had made after saving her sugar rations for the month, chatting with Mr. Kapadia about his newest books and whether Agatha Christie was worth reading when she was so clearly an imperialist, as Fauzia read the words over and over—

We regret to inform you that on the second of February your husband, Omar Khan, was killed in action . . .

In the same envelope came a letter from the chancellor, a standard form issued when Kingston's soldiers died, as a token of appreciation—

We thank you and your family for your great sacrifice. We suffer with your family, for our soldiers are the vanguard of our civilization. . . . We hope you take comfort and pride that their work furthered our great Empire. . . .

When at last I returned home, Fauzia had gone to the bathroom to wipe her tearstained face, and so I picked up the second letter, addressed to me, without thinking, and she came running back out at the sound of my cry. Bhaskar and Omar, gone. They had been our friends, and we had come to love them deeply in our five years of marriage by correspondence. They had survived for so long we began to believe they would survive the whole horror intact, that they were special and lucky—and yet.

"They went together," Fauzia murmured softly, wrapping her arms around me from behind. She tucked her chin onto my shoulder, and I turned my face toward her, breathing in her scent like a balm. "That's what they wanted, in the end. They went together."

And then we cried for our husbands. The small flat we had grown to love now seemed far too large, for we had carried their silent presence here the whole time. We curled toward each other in my bed, holding hands, and I wondered whether Bhaskar and Omar had had the right idea, clinging to whatever love they could give each other because this brutal life could end more quickly than any of us thought.

WE DID NOT know whether Bhaskar and Omar had had revolutionary leanings, but we knew they would not have wanted us to mourn too long, and so we buried ourselves in fighting. At night, we began to sleep with our backs pressed against each other in one bed, our warmth seeping into each other. Though I knew I had missed my chance and Fauzia no longer harbored feelings for me, the nights we spent silently comforting each other only made me notice that my own feelings were changing, even as we redoubled our efforts at rebellion and I remembered why she deserved better.

The next month, Fauzia's second cousin, who was an Anglo-Indian born in England, came to Kingston as part of a government visit. We invited him to our flat one night, hoping we might get information.

"So tell me, Kalki, what do you do?"

"I work in City Hall," I responded, wary that anything outside of a bland script would get me in trouble. Despite the color of his skin, Shameel felt more like a British person than an Indian. He ate with cutlery rather than his hands, and downed multiple glasses of water because he found our food so spicy. I had added only one pinch of garam masala and no chilies—the food couldn't have been more tasteless. He had also told us we could call him Sam instead of Shameel, something I would not do even if the name Sam had meant nothing to me.

"Do you like it?" Shameel asked, putting his spoon down.

The idea of opening up to this white man in an Indian skin did not appeal to me. "I like it fine. It puts food on the table and a roof over our heads." What else could I say? That I for years had been lying to my own people in order to further the cause of those I hated? That I lay awake at night wondering whether what I did for a wage hurt my fellow countrymen in ways I could not fix? That my boss was a lecher and I spent half my time trying to avoid his attentions? No. Better to keep it simple.

He leaned forward, elbows on the table, and I fought back a wince. "What do you know about the situation back in England?" he asked.

I shook my head, because my knowledge of any "situation back in England" was so heavily based on illegally obtained documents that I didn't think I knew the officially sanctioned version anymore. Fauzia jumped in. "Things are better there. People of all races live together peacefully, as equals."

Shameel frowned. "I don't know if I would say people of all races live together peacefully. There's a lot of violence from white people toward other races. Asian people, people from the African colonies. Even southern and eastern Europe."

"You can't group all Asian people together," I said, swallowing a smile. Perhaps he wasn't really white—just naïve.

"It's different here," he said. "But in England, we all have to stick together, because the white people outnumber us."

"How can you say that?" Fauzia asked. "You work for them."

"Well, some of them are on our side. They want us to vote more easily, get the jobs we want, live free from violence. Conditions in England are pretty bad for a lot of us."

This time, I couldn't help but laugh. Fauzia kicked me under the table, and I choked it back. "You're complaining because it's hard to vote?" I asked at last.

He blushed and gulped more water. "I'm not trying to minimize things here. I know they're so much worse." Shameel glanced around as if expecting to see his superiors in the flat. "Honestly, between us, I think it's shameful that we stand for democracy when we have colonies."

Fauzia and I shared a brief look and came to a quick decision to trust him—not enough to tell him about our activities, obviously, but to ask him questions. "Are you saying you stand for independence?" Fauzia asked.

"Yes, of course," Shameel said. "Don't you?"

"That's a very dangerous question," I told him. "It could get us killed."

"Killed?" His voice leaped far higher. "Just for talking about independence?"

I nodded, although the punishment would more likely be jail time or forced labor. "India is a different place from the UK. We are not free here."

He nodded, expression somber. "You're saying that you can't

really do anything about your situation?" Before I could even respond, he continued, "You're right. Those of us who support the cause in the UK need to do our part. How could you be expected to fight back? It's all you've ever known."

"Stop." Fauzia's voice held steel. "People here fight back already. Don't come here and act like we're some pathetic, brainwashed—"

"I'm not saying—"

"Let me finish," she snapped at Shameel. "We're not brainwashed. It's not any feelings of dependence on the British that hold us back. We're not even afraid of the consequences. Every previous effort in India has failed, but it has brought us some small bit closer. Don't you dare come into our home and eat with a fork and spoon and lecture us as if we're weaklings or cowards." Spots of color shone bright on her cheekbones, and she heaved a large breath before angrily dumping rice onto her plate. Fauzia was prideful, and it looked beautiful on her. My heart thumped hard at the sight, and I chastised it—she had made herself clear.

We all ate in awkward silence for several minutes. Finally, Shameel spoke up. "You are right, of course. I am very sorry. I guess I didn't understand how bad things were back here. My parents always spoke of India as though it were a paradise. Somehow, I convinced myself being a colony wouldn't be so bad." And he looked so put out that we didn't chide him.

WE COULDN'T FORGET that conversation, because we had a sneaking suspicion that maybe Shameel had been right in his own misguided way. He had brought us a newspaper from the UK with an article about self-rule proponents on the island, but what we focused on were the quotes from the pro-colonial side, gems such as "We have freed slaves, spared women from forced marriages, liberated the 'untouchables' from the barbarity of their people, and saved many from ritual sacrifice" and "The only value independence might have is in liberating our own country, because it is a drain on our resources to sustain so many backward systems, even though it is our noble burden." It was clear that we could not count on help from that quarter—achieving a true freedom was on our shoulders alone.

We discussed it ad nauseam, whether what we were doing could even be considered fighting for independence. Oh, we were hurting the British and helping our people, but were we approaching freedom? Was it even possible, when the heyday of independence had been so thoroughly stamped out, when the great thinkers were gone, their ideas banned and burned? We all trusted that the people of Kingston wanted independence; we were not like Shameel in assuming them weak and idiotic. But we had fallen into a routine of rebelling, without a plan to get to freedom.

Over and over, we kept coming back to one idea: boycotts. They were a tool from the rebels of old, and we worried they would not be enough. The Indian people of Kingston did not purchase a large number of British goods, but what other option was there?

At last I found myself at Mr. Kapadia's stationery shop, looking for advice. He had never led me astray, and was a veteran of the old times. Surely they must have had a plan then. When I walked inside, his face lit up, and he rose with a tired sigh to greet me. He was getting old, I realized, slowly enough that I hadn't seen it until now. It scared me, that someone I had always viewed as a protector might one day be gone.

"Kalki, how are you? How have you been?"

I reached out to hug him. "I'm good. Busy."

"Of course, of course." He patted my shoulder. "Whenever you come visit your foolish uncle, it is the highlight of his day."

I felt worse now, because I had come here needing something from him. It was closing time, and I looked around. "How can I help?" I asked. "Could I sweep up?"

He beamed even wider. "Are you sure?" he said. "You work so much already. I would not want to waste your time."

"Of course," I told him, heading for the corner where the broom was kept. Mr. Kapadia was too old to be bending for the broom anyway. I began sweeping, content in the silence.

"So, what do you need?" he asked after I had completed one aisle. "I know your moods. Something's on your mind."

I burst out laughing. Of course he had known the moment I walked into the shop. "I've been thinking about the future. About what we're doing, and what the point is."

Part of me hoped that he would reassure me, tell me that what we were doing was going to lead us to the promised future. He did not. I turned around to find him removing his glasses, rubbing at his eyes. "The point is that you are helping your fellows," he said. "But I understand your concern. That has always been the question, ever since the Reestablishment, hasn't it?"

I kept my eyes on the ground, sweeping, sweeping. Even the most mundane tasks were transformed by talk of rebellion, and I was not immune to it. "If we try to mount a large-scale operation, they will simply murder us. They do not care. They would still ultimately profit from being here."

"The old great rebels . . . Gandhi and Nehru and Ambedkar, some of them used your tactics, some of them used shame and pressure, and some of them wrote new policies and messages to prove there was a better way, and together they almost made it unprofitable for the British to be here." Mr. Kapadia leaned on a shelf near me, further limiting the chance of being overheard. "It nearly worked, but they chose to mass murder the rebels instead of leaving."

"We cannot shame them. Perhaps their people can, abroad, but how would we know? We cannot rely on them." I thought of Shameel, ignorant and naïve, speaking of the United Kingdom as though it were a decent place. A democracy. I could not imagine it, nor could I really believe they would allow dissent within their own borders. "But money . . ."

"The rebels of old could protest, boycott, strike. They could speak openly, give speeches. You cannot do that today." He sighed. "To believe otherwise is an old man's foolish dream."

Something he said had lodged in my brain, though. I stood up, ceasing my sweeping. "We cannot do an outright strike, it is true. But the British are neither numerous enough nor industrious enough to run everything alone. There are collaborators here, on our side of Kingston, on whom they rely. If we take down their factories so that the British could collect nothing from them, it would destabilize the whole economy."

"The collaborators have a lot of power. They are also to be feared." Despite his words of caution, Mr. Kapadia did not look worried, and I knew why.

"On this side of the island, so are we."

He smiled at me. "Your father would be proud."

I HURRIED HOME before curfew, bursting with excitement. My mind raced with possibilities. If they ever made a picture of our fight in Kingston, perhaps this would be the scene right before the climax, where the hero runs home with an idea that will change the tide of the war. It was a slim chance, I knew, but I was buoyed with hope. I ran inside, ready to dazzle Fauzia, and found her and Yashu poring over papers on the table.

They did not even look at me, so as soon as I closed the door, I whisper-shouted, "We have to target the collaborators!"

Their heads snapped up as one. "For the boycotts?" Yashu asked. "We could include them, I suppose." She frowned down at her list. "Perhaps these goods . . ."

I took a deep breath. "For boycotts, yes. But also with strikes."

Yashu inhaled sharply at that. "Kalki—"

"Before we start arguing, let's sit in the bedroom. It's more comfortable." Fauzia did not phrase it as a suggestion. I understood her attempt at defusing the situation, but I feared it would not be enough.

Fauzia and I had passed many evenings sitting in each other's beds, for we had a single bedroom with two beds on opposite sides and a curtain between them. But Yashu had yet to participate in that tradition. It was odd, that in adulthood there were things we did not share. As we sat on the long edge of Fauzia's bed, leaning against the wall and pulling the blanket over our legs, I remembered with a sudden flash our old games.

In our first year of friendship, we loved playing European explorers, where we pretended to be the very first colonists traipsing through the swampy marshes of what were then the Seven Islands. We were perhaps a little too old for those games, but we made up for it with an attempt at scientific precision. I was always the leader of the expedition, Fauzia the medic, and Yashu the scholar. We would call out pretend dangers—A tiger was chasing us! A venomous scorpion had felled me!—and dodge through the streets, searching for treasure.

Worse, we would fake encounters with the "natives." One of us, and we took it in turns because fair was fair, would play an Indian we encountered on the island. Some were kind but simple, others devious or murderous, and we as the Europeans would barely escape with our lives. We would howl with laughter afterward as Yashu pretended to recount the encounter from her "notes."

Now we knew Kingston had formerly been a prosperous port city for many empires, bringing in more wealth as a single city than the British had possessed in all their lands at the time. But back then, we thought that the Europeans had civilized us and then begun to commit their crimes—not that they had been criminals all along.

From laughing, sweaty, in the busy markets of Kingston, to plotting treason in my best friend's bed. We were not laughing anymore.

"We need strikes." I looked at Yashu as I said it, hoping she could see my sincerity. "I'm sorry, but we do."

"Strikes, and then strikebreakers, and then it will be the work-

ers in the slums who get beaten up, no matter what they do . . ."
Yashu put her head in her hands. "Can that really be the way?"

"Indians are valuable to the British for their labor, not for
their spending," I said. "And the boycotts would be risky without strikes, because the British might feel they were being targeted. But if the boycott is to support the strikes, it would seem
natural."

Yashu was silent for several long moments. At last she said,
"What choice is there, but to ask?"

"That is all we can do," Fauzia said softly. "We can only ask.
Most people . . . they know we exist, even if they know nothing
more. They know what we're doing. They're keeping their heads
down, but we can at least ask this. It's not action against the British, not really, and it will be temporary."

"Or they will bring in new workers," Yashu muttered, although it was clear she agreed.

"How?" I prodded. "Are they going to allow people from outside in? But they might tell of the outside world!"

For some reason, this set us into a fit of brief, harsh hysterics,
broken only by the hum of the power going out. It was cool
enough outside that it didn't matter, but it sobered us all the
same. "I know," Yashu said. "If people don't want to, they won't.
And if they do, we will organize a general strike. Just until the
collaborators cave. The collaborator industrialists are cruel and
inhumane, but they're also soft, complacent, and afraid of their
margins going red. I think it could work."

In the darkness, Fauzia took both of our hands. "Their loyalty
is to money first, the British second, and us not at all. But we can
compete for second."

THE NEWS SPREAD like wildfire among our circles, traveling
from the main branch—once a vote had been put up—to the others, where there was unanimous agreement to participate.

Smita Deshmukh approached me at lunch the day after Fau-

zia's cell voted—she said she had the day off work, and of course
as the daughter of a collaborator she could travel around Old
Bombay more freely.

"Is there anything I can do to help?" she asked. I knew instantly what she was talking about.

"Whatever your leader told you to do," I replied.

Smita pouted. "My leader told me I'm too close to the issue
and to stay out of it. But I can help, if you tell me more, and
tell me what to do. Wouldn't it be helpful to see what I can
learn?"

I thought Smita might be effective, but I couldn't contradict
Fauzia. She was the head of her cell, and the limits of her authority were the business of her and her members. Not me. "Then
you have to listen to her. Maybe, in time, the situation will
change. And of course, should you learn anything useful, you
should bring it to her."

"I'm just not sure about the plan," Smita said, shaking her
head. "I don't think this is a good idea."

I wondered if I had misjudged her. Or perhaps, in the years
since she had first been recruited, she had changed, the allure of
money eroding her morals. But in response to whatever expression I made, she added, "The workers are going to suffer the
most. I worry about them."

"That's good of you," I said. "But this is the people's decision."

It wasn't as though the workers weren't already suffering; they
suffered every day. There were many factories in Kingston, through
which almost every collaborator had made their fortune. There
was no great wealth to be found serving the British who lived in
India. But using Indian labor to give the British goods that they
could export to their homeland and the rest of the world, gener-
ating the economic power that the UK alone could not—there lay
profit, and power. The Deshmukhs owned a series of cotton textile factories, the Akhtars many foundries, and the Rawals ran

the Indian-side shipyards and docks—these were the most heavily watched and regulated, for obvious reasons, and would be the hardest to organize. There were others as well, the meatpackers who employed only Dalit workers because the work was considered dirty, and construction operations with the highest mortality rates of any industry, but our three targets were the biggest, and where we began our work.

We started whispers, until everyone in Indian Kingston—and definitely the British who surveilled us—knew. *Have you heard? Some of our most wealthy brethren are hypocrites. They would let their workers die if it would save them an extra rupee.* Or, if we were speaking in a more public forum, *They are not comporting themselves the way the British have taught us to behave.* We allowed ourselves some fun coming up with that solicitous line, taking the high ground in a way the British could not take offense to. We planned no strike lines, no pickets, just the quiet refusal to work. The occupation of space without providing labor. And then, beyond it, our promise to not buy their goods. Our clothes could be patched, old handlooms pieced together once more. We could buy fewer goods, not that we bought many to start with. And we could avoid imported foods—yes, buying just from the farmers and fishermen could only work for so long, but people were crafty. We would make it work.

I was nervous as I went to work on the first day of the boycott. It wasn't like the bus routes or any direct British services would be impacted. But that was the trick—for them to think this organic, untraceable, with no shadow of an organized resistance. We wanted them to think that Hindus and Muslims and Sikhs and Buddhists and Jains and Christians and all the others had bridged the divisions among us, the riots of the past year forgiven if not forgotten, because the people of Kingston had decided enough was enough.

At City Hall, though, nobody mentioned a word. The British did not even send a report about it—although, why would they?

They did not need to explain it away, because nothing originating in Indian Kingston was worth explaining.

I was almost disappointed—but why? Was I somehow seeking British reaction, British approval? No, I decided, I was being stupid. The impact on the British was the whole point.

At lunch, though, Yashu came to find me. "Did you hear?" she asked, voice low. I looked around. We were around others, who were obviously trying to listen in. But she didn't seem to care, or perhaps it was on purpose. "There was a walkout at the docks!"

Adrenaline shot through me, even though there was nowhere for me to go and nothing for me to do. There was a press of other women around us, clamoring to know more. "Is this . . . *the strike?*" someone whispered.

"Of course it is," another person responded. "I heard they work them like slaves. Treat them like transported prisoners."

"Same here," said another voice. "I heard people were collapsing in the heat and they threw them in the water to cool them off. They drowned!"

I shared a glance with Yashu. Of course, by design, we didn't know whether any of these women were part of the ILM or not, and so did not know whether they were spreading agreed-upon propaganda. But it didn't sound like it.

"Barbaric," someone sniffed. "Good for the workers!"

There were nods of assent. While it warmed my heart that these women would support a strike, because many of them were from wealthier families, I was more worried about the strikers, who would be targets now that they had walked off. There were vagrancy laws, and gathering laws, and—my stomach was roiling. But Yashu did not look perturbed.

The flock of girls scattered as a few white secretaries entered our lunch area, a casual act of patrolling they reveled in wasting their own precious break on. Yashu bent low to my ear for a moment. "Don't worry. It's all part of the plan. O'Brien says there's no threat." Before I could ask how O'Brien might know any of that, or pass it on to Yashu, she was gone.

I RODE THE double-decker bus home, sitting on top to try to see what I could. Though the city seemed peaceful, I knew this calm could not be everywhere. I switched buses early and got onto another bus to the docks, tucked away on the west side of the island. But the bus halted several stops away from the end of its route, without explanation or apology, and I traipsed out with a good number of people—young and old—who were headed to the docks. They did not look like workers.

Even the lack of transportation could not kill curiosity.

Oddly, though, I did not spy the number of policemen I would expect around the docks on a good day, let alone during a strike. I didn't hear sounds of violence either, no—instead I heard . . . chanting?

Yes, chanting. Like something out of a forbidden book, there was a sea of people, mostly old, grizzled men but a few young women too, who had organized in lines in front of the docks. The air smelled more like salt and sea and fish here than in the city center, but there was something more—sweat, oil, and a frisson of power. Courage.

I approached the picket line, and an older man beckoned me over. "How did you hear about this?" he asked. The mood here was happy, almost infectiously so.

I smiled. "Everyone's talking about it!"

He looked me up and down. "Do your parents know you're here?"

"What they don't know won't hurt them."

"We can always use more people!" He shuffled around, and suddenly I was standing next to him, joining in on the chants as best I could. There were variants of "Safety now!" and "Fair wages for labor!" that were easy enough to remember, but there were others. At the chanting of names, "Remember Varun! Remember Aditi! Remember Jignesh!" I simply raised my fist into the sky, shouting along "Om Shanti!" after each name. How had so many people died at the docks? How had I not known?

Of course, I knew dockworkers had legitimate grievances—that was the whole point of our quiet influencing of these strikes—but hearing these names made the pain even fresher. It was an important reminder that these were people's lives too. The docks were not slums, yet the place seemed downtrodden. The nearby homes were marked with streaks from fumes and exposure, the few shops boarded up. Maybe it was the strike, or maybe the dock gangs that the British turned a blind eye to because the docks were still profitable. The old, familiar anger rose at their selfishness.

In a lull, the man turned to me again. His face was quite worn; he was old enough to have avoided the draft. "This reminds me of my younger days," he whispered. "Before the fire. Many of us were young and fresh, but we haven't forgotten how things almost changed. The whole city was up in arms, before they burned—"

He stopped himself, and I looked away. Even on a strike line, it was dangerous to tell the truth of it. It was also a reminder that it was time for me to leave. I had wanted to see it with my own two eyes, because it was beyond my wildest imagination, and now I had. People wanted to fight. But by being here I was endangering—

There was a piercing scream from far down the street. "Breakers!" someone shouted. "Run!"

There was a crack, like a blunt object hitting a human being, and another scream. "Strikebreakers," the man next to me hissed. "You have to run."

"British?" I blurted out, not following.

"Indian," he said. "People will do anything for a price."

It clicked into place. The British must have hired the gangs, who had managed to keep enough young men in their various hideouts to inflict violence when needed. I had a pocketknife in my bag—our group had learned how to use them in self-defense as a last resort—but I could not fight my way out of this. I could run and almost certainly escape, but I could not abandon the others. A flash of pale skin down the street caught my eye, despite the setting sun behind the figure, and in a moment, I had an idea.

"Please, sir!" I called out, running away from the strikers who were trying to flee. It must be an officer, and I was dressed like I worked in Old Bombay. I was to be a damsel in distress again.

"Miss Divekar?" the British man responded, and recognition hit me. My luck had run out. Samuel Clarke.

"Mr. Clarke," I gasped. This wasn't going to work, but I had to commit or I could end up in trouble too. "I'm sorry, sir. My friend, she wanted to bring dinner to her brother after we left City Hall! She was . . ." I gestured behind me. The gang was almost upon us, and they were clearly taking seriously their mission to brutalize, but not maim, everyone they could find. The dock gates were locked, hemming the strikers into streets that their pursuers knew just as well. "Please, help!"

I expected him to push me away, to tell me to leave, or, worse, detain me. But his eyes grew serious. He reached into his pocket and pulled out . . . a whistle? Why did he have one? Usually only police carried them, but maybe he had one to signal his location if he was in danger. After all, he was probably one of the most prominent white men in Kingston, second only to his father.

It was like I was in another dimension, where Samuel Clarke was helpful. Because when he blew it, *everyone* froze, almost on instinct. "By the order of the chancellor's office, cease this lawlessness at once!" he shouted. Behind us, sirens blared, and the strikebreakers heard them too. They were already running, leaving confused—and clearly alarmed—strikers behind. But Samuel Clarke was running toward the police vehicles, and for reasons that I could not comprehend was pointing them back around in the direction of the fleeing gang members rather than toward the strikers, whom they had undoubtedly come to arrest. He must have been confused by what he saw, mistaking the breakers for the strikers, but his confusion was our blessing. The skirmish seemed to be over as soon as it began. The strikers had taken the opportunity to disperse, and Samuel Clarke was turning back to me.

"It's not safe for you to be here," he said. I wanted so desperately to ask why he was there at all, but I bit my tongue. "Go home."

"Thank you, sir," I managed to force out around my utter shock. And I was thankful, even if I had no idea what had just happened.

I STAYED AWAY from the strikes after that, but Yashu was often at the factories. Much of her extended family still lived in the slums in the northwest. When the city was rebuilt, and the original Dharavi slums burned down, their inhabitants were supposedly given new homes—but only if they had papers, which very few had. Those families, like Yashu's, got crammed into grand homes for show, and the rest shoved their way back and rebuilt farther north. The leather and meatpacking factories followed them, and the sewage plants, and the garbage dumps, and pretty soon—according to the few members of her family that I had met, at least—it was like Dharavi had been built anew, now named Kingston Temporary Housing Number One.

The Deshmukhs owned textile and leather factories and employed half of the slum, and when they had joined with the British they had done exceptionally well. Although the strikers made progress at the docks, and even in the various metalworking factories, they did not make progress with the Deshmukhs. Elsewhere, the strikers did a remarkable job resisting the violence against them and preventing replacements from entering. But the Deshmukhs smuggled in new laborers, children, desperate women, and had them sleeping in the factories. When asked, Smita twisted her hands in her dress, explained that she was working on her father, that he was a hard man. She could do nothing, tell us nothing. The Deshmukhs remained profitable.

Two weeks into the strikes, the Rawals announced that they were increasing wages and safety measures. We knew that was just the beginning—but still, when the news came, I almost skipped home. The whole city seemed brighter, I was sure of it. The announcement came on the radio, and I was sitting near enough the front of the bus to listen in. First was the usual vileness—the chancellor released a statement saying that it was regrettable that some factories had caved to such insidious pressure, since the British already ensured safe and comfortable working conditions for all. But then, as I was about to exit the bus, Samuel Clarke came on for an interview, and I almost stumbled down a step as he called it "noble" to listen to the workers and improve their lives.

Fauzia was excited, too, but something in her countenance seemed off. She finished her dinner quickly and went to the bedroom to lie down. I gave her some time to fall asleep so as not to disturb her. When I finally went in, Fauzia was sitting up on her bed, biting her lip. I went to sit next to her, but she shook her head.

"What is it?" I asked. My mind immediately jumped to all the horrible things that might have happened. Had the boycotts hurt her family's store just when they had finally managed to rebuild?

She shrugged slightly. "You will think me foolish if I say."

"I wouldn't," I protested. "I promise."

"All of this. This great victory—that one of the families has stopped collaborating, that two others have become less lucrative—it's wonderful. It is. But it has made me realize how long this is going to last. If we even survive . . ." She squeezed her eyes shut for a moment, as though imagining Bhaskar and Omar, before looking up at me. "Even if we win. We might be old and gray by the time the fight is over. We might . . ."

I had never thought Fauzia would be one to lose faith. "That's possible," I said. "But we *will* win in the end." I had to believe it.

"I know that." Fauzia pressed her lips together, as if debating whether to say more. "I just mean, our whole lives are on hold. Forever. Sometimes I sneak out, but there's no future out there. I can't adopt children. I can't offer anyone anything, because my life is this, forever."

I had promised not to call her foolish, but I was shocked by her words. "What do you mean?" I asked. I barely stopped myself from saying more, from asking, *Isn't this enough?* Our life together, our rebellion together, was all I could conceive of, was more than enough for me. It was all I wanted.

Fauzia gave me a sad smile. "I love you, Kalki. I love living with you. I love having a life with you. Five years ago, I asked you this question, but we were children then. We didn't know anything. So I ask you again: Don't you want more now? Don't you want a real husband, or children, or some pleasure in your life? Vacations, leisure, indulgences?"

I didn't know what to say. My traitorous mind was dredging up a conversation I had heard my parents having as I played underfoot.

"Isn't it enough?" Aai demanded. "You have a wife, a daughter. Isn't it enough? When do you get to come home and rest?"

"Of course I love these things," my Baba said, in an answer I now understood to be deeply insufficient. "That's why I do the work I do."

"Let someone else!" Aai snapped. "You have responsibilities."

"This is my responsibility. I will rest when we are free."

Aai's face had softened from anger into sorrow. "And if you lose? What then?"

"I'll be reincarnated," Baba said simply. "And if the work is still there, I will still be doing it."

Now I said to Fauzia, "I do want other things." I loved her more than anybody, in a way that sometimes made my heart beat fast and my lungs fail to breathe. Every time I felt that way for her, I stopped myself short, because I couldn't stop thinking about the rebellion—but now that Fauzia was asking, the words poured out. "I do. I understand. Sometimes, I imagine a future together. A future with more."

I forced myself to look at her as I spoke, so I could tell the moment she understood what I was admitting. Emotions warred in her eyes, and I glanced away, not wanting to see another rejection from her. But she grasped my chin, gently tipped my face back toward hers. In her face, I saw caution and . . . desire.

She released my face, took my hand. "Kalki . . ." I leaned closer to her, pulled by the temptation of finally, finally, just for a moment, giving in.

Fauzia closed the gap, her lips pressing against mine. A spark of electricity ran through me, from the crown of my head to the tips of my toes. My heart pounded in my rib cage, and though I could hardly breathe I craved more. Craved her. She tasted sweet, like sugar and mango, like everything good in the world. She huffed a laugh against me, and I pulled back, embarrassed at my own inexperience. "What?" I asked.

"I just—I can't believe this is real," she said. "That you . . . that we . . ."

"I'm slow to everything except anger," I told her, honestly. "Including this. I've thought about you for many years . . . but I knew it wasn't fair. Not when I wanted freedom more than any other desire. Not when you seemed not to want me."

Fauzia gave me a small smile. "I always thought you were out of reach," she admitted. "Sometimes, I see the future of fighting for decades stretching before me and I wish I could do anything else. You are so *happy* fighting—I'm not. But this, Kalki? Some happiness today, even as we fight for more happiness tomorrow? This is more than I could have ever imagined."

I pressed myself to her then, my lips to hers, my tongue to hers, my heart to hers. All of it was hers. We found our way to her bed, kissing and laughing until we were too tired to keep our eyes open. I took her hand, and sleep called us home.

I HAD NEVER been with someone in that way before, never enjoyed such closeness, never wanted to except with Fauzia, and now—it was as though we moved as one, our souls entwining. I had not understood what it could mean to connect with someone, the ecstasy of touch, the ache of even a moment's separation.

At times, though, I felt like I was outside of myself. That I was watching someone else with Fauzia, watching someone else's hands caress her body, someone else's mouth on hers. I wanted to be there, in my body, but even as I tried to lose myself, in the end my mind returned to the rebellion. One moment, I could hardly breathe unless it was her scent, could think of nothing but the softness of her skin, could feel her touch like a ghost when I closed my eyes. The next, my mind leaped to the fight, to the Akhtars and the Deshmukhs and all that was left to do. But I knew that Fauzia wanted this, that she was happier now than I had seen her in years, and I tried to force such thoughts from my head.

We heard through the grapevine—Fauzia and others—that the Akhtars had lost a major contract supplying parts to the British armies. That was a blow to the Akhtars but especially to the British, who relied on their collaborators for a mutually profitable relationship. We believed the Akhtars would cave soon enough, especially now that there was informal pressure coming from the mosques. The Akhtars had thrived on a strong relationship with both the British and the Muslim community, and now having lost one, they would be at the mercy of the other.

The Deshmukhs, however, had only gotten worse. I floated the idea of using Smita Deshmukh to push her family, remembering how she wanted to help. But Fauzia reiterated that she didn't think Smita had the influence or the discretion, and though I disagreed, I quickly caved.

There were better things to do with Fauzia than discuss Smita, and I lost myself in sensations I had never before experienced. Fauzia was gentle but hungry, approaching each day as though it might be our last, as though making up for all the time we had not crossed this boundary. Occasionally, I lost myself for whole evenings with her, not thinking of the work, or the strikes, and then after she slept I lay awake, guilt weighing heavy on my chest. Guilt that I had forgotten the fight even for a moment, guilt that I felt any regret over the time spent with Fauzia, guilt that I might not be committed to happiness the way Fauzia wanted me to be.

The Deshmukh strikers had now lost their jobs, and the new conditions for the workers who were forced to labor at the factory were beyond despicable. They were dragged from the slums, locked in, made to sleep on the floor and eat what little was provided to them, all so that production could go on. What could we do?

Then Simran brought in plans for homemade bombs, things we could assemble ourselves. She refused to say how she got them, but they were obviously well traveled by the time we found them in our possession. Her hard, determined face had nothing of her usual joking. She had changed since Abhaya was transported for the Mountbatten Electrical Center operation, so much so that she had stopped going by Simi. She was still an engineer, but she had become more like me—to her, there was no purpose to life other than freedom. She seemed, in this moment, more like me than myself.

"Bombing the Outpost ended in the destruction of the first ILM here," Fauzia cautioned immediately. "It achieved nothing."

"We can't bomb the factories with people inside," I added. "We can't kill our own citizens."

"Bombings work for a reason," Maryam argued. She was usually quiet in meetings, since she was the only addition to our core group, but now she was flushed, excited. "I heard that there have been bombings in the west for months now, and the British are retreating. The people there are celebrating."

"If you're talking about Balochistan," Fauzia scoffed, "that's fundamentally different. They can flee into Iran if they have to.

And information from there is unreliable at best. I read a confidential bulletin that things are worse than ever, and everyone lives in fear of being attacked." It was hard to forget that there had been bombings before the Reestablishment too, ones the British still remembered. We learned in school of Bal Gangadhar Tilak, who supported bombings to liberate India so Hindus could continue child marriages. Even though I no longer believed their blatant propaganda about him—had learned instead that despite some of his backward views, especially on women, he had been a tireless advocate for self-rule however India could win it—I was conscious of how these things could be so easily spun to the empire's advantage.

"Other branches of the ILM are fighting, actually fighting," Simran said. "Didn't we decide to start these strikes because we wanted to do the same? Now we have to step up and help."

"Are we really to kill our own people?" Fauzia asked. "We would be no better than the British."

"Someone has to decide," Simran said. "Would you rather the British keep killing us indiscriminately, keeping us as their servant colonies so they can forever prosper? At least if we do this, we will be one step closer to freedom. It is not the same."

I looked toward Yashu, who had been very quiet, but her face betrayed nothing. Fauzia turned to me. "Well, Kalki?" There was no gentleness in her now, but every aspect of Fauzia was one facet of a gem; I recognized in her hard command the same woman who softly kissed me at night.

Wasn't this what I had wanted? To make the decisions when nobody else would? Simran, and Maryam, and the rest supporting them, were right. To sign the warrant for another's death, for our own kinsmen's, should have been unthinkable, but my moral compass had always been flexible when it came to independence. Fauzia looked away at the set of my jaw.

"We could bomb the lorries transporting the products," I said at last. "It will be easier that way, to set the bombs on streets. We can evacuate the streets beforehand, using our usual methods. We can minimize the damage."

"And the drivers?" Fauzia demanded. "What gives you the right to decide that they should die?"

"We can observe the patterns of the trucks and the drivers, try to time it so that the products are destroyed but the drivers might live. We can try our best, but know that there is the potential for lives to be lost. I do not take the decision lightly," I said. "And I leave it to a final vote by our group. But we are leading the movement to remove the British from our city. We are the ones who decide how it happens. I would be willing to lay down my life for freedom if the time came." It was true, though I hoped it would never come to that. Did not every one of us have to be selfish to want rebellion instead of survival, and I even more selfish to be willing to endanger lives for the hope of freedom? Sacrifice was necessary for the greater good, I knew it.

"They're not laying down their lives, and they're not collaborators. They're innocents, just trying to survive." Fauzia knew she was in the minority, and she was also right. There were no good options, when either way innocents could die.

"No matter what, our people will suffer," I said. "That is the curse of the British, is it not? Unless anyone else has anything to say . . . we will vote."

WITH HEAVY HEARTS, we studied shipment routes. The Akhtars caved, agreeing publicly to pay higher wages and privately to stop supplying the military—religious pressure had worked, apparently. But the Deshmukhs only got worse, rubbing in the strikers' faces that they had been replaced, that costs were lower, that production was better than ever. It was said the factories were like graveyards, with the numbers who died, and yet the Deshmukhs continued to find more workers. We studied their factories, watching as on Sundays they loaded up their trucks with garments, observed the precise times at which the trucks, headed to the three different major warehouses in Old Bombay, rolled over the least crowded streets. We tried to calculate the best timing to destroy only the cargo. Fauzia and I did the surveillance, and afterward we went home to each other's arms, seeking in vain some comfort from what we were about to do.

I did not help build the bombs. I did not help give out the warnings. It was Yashu who volunteered to lead the action itself, saying if she must condemn her people, she would not let her hands remain clean.

And then, in a sick echo of an earlier triumph, Yashu came running into our flat the morning of the bombings. Fauzia and I had been so tangled up in each other that at first we did not hear her. Though we had not forgotten what was happening today, we couldn't help but try for a moment of goodness before we went out to bear witness to the aftermath.

"What are you thinking about?" Fauzia had asked me when she woke to find me staring at the ceiling.

In truth, I had been thinking of the bombings, of all that could go wrong. But as she threaded her fingers through mine, I knew she wanted me to say I was thinking of her. "I was waiting for you to wake up," I had told her, and her open smile was all the reward I needed. In those moments where I could not help but think of our cause, I reminded myself that Fauzia wanted me, and in being hers I could make her happy.

Each moment between us felt stolen, but despite my distractions, my time with her still held a feeling of rightness. We fit together, body and soul, and sometimes I could not believe we had done this for only a few weeks, that this was not how we had always been and always would be.

Yashu's knocking broke through our haze. I thought of how Bhaskar and Omar might have felt when Fauzia and I knocked at their flat all those years ago. We hastily smoothed down our clothes and our hair and made for the door, where Yashu stood, hands trembling. She forced her way in and slammed the door shut before whispering, "It's a trap. Look."

She shoved forward a scrawled note—*They're putting humans in the trucks. Something about foiling the ILM's plans.*

Fauzia paled. "No. No. It can't be. How—how would they know?"

"Are we sure it's real?" I asked, but what else could it be? The trucks, the warning. "Maybe they're trying to flush us out."

"It's his hand," Yashu said. "O'Brien's. I heard a knock on my door, and it was dropped there. I ran straight here. I didn't know what to do—the trucks have already left, the bombs have been set . . ."

"We have to go," I said, making a split-second decision. "We have to stop the trucks. They might be waiting to arrest us, or . . . no. I'll go. You both see if there's a way to disarm the bombs."

Yashu stepped past me and stared at the clock in horror. "I— I don't think we have that kind of time."

And then we were all running, all headed for the route nearest to my and Fauzia's flat. It was raining, and the roads were slick, but we sprinted, hoping against hope that we could stop the trucks in their paths. Even stopping just one of the three planned blasts—we had to try. I could see the plan now, the one that would result in total devastation. This particular target was a set of three wide lorries, and we would have three small bombs, disguised as rubbish, go off at designated intervals after the weight of the front truck triggered a trip wire. The goal—though we knew we might not succeed—was to spare the drivers' lives while destroying as much product as possible in coordinated citywide explosions as the Deshmukh factories moved output for their Monday shipments.

I wondered how my Baba and his comrades had felt when they set up the Outpost bombing. Apparently one man had volunteered to drive a bomb inside and blow it up there. Had Baba waited a few streets over, wondering whether it would go to plan?

Whether it should have been him in the van? I wished desperately that I could remember how he had seemed that day, but I had been at school when the news came through, and the whole event had blurred. My memory of the past was slipping away the deeper our rebellion got. Perhaps the past could no longer guide me. I had not heard from my Baba in months, after all.

The ground shook, followed by a sound so loud it momentarily deafened me. *Too late.* We were too late. Ahead, a steaming blaze came into view, a plume of fire and smoke up the way. There were fragments of twisted metal on the ground, and big pieces of something unidentifiable floated in the sodden air.

Then there was a scream from the direction of the blast. Could someone have survived? The fire was almost out already, the rain doing its work, and as we got closer, we heard cries: "Help! Help!"

A large piece of debris blocked my path, and I pulled up short, trying to figure out which way to go. Behind me, Yashu cursed. The back part of one of the lorries—likely the last one—had been blown clean off and thrown into a nearby building. There were flames, sheltered from the rain, blocking my line of sight, but I heard again, "Please, help!"

Without thinking, I dove toward the half truck. "I'm coming!" I shouted. The metal of the truck was sharp, warped, and extremely hot to the touch, but I pulled myself up all the same. The smoke was immediately so terrible I couldn't see, I couldn't breathe. Before me was a barrier of flame, and beyond that . . . someone moved. Oh, gods. Something wet touched my hand. I turned to see Fauzia, handing me a scarf. Yashu had disappeared.

I wrapped it around my mouth and then, before I could second-guess myself, plunged forward. It seemed the fire had not spread to the back of the severed lorry, where several shapes were huddled. Most weren't moving. "Help," called the voice, sounding weaker, and one shape stirred. I ran toward it.

It was a young woman, I thought, her leg at an unnatural

angle. She coughed. "I'm going to get you out," I told her. "All of you."

"There's not much . . . to get out . . ." she said as I tried to determine the best way to move her. The lorry was at an angle, filling with smoke, and the fire was going to keep spreading, where the rain couldn't reach.

I grasped her arms, and she screamed, an involuntary sound, as her leg jostled. But I hauled her up with strength I didn't know I had and began to tug her back. There was no way to get her through the fire without burning her, but perhaps if I put the scarf around her face, she wouldn't be too badly injured.

"Kalki, when I throw, you run!" Yashu shouted. I had no idea what she meant, but I trusted. There was the sound of sizzling, a patch of fire briefly dimmed, and I dragged the screaming girl through. Yashu was there, with others, and . . . buckets. How in the world she had found them, I didn't know, but I didn't have time to question.

"No," Yashu whispered, her hand covering her mouth when she saw the girl. "Lakshmi?"

The girl didn't respond. She seemed unconscious. I hoped she was only unconscious. "There are others," I said. "Many others."

I turned around and plunged back through, trusting they would get Lakshmi down and tend to her. There were some noises of argument behind me, and then Fauzia was in with me too. "They're going to do what they can against the fire," she said, already passing me to crouch by one of the bodies. "Breathing. You take her."

When I got her into the light, I saw a chunk of her skull was missing. She was breathing, shallow gasps, but I shared a devastated look with Yashu. Then I went back in. We went back again and again, for the living bodies and the dead. There had to be more than twenty, and nobody else was willing to go into a burning vehicle. I didn't know what was in the other lorries. I couldn't know. By the time the fire brigade showed up to investigate, we had freed the last bodies from their final prison and knew we needed to go. We ran through the rain-soaked streets, trailing mud and blood and who knows what else.

I don't know why we stopped, other than that I couldn't run anymore. My lungs burned. I coughed and coughed, and with each spasm, I remembered. There was a boy, severed almost in half. Young women, heads caved in, limbs twisted, necks snapped. Others with no discernible injuries, barely breathing. We had done that. I had done that. Was this the sacrifice on which we would build a country?

"They knew," Yashu said to us. To the wall. To the sky. "They knew, and they wanted to punish us. Only a few of us knew, right? Our core cell, and those who built the bombs. Do we have a traitor? How? Who?" She was angry, and now I was angry.

"If there was a traitor, we'd be dead," I spat back. "No, the Deshmukhs must have guessed we would do something to harm them and devised this plan. And they guessed *right*. They knew what we were willing to try."

Yashu punched me in the stomach. I doubled over, groaning. The pain felt right. It was what I deserved. "I thought this was right too," she said, and I thought she was crying in the rain. "What have we done? Fauzia, you were right. You were right."

Fauzia was slumped against the wall, in a crouch. She stared right ahead, unblinking. We waited there as the city learned what had happened. Learned that the strikers had tried to kill the temporary workers out of revenge. Learned our own acts again, the story that would now be the truth.

I sleepwalked through the next few days, my mind fixated on what I had seen. What I had done. The half-burned face, the bone sticking out of the leg. And more, from the pictures in the paper of the bodies at another bombing site in the city. My hands shook and I had to hide them under my desk so Mr. Jenkins wouldn't see. I felt my guilt was written all over me. I had been the one whose approval made the difference, and the consequences were on me. I had wanted to be a leader. I had asked for this. We learned, in time, that the Deshmukhs were finally under fire from the British for failing to fulfill their contracts, but the toll—gods, the toll. I knew we would not do it again, no matter what happened.

"Are you all right?" Fauzia asked me four days after the bombing. "You just said yes when I asked you if I should cut off all my hair."

"Oh. What? Don't do that." I tried to look at her, knowing she was struggling too, but I felt a small kernel of bitter judgment that Fauzia was joking at such a time. It filled me with guilt, remembering what Fauzia and I had been doing when Yashu came to our door. We had been about to murder dozens, and we had—

"Stop looking at me like that," Fauzia said softly.

"Like what?" I asked, looking away, then glancing back at her.

She studied my face for a few long moments before pushing her chair away from the table and sighing. "I worried . . . I should have known. You can't allow yourself happiness without feeling guilty, not until the work is done. I knew that—I just thought maybe you could. For me."

"Fauzia—"

"I'm not mad," Fauzia said. She was smiling slightly at me. "If you weren't who you are, I might love you less."

I stood, cupped her cheek. But she shook her head, taking my hand in her own and putting it on my chest as though giving it back to me. "No, Kalki. This was not a bad idea because it was so . . . it was indescribable. It was everything. And one day, that time will come for us again. But I cannot be with you knowing you will feel guilty for any happiness you feel. That you might regret spending time with me. It hurts me more than I can say. I am not indifferent to the horrors of our world, of what we have done. But I cannot feel guilt for my happiness, and I cannot have a partner who does, either."

My heart twisted in my chest, even as I knew I could not refute her words. Even though I loved her, I regretted the distraction. "That has nothing to do with you," I protested instead. "I want to make you happy. Let me make you happy."

"I know it has nothing to do with me," Fauzia said. "But I cannot be something you regret. I do not want you to be with me to make me happy. I want you to be with me for yourself. So think of this as a promise for the future, all right? When the British are gone, we can be free too."

Her eyes were filled with tears, and she turned abruptly from me to go into the bedroom. I sat heavily in the chair she had vacated, knowing she would want her privacy even as all I wanted was to hug her. I knew I hadn't lost her, that I could never lose her, but knowing that—at least for now—being with me was too painful for her to bear felt like a loss in itself. And, too, I knew she was right, because my mind kept turning back to the movement, to all that had gone wrong and all the work left to do. Fauzia and I had only had a few precious weeks trying to seize some new, priceless happiness, but I had not deserved it. Not yet. Not when that future she spoke of was still only a thought. It felt as though my heart were splitting in two, as though I had finally found a sacrifice too difficult to bear.

I tried to remind myself of what my Baba would say. That sacrifice was necessary, that lawbreakers were heroes, that all heroes had to go through trials to triumph over evil.

"Once upon a time," he would begin, and I would scamper onto his lap, a child with the conviction her father was never wrong. "In the kingdom of Ayodhya, there lived a great king. The king had three wives, and from these three wives, four sons. His eldest son, Rama, was a great prince who brought the king much joy. The king felt Rama was ready to ascend the throne and started preparations for Rama's coronation. But the king's wife Kaikeyi, who was mother to the second-oldest son, saw that Rama was not ready to ascend. He would make a fine king, but the greatness within him lay untapped." Here he would look at me, and he would wink, and I would try to believe.

"This wife, Kaikeyi, had once been a great warrior and saved the king's life. In gratitude, the king granted her two wishes that she could use at any time. So as the preparations for Rama's coronation began, Kaikeyi went before the king. With her first wish, she asked that Rama be exiled into the forest for fourteen years. With her second, she requested that her own son, Bharata, take the throne in Rama's absence, knowing that he would keep the kingdom safe until Rama's return. The old king begged her to reconsider, but she knew what she had to do and held firm.

"Heartbroken, the king sent Rama away. Rama's wife, Sita, and brother, Lakshmana, joined him in exile. For years they lived in the forest, until one day another woman fell in love with Rama, and later his brother Lakshmana. When she would not take no for an answer, Lakshmana cut off her nose while Rama stood by. For this insult, the woman went to her brother, the demon king Ravana, and asked him to avenge her."

Rama had not done anything as horrible as we had, but he had done wrong and his people had suffered for it. Maybe as a child I could have found solace in that, but now it was a cold comfort. I had consigned my people to die. If Rama could bear to live apart from his whole world for fourteen years, I was making no big sacrifice for my crimes—I still had Fauzia by my side, her friendship and support. My pain was nothing.

"When Ravana came to the forest to investigate, he saw Sita and fell in love. He engineered a plot to lure Rama and Lakshmana away from their house. Ravana kidnapped her and took her to his palace in Lanka. When Rama and Lakshmana discovered what had happened, they followed Sita and Ravana to Sri Lanka.

"As they journeyed across India, Rama and Lakshmana created their own band of misfits and rebels. The chief among these was Hanumana, a monkey with great strength and powers, who was fighting against the unjust ruler of his family's citadel. Rama helped him overthrow this ruler, and in return, Hanumana and his armies marched with Rama. Even one of Ravana's brothers, a good and kind man who had tried to change his brother's mind, defected to Rama's side.

"These allies worked with them every step of the way, building a bridge to Sri Lanka, setting fires in Ravana's palace, and even flying to the Himalayas to obtain a lifesaving herb for Lakshmana. The battle raged for days, but finally Rama's arrow struck true. Rama rescued Sita and headed for Ayodhya a changed man. As he returned, making his way in the darkness of the new moon, all of India united to put out lamps to light his way home."

8

KRISHNA, PATHFINDER

I learned how to endure at twenty-six.

I could not forget the horror of our bombings, and neither could the city. Although the ILM was never identified as the culprit, I knew I was responsible. Throughout the city, almost fifty factory workers had died. In losing that skirmish, we had won the battle, because in the end the collaborators had given in to the strikes or lost their contracts following production failures. We continued to commit sabotage large and small as the welfare of our side of the island improved. The blood price had brought a better future—but was it worth the lives? I could not forget what we had done. What *I* had done.

In time, the sharpness of that shame and grief faded to a dull throb, and I found myself emboldened by news farther afield, from the faraway country of South Africa. We knew of this country vaguely, because Gandhi had once lived there, and because native prisoners were sometimes shipped there for forced labor.

None of them ever returned, but occasionally one would manage to slip word to their family in India. And now momentous news had trickled in through the gaps in the British net.

For South Africa was free. After a failed attempt in 1960, the native population had risen up almost a decade later to both end the British occupation and throw out the other white settlers on their land. The Africans there could govern themselves. This news was banned in India, but that didn't stop us. We wrote by hand a beautiful flyer advertising the "newfound freedom of our brethren" that urged people to "end the occupation," made copies, and plastered them across all our networks spanning the whole of the sprawling metropolis on Salsette Island.

This, perhaps, gave me more joy than anything else in my life. Of course Fauzia brought me happiness, our old, easy friendship still intact with the occasional lingering look, the hopeful anticipation. But this was what I lived for, what we had at long last achieved: The ILM Kingston was finally, *finally* a truly citywide network. Each of the women in our original group had created her own cell, completely separate from our first group and anonymous to all others. I myself did not run a second cell—the original was my own. But by now, many members of the secondary cells had created their own new cells, and perhaps members of those cells would then create their own.

To preserve both anonymity and autonomy, we had decided in our very first meeting that each new branch could decide their own actions based on their personal connections and locations, so long as they fell within our parameters of caution, advanced our cause, and did not jeopardize any broader missions. Now, at last, this dream came to life, spawning a system of specialized roles and functions. Some were skilled at breaking into British stockpiles, some were masters at smuggling things and people out of the city, and some were even specialists in the newest technologies—computers, communication devices—and used their skills to our advantage.

After the strike, our main group had decided to leave decisions of people's fates to their own communities—some of which ended in violence, which we told ourselves was not our fault. Instead, we turned to an information campaign, like the rebels of old. Hearts and minds, Fauzia said, and after our failure, we listened. We wrote about the past, about women like Bhikaiji Cama, a Parsi woman from then-Bombay, who fought for independence on British soil until she was exiled, and Savitribai Phule, who along with her husband fought for the rights of women and lower-caste people, and we posted the poetry of Sarojini Naidu, who marched with Gandhi and fought for women's education before she disappeared from our records.

In our last operation, at Yashu's behest, we had printed tracts of a text by Dr. B. R. Ambedkar, long since killed by the British. Freedom was an illusion, he had said, without the annihilation of caste. There had been rumblings of dissent about using the full network for this, but I trusted Yashu. She had pointed out that there was a problem of segregation in our branches, that the cells would be Muslim, like much of Fauzia's, or Sikh, as Simran's was, or lower-caste, like her own, but never mixed with upper-caste Hindus or with one another. We were even divided by language, with a lone Gujarati cell, made up of the descendants of those the British had brought here half a century ago when the Marathi population proved too troublesome to be good servants—although some Gujarati people, like Mr. Kapadia, were part of other cells. While the branches wanted to be that way, and I didn't see any point in forcing change, I knew Yashu was right: We had to free ourselves from our failures as well as those of the British, and caste was the greatest among those.

Now, though, we had reason to hope for a better future. Almost every street in the city had a notice about South Africa, and notice people did. Everyone knew about what had happened, despite nobody talking about it.

I studiously ignored the signs on my walk, climbed right up to the top level of the dirty red bus, and kept my head down while we rumbled through the streets. I loved sitting at the top of the double-decker bus and looking out on the city, but today I stared fixedly at the ground, trying to listen carefully to the conversations around me. The bus as usual managed to hit every pothole on the hour-long journey, and I overheard many veiled conversations about the flyers. People did not speak as quietly when they thought the bus drowned them out.

"Did you see—" and "Wasn't Vishesh sent to South—" and "Have the boys on the front heard—" This last sent a pang through my heart, for although it had been a year since Bhaskar's and Omar's passing, occasionally something would remind us and we would feel a shock of sadness. But by the time I walked into City Hall, the feeling had lightened. Inside, I spotted Samuel Clarke talking to someone. This was a fairly common occurrence, and I always tried to duck out of view on the off chance I sparked some recognition. Today, though, he was looking right at me.

"Mrs. Divekar!" he called, waving me over. I had failed to change my last name after my marriage—and in the chaos of the war nobody had cared—so I wondered why he now remembered I was married.

I considered pretending I hadn't heard him but knew he would just chase me down. Instead, I walked over, trying to calm my breathing. I had put up maybe ten flyers, only symbolically. He couldn't possibly know. Or had they found evidence linking me to the ILM after all? No. If he knew that, he would have more than one security person with him.

As I approached, I took stock of his somber expression and slightly hunched shoulders and felt relief. He probably needed help finding Yashu for some urgent, dire task. "Hello, Mr. Clarke. What can I do for you today, sir?"

He turned to the British security guard at his shoulder. "We won't be needing your assistance."

"But—" the guard protested. Samuel Clarke cut him off with a sharp shake of his head, and the guard turned smartly on his heel and walked away from us. It occurred to me that perhaps he was this brusque with everyone, not just Indians.

"Please accompany me to my office. And call me Sam." Without waiting for my response, he took my elbow and started steering us out of the crowded atrium and down a hallway.

"Your office?" I echoed, now thoroughly confused. "Is something the matter, sir? I'm sure my supervisor could be of more help."

"I don't need your help," he said. His voice sounded strange, as if he had swallowed something sharp. His tone made me stop asking questions, and we walked silently the rest of the way. His hand, oddly gentle, never left my arm.

He opened the thick wooden door for me and gestured me inside. "Have a seat." I sank into the chair across from his desk. Samuel Clarke—Sam—went around to the other side of his desk but remained standing for a moment. "Can I get you something to drink? Water? Coffee? Tea?"

A white man, offering to serve me? I couldn't pass up the opportunity. "Water, please. Thank you, sir."

He opened an icebox and handed me a cool glass bottle before sitting heavily behind his desk. "Mrs. Divekar, what do you know about your father?" He seemed like a different man in that moment, not the cold superior I saw in the halls sometimes, but a real person.

"He left home when I was very young. I haven't seen him since."

"Do you know why he left?"

"No, sir." I realized he probably had all the records of that day, so I added, "Not really. An officer came looking for him, though. My mother always told me that he became a bad man, and that we were better off without him." In fact, when I was young Aai and I had practiced what to say if anyone asked me about Baba at school. The lie rolled off my tongue.

"At the time, we had reason to believe that your father was

part of a violent fringe organization called the Indian Liberation Movement. Have you ever heard of them?"

I suppressed a snort at Sam's use of the word *we*. As if he, as a teenager, had been involved in tracking down enemies of the British state. I knew this was going nowhere good, and I was beginning to panic. I tried to breathe inconspicuously. "Yes, vaguely. People have mentioned them in passing, on the street and the like."

Sam gave me a curt nod. "We take any allegations or incidents of treason very seriously. The ILM has primarily been active on the outskirts of India for the past few decades. I myself have been quite involved in helping track down such enemies of the state. We recently identified a potential cell, and one week ago, members of the British military undertook a surprise raid on an ILM hideout in Peshawar." He swallowed hard. "We identified one of the bodies from the raid as your father."

For a long moment, I did not understand. Could not. "So he's been taken prisoner?" I blurted out.

Sam looked me in the eyes and said, "No, I am sorry. He was killed."

I made a little sound, something like *oh,* and then, before I could stop myself, began to sob. My whole body clenched up as I gasped for air, and I might have let out a keening noise. I would never see Baba again. We had been rushed on our last call, a few months ago, because Baba was afraid the call might be traced. Had I remembered to tell him I loved him? I couldn't remember anything, not the words we exchanged or even the sound of his voice.

And to think, when I had seen Sam standing there grimly, I had felt relief that he hadn't found out about my part in the flyers. I would rather they discovered everything I had ever done than—

Oh, gods, this was my punishment. Some karmic retribution for murdering all those people. It was my fault, all my fault. I had gone too far, been too selfish. I had as good as killed Baba. I became aware of Sam crouching down next to my chair in concern. "Mrs. Divekar? Can I call someone in here? Miss Kamble, perhaps?"

Somehow, the strangeness of this British man showing concern for me snapped me out of the paroxysm of grief. "Why are you being so nice to me?" I demanded, unable to hold my tongue. I could not bring myself to call him sir anymore. "I'm mourning a traitor."

"He was your father," Sam said quietly. "If tomorrow my father was found guilty of corruption and hanged, I would still mourn his loss."

"I haven't seen him in years," I confessed. "Why am I so sad?" Internally, I added, *Why am I asking this of a Britisher?*

"You had hope." Sam stood up and went back around to his desk. "Normally, we would not inform families of the deaths of . . . traitors. But I advocated for an exception in this case, because you are so loyal and such a shining example of the future we want to build for all Indians." Now he sounded like he was reciting a speech or a press line. Whatever sympathy I had seen or imagined in his features was gone.

Nevertheless, I choked out, "Thank you."

"Don't thank me," Sam said sharply. "Not for delivering such news. I know from your file you have already lost your husband. I am sorry for this compounding tragedy. I spoke to your supervisor to let him know you would be completing an urgent project for me today. If you want to go home, I can find you a taxi."

THAT NIGHT, I went to my Aai's flat. By then my sorrow had congealed into rage, a familiar friend flowing white-hot through my veins. Why should the British get another moment in my motherland when my Baba would never see a free India? I wanted to destroy something, to tear down the Outpost that Baba had always wanted to fell brick by brick, to make someone feel the same pain I did. But instead I sat on my Aai's ancient sofa, hands shaking, waiting for her to come home.

I didn't notice her open the door. She must have looked at me and realized something bad had happened, because she asked, "Did you lose your job?"

I shook my head, at a loss for words. She put down her bag and hugged me to her chest. "Tell me what happened, beti," she said.

The word *daughter* undid me, and tears began pouring down my cheeks. "Baba is dead," I managed. "They killed him. He's dead."

I heard her slight gasp and then she bent down to eye level, her knees cracking. "Kalki, how do you know this?"

"Someone in the office informed me this morning. He died over a week ago. In a raid."

Aai collapsed onto her knees and bent forward. Her entire frame trembled, but she did not shed a single tear. She placed her hands together on the floor, rested her forehead on them, and whispered, "Please accept his soul. Even though he was not cremated, he was a good man." Normally, I rolled my eyes at her prayers and superstitions, but I found new tears pricking my vision as she spoke. She continued to murmur for several minutes, Sanskrit prayers I had never bothered to memorize. I pressed my hands together and listened to her whispers, and with every word my heart beat faster. We could not even properly mourn him according to our custom, because we could not publicly acknowledge what we knew. It was wrong that Aai had to feel this pain, so very wrong.

After several minutes, Aai rose onto her knees and hugged me tightly. "Do not do anything foolish," she said. "That is not what he would have wanted."

I pulled out of her grasp. "He would not have wanted to die!"

"Your Baba was willing to lose his life for the cause. He would not have wanted you to lose yours," she said, her voice wavering.

"You don't know that," I said, feeling the words rise in me like poison. "He would be ashamed that I have not done more."

I remembered that after he took me to the Outpost, he had led me to a street I had never walked down before, until we found ourselves next to a patch of poorly maintained grassy park. At one corner of the park stood a small temple enclosed by three walls and a rickety wooden roof that let in slivers of light. My Baba ushered me inside, and we slipped off our shoes to stand before three statues. There were flies buzzing around old bananas that had been left as offerings, and I tried to breathe in the musty smell as little as possible. Perhaps this was the Baba that Aai spoke of.

Aai pressed her lips together, and I saw them tremble. "He wanted you to be safe."

"Is that why he brought me to the creek? Is that why he taught me our true history? What about that was safe?"

In the hallowed place my Baba brought me to, he did not call for violence or resistance. He pointed out each statue in turn as I fidgeted: Mumba Devi, fashioned out of marble and sitting on a bronze bull that someone had taken the time to polish, the mother goddess of the tribes that had initially lived on these islands and still the patron god of our city. Annapurna, the goddess of plenty, holding a bowl in one hand and a ladle in the other—the fruit had been offered to her. And Shiva, whom even I could recognize, with his trident and a snake around his neck, the destroyer, husband of Parvati.

"He wanted you to know the truth, but he did his work so that you would be safe. Your Baba would never want you to be in danger. Trust me."

Aai knew *nothing*. It was my Baba who had inspired me to start a new ILM chapter. He had wanted me to follow in his footsteps. I could not tell her the truth and put her in danger, but she could not act as though I had no choice. My anger boiled over. "I get to decide what I want and what I don't want. Baba's wishes don't matter anymore, because he's dead!" I shouted.

Aai recoiled from my words as though they hurt. "Your Baba still matters. Without him, you wouldn't be alive."

"Well, maybe it would be better to never have existed in this horrible world. Why would you even have a child in an occupied country? You knew I would be raised in oppression, and you still had me because you were selfish. I never asked to be born."

Aai sat down on the sofa I had vacated, and tears at last began to roll down her cheeks. "Would you—do you really fault me for having you, Kalki?" she asked in a small voice.

For a moment, again, my Baba's voice rang in my ears. "This is a place of goodness," my Baba had said after he finished praying. "The kind of place to look upon with awe."

It was very hot, and I kept hopping from foot to foot so bugs wouldn't land on me. "It's the same as any other place," I told him, although truly I thought the clean and neat walls of British constructions might be preferable.

"And?" my Baba asked. "This is what you should be proud of. That we are still here, worshipping our gods. We can endure anything. We can still find joy, and hope, in our survival."

I looked up at him, confused. This was an old and mostly forgotten temple. There was nothing here to be so emotional about. Baba shook his head. "Ignore me," he said. "I'm talking nonsense."

Now, looking upon Aai's tired, sorrowful face, I regretted everything I had just said. She had lost her husband, and I was shouting at her for having me, something I could not actually fault her for. I was getting carried away and being selfish, as always. I sat down next to her. "I'm sorry, Aai, I didn't mean it. I am so glad you had me, and that I had the years with Baba that I did."

She pulled me closer to her, and I snuggled into her shoulder, inhaling deeply. Aai always smelled slightly like turmeric and cumin and other spices she used to cook, and it was one of the most comforting scents in the world.

"Stay for dinner," Aai said, in a tone that brooked no argument. She got up to begin preparations, and I phoned Fauzia to let her know that I would be spending the night with Aai. I hung up before she could ask any questions, for I couldn't handle telling anyone else tonight.

We chopped vegetables together in silence, and then Aai prepared the bhaji as I rolled out chapatis and heated them over the stove. I slathered extra ghee on each one, and if Aai noticed, she didn't mention it. The potatoes and green beans filled my stomach pleasantly, and at the end of the meal, I felt better. I was too full to rage, if only temporarily.

I WAS DETERMINED to get back to work, for my Baba's memory if nothing else. I first went to Mr. Kapadia's store at opening hour. Somehow, when he saw my face, he knew. "Oh, Rajendra," he said, holding me close. "He will be reincarnated into a free world, Kalki. I know it."

Tears sprang to my eyes again at that, and I tried to dash them away. "I know he would have wanted to thank you, for everything," I managed to say.

"He would not have thanked me," Mr. Kapadia said, pressing a candy bar into my hand for the road as though I were a child. "That is what family does. Now, do not miss the bus."

Somehow, I left. As the bus bumped along the road I remembered meeting Adi in a place similar to this three years ago. Adi, who had carried me messages from my father not once but twice. Had he died too? He had been working with my father, but perhaps then he had remained on the Deccan plateau. I hoped he had someone to mourn him, because I knew that, like me, he was devoted only to the cause. There might have been a spark between us kindred spirits; perhaps if I knew him the way I knew Fauzia I might have felt for him as I did for her. *Perhaps, in another life,* he had written.

My Baba was in another life now. I hoped Adi wasn't.

I got in to work early, trying to force myself to care about doing my job, since I had already missed a full day. The highest-ranked members of the department were of course all white, but I had gone from a data-entry worker to a personal secretary to a drafter for the press relations team of the Office of Rations and Civil Supplies—one of the perks of being the object of my boss's obsession. Even though the work itself was evil, it at least felt useful because of the way it helped the ILM's operations. I told myself spinning rations to an already skeptical public in order to get advance notice of those rations minimized the harm.

I checked the intake basket on Mr. Jenkins's desk and began working through the requests that had come in during my day of grief. There was nothing of interest—mostly explaining continuations of the flour ration as its three-year renewal approached. I lost myself in the mindless task of writing inane British propaganda. I knew that the ILM had its own supply of flour stored for distribution to those families who could not afford the black-market prices. It was harder for us to circumvent the water rations, as liquids were far less portable, but we had designed our own containers to hook up to water lines and transport to the desperately ill. The ILM's day-to-day work was less than glamorous, but it kept our people alive.

Sometime around eleven, Mr. Jenkins strolled into the office. "Good morning, Kalki," he said, maneuvering into his desk. "We missed you yesterday."

I clamped down on the urge to roll my eyes. What he meant was *I missed the opportunity to stare at your legs.* "Good morning, Mr. Jenkins. Mr. Clarke from the legal department requested me just as I entered the building. My apologies."

"Sam sent me a letter saying he needed you two nights ago." He leered at me. "So why do you think he asked for you?"

"I'm friends with some of the girls in his department." This was a clear truth, which he could ask anybody else to confirm, so I hoped it would be enough. "Maybe they recommended me? I don't know, sir."

Mr. Jenkins subsided and began flicking through his paper-work. I tried to return to my work when he asked, "Do people really believe this shite about the Indian Liberation Movement?" He laughed, and I swallowed down a sudden surge of bile, focus-ing on a fixed spot above his head. He repeated, "Do you believe this?"

"I guess I've heard of them," I hedged, wondering where this was coming from. "They always seemed like a myth."

"Yes, yes, they are not much more than that, my girl." He nodded sagely at me. If only he knew. "After all, are you not happy with how things are?"

A smile crept across my face, what Fauzia liked to call the British Smile. Too much teeth, never quite reaching the eyes, but enough to mollify any arrogance-blinded Britisher. I had prac-ticed it with her and Yashu after we started the ILM, just in case we ever fell under suspicion. "I am happy, sir," I said. "Thank you for the opportunity to work here. I feel so . . . fulfilled."

Mr. Jenkins had a short attention span and little capacity to think for himself. Evidence suggested, then, that he had received a memorandum about the ILM. I slowly rolled over to his desk, and he did not complain.

"You are a good employee, one of the best natives we have here," he told me, smiling. I was close enough now to see the ubiquitous beads of sweat on his face. He reached out and patted my leg, a little too close to my crotch for comfort. I forced myself to relax and let his hand rest on my upper thigh, remembering the way Smita had put him in his place the one time he had tried to do anything more. He had not tried again—even though Smita had become a housewife, abandoning her job and the ILM after her fleeting fancy with it apparently subsided, he recalled getting caught. He would not go further.

"Thank you, sir, I appreciate it," I lied easily. "Why do you ask about the Indian Liberation Movement?" My chair was now close enough for me to see his papers. I leaned in a little and subtly pulled down the front of my V-neck blouse. Sure enough, as I exposed the tops of my breasts, his eyes followed. He gestured vaguely to his desk.

"May I?" I asked, brushing my hair to one side and exposing my neck. "I'm curious." He didn't respond, and a stray glance at him revealed a slack jaw and glazed eyes.

I did not have time to marvel at how well my clumsy attempt at seduction had worked as I read the document. It was a travel advisory for all British citizens warning against visiting certain parts of India's heartland because of the violent extremist activities of the Indian Liberation Movement. The message reassured readers that there was no evidence of activity in Kingston, and that although "some natives are taking it upon themselves to post political leaflets," British intelligence did not suggest this had anything to do with the anarchist movements on the mainland. The message then detailed extra protective measures that would be taken to watch for any signs of the movement: special patrols, phone taps, and contraband checkpoints.

I absorbed it all quickly and rolled back to my desk. Pulling the information out of him had been as easy as slicing warm butter. Mr. Jenkins snapped out of his haze and returned to his work as well. He didn't speak of the incident again but kept sneaking sidelong glances toward me.

At five, exhausted from the past few days, I headed back to my flat. Mr. Jenkins had already left after dumping several documents on my desk that I intended to deal with tomorrow. We had a whole group meeting tonight, but Fauzia had a network group gathering just after work. I was fine with that; on a day like this it would be too much to be in her presence, too much to remember our dream of a future together, when my Aai and Baba had dreamed of a future that would never come. I itched, deep in my skin, for some sort of adrenaline rush to wash away the pain and anger. I couldn't wait until our midnight meeting.

After curfew set, I slipped out of the flat. Even though the streets where I grew up would always be my first love, Cotton Green—near where Yashu had grown up—had its own charm. I especially loved the fresh mint color of the Cotton Building, which looked an almost ethereal white under the streetlights. I had my own well-worn routes through the area at this point, so I barely thought about turning the corner into an alley shortcut.

And bounced off of someone.

Biting down an oath, I lashed out to hit the person, and he laughed. I recognized the noise, my blood chilling.

Mr. Jenkins.

He grabbed my wrists in his beefy hands and said, "Oh, Kalki, I was waiting for you. I'm so glad you got my message."

"Your message?" I asked.

"That I left for you in your inbox. To meet me outside your flat. I've been dreaming of this moment for so long."

Before I could protest that I had no idea what he was talking about, he leaned forward to kiss me. I smelled his hot breath and shoved him without thinking. He stumbled back a few steps, blinking as if stunned.

"Stay away from me," I said as loud as I dared. My own voice sounded foreign.

"Slut," he growled out. "What are you doing out here if you didn't want this?"

"I—changed my mind." I knew even as the words left my mouth how hollow they sounded.

"You're out after curfew." A smile twisted his mouth. "It is my duty to report that. But I could reconsider . . ."

He unzipped his pants and walked slowly toward me. I backed away, disgust filling every inch of my body. We stared at each other for a long moment as my limbs filled with ice. And then—

He zipped his pants back up. "I'm not unreasonable, Kalki. I'll give you a choice. Either you can do what you came here to, or you can expect my full report in the morning." He grinned at me, that leering smile, and knew it was no choice at all.

Rage pounded in my ears. Baba was dead but Mr. Jenkins still lived. This repulsive man breathed air my Baba never would. I took a step toward him, and he gave a self-satisfied smirk, reaching again for his pants. Time slowed. It was as if a long line of British men stretched beyond him. Their uniforms mocked me. I reached into my purse and grabbed my pocketknife. I could imagine my Baba kneeling before my younger self, tapping his own neck, telling me the best place to attack a critical artery as a last resort. I would do what my Baba had taught me. I would fight.

And then the world came roaring back into full speed, and I stabbed Mr. Jenkins's neck, the blade puncturing the vulnerable flesh.

He collapsed instantly onto the dirty alleyway ground, arms twitching, looking up at me with an expression of terror as blood glugged out of him.

I backed away, horrified by what had just happened. No. What had I done? I looked down at my hand and all I could see was the blade, covered in blood. I dropped it to the ground.

Mr. Jenkins made a noise of pain, and I started in fright. He attempted to pull himself toward the street, looking to be in agony, and I knew he would not make it till morning.

The same cold clarity of the power plant came over me. I wrapped my scarf around my hands and ran up to him, pressing down hard on his throat. He choked silently, unable to make any noise as all air left him. He convulsed once, twice, under me, and then went still. I squatted down next to him, rocking back and forth on my heels, afraid to touch him with my hands and leave any recognizable mark. Just as in the power plant, I was watching myself outside of my body. I felt nothing.

I picked up my knife and wiped it as clean as I could on the already bloodied scarf. My clothes and shoes had flecks of blood on them, and I thought my skin had some too.

Somehow, the moon had moved far in the sky. I was nearly late for our meeting. I dashed through the streets, not caring who might see me, and burst breathless into our meeting place for that evening, underground and secure.

The other women were all milling about, chatting, but they looked up as I slammed the door.

"Kalki, what happened?" Fauzia asked, already heading toward me.

"I just killed my supervisor" slipped out of my mouth. "I did not mean to." My scarf, clutched tightly in my hands, fell limply onto the ground.

I saw their horrified expressions, and suddenly my stomach roiled. Before I could even stop myself, I had emptied my dinner onto the floor. I stayed bent over for a moment, and as I straightened up, someone pressed a glass of water into my hand. I looked up to see Yashu.

"Drink," she said softly.

"I—" How could I face her? I had killed, again, and for what?

She gave me a slight smile, free of judgment. "I've seen worse. You need to drink." She helped me lift it to my mouth, and then I gulped greedily. When I lowered the glass, she was gone, replaced by Fauzia.

"You killed someone?" Fauzia asked. I heard the unspoken *again?* Somehow, I had ended up sitting in a chair, and the mess of scarf and vomit was gone. How much time had passed? Fauzia crouched down in front of me, her hands warm on my thighs.

"My supervisor. He was in the alley, waiting for me. He thought I had come there for—to—he wanted to—he unzipped his pants and tried to come for me. I pushed him away, but he kept coming. I told him no, I did, but then he threatened to report me for being out after curfew and I couldn't stop thinking about how he gets to live in this world while my Baba is gone and—"

"Your Baba?" Fauzia interrupted.

I hadn't told her. "He was murdered in a raid a week ago. I just found out, yesterday. They told me at City Hall. That's why I didn't come home."

She inhaled sharply. "And then what happened?"

"He was there, and my knife was in my hand, and before I knew it, his throat was open. He tried to call for help, but I— I choked him."

"You're sure he's dead?" Fauzia asked.

I nodded, unable to speak.

"Where is the body?"

I forced the words out and the rest of the team sprang into action around me, going to dispose of the body and get me cleaned up. I vaguely heard Yashu's voice giving orders, instructing people where to go, and I thought I heard Simran expressing admiration for what I had done, but I could not feel anything. I stayed mute, unable to move, until Fauzia bundled me up and took me home.

Back at our flat, I sat on the couch as she made me tea, and in the quiet, I finally found the voice to ask, "Why aren't you furious with me?"

"What do you mean?" Fauzia asked, pressing the cup into my hand and helping me drink.

"Last time, with Mountbatten, you were furious."

"This is different. Or maybe I have changed. But you did not have a choice. If he had reported you—" She shook her head and drew my head to her chest, her face pressed into my hair. My heart skipped a beat at the sensation, at the memory of our brief time together. "I am just glad to have you here with me, safe."

She held me until the morning light, and I stayed leaning against her, my thoughts spinning. Relief warred with disgust. It was too much to process, and even as Fauzia fell asleep I stayed awake. Were these the actions of a hero, as I had always wanted to be, or something else altogether? Who was I?

I walked into work the next day as if nothing had happened, but already our office was swarmed with investigators. One of them asked to see my badge and credentials, and then led me for questioning into the office I had previously shared with Mr. Jenkins.

He sat himself at Mr. Jenkins's desk, and I wondered perversely if he felt the shadow of a dead man over him. I took my own chair across the way from him. Belatedly, I realized I shouldn't know why investigators were in our department and asked, "What is this about, sir?"

"Madam, this is a sensitive issue, and it may be disturbing to hear. I recommend you prepare yourself. Christopher Jenkins was reported missing by his wife around four o'clock this morning. We are treating this as a homicide investigation."

I gasped and put my hand over my mouth, attempting a facsimile of surprise. He bought it, his posture relaxing slightly. "How awful," I said. "What happened?"

What evidence did they have? I knew that Yashu and some others had gone out to do cleanup, and I doubted they had left a trace. We were thorough if nothing else.

"That is what we're trying to find out. As such, we are talking to everyone in this department to determine how and why this might have occurred."

"I absolutely understand, sir. How can I help?"

The officer opened his file. "How long have you been working for this department?"

"About five years, sir."

"And how long have you been working for Mr. Jenkins?"

"The same amount of time, sir."

"Would you consider yourself close to Mr. Jenkins?"

"Well, we shared an office." I tried my best to strike a balance between sad and casual.

"Really?" He paged through my file. "I don't see that here. Your desk number is marked as one of the cubicles outside."

This time, I did not need to feign surprise. "This is my desk and cabinet and processor. Mr. Jenkins had me move in here a couple of years ago. It was . . ." I could not say anything even slightly suspicious. "Easier for him to dictate to me when necessary."

"Hmm, interesting," he said to himself, and marked something down. I angled my head but couldn't glimpse what he had written. "Did he ever indicate to you that he was worried, or that someone disliked him?"

I shook my head. "No, sir."

"Did you see any evidence that someone, in this department or outside of it, might hold a grudge against him?"

"No, although he did occasionally get into arguments with some of the other department heads," I offered. I figured if I could provide an alternate direction, however improbable, they would no longer suspect me—if they did at all. They were looking for a scapegoat. My suspicion was proved correct when the officer wrote nothing down.

"Did Mr. Jenkins tell you what his plans were for yesterday evening?"

"No, sir." And then, because I could not resist, "Why are you treating this as a homicide?"

He sighed and closed my file. "High-ranking officials like Mr. Jenkins are targets for anarchist organizations. We have no reason to believe he would just abandon his family and home."

"I understand," I said.

"We are going to be interviewing every member of this office. If you are withholding anything"—here he leaned forward and stared into my eyes, as if accusing me of doing that very thing— "there will be serious consequences. Please let us know if you think of anything, or if anybody tries to contact you."

"Contact me?" I did not need to fake the quaver in my voice.

"Yes. To extort you."

"I thought you said he was dead," I said.

"That is how we are proceeding." He stood up to leave and the message was clear. Conversation over. My mind raced, trying to determine whether anybody would have information linking us beyond sharing an office. It looked like nobody had gone through my things yet, probably thinking I was no real threat, so I would have to surreptitiously find the note Mr. Jenkins said he left me and pass it to Yashu to burn.

He turned back to me in the doorway. "You will need to move

back outside. We will require this office for the next few days to conduct our investigation."

I picked up my bag and grabbed my important files and loose papers, hoping they included the note. Unbidden, a British newspaper article from last year appeared vividly in my mind. They had managed to track down several of the orphans of our bombings—the Deshmukhs had certainly helped—and taken a photo in the worst of the squalor of the slums. The children were small, serious-faced, sitting in a neat row. Their haunted, empty eyes would chill any soul. They had lost everything, and would never be whole. That the ILM was responsible for these things could not come to light, or the movement in Kingston would be over—I did not think our people would be able to stomach such a thing. In total, thirty-two adults and sixteen children had been killed.

I was an adult with a steady income and a surviving parent, and I was lost. I was lost. Baba's death could not even be karma for what I had done, because I deserved suffering over several lifetimes before I could begin to atone. Forever there would be these children whose lives I had destroyed.

I passed the note to Yashu in a haze, and then sat outside the building, unable to stay within its walls. People knew what had happened and allowed all of us in the rations office a wide berth. It was there that Fauzia found me hours later, deep in the blankness of my soul.

"Come, Kalki. It's time to go home." I could not rise, remembering again how many I had killed, how many in my life had been killed. Was that balance, justice? Or was it just chasing pain with pain in an endless night?

"Let me tell you a story," she said when I did not move. She sat next to me, and our forearms pressed together with a comfortable warmth. "About Krishna. I know you love his stories, and even I know them."

When I didn't say anything, she continued, "A long time ago, in the kingdom of Mathura, the power-hungry king Kamsa imprisoned his sister and her husband, afraid of a prophecy predicting that their eighth child would overthrow him. He murdered each child his sister bore. On the night the eighth child was born, a great storm passed over Mathura. When the son, Krishna, came into the world, his father bundled him up and ran into the night, determined that one of his children would live. The swollen river parted to let Krishna through, and his father exchanged Krishna with a baby in the village of Gokul. Kamsa tried to kill this baby, but she took the form of a goddess and escaped.

"Krishna grew up happily in the village. But across the river, Kamsa began to hear of a mysterious boy in Gokul, and of his extraordinary deeds. For Krishna was not a normal boy. When a mighty rain fell upon the village, he led the villagers to a mountain, which he lifted with one hand to provide shelter for all the people and animals. When a monstrous snake with many heads came to poison the village's river, Krishna fought the snake and danced on its hood until the snake agreed to leave and never return.

"Kamsa became suspicious, paranoid that someone might have the strength to overthrow him and the will to carry it through. He invited Krishna to a wrestling match in Mathura. Krishna sensed something was amiss, but still he agreed to go. At the match, Kamsa set his two strongest men against Krishna, but Krishna easily defeated them. Then Kamsa himself entered the ring. He lunged for Krishna, but Krishna sidestepped and slammed Kamsa's head into the ground, killing him and ridding Mathura of a tyrant."

I turned to look at her, tears in my eyes. Was that her point? To compare murders? To tell me that if the gods had suffered, my suffering could be borne? But then she continued, "After he freed his parents and restored his grandfather to the throne of Mathura, he did so much more.

"He founded his own kingdom, Dwarka. He rescued thousands of women from the clutches of a demon. He fought evil throughout the lands. And then, when all this work was done, he befriended a set of brothers, the Pandavas. When the Pandavas went to war against the Kauravas in the war of the Mahabharata, the great war for India itself, Krishna refused to fight or kill. Instead, he became the charioteer for the Pandavas' greatest warrior. When that warrior faltered, uneasy at the thought of fighting his own cousins and killing his fellow countrymen, Krishna exhorted him to do his duty. To achieve greatness. He had lived a long life filled with complexity and sacrifice, and he knew the price that had to be paid for a better future.

"Krishna no longer needed to fight or kill. His words and thoughts were more powerful than any physical blow could be. The righteous Pandavas won the war, and goodness triumphed. Krishna returned to his kingdom and lived out his days until the world no longer had need of him."

9

BUDDHA, ENLIGHTENED ONE

I learned how to forgive at twenty-seven.

After the disappearance of Mr. Jenkins, the British looked for us. They hunted us. They had blamed Mountbatten on a sole defector, and the bombings on disgruntled strikers, but the killing of a high-ranking official had convinced them that there were larger forces at work. O'Brien passed us information at breakneck speed, trying to help us avoid detection, and Yashu ran the information to us as fast as she could. He would warn us just hours before a meeting that there was a planned raid, or let us know that officers were waiting for us at a planned operation target.

We survived this way for months, dodging and working even more brazenly now that our chapter had been found. One day, Adi smuggled us a message—he was alive, and planning to infiltrate and hold Pune as the West Deccan ILM's new base. He requested that we find a way to concentrate soldiers in Kingston. We spread rumors for weeks of a plan to assassinate the chancellor and take the Outpost, including leaving fake plans in an abandoned warehouse, until one could not walk five feet in Kingston without coming upon a soldier. And although I did not hear from Adi afterward, I learned at work that the rebels had dug so deep into Pune that the British saw little chance of taking it back.

When they came for us, we had no warning at all. Fauzia and I were sitting at the table playing the card game saat-aath, or seven-eight. Just as Fauzia took her ninth hand, putting me in debt to her for the next round, a knock sounded on the door. Three sharp raps.

Both of us stiffened. We could spot official business a kilometer away.

"Police, open up!" came a voice from outside, and then, without a pause, the door burst open. Five officers raced through in combat uniform, guns drawn. Instinctively we both raised our hands into the air, watching in growing alarm as two bureaucrats in unwieldy vests filed in behind them.

"Mr. Clarke?" I asked, confused. What was he doing here?

Sam looked at me, expression unreadable. "We have reason to suspect that leaders of a rebel cell known as the Indian Liberation Movement can be found here."

Fauzia swallowed. "There's nobody here but us, Mr. Clarke."

"I know," he said.

"Enough of this nonsense," the older man cut in. "You are both under arrest for crimes of treason against the British Empire. If you cooperate, we will be merciful."

"We are innocent, sir," Fauzia said firmly. "You have no proof. This is a country of laws. You cannot just break in here with no evidence."

That was, of course, untrue, but it was a good line to stall for time as we determined what we should do. And then Sam stepped forward to hand Fauzia a piece of paper. I recognized it as a letter she had written to request supplies from one of our contacts at a warehouse, although it was signed only "the people of

Kingston"—her handwriting was distinctive to me. It was clearly treasonous, but there was no proof it had anything to do with us.

"We were told by a confidential informant that you sent this," Sam said. "They have provided testimony. Your superiors and handwriting analysts have confirmed this is your script."

I began to panic. I glanced over at Fauzia, hoping my face looked as innocent as possible. How had they learned about us? Now that we were under suspicion, there was little chance of our survival. Could we still prevent the rest of the ILM from being found?

I opened my mouth, knowing silence was an admission of total guilt, knowing I had to do *something,* when—

"You're right," Fauzia said. "That is my hand. I am the head of the ILM here in Kingston. Kalki, I'm so sorry. Please know I never intended to put you in any danger—"

"No," I whispered. "No, Fauzia."

"I'm sorry," she said.

"How could the friend not know?" the older man demanded. "Bring them both in."

"No, wait," Fauzia said. "I promise—"

"What use is the word of a traitor?" the man hissed.

"I can prove it," Fauzia said, her voice calm. "You've found me, so there's no use in lying. I'll give you the names of my people, and you'll find none of them know Kalki. I worked hard to hide it from her. I would always tell her I was visiting my family. You have proof of my actions, but nothing implicating her."

"You'll give up your fellow rebels for a friend?" the man sneered. But he was starting to sound convinced. "Some leader you are."

Fauzia turned to me then, even as the police grabbed her by the shoulders and started to pat her down. "I love you," she said. Her eyes darted toward Sam and the other man, then back to me. Her gaze had a new weight. A finality. "I wish I had the courage— I love you. And I'm so sorry."

I didn't know what was on my face, but it must have been

shock, because Fauzia added, "I'm sorry I never told you, Kalki. I knew you didn't feel the same way." It was for the benefit of the British, but it hurt so badly I thought I might be dying. I remembered the feeling of her lips on mine, those few blissful weeks in the oasis of our love. I remembered, too, our promises that when this was over—and now—

It should have been me saying those words to her, me who loved her enough to save her. She was doing this to protect me. Yet my mouth wouldn't unseal itself, my tongue stuck to the roof of my mouth, while my conscience distanced from my physical body.

"Well," said Sam briskly, as if he were now observing a cricket match instead of the end of two lives, "I think that's all there is to it, then. I'll question Mrs. Divekar myself tomorrow, but I doubt she has anything useful to say. We should search the flat to confirm her story, and bring this traitor in for questioning."

"If this other girl is part of it, she cannot have the opportunity to escape," the man said. "That's against protocol."

"How would she escape when she's under guard?" Sam asked coolly. "It will take at least the rest of the night to search, and one of you will bring her down to City Hall in the morning."

I stood rooted to the spot as Fauzia was cuffed, as she smiled up at me from the floor and the police dragged her out into the night. It happened so fast, and I was voiceless, spineless, useless. Two men stayed behind, tossing our flat, banging in and out of our bedroom, shouting when they found the knives we had hidden under Fauzia's bed in case we ever needed to defend ourselves—further damning her, I knew. I stayed standing in the same place, staring at the door as it swung slowly on its hinges, until my knees buckled and I pressed my cheek to the floor where I imagined I could still feel Fauzia's warmth for the very last time.

When we were children, we learned that we did not feel the earth's rotation because we rotated with it. But I felt in this moment as though I had stopped moving and the earth was turning without me. In another second, I would roll through the wall, and in a minute, leave this city. I would travel around the world, and after a day, I would be back here in this destroyed flat. And a lifetime would have passed.

I SPENT ALL night immobile on the rug, until a guard tried to wake me with a poke of his boot. I was already awake, my mind recalling memories of Fauzia over and over again, but he could not tell. I was not allowed to change or freshen up, and was instead escorted to the car parked outside our complex, shoved into the back seat, and driven to City Hall. I still felt as shell-shocked as I had all those hours ago, disconnected from the world. Samuel Clarke was waiting for me in the lobby, and he frog-marched me all the way to his office, leaving my police guard behind.

"Sit," he ordered when we arrived. He sat behind his desk, his hands clasped so tightly in front of him that his knuckles had turned stark white. "I'm sorry for handling you like that. I can't be seen to go easy on you, even if I've seen enough of you to know you're no traitor."

I said nothing.

"I need to ask you some questions. Pending the results of our discussion, we may ask you to testify."

"No, sir." I hardly recognized my own voice.

"Did you just say no?" He kept his voice remarkably even.

"I will not testify against Fauzia." Here my voice hitched, and a slight piece of Kalki forced its way through.

"Be that as it may, Mrs. Divekar, the British government will decide whether you testify."

"May I see her?" I asked before I could gain control of my tongue. I knew I was making myself look suspicious and failing to follow ILM procedure, but I could think of nothing except Fauzia.

"She is being held in solitary without bail. So no, you may not see her." I slumped in my chair, and he asked, "How long have you known Mrs. Naseer?" Fauzia, too, had kept her last name. Now she would die with it.

"Since I was twelve or thirteen. We went to the same school, had the same friends."

"Did you know about her . . . tendencies?"

We had rehearsed these answers. In the event that one of us got captured, the other would disavow our connection and act as though she didn't know her all that well. The one who got caught would be put to death regardless, and any attempt to mitigate that sentence would only result in more death. At the flat, Fauzia had thrown all rules to the wind to save me. I had always thought I could sacrifice myself. That I would sacrifice myself, if it was called for. But, to my great shame, I had not.

Finally, my training kicked in, and I responded, "No, sir. She kept it well hidden."

"You lived together, though, did you not? Slept in the same room?"

"We met two friends at our school. Bhaskar and Omar. They rented that flat, and so when I married Bhaskar and she married Omar, we all moved in. When they got drafted, we both stayed in the flat. But we kept to ourselves. We stayed on our own sides of the room, and I often stayed with my mother to make sure she was all right—she's getting older, and she has only me. We were friends, but I had no idea about her leanings."

"And what about the feelings she expressed last night?"

"I had no idea. We were married, to men." My voice was flat, lifeless.

"Did she ever hold any gatherings at your flat?"

I shook my head. "We held a few parties, for some of our mutual college friends. Other than that, none that I recall."

"Do you remember her ever leaving the house after curfew?"

"No. Like she said last night, sometimes she would not come home at all, but I assumed those nights she stayed with her family. I did that too."

He did not look up from his notes. "Did she ever talk to you about any illicit activities?"

"No, sir."

"Did she ever bring home any suspicious materials, such as firecrackers or pamphlets? Or any dangerous items? Weapons?"

"No, sir."

"In your opinion, did she have the type of personality to break rules or commit treason?"

What spilled out of my lips wasn't my own laugh, but that of a stranger. High-pitched, fast, uncontrollable. "Fauzia was always orderly and proper. She kept to herself. She wasn't the type." *Her best friend was. She was the type to commit murder and arson and drag Fauzia into it. You have the wrong woman. I'm the reason she was there, the reason you were looking for her at all.*

"Mrs. Divekar, I have to ask this as a matter of procedure. Are you, or have you ever been, affiliated with the Indian Liberation Movement?"

"No, sir." The words were out before I could think twice.

"And yet first your father and now your flatmate were?"

"I must be extraordinarily unlucky." I stared him in the eyes, projecting all the confidence I could. I knew just how flimsy my excuse was.

"All right." He made a few more notes on his pad, then said, "Thank you for your time." Just like that I was safe again. "I do not think we will need your testimony at the trial, but I will notify you should we require you after all. Please stay in the area until noon, and be home before curfew."

"It's today?" I managed to get out. Now that we were outside of my practiced framework, my world collapsed again. If I glanced too quickly at the corners of my vision, would I see darkness encroaching?

"The trial is set for this afternoon." He paused, then added, "It's best to finish this business as quickly as possible and send a swift message. One of our best judges will preside."

I knew I shouldn't ask, but I had to try. "Perhaps I should testify after all? To say I never saw anything—"

He held up his hand to stop me. "You said yourself you had many gaps in observation."

"May I watch the trial?" I asked instead.

"It will be closed to the public," he said. "It's being held in the secure Outpost courtroom. But if the verdict is typical for this situation, you may be able to attend the . . . dénouement."

"The dénouement?" I asked, tripping over the word. It had an ominously heavy feeling to it, despite the light pronunciation.

"Oh, yes. Do you recall your former boss? Mr. Jenkins?" He did not wait for me to respond. "We believe that she was responsible for his death."

"What? Why?" *No, no, no—*

"I'm afraid we can't share that with you, but as a consequence, she will almost certainly hang."

I barely made it to his waste bin before vomiting. He watched me impassively from his chair but handed me a bottle of water when I was done.

"Thank you, sir," I gasped out, surprised.

"We are not animals," he said quietly. "I am sorry for the friend you thought you knew."

I WAS NOT expected to work. Evidently Sam had made excuses for me, so I left the claustrophobic building to feel the sun. Yashu found me on the steps of City Hall and tugged me into a hidden corner before throwing her arms around me.

"You're safe, thank God. I thought I would lose you both." Her whole body was shaking.

"Fauzia—" I wanted to explain that she had given herself up, but my voice broke and I couldn't go on.

Yashu pulled away, her eyes bright with tears. "I know," she whispered. "I feel like I can't breathe."

"What do we do?" I asked.

"What she would want us to do," Yashu said, rubbing a hand over her face. "Keep fighting. I will handle our cleanup. Since our friendship wasn't public, I'm not under suspicion." I had meant *How do we save her?*, but Yashu had a better head on her shoulders. Her love for Fauzia would lead her to do the right thing.

I embraced her once more, then let her go. I was a liability to her right now.

Once noon had passed, though, I had to do something. I had to save Fauzia, as she had just saved me. But how? Fauzia would be under maximum security, held in detention at the Outpost. I remembered Baba's lament that British rule would never fall until we destroyed the Outpost. But it was impenetrable.

And that gave me an idea.

I took a long route to my target, keeping an eye out for anybody who might be tailing me. White officers would stand out, but there were plenty of Indians on their payroll. In time, once I felt confident that any doubts about me were not serious enough to extend to a tail, I ducked into an alleyway and loosened a brick from the side of a building. There was a package stowed away for anyone needing a disguise—nondescript clothes, a patterned dupatta that blended into the night but was still memorable, makeup, and more knives. I changed, wrapped the dupatta around my head, painted my lips red, and stowed the knives under my blouse, hiding my original clothing behind the brick.

I had done this before, playing the damsel while Fauzia was in true danger. But what other choice was left to me?

I headed toward the Outpost. When the awful prison came into sight, I began running toward the officers in front, waving my hands to get their attention. "Sir! Sir! A man stopped me on my way to lunch and told me—told me I had to warn you—" I pretended to pant, as though in desperate shock. "Bomb! They're planning to bomb you!"

As I had predicted, this immediately started a flurry of activity at the entrance of the Outpost. Within seconds, sirens went off inside. The British and their procedures could always be relied upon.

"This is very important," the officer said, holding me by the shoulders. "What did he look like? What else did he say?"

"Beard," I gasped out, gesturing to my face. "Long beard. Short hair. Black. About your height. He said—he couldn't have it on his conscience. Just grabbed me, and yelled at me, and ran."

In front of me, people began streaming out of the building, chaos swirling all around us. The officer swore and turned to grab a colleague. By then, I was already gone. I pulled off my scarf as I entered the crowd, letting it fall below people's feet, and rubbed my lipstick off in a quick motion. I stood straighter, giving myself an extra inch or two of height, and ran around the building. They would be evacuating from every point, but I was willing to bet Fauzia wouldn't be led out the main entrance. After a few moments, a side door swung open and men in black robes and armed officers began filing out, then people in smart suits. I held my breath, and then—

My knees nearly buckled at the sight of Fauzia. Her hands were cuffed ahead of her, and she wore what looked like light blue pajamas. She was flanked at all four corners by large British security guards. Her chin was held high, and despite a yellow-green bruise blossoming below one eye, she did not appear to be in any pain. There were a few other Indians, servants and stenographers by appearance, filing out too, and I slipped into their ranks, blending right in. I kept my eyes trained on Fauzia, taking small steps toward her. Everyone was crowded together, pushing forward and away from the Outpost, but the guards were a problem.

Then one of the judges said something, pointing in the not-so-far distance to where a plume of white smoke was rising. I had no idea what that was, but several of the guards ran ahead to assess the danger, leaving an opening next to Fauzia.

She turned her head slightly when I filled in the gap, and gave a small, soundless gasp before snapping her head forward again. Was that anger on her face?

"On my count," I whispered.

"No." She did not look at me.

"We have to go," I said. Nobody was looking at us, but for how long?

"You need to leave," Fauzia said. "What is wrong with you? Go!"

I ignored her, reaching for a knife, but despite her bound hands she managed to drive her elbow into me. I doubled over, winded. "Do you want us both to die? Do you not care for my wishes?" she hissed. "For once in your life, quit being selfish." It was as though I were on fire, my whole being in agony. I couldn't understand what she was saying.

Fauzia walked away from me, facing her guards, who at that moment had turned to check on her whereabouts. They grabbed her arm and yanked her forward. Just before she disappeared from view, she looked over her shoulder to where I stood, stunned, and mouthed a single word: Go. Then she returned her attention to the people who held her life in their hands, and walked out of sight.

I COULD NOT remember what happened after that. I sat at my Aai's flat until a British officer knocked on the door, seeking me out. He asked me more questions, about Fauzia and her habits, about how I had met her and how long I had known her, about our dead husbands. I answered through numb lips, whatever I said slipping from my mind as soon as I had said it. He escorted me back to my flat before curfew, and I slept on my tattered bed as guards continued their work in the living area. The next morning, I found myself at City Hall. A few people were already milling about, but I ignored them and marched straight to Samuel Clarke's office. He was already there, and he stood when he saw me in the window of his door.

"Please, sir. I want to see the execution," I said. "She should have a friend, however distant, out there."

"The hanging is to be public," he told me. His eyes seemed almost sad, and I resisted the urge to jump across the desk and claw them out. Instead, I clenched my fists so hard that my nails left little crescents in my palms. "You will be allowed. I will let your department know. You can accompany me."

"No!" I shouted without thinking. I could not imagine bearing witness to Fauzia's final moments with this man beside me. "No, that would be improper. After all, I bear some responsibility for—" I choked.

"For what?" Sam asked. "Yesterday you said you knew nothing." His tone held a warning.

"For not realizing what was under my very nose. I don't deserve to accompany you. I will attend as any other."

"It will be at nine, in the square." He returned his attention to the papers on his desk.

"It should be him," I whispered to whatever gods might be listening.

"What was that?" he asked.

"I said, thank you for your time, sir." My voice rose far louder than necessary. He flinched back ever so slightly, and I swept out of the room, consumed by the vision of Samuel Clarke hanging. His playing at humanity when my father had been killed had been a farce. He was who he had always been from that first day in the alley.

The thought kept me occupied as I left City Hall and headed for the square. My stomach turned with nausea. Though I had not eaten in almost a day, I felt full with fear and grief. I thought time would creep in awful anticipation, but it raced by so quickly I could barely keep track. I was lost in my imaginings about her last hours—Would they give her a last meal? Would they allow her nice food, like the paneer she loved so much, or would it be some moldy bread and water? Would she be allowed to bathe?

To pray?—and before I knew it, the clock showed ten minutes to nine and the square was packed.

I stood at the very edge of one of the crowd-control railings, so I could be sure to see everything clearly. Behind me, people morbidly bumped and jostled for a better view. The British had hastily constructed a wooden stage and gallows. It all looked so medieval. I could not believe people still died by hanging—but, of course, it was the best way to make an example out of someone.

At nine precisely, three cars drove up a specially cleared pathway. Fauzia was removed from one and taken up the steps to her fate. A man stood off to the side, reading the charges against the unnamed rebel to the assembled crowd, but I only had eyes for Fauzia.

She was dressed in those same prison clothes, with her face washed and hair brushed, and I was grateful she'd been allowed that much. Samuel Clarke's *We are not animals* rattled around in my head. Her hands were still bound in front of her, but her back was straight and proud. Two men tied objects around her ankles. Weights, my mind supplied, so her neck would snap.

"Do you have any last words?" the man asked. I wondered why they would allow a traitor final words—unless she had agreed to publicly repent in exchange for something. Clemency for the other people caught in the sweep, perhaps? I was sure Yashu had done everything she could to avoid this, but the confidential informant who had given up Fauzia would have at least had information on the circle she led in the ILM. And I knew Fauzia would have traded her own last moments to commute or downgrade others' penalties from a death sentence to imprisonment.

He handed her the microphone, and she began, in her clear, beautiful voice, "I would like to say to all my fellow Indians, let me serve as an example to you. And a warning for if you try to resist."

The man nodded approvingly. Tears pricked my eyes. I had

not yet cried, but the idea of Fauzia giving in to the British now broke me.

And then she said, "I beg you to remember this. Remember that they will stop at nothing to deprive us of our independence, but we will still prevail! Remem—"

The man yanked the microphone away from her, but cheers had already broken out in the crowd. I looked around me, shocked, before remembering that these were the last moments I would ever see her. I turned back toward Fauzia to find her facing the crowd. Her chest heaved, and then she began to sing.

"Sarfaroshi ki tamanna ab hamaare dil mein hai. Dekhna hai zor kitna baazu-e-qaatil mein hai." Her voice, high and steady, soared above the other noise and carried straight to my ears, as though we were back in our flat, our lives still intact, planning an operation. Fauzia had found a ghazal written by a revolutionary decades ago, after the massacre at Jallianwala Bagh.

We had learned in history classes that the brave General Dyer had tracked down and killed rebel leaders in Punjab. But recently, we had found a document by the British themselves, passed to us through Yashu's friend O'Brien, that revealed the truth: British troops had killed more than fifteen hundred Indians that day at a peaceful protest, blocking the exits and massacring them where they stood. Afterward, some of the British were horrified, but more of them viewed General Dyer's actions as the correct approach to Indians.

We had been excited to discover that significant radical art and writing had come of the incident, even if it had been swiftly suppressed. Fauzia had fallen in love with one poem in particular, this ghazal, which she insisted we translate, print, and post. I wondered if anyone else here recognized it, if they understood that it had been written about the strength of rebels, about how death was not the end. *The desire for revolution is in our hearts,* the ghazal went. *Let us see what strength there is in the arms of our executioner.*

Had she known, somehow, what was coming? I had always known how much better Fauzia was than me, but in this moment, I realized that she was more than human.

"Karta nahin kyun doosra kuch baat-cheet? Dekhta hun main jise woh chup teri mehfil mein hai . . ."

And then, improbably, I heard others begin to sing. Fauzia had set the words to a simple, well-known melody, and now all around me people were showing that they too knew the lyrics. That they had read the postings, learned the song, and recognized it now. That they too were rebels, at least in some small way. They might not have known Fauzia's name, for the British wanted her to die in anonymity, but the people of our city knew her spirit. The British didn't seem to know what to do. There were too many of us here, and too few of them to effectively stop us. As I watched them look around in panic, part of me considered running up, grabbing Fauzia, dodging the British and fleeing. I couldn't achieve it, I knew, but still I wanted to. The only thing that stopped me was Fauzia. She was sending us a message, that we couldn't let her sacrifice be in vain.

At last, someone shoved Fauzia up the steps to the trapdoor, but still she kept singing. They looped the noose around her neck and tightened it, but she did not move except to keep singing, her voice growing more strained. I knew that Fauzia would have wanted her last words to be her declaration of faith, but she was giving that up. Tears ran down my face as the whole crowd behind me sang with her. "Wo jism bhi kya jism hai jismein na ho khoon-e-junoon? Kya lade toofaanon se jo kashti-e-saahil mein hai?"

She took a breath as if to continue, but at that moment the trapdoor gave way underneath her, and she fell sharply. The crowd gasped. I watched the body twitch, but it didn't even feel to me like it was Fauzia's.

Silence fell over the assembled, and then, as one, we all continued, "Sarfaroshi ki tamanna ab hamaare dil mein hai. Dekhna hai zor kitna baazu-e-qaatil mein hai."

IN THE MONTH following the swift murder of Fauzia Naseer, the Indian Liberation Movement in Kingston lay low. Or at least, that was the official party line. Our original network met every week, sneaking here and there with the confidence of night, although I was too steeped in grief to attend meetings. Occasionally, my friends would come to my flat instead, in broad daylight, and I attended those gatherings solely by virtue of living there. I mostly stayed curled up on the sofa, breathing in the smell of Fauzia that faded further from the two-room flat every day. Sometimes I would rise to sleep in her bed instead, desperate to grasp at memories of our time in each other's arms. How had I been so foolish to wait? To think that we would have a future? I wanted to beat myself, to tear my hair out, to sleep and never wake. But then my friends would bustle in with fresh dishes and stock up the pantry, throwing away the previous weeks' picked-at leftovers without judgment, and I would open my eyes. Yashu would come too, but she held herself apart. I did not fault her for it. Fauzia had been her dear friend too, for nearly fifteen years.

Our flat was likely under whatever surveillance the British still had the resources for, and I was sure that they had at least briefly investigated every friend Fauzia was known to have. But we had been sufficiently paranoid, and besides the informant who had given up Fauzia, there was no evidence connecting any of us to rebel activities. I went once to visit her family, to return her prayer rug and other possessions that hadn't been confiscated. Her parents would not even talk to me, but I read the condemnation in their drawn, grieving faces: *We know this is your fault.* It was Basma, her younger sister, who took my offerings and gave me a brief hug. "Thank you for being such a good friend," she whispered in my ear. "I know Fauzia is with her husband now." I managed to make it onto the street before weeping again.

Often, my friends would simply sit with me. Maryam would bring a warm blanket, and Simran would pull my head toward her and card through my hair, cracking lame jokes about the tangles she found. In hushed tones, they would give me the latest updates. Some of them I had put together based on my work assignments, but I liked hearing the comforting hubbub of my friends' voices describing the fall of the British.

For that was what happened all around us. Though the British kept pumping out soldiers to gods only knew where, we knew they were losing their grip on us, that these were their death throes. And the effects were felt everywhere. The rations for Indians grew sparser, and even British citizens in their glossy stores had to obey rations.

Better yet, Nigeria in faraway Africa had broken out into open rebellion over the past year. Our Nigerian brothers and sisters linked arms, each and every one of them united against the British. Some of the Indian troops sent there as peacekeepers had even laid down their weapons, or turned them on their generals. The country was now in open war against the British—and they were winning.

But I had lost my will to fight. All I could think of was Fauzia, the last thing she had said to me. *For once in your life, quit being selfish.* Looking back on every action, I could see it, the selfishness that had brought the British to our door. I had been thinking of myself, of what I could do, and Fauzia had thought of everyone else. She was dead because she deserved to be alive, and I was alive because I deserved to be dead. I understood at last, deep in my soul, what I had done the day I approved the bombings. This was what I had inflicted upon someone else. This was what I deserved.

I found myself instinctively leaving my flat at night to run some foolhardy operation, only to turn around and around, unable to act. Unable to endanger others again. Instead, I would punch discarded debris or walls, or kick objects in anger until I was spent, returning home a hollow shell. There was so much anger in me, at myself, and I couldn't seem to vent it.

I would find myself wandering the streets in daylight too, aimlessly returning to places that had once held meaning, to play pretend for a minute or two. Today I found myself near the mango stall where I had spotted Adi Naik all those years ago. Adi had managed to send me a note with the words *I'm sorry. It will not be in vain.* It had warmed me that he had taken the risk to send me a message just to comfort me, and it was indeed some small comfort to read that Fauzia's sacrifice was known beyond our island. But her memory could not bring her back.

Lost in thought, I almost thought I imagined a cry from the alley. My favorite place.

Around me, people ignored the noise. Perhaps it was my mind playing tricks, considering that this was the alley where my encounter with Mr. Jenkins had occurred a year ago. Was this where that first encounter with Fauzia had happened? Fate worked in strange ways. As I walked past the alley, resolutely not turning my head, I thought I heard a voice shout, "Mrs. Divekar? Kalki?"

Too curious to ignore it now, I ducked into the narrow corridor. It took a moment for my eyes to adjust to the shadowy alley. I blinked rapidly, and after a moment, my vision cleared.

Before me lay Samuel Clarke, dressed in an officer's uniform. His head was thrown back against a pile of garbage, which must have smelled something awful, but he didn't seem to care. His hands pressed against his thigh, and a sharp, bloody protrusion of broken bone pierced through his dress pants.

"Oh, thank God, Kalki," he moaned. "It is you. Thank God. Please, help me."

I looked down at him and felt power. Control. Pleasure. Now he was the one in distress, and I was cold and unfeeling. "Who did this?" I asked, rather than responding to his plea. "Who did this to you?"

"Please. I never saw them. Some people came upon me from behind. They beat me with a cricket bat, they shouted horrible things—" He shifted slightly and hissed in pain. "Please, I have worked here for years."

"Why did they beat you?"

"Because!" His desperation heightened the pitch of his voice. "Because I am British, and they hate people like me."

I approached. "So?" I asked, looming over him.

"I have tried—so hard. So hard. To do the right thing by all of you."

I placed a deliberate hand on his bad leg and patted it a couple of times. He writhed in pain and gasped for breath. "You have worked here for years," I told him, bringing my face very close to his. The stench of rubbish filled my nostrils, but the scent of power overwhelmed it. "Every day, you do something wrong. You killed Fauzia."

His eyes, previously full of unshed tears, began spilling their burden down his cheeks. "Please, help me. I have a family. A wife. Surely you wished for your husband, for the man you loved, to come home."

I recoiled backward, disgusted that he would use Indian soldiers for his own gain. "My husband is dead. You know that, and you use it against me? Your kind saw to his death." And inside me, there was a voice waking from its slumber, saying, *I truly love only one thing, and it is not a person.* In its service, I should leave this man here.

But behind Samuel Clarke, hovering over the trash, I saw my Baba. He looked exactly as I remembered him looking eighteen years ago on the day the British drove him out. Eighteen years—an adult life separated me and my Baba. He seemed solid, and real, but I knew it was a cruel delusion of my mind. "You're dead," I told him aloud. "Go away."

Sam looked down at himself, scrambled slightly to turn his body, and then glanced back at me, aghast. I saw the thought in his eyes: *My only hope is a madwoman.*

My Baba merely smiled at me, the way he used to when I said something particularly precocious. "Beti, is this the India you want to live in?"

"You murdered so many of them!" I shouted. "And it never bothered you. This man's blood is not on my hands."

"And then I was murdered in my turn. I did not live to see a free India," he said calmly.

"Neither did I," Fauzia said, appearing from behind him. I cried out, reached toward her hand, but her fingers shimmered against mine. I was imagining her. "I forgive the man who sent me to my death. He did his job, Kalki. Just as we do."

"You are the leader of the independence movement in Kingston," Baba added. "Do your job. Your free India should be better than our British world."

I closed my eyes, trying to scrub away the ghosts. The hallucinations. But my mind was a traitor, and instead I heard voices. Heard my Baba, all those years ago, when he brought me to a meeting after taking me to the creek. I had struggled to recall what had happened for years, and now it all came flooding back: jolting awake, on the floor in an unfamiliar room, and in the next room, Baba's voice. Something was different about it, and I could not make out the words. His tone frightened me, made me want to shrink back against the floor.

Another man's voice responded to him. "Samuel Clarke has just arrived from London, and that's why they've changed their security patterns. To accommodate him. I have it on good authority that his father insisted he be educated here, in the Old Bombay schools."

"He's being groomed to take over," my Baba said.

"Why else would he be here?" the other man said. "He's the princeling of Bombay." The man chuckled, a sound that reminded me of an asura from a bedtime story. "Rumor has it he's a brat and has been begging to go back. The chancellor is distracted. If we acted now—we could wipe out that whole line."

There was a long moment of silence, then my Baba said, "We cannot target the child."

"Are you losing your nerve?" a third voice asked, rasping. "You, of all people?"

"It is not nerve, it's intelligence," my Baba hissed. "You think killing a child will help our cause?" At this I gasped. What was my Baba talking about? But nobody heard me. I clenched my eyes shut, hoping the conversation would end soon. "No! They will call us barbarians as they always do, take their vengeance. Again. Who will be left this time? Our people will be beaten and gassed and worse."

"Or they might—" a high voice began, before the rasping voice cut him off.

"I swear, Jitendra, if you say the people will rise or some such nonsense again . . ."

"There's no need to fight," Baba cut in smoothly. "But that is exactly what I mean. We are alone, and few. Better to survive than to lose more support in some desperate attempt."

"Are we truly to be controlled by them forever?" Rasping-voice sounded sad, and I found myself relaxing, less afraid of these men. "This sort of action is what *they* would have done."

"And that is why we are here and they are gone," my Baba replied. I had not understood as a child. At last, now, I knew. The rebels of old might have considered something like this, but they were no longer with us. It was our choice whether to make something better of our world.

I opened my eyes. My Baba had spared the life of this man, and now Fauzia was dead.

Beneath me, Sam Clarke squirmed. I crouched down beside him again, considering his fate, but my eyes were drawn to the memories of the people I loved, standing above me. I could not stop looking, drinking them in. Something tickled my cheek and I slapped at it instinctively, not wanting a mosquito bite on my face. But my hand came away wet with tears I didn't realize I had shed.

Is this the India you want to live in?

Quit being selfish.

They both disappeared as I made my decision, and I made eye contact with Samuel Clarke. "I hate you too," I whispered to him. His eyes widened in shock, but he smartly said nothing. "But I am going to save you. Because I am not an animal."

At the corner of the street was a phone booth. I strolled over, taking my time, and placed a request to dispatch. Then I returned to stare at him in frigid silence until the wailing cry of the ambulance pierced our ears.

Only then did I crouch down next to him. "You stole my best friend," I told him. "What you did was unforgivable. You might live, but I hope you die a thousand deaths every day knowing that."

He began to cry again, snot dripping down his face pathetically. "I'm sorry," I think he said, but it was masked by the sirens and the raw pain in his voice.

Then the emergency attendants were upon us.

They asked me questions about how I had found him, but I stuck to my story as they examined him and determined how best to move him. The lie stayed simple enough: I had been on my way to buy some mangoes when I heard someone crying out. Investigation revealed that an upstanding British officer had been attacked by some hooligans, so I did what any good citizen would do and called the authorities. Sam stayed conscious enough to insist I come along, and so I stood in the corner of the ambulance as we tore toward the British hospital. They whisked him off, and I sat in the waiting room. An orderly told me Sam would be fine, but he needed urgent surgery, and I wondered why I had been brought here at all.

I lost track of time, staring at the wall feeling sick to my stomach as my thoughts looped in a steady pattern of *I saved Fauzia's killer,* and *She would have wanted me to,* and *She would have wanted not to die.* Then Sam's father, the chancellor, swept in. Well, he arrived in waves. First his bodyguards, who cleared the waiting room of all but me. They must have known who I was, because I was the only brown woman in the area, and they let me sit. Then two aides walked in, followed by the chancellor, and behind him a veritable entourage.

One of the guards prodded me in the back and I realized, belatedly, that I should stand. I rose to my feet, aware for the first time that I smelled like I had rolled around in a garbage dump. I felt curiously ashamed. I despised this man, his posse, and everything that they stood for, and yet my cheeks flushed in embarrassment as I imagined what I might look like.

"So you're the girl who found my Sam," he said, crossing his arms in front of him.

Woman, I corrected in my head, but aloud I said, "Yes. Sir. Chancellor."

"The doctor said it seemed like the attack had happened a few hours before he got to the hospital. If any more time had passed, Sam's prognosis would be far worse." It wasn't a question, so I silently studied him. He had lost weight in the years since I had last seen him up close. Dark rings circled his eyes, and his forehead appeared permanently creased. I hoped I had something to do with that.

"Why did you stop?" the chancellor asked me.

"Excuse me, sir?"

"Apparently several people walked past him before you," he said.

"Apparently," I echoed.

"So why did you stop?" His voice had a strange quality to it that I could not place.

"He called out to me. I know him, from working at City Hall. And when I saw him—I could not leave him there."

"I received your file on my way here." He pulled himself together so abruptly and sounded so matter-of-fact that it took me a moment to realize what he was saying.

"Oh. Okay."

"It says that my Sam prosecuted your roommate for treason just a few months ago." He put his hands in his pockets and stared straight at me.

"Yes, sir. She was hanged." I kept my voice level and marveled at my own restraint.

"And you still chose to save him?" He studied my face, as

though some answer to another unspoken question could be found there.

"Yes, sir." I could not for the life of me figure out the purpose of this questioning.

"And he insisted you come along."

"Yes," I answered, even though he had made a statement of fact.

"Mrs. Divekar, are you having an affair with my son?" he asked in the same monotone.

I choked on my own spit. "I'm sorry, what?"

He sighed, shook his head. "That tells me all I need to know. I had to ask."

Did you? I wondered. I babbled, "I'm just an acquaintance. Our paths crossed at work. A work acquaintance."

"A work acquaintance who saved his life."

"Someone else might have stopped."

"He had been attacked in an alleyway. They took his radio and left him there. It would have been hours before anyone even went looking for him."

"Okay, sir." I did not want to sound obstinate, but more than that I wanted this conversation to end.

"Thank you," he said at last, releasing a shuddering breath. "Thank you for saving my son." To my horror, I saw tears in his eyes.

"Really, I just did my duty as a citizen." Despite myself, I felt some slight sympathy for this man.

The chancellor rubbed at his eyes with his hand. "Forgive me. It has been a difficult few months. Not all Indians are as good as you. Some might be angry, especially since your file says your husband also died in the army. That was a bad mistake, that campaign. Many soldiers died, and for what?" He clicked his tongue.

I had almost missed my omnipresent friend, anger, but here it was again. "What happened to my husband?"

"A mistake was made. His division was sent without protection to a hot conflict area. A regrettable affair."

I could hardly believe my ears. Bhaskar and Omar had died for—a mistake? "Thank you for your apology," I said at last.

"This is not an apology," he replied promptly, although it seemed to weigh on him. "The government cannot apologize for such things, or there might be implications. We cannot debase the value of apologies with such trivial matters, you understand? But know that I am very thankful for your conduct today."

I understood I wanted to punch him in the mouth, but behind him, my Baba slowly came into view. "He is telling you a truth nobody else would. If a British man saved your life, I would be grateful to him too, beti," he said. "That is the India I wish to live in."

The chancellor turned to look over his shoulder at where Baba was standing, then faced me again. "Is there something on me?"

I shook my head. "No, sir. I was just thinking."

"Thinking?" he asked.

"About why I stopped."

"Oh?" He sounded genuinely interested.

"I stopped because . . . leaving him there would have been wrong. Because that is not the India I want to live in. That is all," I said, as if it were a simple choice.

The chancellor tilted his head slightly, then nodded at me once. "Thank you, Mrs. Divekar. You are a good girl." *Woman.* "I would like to give you a gift." He gestured to one of his aides who handed me a thin envelope. "A check. As a measure of our appreciation."

I resisted the urge to look at the amount, deciding instantly that I would send the funds to the ILM front in the north as repentance for benefiting from saving a murderer. Oblivious to my inner turmoil, the chancellor sat himself down in one of the blue waiting room chairs.

"May I stay until he is out of surgery?" I asked. I did not know why, but now I felt I had to see this through.

"Of course."

I sank back down into the British hospital's nice cushions and waited. All the while, I could not help but notice how the chancellor had never seemed more mortal. More vanquishable.

SAVING SAMUEL CLARKE, and waking from the fog of Fauzia's death, only sent me further into a depression. For now I could feel every emotion, could truly comprehend how I had failed my friend and my city. A few months after Fauzia's death, after no further retaliation or investigation from the British, Yashu made the decision to fully resume normal operations, and I didn't stop her. Our meetings had become more frequent now—all of us had a sense that we were nearing that terminal goal, if only we could push through.

One evening, we were to meet at Mr. Kapadia's store. Something told me to arrive early, and despite feeling like I would rather die than move, I dragged myself there. When I entered the back door, three figures stood inside, talking in hushed tones. One of them I easily recognized from his stoop as Mr. Kapadia.

"Hello?" I whispered. One of the other men with him startled, whipping around and brandishing a gun. "Whoa!" I said, holding up my hands.

"Kalki?" The man holstered his gun and was upon me in two short strides, hugging me tight. "Oh my God, Kalki, you're alive." Something about his voice sounded familiar, but I still could not place this man who trembled in my bewildered arms.

"Just as I told you, Bhaskar," Mr. Kapadia said in a calm tone.

"Bhaskar?" I all but shouted, pulling myself away from him to get a better look. Sure enough, Bhaskar stood before me. I could hardly believe it, and I pressed a hand to his chest to confirm he was not a ghost. Mr. Kapadia could see him, and I could feel him—this was real! I threw my arms around him again. "You're alive!"

"Kalki, it is so good to see you again."

We finally separated, and I turned to the second man, now easily identifiable as Omar. He watched Bhaskar and me with an expression of pure misery. "I am so sorry," I said, touching his shoulder. "She died bravely. Fighting. I am so sorry."

Omar mumbled something to the effect of *not your fault,* and I embraced him too. He stood stiff for a moment before relenting and wrapping his arms around me.

I realized, as Omar held me, that I was shaking. They were *alive.* Fauzia was dead, my father was dead, but Bhaskar and Omar were somehow, improbably, alive. The ravages of the British had not been absolute, because here stood my friends. Survivors.

"We did not mean to cause you a fright," Bhaskar said when Omar released me.

I rubbed my arms, feeling suddenly cold. "We thought you dead," I said at last. "We received letters. Fauzia . . . I wish she had known."

Omar clenched his jaw and looked away. "I wished we could have told you," he said at last. "We faked our own deaths during a massacre so we could leave. So we could fight."

It all clicked into place. "You deserted," I said softly. "You're in the ILM."

"Don't be angry," Bhaskar said at once. "It was better everyone thought us dead, so we could keep you safe."

"Don't be angry?" I repeated, incredulous. But as I said it, I realized I was not angry. How could I be? We all had to keep secrets from our families and our friends to keep them safe. It would have been monstrously selfish of them to risk sending news back to us, especially since they did not know that we were leading the Kingston branch of the ILM. "I'm not angry. I wish I could have known, but I'm not angry."

Bhaskar gave me a small smile. "I guess we have all grown up, then. I heard you are head of the ILM Kingston—you must have learned some calm, seeing how long your chapter has survived."

My body tensed at his words, thinking back on all I had done in the past few years. I had gotten lucky, rather than learning any lesson. But that did not matter. Bhaskar and Omar were here, and members of the rebellion to boot. This was a happy moment. The opportunity to reunite with long-lost friends was so unfathomably rare. "How did you learn that?" I asked at last.

"A man by the name of Adi Naik," Bhaskar said. "He's the head of the West Deccan ILM, and if I'm being honest, I think he has a bit of a thing for you."

"Excuse me?" I asked, even as I ducked my chin and my cheeks involuntarily flushed. Adi had sent my friends back to me. So many survivors, and yet Fauzia, Fauzia whom I had loved more than any other being in the world, was still gone.

Bhaskar shrugged. "I'm only speaking the truth."

I laughed, then asked, "What are you doing here?"

They both shared a glance. "The West Deccan ILM has recently reestablished a long-forgotten route into the city in order to assist your chapter. They thought you might need military experts, so that you could finally push the British out," Bhaskar said. "But when we heard what happened to Fauzia, we begged to be sent."

"We dealt with your traitor." Omar spoke with a dangerous intensity, one that made his face look almost foreign to me.

"My traitor?" I repeated.

Bhaskar gave a grin that bordered on feral, and I took a step back. Suddenly the hollows of his cheeks were filled with shadow. "Smita Deshmukh. The girl who gave Fauzia up."

It was a wonder I stayed standing, because my heart dropped out from my chest. Oh God, of course it was her. She had been at the power plant when Abhaya had been betrayed. She was in Fauzia's cell. I covered my mouth with my hand, feeling the acid guilt rise. How had I not seen it? Smita had killed Fauzia, and by inviting her, I had killed Fauzia too.

"You didn't know?" Omar asked. "She admitted it to us, before she died. That's how word got to us that the hanging was Fauzia's, because one of the Deshmukh men was bragging about giving the tip-off."

I felt disconnected from reality. I hadn't thought of Smita in years, not since she left her job and Fauzia ruled her out of aiding with the strikes. She had been beneath my thought. My utter, disgusting hubris. I must have gotten lucky that there was only proof implicating Fauzia. Or perhaps Smita had not mentioned me, because—what? I had been nice to her? My stomach churned.

I could not speak, for any word would be incriminating, or worse. These were not the men I knew. Their actions were unfamiliar, nothing like I remembered. They had changed. It wasn't just the beards and the clothes and the dark circles under their eyes. They had been altered on a deeper level—and perhaps I had been, too.

"There must have been others," Omar said. "Officials who helped? Surely you want them to pay."

Getting revenge for Fauzia's death might once have been appealing, but after everything that had happened with Sam I had no stomach for it. And I was scared that where once our interests had been personally aligned, we were now divergent in rebellion. "I don't know," I said. "The only way to get true revenge is to tear it all down." There was a brief, uncomfortable silence, and I rushed on. "What kind of military expertise?"

"Explosives," Bhaskar said, one hand hitting the other in a sharp gesture. "And we can train up your people, bring in weapons along the same route we came."

Maybe, years ago, I would have welcomed the opportunity to make our ILM more outwardly violent. But I had witnessed the results of such untargeted destruction in our city, and I knew that reckless militarism from the front couldn't work here. I swallowed. "I am not sure the ILM Kingston's members would be much good at that," I said at last. "We are effective without that, at the least."

"How can you say that?" Omar demanded. "If you had been armed when—"

"Fauzia would still be dead, and I would be dead too." I met his eyes, trying my hardest to project confidence. "We cannot fight them, not like that. You are welcome to stay here, and teach self-defense—"

"Since when are you a coward, Kalki?" Bhaskar interrupted. "The Kalki I knew was always itching for a fight."

"Since I learned that stealth is safer. We've tried violence—and all it did was end lives, without making progress. We will destroy them from the inside, use their own weaknesses against them." My anger began to swell. "Who are you to act like you knew me so well? We were friends for what, a year? Do not presume to know me."

Bhaskar reared back as if struck. "You don't mean that. For years, you were our lifeline. All those letters . . . You both meant so much to us—"

"Leave it," Omar spat. "So you'd rather cooperate? Is that who you are? We know you work for the British. We just didn't think you would have such a soft spot for them."

"Everyone, please take a deep breath," Mr. Kapadia interjected. I had almost forgotten he was there, sitting on a chair by the wall. "You all want the same thing."

"I want the people of this city to be safe," I hissed, so mad at being accused of cooperating that I could almost see red. "Bhaskar and Omar clearly have other priorities."

"Ah, yes," Omar said softly. "The way you kept Fauzia safe."

My anger spilled over so fast that I moved to slap him. He caught my wrist like it was nothing, his grip crushing. We glared at each other for a moment, and then he shoved me hard, sending me tripping over a chair. The side of my face collided with the floor and my vision briefly dissolved into sparks.

"That is enough!" Mr. Kapadia snapped. I tried to get back to my feet. Tears were flowing down my face as the rage and the hurt came pouring out. Omar had hurt me. And maybe I had deserved it. Maybe this was punishment for letting Fauzia die. Maybe they had a point.

And then Omar was at my side. "I'm sorry, Kalki. I'm so sorry. I shouldn't have—I'm so mad. I'm so mad. She's dead, and it's not fair."

I held up a hand to stop him from touching me. "I know. But more death cannot pay for death."

"Death is inevitable in a war," Bhaskar said. There was silence as the three of us stood facing one another, each closing in on ourselves. The empire had changed us all for the worse. "Perhaps she would have died in any world where the British still reigned. But she would want us to finish this, wouldn't she?"

This, at least, I knew. "Fauzia would not have wanted another soul to die. I know that for sure. I . . ." I took a deep, steadying breath, trying to find the Kalki who was a leader. "I love you both very much. And I am glad to see you. But your skills are of more use to Adi. Please tell him that we appreciate the offer, but we will fight on our island the way we know best. And when this last war is over, we will be together again."

Bhaskar stepped forward and embraced me, but this time it was the sharp squeeze of a goodbye. Omar had tears in his eyes. "I'm so sorry, Kalki. I don't know what came over me."

"It's okay." I touched the side of my throbbing face. "If anyone can understand, it is me." Had I not told myself I deserved a thousand more hurts for what had happened to Fauzia? "Please, stay safe."

There was nothing more to say. They both bent to touch Mr. Kapadia's feet and then they were off into the night. Mr. Kapadia got me a compress with a heavy sigh. "I think they just wanted to see that you were all right."

I thought about how they must have felt hearing of Fauzia's execution. When they heard the name of the dead woman, they would have known I was part of the rebellion too, for we went in all things together. Not long ago, I might have done the same foolhardy thing as them. I could understand the lengths we were all driven to, to keep those we loved safe and proud. "I am all right," I said at last.

He gave me a kind smile, though he somehow looked sad. "I think you are, now. You have no idea how happy that makes this old man."

I pressed the ice to my face, trying to understand what I might be missing. "What's wrong?" I asked.

"I am old, Kalki," he said. "I was older than your Baba, and I am nearer seventy than sixty." His hand trembled. "I just want to live long enough to see us freed."

"What is it?" I asked.

He sighed. "Cancer. It started in my kidneys, but now . . . well, sometimes, the British aren't our killers."

"Where are you getting treated?"

"You don't want—"

"No, I do want to know."

"At the Catholic Hospital of Kingston."

"That piece of shit?" It was as good as a death sentence. "At least go to Old Bombay Medical Center."

"I can't afford it." He left it there, but I heard the unspoken words behind it.

"Because all your life savings have gone into our operations. Because you have helped us pay to smuggle people out and buy materials on the black market, and you have closed the store early to help with meetings and printed our pamphlets for free."

"It is worth it."

"No, no, it's not." I prayed, to whoever listened, Vishnu or Ganapati Bappa or Allah, for a miracle. We were due for one about now. "I can find the money for treatments at Bombay Medical. I have some savings from my salary. Let the British money do that much."

"I am afraid that it is far too late. I waited to go, like a foolish old man, and now I fear no matter where I go, it will not matter. Some things nobody can change."

"No. You are fighting here, you will fight this too. Promise me. And in return, I promise you this: You will live to see India freed." I had not promised such a thing to anybody. Not Aai, not Baba, not even Fauzia. I could not guarantee anybody's survival to our independence day. But Mr. Kapadia had fought for longer than any of us. By my estimation, he had now fought even longer than my Baba. And so, to him, I would promise the near impossible.

"I do not know how much I can fight," Mr. Kapadia said softly. "Perhaps I have expended it all on the British."

"Imagine if I was the one saying this to you."

"Well, you are young, and I am very—"

"No. You are not giving up now, Uncle. You will not." I would not lose him too.

AFTER THE MEETING, I took the long way home despite it being well after curfew. Mr. Kapadia's news had given me the odd urge to visit the gods, and my feet bore me to the temple I hadn't visited in more than a decade. Mumba Devi looked tired, or perhaps that was the effect of the low light from the streetlamp. But still she sat there, implacable. Worn but unyielding. It brought a small smile to my face. The Outpost was still standing, yet so were we. I didn't really believe anymore, but I could appreciate the symbolism enough, standing here tired and alive in the moonlight.

I bent in a moment of respect and then went back to my flat, noting each familiar structure. We were here. I was here. I didn't have to be a hero. I just had to resist, to fight. That was a privilege, something Fauzia had died to give me. I had to honor her love.

At last I found myself in my building, feeling calmer than I had in a long time. When I entered my flat, there was a familiar woman waiting for me.

"So are you going to explain why you were at the meeting with a giant bruise on your face?" Yashu demanded.

"How did you get in here?" I asked, looking around.

"I have my ways. Answer the question."

"It's nothing," I muttered, half hoping she would insist on knowing and half hoping she would drop it. I didn't want to confess that I had been castigated by my late husband and my friend for my failures.

She dropped it. "Okay. Whatever trouble you're getting into . . . it can't reflect back on the ILM. We're starting to get close, actually close, and the last thing we need is for someone to get reckless in their anger and bring us all down."

I recognized her words with a sort of horrified detachment. It was a conversation all of us in the leadership cell had practiced many times, when greener or more aggressive members of the ILM needed talking down. It was meant for the cell leader to give. And Yashu was here to give it to me. "Was it a group decision?" I asked at last. "That my grieving wasn't up to standard?" I kept to myself that I did not deserve to grieve. That I had introduced Smita to Fauzia, and Smita had betrayed her, just as Yashu and Fauzia had warned. That was a shame I would take to my death. Omar and Bhaskar had enacted their justice for it, but it brought me no pleasure or peace.

Yashu frowned a little. "Fauzia was my friend too. You both were my best friends. We're all grieving. But you need to snap out of this, hard as it might be. You're a good leader, Kalki. We need you back. We're all suffering a million griefs, and you have the power to help that end."

She was right. And perhaps worst of all for my ego, the ILM was thriving without me. I was not necessary.

"Are you just going to stand there?" Yashu asked after a long minute.

"How have you been doing?" I said instead.

"Is this because I said I'm mourning too?" she asked. "Don't worry about me. I am fine."

"No," I said. "I ask because I've finally realized how selfish I have been. I made you promises six years ago, and I never checked if I kept them. I never bothered to do anything other than what I wanted to do."

"I'm not going to stand here and tell you you're perfect," Yashu said. "But I meant what I said. You're a good leader, strong and dedicated and smart. And you knew when to delegate, because you knew you couldn't be a good leader for every group. Do you remember that girl, Lakshmi, who you saved from the burning truck?" I nodded. I could not forget. "She has joined up, now. She asks me about you. You're her hero."

"I shouldn't be," I whispered. "You should be her hero. It was my fault she was hurt at all. I haven't done enough. All our problems are still here."

"It is true that nothing short of the abolition of caste can be enough," Yashu replied. "But you have kept your promise, and the most oppressed of this city have not been forgotten. Do you remember when I took you to the factory dormitory?"

It was hard to forget. About a year ago, shortly after the Mr. Jenkins incident, Yashu asked me to come to a meeting of one of the cells she ran, which met in an Indian-owned leather factory that profited immensely in the British markets and had its own living quarters. Enough time had passed from our bombing, and she wanted to show me the state of the places we had targeted. The quarters turned out to be filthy cots crammed together without latrines, and the meeting was less about overthrowing the British and more about self-protection within the community. I sat in the back and listened with growing horror as the workers described countless atrocities: working conditions that had killed or maimed many of their cohort, and assaults at the hands of the factory's managers. I remembered Yashu's calm after Mr. Jenkins. How many traumatized women had she comforted? How could this be happening at the hands of our own people? I did not know what to say about the absolute inadequacy of my ability to help. "I remember."

"I brought you there so you could learn, though the workers didn't believe someone like you would come at all. But when some of the worst offenders suffered their . . . mysterious changes in fortune, they knew you had not only come, but listened to them."

"They were testing me?" I asked, confused. I had done little. A few words here and there, to try to determine whom we knew who held the debts of the worst perpetrators, using the vast network of the ILM to enact a small pittance of the justice that was due. It was not enough, we both knew. It was possible only because they were managers, and not the protected collaborator families. I did not understand how I could have possibly passed.

"That was their life, their every day. Before they aligned themselves to such an abstract cause as independence, they also needed to know that its leaders weren't just leaders for certain people. This evil existed before the British, and it will exist after."

"I know," I said softly. "I agree. You were always right. I was only slow to see it."

Yashu gave me a small smile.

"So I need you to get back to work. Whoever is our leader at the end of British rule is probably going to be our leader at the beginning of independence, and as much as I have come to like and respect the others, I trust you, Kalki. And even if the last few weeks have been difficult, the plans are working. The smaller collaborators are suffering, the British are suffering because of them, and there are more targeted strikes happening among their servants now. Her death . . . it changed things. They made a mistake, and we're close now. Your work is continuing on, and when the time comes, I'd rather it be you."

"No," I said.

"Excuse me?" Yashu demanded. "Look, I'm being nice to you, but I'll yell if I have to!"

I laughed, because it was so very Yashu and I had missed her. I had missed this.

"This is not funny. What has gotten into you, Kalki? You're acting with all the sense of a pig rolling in shit, and you don't look much better—"

I grabbed her hands before she could truly get started on her rant. "You're already leading the ILM Kingston. It's you. You're better at it than I am—"

"Do you hear yourself?" Yashu said. "Is this some misplaced upper-caste guilt?"

"No," I broke in. "I can see this clearly. It should have been Fauzia as the leader all along, not me. And now it should be you who leads. You're already doing it. Look at you! You didn't believe at all in the possibility of change, you did not think we could do anything but curl up in a ball and try to protect ourselves. You got mad whenever I mentioned independence. You thought it was a fool's errand, and now you're leading us all on the march to victory. You believe that you can change things, for the city and for your people. You have changed, and I have not, and that's why it has to be you. Because you have been right all along, about what our people need to truly be free." I hoped she could tell how much I loved her as I spoke, how much she impressed me with her courage, because now, thinking back on it all, I was in awe of her.

Yashu took a step back from me as though I were infected with some contagious disease. "I don't want to put myself in that position."

"If you're worried about others, then I'll—"

"It's not just that," Yashu said. "You can't just decide on your own that you want a radical power change in the middle of a conflict."

I shook my head. "I already decided, with my actions. You stepped up, and we've accepted you."

"I don't want to do this alone," Yashu said slowly. "If this is you asking for help, then I'll help you. I'll stand beside you. But you cannot shirk your responsibilities either."

"This is really what you want?"

Yashu nodded. I extended my hand to her in the British custom, and with a grin she clasped it.

"Your face really does look awful," Yashu said after a moment. "Does it hurt?"

"It doesn't not hurt." Yashu rolled her eyes, and I went to find something for my bruise. "Distract me, Yashu. Tell me a story, like when we were kids."

I rubbed some of Aai's all-purpose herbal oil on the injury, wincing at the pain, and she heaved a sigh. "Very well, if I must. You know that many Buddhists were Dalits who converted, and I'm named for Buddha's wife."

"You've mentioned it once or twice," I said.

"It's a good story," she said. "Although it may not be violent enough for you."

"I've had my fill of violence," I told her honestly.

She squeezed my hand. "Once upon a time, a prince named Siddhartha Gautama was born into a great kingdom in northern India. His family needed a child to inherit their kingdom, and his coming was celebrated across their territories. On the day of his birth, his father, the king, consulted a seer about the prince's future. The seer had never before encountered such a future, for he saw that this baby would become either the greatest king the realm had ever known or the greatest holy man in the world.

"The king wanted his son to become a great king, not a holy man, so he sheltered Siddhartha from all suffering and prevented him from learning any religious teachings. The king thought that in this way Siddhartha would have no reason to become holy. To keep his child happy and content, the king provided his son with all the material goods he could ever want.

"But Siddhartha wanted to know more about the world beyond his walls. One day, the young prince escaped out into the city with only a servant as his companion. Outside the palace, he encountered an old man, suffering from the usual maladies of the elderly. The prince could not understand what he saw, for those in pain had always been spirited far away from him. His servant explained to the confused prince that all men grew old after a time. Even he would grow old. Horrified, Siddhartha pressed deeper into the city. There he saw someone struggling with great illness, and a woman in deep despair over the loss of her child.

"The prince had never known that such suffering existed in the world. He vowed to find an end to this pain, and by night escaped from the confines of his home. He struggled to make his way in a world he had never known, and for a time, he became a wandering ascetic, reliant on the charity of others. He pushed his body to every extreme possible in his attempts to transcend the ills of humanity. Finally, he threw himself down at the base of a pipal tree and resolved not to rise again until he had discovered a path forward or perished.

"He stayed exposed under that tree for forty-nine days and forty-nine nights, his body wasting away but his mind free and searching, until at last he gained enlightenment. Through his dedication and tireless pursuit, he achieved liberation from the cycle of birth and death and rebirth that plagued the rest of humanity. Dissatisfied with achieving only his own enlightenment, he then went out into the world to spread knowledge of this path to others, so that they might follow him into such liberty."

10

KALKI, RESTORER

I learned how to believe at twenty-eight.

In the months following Fauzia's death, the mood of the city changed. People could no longer bear the weight of the curfews, the drafts, the rations, the abuse, the restrictions, and the subjugation, and finally decided that fighting for independence was worth the risk.

We stepped up our outreach, posting myths in alleyways with small details changed, a code giving information on how to contact us. People sought us out, putting up discreet flyers with complex messages asking for us to contact them, or scrawling graffiti in alleyways using glow-in-the-dark paint and Devanagari script to conceal their information. We began making daylight sweeps to retrieve the information, and even got a few new UV lights. At first, we thought it might be news of the ILM's military victories in Peshawar and Jammu that spurred new members to take a stand. But when we asked people, in their initial interview, what had inspired them to join, they answered over and over: "the

Great Revolutionary Hanging." They did not know the name Fauzia, or what she had done for the cause, or what exactly had led to her execution, but the image of one of their own singing into the face of death did not go unnoticed.

Progress was slow at first, and then exponential. The home-grown movement respawned without our even planning for it, with people manufacturing their own clothes and sneaking down to the salt flats at night to make their own salt. The British knew what was happening, but they now had little manpower in the heartland and could not manage to mobilize more troops with all their other conflicts. One day, more than half the Indians work-ing in City Hall came dressed in kurtas and saris, an offense that should have resulted in firing but was too widespread to punish. It was a message: *Your time is limited. This place is ours.*

After Fauzia's death, I finally came clean to Aai. I still lived in the empty flat I had once shared with Fauzia, but I went home much more often. One night, I beat Aai home and made a veri-table feast out of what little good food we were allowed. I made batata bhaji, with a little more onion than potato. I fried puris in our saved-up old oil and created a raita out of beets, which were far cheaper than cucumbers. And I made a single puran poli—inefficient, given how much I had to grind the filling, but we did not have enough jaggery to make another.

Aai came home and inhaled the scent deeply, eyes closed and smile beatific, before coming to kiss my forehead. "Is today my birthday?" she asked, stealing a slice of chopped beet from the bowl.

"No, Aai." Breathe in, breathe out. "I have something to tell you."

"I know what it is," she said. "I am proud of you."

My mouth dropped open. "You do? You are?"

"You joined the Indian Liberation Movement. After that poor girl's murder, who could blame you? I think your Baba would be very proud of you. No—I know it."

"Oh." I busied myself in setting the table, moving the food out of the kitchen, and heaping both plates high. She sat down, smiling to herself, and we began eating in silence.

After a few minutes, I finally blurted out, "Aai, I didn't join the Indian Liberation Movement. I mean, I guess I did, in a way, but . . ." My voice shook. I could lead thousands, but not confess to my own mother.

"But what?" Aai asked. Her smile had vanished.

"I started the ILM. The Kingston chapter. Well, restarted it. Me and Fauzia and a few other girls. And Fauzia's death . . . it wasn't a traffic accident, like I told you. She—"

"Was executed," Aai finished. Her entire body trembled, with fear or rage or shock I knew not.

"How long?" she whispered at last. "How long have you . . ."

"Seven years," I said. "Formally, it has been seven years. Baba told me to, one day—"

"Your Baba told you to?" she asked, tears in her eyes. "After all that happened, he . . ."

"Maybe not. Perhaps I misunderstood."

She knew I was lying. My Baba had given everything for the cause. He would not have hesitated more than a moment before suggesting such an undertaking to me. "Seven years," she breathed. "Why didn't you tell me?"

"I did not want you to be implicated, should something go wrong."

Aai shook her head. "You did not want me to tell you to stop. You were afraid of my reaction." I stayed silent, knowing she was right. "Would you have stopped if I asked you to?"

"Maybe," I said, truthfully. There was another secret on my tongue, and before I could stop it, I let it slip out. "Once, another ILM member came to the city and offered to take us to Baba. I said no. I'm so—"

Aai raised her hand to stop me. "There is no more you need to say. If we had gone, you would be dead now too, Kalki. And you are all I live for."

She forgave me so easily, so casually, for a moment I hardly understood what she was saying. If we had gone with him, we would all be dead. The Kingston ILM . . . what would have become of it? But I had not known that when I had kept this from her, and I deserved her anger. "Aai—"

She had already moved on. "And Fauzia, she was really killed for it?"

"Yes."

"The hanging that everyone has been talking about. That was Fauzia?"

I nodded, grief aching in my throat.

"Oh, baccha, I am so sorry." Silence descended, and we resumed eating. When she finished, her plate almost shining, she said, "I have joined a cell. I will not tell you which one, as per protocol, and all I really do is help make clothing."

I leaned back in my chair, stunned. "You *what*?"

"Yes, Kalki. It is time, now."

I blinked at her, once, twice. Aai, like Yashu, had once spoken of liberation as a near-impossible task, a fool's errand, and now here she sat before me, confessing her own secret. It became clear to me in that moment, like looking through a freshly cleaned window. We had finally crossed the line from resistance into rebellion.

"Yes!" I shouted, throwing my arms up and dancing out of my chair.

Aai laughed at me. "What's gotten into you?"

I whooped. I could not begin to explain the incandescent joy that propelled me to lift Aai clean off the ground and spin her around despite her protests, before letting her go to shimmy around the flat.

Aai let me celebrate for a few moments, then called me over to her. She had pulled out a length of black thread, which she looped around my left wrist and knotted. "To ward off nazar and protect you from harm," she said. "This family has made too many sacrifices for the future we hope to see. Promise me that there will not be any more."

I swore it to her and touched my head to her feet. She passed a hand over me in blessing, in absolution.

THE BRITISH WOULDN'T tell us this, and of course our information could never be perfect, but we heard that they had been defeated in the north. Jammu and Kashmir and other territories had not only driven out the British entirely but established their own rule. They were self-governed, and it made us believe that we could achieve that for Kingston. These new—Countries? States?—had allied themselves with the Indian Liberation Movement. Through them, the ILM was acquiring supplies: tanks, machine guns, and even, rumor had it, a few helicopters. The British had been forced into the interior of India, abandoning hope of maintaining the frontier, and they openly admitted that the Chinese armies were no longer threatening the border, and perhaps had not been there for some time. But the British returned to safer harbors to find their cities roiling in secret rebellion.

All that was left to do was push through to the finish, a task for which Yashu, with her impressive organizational abilities, was well suited. We spent our evenings planning, clandestine operations forgotten in favor of deciding how we could force the occupiers out in one decisive blow. We planned a date, requested assistance from the ILM's military branches, and reviewed every contingency. I spoke to Adi, using random telephone booths, our short calls a constant patter of energy.

"We can send soldiers by boat to City Hall," he said on our first call. "We can secure Old Bombay that way."

"We must take the Outpost too," I said. "That is the true enemy."

Adi hummed. "I know. We have lost too many to that place." I heard the odd tone, knew we shared this pain. "We can give you weapons. But we would have to fight in the streets for the West Deccan ILM to reach the Outpost. The cost . . ."

I could also not countenance jeopardizing innocent civilians, not ever again. "We will handle it ourselves."

"We can do this, Kalki. You *will* do this."

I found myself, strangely, smiling. Everyone was a believer now, it seemed. The ember of hope had well and truly caught.

But two days before the agreed-upon date, I opened the door of my flat and immediately sensed something was wrong. The shadows were strange, and—a man sat at my table.

I flicked on the lights. Samuel Clarke had grown a beard. That was all I recognized before I grabbed a knife from under my dress and advanced on him. "I saved your life once, but I have no problem with taking it now. Why are you here?"

"I needed to talk to you," he said softly. "Away from prying eyes and ears."

"Get out. I have nothing to say to you."

"But I have something to say to you," he said. "Please. Please hear me out." I advanced on him with the knife. He swallowed, his throat bobbing, and then he said, "I am sorry. I am so very sorry. I—"

"Shut up!" I all but shouted. "What the hell is your problem? Get out or I'll scream. I don't care if the police take me too, as long as they get. You. Out."

"Listen," said a voice. Fauzia's voice. I spun around, but she was nowhere to be seen. "Listen to him."

He shifted uncomfortably in his chair. "Why is this so hard to say?" He took a deep breath. "Old habits die hard, I suppose." His eyes met mine. "I am O'Brien."

I tipped my face back and laughed. I laughed and laughed and laughed. "No," I said. "No."

And then, as if on cue, someone knocked on the door. "Is that the police?" I asked him. "Now that you have confirmed I know who O'Brien is, will they take me too?"

From the other side of the door, though, Yashu's voice called, "Kalki! Open up!"

"I asked her to come," Sam said softly. "I knew you wouldn't believe me. That's my contact. One of my employees."

"Yashu," I hissed, then went to yank open the door. "You have got to be kidding me."

Yashu's eyes were filled with tears. "I'm sorry. I'm so sorry to have kept this from you, but the information was good, and then Fauzia died, and—"

I grabbed her forearm with my free hand, and she flinched. But I knew there was only one appropriate response. "Don't be sorry," I said.

Yashu took a deep breath. "His information saved hundreds of lives. Maybe thousands. He didn't learn her cell had been compromised fast enough to save her, but his work almost single-handedly saved the ILM Kingston. I didn't know that he would be involved in—in what he did. I could never tell you because . . ." Here she swallowed, hard, and looked at a point over my shoulder. "I know how you feel about them, but I knew we needed people on the inside to win. So I made the decision."

I could see why Yashu would have wanted to work with Sam, even though I never would have. The fault was not on her for choosing her method of liberty. It was on Sam and his people for forcing her, for forcing all of us, here in the first place. In the end, I knew that Sam had not given Fauzia up. It had been a random daughter of a collaborator family, a nobody. Finally, I said, "I understand."

"Thank you," she said, squeezing my hand. "He has important intelligence, he said. Could only tell us tonight."

"It's time-sensitive, but a few minutes won't hurt," Sam said. "I think Kalki deserves some answers first."

At this, I whirled on Sam. "When did you start?" I asked. "No. *Why?* Why would you do this?"

Sam's face flushed. "It is a truly horrible story, one for which you may judge me quite harshly."

"Go on," I said, and I made sure my face conveyed the message *I will pass judgment.*

"My friend convinced me to try to rape a girl."

I choked on air in an effort not to laugh hysterically, but he interpreted that as horror.

"Yes, I know. We were fifteen or so, and obsessed with girls. My friend told me he had an idea, and eventually I agreed. One afternoon we picked this random girl walking home from school alone. My friend had done it before, said nobody would stop us, it would be fun. I was young, randy, and unthinking. I went along with it. And then . . . well, then some other girl ran up to us and beat us up, and the two fled the scene. But as I lay there on the ground, it almost felt like my soul entered my body for the first time. All this time I had been walking around with no conscience, no ability to think for myself, unquestioning, and then it snapped into place. I could not believe what we had almost done, and I realized that the Indian girl who had saved her friend was so much better than we ever could be. Why should us heathens, soulless heathens, get to rule over this country?"

I closed my eyes, and in my head I could see Fauzia, alive and well. "The girl who came to her rescue wasn't her friend. The rescuer didn't even know the girl."

"What do you . . ."

"That girl you tried to rape? Her name was Fauzia Naseer. That was the day we became friends."

For the first time in this interminable conversation, true horror dawned over his face. "The same—" He answered his own question with a shake of his head. "My *God.*" I waited, impassive, for him to continue, until he released a shaking breath. "I am sorry, then, triply so. After that incident, I began to remember things. Things from my childhood that I had tried to forget. My mother, she never came here. She refused to. She was half Irish, and when I was a child, I remember she took me to this awful jail back on the isles. While we went on a tour describing how they put down rebels in Ireland, my mother whispered in my ear that my great-uncle had died in that prison. She told me things I didn't want to believe, but . . . I began to see they were true, and we were doing all that here too. She killed herself and they sent me here to escape the shame.

"But I didn't know what to do once I realized what we truly were, because I was stuck here, being groomed for the chancellor's position. I plotted and schemed on my own about how to make what I knew useful to you. Then one day, I passed Yashodhara in the hallway, and I just had the strongest feeling in the world that this woman who seemed perfectly ordinary would know what to do with clandestine information. How do you explain that?" He shook his head.

"I don't know," I said. "But why did you help with raiding the ILM? If you are so devoted to the cause . . ."

"Not participating when given the choice would have appeared suspect. I had to protect my position. At first, I didn't even tell Yashodhara who I was. I wrote her notes with my nondominant hand and went to great pains to disguise my identity, until years had passed and I knew I could trust her. And as O'Brien I am able to help so many more—"

"Who are you to say that your work mattered more than the people you hunted down?" I demanded.

"Kalki—" Yashu began, but Sam beat her to an answer.

"Nobody. I will regret it every day of my life," he said without hesitation. "And then there was Fauzia. Your friend. She confessed so easily, and I thought perhaps you really were innocent, and I wanted to at least spare you if I could. We had barely gotten to the Outpost when she confessed to the murder of Christopher Jenkins, and I wondered what else she might give up if given the time, and so I knew I had to move quickly," he continued. The breath had been knocked out of my lungs. "I did not want her to give up any more information, information that might actually be critical to the cause."

For a moment, I could hardly think. "She—she confessed?

No, you pinned it on her. She wouldn't have!" My throat was swollen, the words forced out with effort.

Sam looked at me like I was the crazy one. "We asked if she had any information about his death, and she admitted to it immediately. She even told us how she did it. She—no." I nodded, clenching my eyes shut so I couldn't see the recognition dawn on his face. "She was covering for you, wasn't she?"

For a horrifying moment, I thought I would burst into tears, at this pain, at this awful joy that she had loved me so much that—

"I am sorry, truly I am," he said. "I told her, right before the end, who I was. That I was O'Brien and that I was sorry. She laughed a little bit, and she told me—" He paused and looked at me, uncertain.

"What did she tell you?" I ground out. The idea that they had shared anything—that Fauzia had died for me and been kind to her killer—was unbearable. My only comfort was that he did not hear her last words. Those had been for all of Kingston.

"She told me that she forgave me. That she understood why I had to do it, and that she hoped this would give me enough cover to keep working. She said she was glad for it. She asked me, 'How many others get to save so many lives with just their own?' "

I could barely control the rage under my skin. "You saw that display of selflessness, and you *still* decided to murder her?"

His face fell, and he looked down at his hands.

"Answer me!" I shouted, restraint slipping.

"I did it because I was afraid," he said softly. "I thought I had a duty to do my undercover work, and I was afraid of compromising my own position. I could have saved her, but I would never have been able to help the ILM again. It was easy for me to trust my intuition, because I needed to be right about this."

I took two deep breaths to prevent myself from punching him in the face. I wanted to hurt him, I wanted to pummel him, to end his miserable life. "And you, in your cowardice, decided to kill Fauzia?"

"It wasn't cowardice!" he insisted, meeting my gaze. "Yes, her death protected me, and I wish that hadn't been necessary. But have you ever considered the possibility, even once, that maybe Fauzia's death is pushing this city to independence?"

"Shut up," I snapped. He had no right to say it, right though he might have been.

"Kalki," Yashu said again, her voice soft and sympathetic. She placed a hand on my shoulder, light as a feather. "You know it's true. I would never have wanted this either, but . . . we both know. The tide shifted. And Fauzia would have gladly made that trade."

I couldn't scream at Yashu, but Sam was still fair game. "What right do you have to claim you had to murder Fauzia on behalf of her own people? She was Indian, and you're just a pathetic British man. You're all the same. You would do anything to save your own skin."

Sam merely bowed his head, guilt written on every line of his face. I felt a brief flicker of shame, but pushed it aside. He deserved this. He deserved it, he had to, because the other option, the possibility that this had all been helpful, or worse, *necessary*— I couldn't take it. I couldn't stand for Sam to be some hero.

"I'm sorry." Yashu's eyes were bright with sorrow. "I'm sorry to have sprung it on you like this. I thought I would tell you after. But the reason we are here is because Sam said he needed help to accomplish something. And I thought of you. The movement needs you."

I could pull myself together. I could be selfless. I could, I *could*. I took a deep breath and squeezed Yashu's hand. "No, I'm sorry. This is about more than—the present is more important than the past. What can we do?"

"Our intelligence knows what you plan to do in two days." Sam spoke so calmly we couldn't understand him for a moment. Yashu made a choking sound, one hand going to her heart. Sam's eyes widened and he raised his hands. "Don't worry! They know they can't win and have been quietly evacuating for a few days now. They're going to flee and say they granted you independence in their benevolence."

Yashu released a stuttering breath. "Then what's the problem?"

"The problem is that they've come up with a plan to cover their tracks. Operation Save the Queen or Crown or something like that. For the next forty-eight hours straight, the furnaces in the Outpost are going to be filled with every single piece of paperwork we have."

My mind was working double time. I understood what this new battle was. It wasn't the last battle for independence, really, but the first one for our future. "So there will be no record of what happened but our memories," I said. "No sham trials or interrogations or disappearances or special intelligence units or assassinations or—"

"We get the picture," Yashu interrupted.

"They'll get away with it all," I whispered. "They'll pretend it never happened."

Sam shrugged. "They'll get away with it no matter what, the way they always have. But it's still important to preserve. The truth matters. The evidence matters. If you were stealthy about it, I could get you in, and then you could try to save some things. Some proof."

I saw in Yashu's face the same determination I felt. "Lead the way," I muttered. The words tasted less like poison than I might have guessed.

WE COULDN'T SEE smoke in the darkness, but we could certainly smell it as we approached the Outpost. "It's already begun," Sam whispered. He had explained how the Outpost had created teams to sort the most damning documents and burn them in the furnaces they had throughout the building.

"That's okay," Yashu said, even though my body had already begun to tense. "We can't stop it all."

"We could have," I said, spite rising again. "If we'd had notice."

"I'm sorry," Sam said. "I couldn't figure out how to delay it without losing my—"

"If this is the end," I argued, "why would you care?"

"If I was in jail, I couldn't warn you, now could I?"

A hot spike of shame burrowed into me. Had I not had the same thoughts, and let Fauzia go to her death as I stood unmoving?

Yashu didn't respond to either of us. "There's nobody at the side delivery entrance," she said instead. "Sam—"

"I took them earlier," he said, holding up a heavy set of keys.

We broke into a jog across the street to huddle by the door. I kept lookout, but the streets were deserted. Not even officers came around this way. "Where is everyone?" I whispered.

"They've been evacuating for days. Only essential staff remain. Old Bombay is a ghost town." Sam finally managed to find the right key, and the door slid open.

"Of course," I muttered. Of course they would all escape any justice, now and forever.

"Better we don't start off with vengeance," Yashu said sharply. "You might not like where that ends up."

She and Sam stepped into the building, and I followed after a moment of hesitation. For all that I had lived in this building's shadow, I had never set foot inside the Outpost. But when I stepped into the dim hallway, the stone underneath felt the same as any other stone. What had I expected? The fiery depths of what the British thought of as hell?

I followed behind Sam, wondering what my Baba would have thought. Perhaps he would have been disappointed I wasn't here to tear the Outpost down. As satisfying as that might have been, though, what could it do?

Voices floated from a room, and instantly we stiffened and went silent. Sam had volunteered to go in first, to tell the men there was an emergency on the next floor up, and clear the room for us. Yashu and I hung around the corner, watching as Sam opened the door and light spilled out.

Sam had lines, was supposed to pretend to pant and immediately direct everyone upstairs. Instead, there was only silence.

Yashu and I looked at each other, wearing what were probably identical looks of terror. Had Sam betrayed us after all?

"I don't know what this is all about," Sam's voice said after a moment.

"Oh, give it up, Clarke," a low voice said. "You're a softhearted fool. Don't make this any worse."

We hadn't been betrayed. Sam had been discovered. Somehow, I found in myself a deep calm, and the knowledge of what to do. I hadn't saved Fauzia then, but I could save Yashu now. "You have to go," I said to her. "They don't know we're here, because this place isn't set up like a trap for multiple people. But in a moment they will close off the other entrances to prevent Sam from escaping. And we can't both die here tonight."

Yashu shook her head. "They don't know we're here. We could both go. We should both go."

"Someone has to save our man on the inside," I said. "I have to try to see the mission through." And who better than me? If I died, I knew Yashu was more than up to the task of the future. In fact, she was meant for it—and I wasn't sure I was. I had saved Sam once, and I would do it again, if for no other reason than we had to try.

"Kalki—"

"Yashu," I said. "You know I'm right. For once, I'm right. It seems they believe Sam acted alone, and they don't have the manpower left to do a complete flush of the building. We have to take the chance. You have to go and I have to stay."

I could barely make out her face, but still I could see when her expression hardened with determination. "I'm coming back," she said. "Don't do anything stupid. I'm coming back for you."

"I love you," I said, pushing her away, back down the hallway. If I never saw her again, I needed her to know. "But don't come back." She began to run, and I turned toward the door, creeping forward. Somehow Sam was still arguing with the men; I could see his back framed in the doorway.

"We're leaving," he was saying. "Why is this necessary?"

"What did you think you could accomplish here tonight?" the other man said. "You're a bit early, I'll grant. We thought you'd get here later."

It was as though Sam hadn't heard the question. "You don't have to do this. You could just walk away and nothing would change." I had no idea how I was going to get him out of there.

A voice from behind me shouted, "There's another one!"

My time was up. I didn't even bother to turn around, just dashed forward and grabbed the back of Sam's clothes, dragging him after me into the hallway, the deafening sound of gunfire behind us. We needed to remain one turn ahead at all times, but this place looked like a maze of fluorescent lights. I kept running, pulling Sam along with me, conscious that there were several officers behind us. I could hear the occasional gunshot when they turned a corner. All we had was the element of surprise, and, I hoped, a bit of luck.

"I don't—" Sam panted. "I don't understand."

I had no breath to waste on words. I pushed through a door marked Exit and found myself at the bottom of a staircase, spiraling upward, with one small exit to the outside painted shut. There was no escape.

We looked at each other and then as one began taking the stairs two at a time.

"Third floor," Sam managed. "Hiding spots."

I heard the slam of a door and shouting as the officers entered the stairwell. I could only hope there weren't more waiting for us at the top, that there was nobody to be radioed.

My legs were burning, but I pushed myself on, following Sam as he took the lead. I spared a glance behind us and didn't see anyone. They were still one turn away, unable to shoot us. Could we lose them?

Sam opened the door as quietly as he could and ushered me through, and we both eased it shut. The lights were on up here too, and there was enough smoke to make things hazy. Sam darted forward, taking the first left, then a right, and opened a door. He shoved me in, then closed it behind us and began searching through the keys he had brought with him.

The room was dark, the only light coming in through a small window in the door. My heart was racing. "Where are we?"

"Janitor's closet. I once thought I could hide prisoners here, so I had the location memorized. It was the first place that occurred to me."

"So there's no way out."

"No." Sam found the key and turned the lock.

"We're going to be found. We're going to die in this janitor's closet." I was becoming more furious as I spoke. "What is wrong with you? This is the worst strategy! We could have at least tried for the roof. And all because you got caught out."

"You didn't seem to have a better plan in the moment," he said. "I'm sorry. Where's Yashodhara?"

"I told her to go. As soon as we realized you were compromised. I stayed behind to—"

There was noise from outside and we both ducked down, watching as an officer jiggled the doorknob, then ran past us.

"I'm sorry," he offered again. Useless.

I opened my mouth to respond, and realized I had nothing to say. If we were going to die here, I didn't want to die berating Samuel Clarke, a man who had done something when others had done worse than nothing.

"Did your wife get out?" I asked at last.

In the scant light, I could see the odd expression on his face. "Yes. My wife took what she could of my files back to England. I was supposed to turn them in . . . I wonder if that's what made them suspicious. I had changed her mind on the whole project, you see."

"How many do you think there were?" I asked him. "How many people like you?"

"There are enough back in England," he said. "But we're usually not allowed out to the colonies. It's all safe and good to have dissent as long as it stays just words, across the ocean. Besides, with everything that happened in Ireland, that continues to happen, most people are too afraid of the colonies and independence to ever push very hard."

"They'd rather be comfortable," I said.

"Yes. They're scared of retribution. And they don't know how bad it is. They still think this is a good thing, that we must civilize by any means. They must believe that. Otherwise, they're . . ."

"Monsters," I finished for him. "If they allow themselves to remain complicit with no effort to help us . . . they're monsters."

We were pressed together, in a way I had never been with any man. He smelled rank. "Not that I don't agree, but your people aren't—"

"Don't finish that sentence," I snapped. If he lectured me about caste or interreligious tensions, I might actually beat him. I peered out the window instead. "Okay, I can't see anybody. We should go."

"Go where? I'm sure they've secured the entrances by now."

"Anywhere but here. We have to try." My instinct told me to go up, higher. They would expect us to flee, and would check higher floors last. Or would they check them first and clear them top to bottom? It didn't matter as much as making a decision. And that was something I was well-versed in.

"Staying here—"

"They'll check this room eventually. Don't be a coward." He flinched at that and pulled out his key ring. I pushed open the door a crack and peered out. The hall remained clear, but I heard the distant echo of footsteps.

"Come on," I whispered, and walked farther down the hall without looking to see if he was with me.

"You don't even know where to go," Sam whispered from behind me.

"Up," I said. "That's the only way we can go."

"This way." I followed him in silence as he led me to another stairwell. He poked his head through the entrance, listening carefully, and then beckoned me after him up to the next floor. Behind us came the sound of a door opening. "Shit," he muttered. We darted into the fourth-floor landing and heard voices approaching. Sam froze, looking to me.

Of course. I lunged for the first doorknob I saw. It turned slightly, then stuck. Was it locked? Jammed? The voices were getting closer. I pushed harder, hoping against hope, staring down at Aai's black thread stark on my wrist, meant to protect me. *Please. Please.* Sam's hand covered mine, and together we pushed again.

The door gave. We tumbled through and found ourselves in a room with stacks of paper everywhere. Tables groaned under the weight of files, and there were others piled on the floor. I remembered, with a flash, breaking into City Hall's files almost a decade earlier. How far I had come.

A door slammed nearby, and we both crouched low, watching as a figure rushed past. I slowly edged out of sight of the window before looking around. "We shouldn't have come here," Sam said. I barely heard him. I had grabbed a packet, a handbook really, off the nearest stack, and couldn't tear my eyes away. *Interrogation Techniques for Native Populations.* I flipped the page. There was, laid out in the table of contents, every one of my worst suspicions and fears. Chapters upon chapters about physical torture. Discussion of native physiology. A section on psychological manipulation, a subsection on religious pressure points. I could only imagine what it might say. *Tell the Hindu their Muslim neighbor turned them in.* A handbook of evil, because if anybody would systematize such things, it would be the British.

"We must be in a burn room," Sam said, examining the files. "Look, here are records of specific people's interrogations."

I turned to look at his pile, and grabbed several yellowing pages off the top. "These are from the 1930s," I said. "Vinayak Savarkar, imprisoned 1910 for the assassination of . . ." The words were blurry, but Sam let out a low whistle. "You know of him?"

"His followers assassinated several British officers in the state, before the Reestablishment. Rumor has it he's the one who gave up Gandhi while he was in prison, hoping for his own release, but that rumor circulates about a *lot* of people."

I scanned the paper. "It doesn't say." The name Savarkar rang a bell, not for Gandhi, but for wanting to split India and rid it of its Muslim population.

"Well, it wouldn't," Sam said. "You would note something like that in a different file."

And what could I say to the administrative habits of the empire? I picked up something off another stack. "We need to save all of this."

"I don't even know how we're going to get out of here alive," Sam said. "But if we do, records of individuals are less important than the overarching policies."

I flinched. Fauzia was a file. This man had been a file. How many people were there who had possessed the audacity to fight for their own freedom, their fate now just a few papers in a burn room? Sam had no right to tell them the policies were more important. I was about to tell him so when we heard loud voices through the door.

"Anyone checked here?" a voice called.

"That's the last one on this floor," someone replied. "We better move fast. Those heathens aren't stopping."

"We should go help hold the gate," the first voice said. They had stopped just outside the door.

"The gate is going to fall," the second one said. He spoke quickly, like he was in a panic. "Let's clear this room, and then we go to the top for the helicopter. It's over."

"Maybe we should go now," the first man said.

The doorknob wiggled but didn't turn. "What are we going to do?" Sam whispered.

I remembered how Fauzia had looked, facing death, and found within myself that same sense of calm. I crawled behind a stack of papers. It wouldn't provide much cover, but I wouldn't be obvious at first glance. And if I died now, here, then I died. I could accept that.

"I can negotiate with them, make them see reason." They were continuing to fight the doorknob. It was only a matter of time.

"They'll shoot you," I whispered. "Hide. At least try to survive."

"I'm not a coward," Sam said, rising to his feet just as the door gave way.

"Oh?" said voice two. "Look here, we've got a not-a-coward traitor."

"You don't have to do this," Sam said. "Don't be monsters. You're better than this. I know you are."

"They've breached the gate," said the first voice.

"Come with us as a prisoner or die now," the second voice said. My ears were buzzing, a rushing noise filling them up. "You have three seconds, traitor."

I could see the cut of Sam's jaw, that odd mole on his brow, as he declared, "No."

Two things happened at once. There was a bang and shouting from down the hallway. And a puff of red came out from behind Sam as he collapsed beyond my sight.

There were more bangs, more shouts. They sounded . . . Indian. And angry. I couldn't understand what was happening. "Get out!" people were shouting. "You're done! Monsters!" The officers ran. I heard screams. I waited for another moment, then, when no new officer appeared, crawled toward Sam.

There was a hole in his chest, making an awful sound as he wheezed for breath. I tried to press on the wound, but I knew it was hopeless.

"I'm sorry," Sam whispered. His bloody hand covered mine. He mumbled something more, which I thought might be *wasn't enough*.

I wanted to cry, but there were no tears in me for him. How stupid it was, how senseless, to die now. I swallowed my anger, my pride, and looked down at his pained face. "Thank you, Sam. Thank you."

His last breath left him. I thought he might have smiled.

"Kalki?" Yashu's voice reached me before she did. I turned to see her appear in the doorway.

"I don't . . . I don't . . ." How was she here?

"I told you I was coming back. We sent out the signal, throughout the ILM."

"I don't understand."

As if realizing I needed more, she crouched down next to me. "I found the first sympathetic house I knew. I banged on it, and I told them. Kalki Divekar is in danger. She's the head of our rebellion, and she has lost everything for you. Please come to the Outpost. And . . . they followed me without a second thought. They called their cell members, and their members called others, and before I knew it, there were hundreds of us. Thousands, maybe. They came for you."

They don't know me, I wanted to say. *They came for you.* But I stayed silent, gesturing for her to continue.

"You both had been in here for an hour when we decided to move. We swarmed the gate and they shot at us, but we were too many to kill. We overwhelmed them, grabbed their guns. The few British remaining ran away and fled to helicopters on the roof. It's . . . I can't believe this, but I think it's over. It's really over." She reached down to close Sam's unseeing eyes, her face clouding with sorrow.

"How—"

"It's too fast to comprehend," Yashu said. "I could hardly believe it myself. I just kept telling myself you both would hold on, that you would make it."

"He was so close," I said. "Seconds away. And it wasn't even *for* anything. We would have kept all these documents, all this proof, either way. He was trying to convince them to lay down their weapons."

"That was stupid," Yashu said, laughing wetly.

My brain was starting to catch up. "Have there been any casualties?"

"A few. But we decided . . . we had to do it. They were surprised. And I told them to let the helicopters leave."

Not so long ago, I would have wanted to shoot them down. "You're right," I said. "Let them go. Their last act was murder, but our first shouldn't be. Not when it's unnecessary."

"Come on," Yashu said. "We'll come back for Sam, but we need to secure the building."

As I stood, I felt a tugging on my wrist. Sam's finger had tangled in the string Aai had tied for me, and the black thread gently unknotted, falling back onto Sam's chest.

Outside the room, I saw ILM members at each corner. Maryam came running down the hall and raised her hand to Yashu in greeting. "Someone said I could find you here! It's done. The Outpost— Kalki, what *happened* to you? Do you need a doctor?"

I looked down and saw blood on my hands, glistening patches on my black shirt. "Not mine," I said. "What is it?"

Maryam's eyes darted between us. "The Outpost is ours. We've cleared it. And . . . there's something you both should see."

I felt within me some sort of crumbling. Though the British had managed to burn a few of their documents, they hadn't been anywhere near finishing. We had won the Outpost, and we had won the truth.

We followed her through the corridors, and I wondered at how impersonal they felt. Like a building had been brought from elsewhere to be this maze of British control. It wasn't even all that nice, reminding me more of Kingston's community hospital than anything else. And it was filled with Indians, nodding as we passed as though they knew who we were. Perhaps now, at last, they did. Once that had been my dream, but now it didn't make me feel anything at all.

"Kalki?" Maryam asked, and I realized she had been speaking to me.

"I'm sorry," I said. "It's all just . . ."

"I was talking about the Outpost, and all it's meant, but— it hardly matters now, does it? Now that it's ours." She pulled me forward, catching us up with Yashu. We entered a much nicer area, an atrium of sorts for the floor, where Simran stood transfixed by a large, thick window. A roaring noise was coming through the glass.

"Oh my God," Yashu whispered, raising a shaking hand to her mouth. As far as the eye could see there were Indians standing outside the building, raising flashlights, chanting and shouting. "What in the—"

"Word spread fast," Simran said.

"It's like all of Kingston is here," I said, half disbelieving.

"It's real," Yashu said, and then she let out a choked sob, her hand grabbing my shoulder. "It's real. Sam's dead and you're alive and we're—we're free."

I looped my arm around Yashu and the both of us stood there, shaking. Beside us, Maryam and Simran clung to each other, their grins wide enough to split the world. At last my own tears were coming, the fever of the past hours breaking. I had survived to see my city liberated. And in the end, I had been in the Outpost while it happened.

"You should go out," Yashu said after a moment. "Go out there and make a statement."

"I should," I echoed, but did not move. My mind caught up to me. "No, I shouldn't. Yashu, you should go."

"Kalki, they know you, this is your—"

I shook my head. "No. This is your moment. I am honored that . . . that I got to play a part in your victory. But it's not mine. Yashodhara Kamble is the leader they need now."

"Kalki," she said softly. She held my hand in hers, ignoring the blood. I saw the moment she agreed, not just to give the speech but with what I had said. Because it was true, if Yashu became Kingston's new chancellor, or whatever we decided was next, she would be unstoppable. I was not meant to do that, to be a leader in the open. "Come join me, okay? When you're ready." And then she was gone, Maryam and Simran leaving with her. I stood alone in the atrium, looking through the shaded window at the street. If I squinted, I could make out details of the figures below, lit by the torches people had brought with them. There was the most familiar woman in the world, pushing a man in a wheelchair through the crowd, aiming for the entrance. I pressed a bloody palm to the window as though Aai could see me. I would join her and Mr. Kapadia in a moment, to revel in the fact that we had all lived to see independence. I had kept my promises to them.

"I knew you would do it, Kalki," Fauzia whispered from behind me. "I never doubted you."

I turned to find her smiling at me, tears slipping down her face, and then her lips ghosted over mine. I could almost feel it.

"I will make sure everyone knows your name," I vowed. "We will never forget."

She reached out to cup my face, and then she was gone, and behind her was—

"Beti," my Baba said. I raised a forearm to my mouth to cover a sob. "I told you the Outpost would have to fall. I am so proud of you."

I took a step toward him, but he too disappeared, and I stood alone. My hands were still wet with blood, Sam's blood. I had lost more than I could ever regain. I had mountains of proof to sort through, crimes to relive, to help bring this city into the future. I had killed my own people for this moment. And all I could think about, all every cell in my body cared about, was that we were *free*.

Did I understand, then, what freedom would mean? What it would cost, whom it would hurt, how we would fail a million times over? No. But I knew that we could overcome any tribulations, because an Indian woman with a dead rebel father and a hanged rebel heart could stand in this building and know her land now belonged to her.

WE BUILT THEM a monument. Two months after we drove the British out, we erected a temporary structure in front of the Outpost, just names hastily carved into marble torn from City Hall. Similar ones were going up all throughout the country, but I cared only for the one in Mumbai, our city reborn. In time, there would be statues and celebrations and far more than this, but I knew we needed this now, an act of memory to end the rebellion and begin a new era. A remembrance to ensure every citizen would know those who had laid down their lives so that we might reach this day: Abhaya Bhosle, Rajendra Divekar, Fauzia Naseer. All those who had died in our bombings.

Samuel Clarke was on the list too, and though I did not weep for him, I knew Yashu did. Yashu, who had just been elected our first commissioner, the leader of Mumbai, the one who had the task of reuniting us with the mainland. Soon the presidencies would be states, and Mumbai would be fully a part of this new country, the future we had wished for but never truly contemplated. I was happy for her, although it was a responsibility I did not envy. Simran and Maryam and Asha and others of our original cell had run for council elections throughout the island and won, others had left to find their families in the rest of India, but I had stayed behind. There was nothing left for me to do.

Mr. Kapadia's name was etched in the marble. He went to his next life the week after our freedom was won.

"I kept my promise," he had said when I entered his hospital room. "And so did you."

"I'm sorry it wasn't sooner," I whispered. "It's not enough time."

"It's never enough time, but it is enough for me. I did what I was meant to do. I watched over you."

I wanted to tell him that he should have gotten to do so many things beyond that, but before I could, Aai said, "Dudhapeksha dudhachya saayila jasta japaycha asata." *You have to cherish the cream on top of the milk.*

It sounded like gibberish to me, but Mr. Kapadia smiled. "Rajendra liked that saying. He would say it about you—'We have to protect the younger generation.' And just look at what you have done. I am so proud of you, beti." My heart had clenched at his use of the term. *Daughter.*

Aai and I sat vigil by his bedside as the rest of the city rebuilt, and Kingston lost a hero.

Bhaskar and Omar came back as soon as the British announced their full withdrawal, and they looked the age they had been when we married, the years lifted off. They wept for Fauzia when her name was read, but they also ribbed me about talking to Adi Naik.

Adi had found me before the dedication, a man on a mission. "You did it," he said, and in his mouth the statement turned to the highest praise. "I have something for you." He reached up to his neck and unclasped his pendant. The silver wheel.

"That's yours," I protested. "I couldn't take it."

He moved behind me, gently sweeping my hair aside, and looped the pendant around my neck. "Your father gave this to me when I became a lieutenant," he said, his breath tickling my skin. "I know he would have wanted you to have it."

I touched the pendant, imagining Baba's hands grasping it, passing it on to a promising young fighter. The spinning wheel of self-sufficiency, the wheel of enlightenment and time. *Thank you* seemed inadequate, but when Adi saw my face, he smiled, and I think he understood.

"I was with your father before the raid," he said. "He and a few others, the elders, decided to make a stand. A distraction, so that the rest of us could escape. It was his idea, for them to sacrifice themselves so that the rebellion might live on."

We have to protect the younger generation. "That sounds like him." My voice was choked, but I pushed on. "His faith was not misplaced."

"It is not fair that I got to see so much of him and you so little," Adi said. "Maybe later I might tell you more about him? Perhaps over dinner?"

"I would like that," I told him, and I was surprised to find I meant it. I could tell he was struggling like I was to know what came next now that our people were free. It wasn't right that Fauzia, who had dreamed a whole life for this day, should not be here, and I, who had never thought beyond it, should.

I stood with Aai as the names were read, our hands clasped together until it was over. "What would Baba have done now?" I asked her. I knew she understood my true question: *What do I do now?*

"He would have celebrated," she said. Her hair was gray, and she was beautiful. Her eyes alighted on my new pendant, and she smiled. "And then he would have found his next cause. Some people . . . that is who they are."

She squeezed my arm and left me alone.

I stood there staring at Fauzia's name until an arm looped around my waist, and Yashu laid her head on my shoulder. "Madam Commissioner, don't you have work to do?" I asked.

She laughed. Despite the new weight on her shoulders, she seemed lighter. "The memorial is built. There's so much left to build."

"I know."

"Kalki," she said, and at her exasperated tone I turned to look at her. "When I didn't believe there was any hope at all, you made me believe in your vision. You gave me a place to put my trust, and now look at our city. So let me repay the favor. There's so much to build, and I have a vision. If you don't trust yourself to know what to do, then let it be your turn to trust in me."

"Are you offering me a job?" I asked. "I think that's favoritism."

She laughed again, and pinched my side. I marveled at the

change in her, and wondered when that change would come for me, if ever. "I'll give you some time to think." And then Yashu too was gone.

I didn't need time to think. I knew that she was right. It was what Baba and Fauzia would have wanted. It was what I wanted. The memorial was done, this chapter closing. It was time to get to work in the new world now, a world where we were still divided by religion and caste and gender, where we were still reeling from the endless poverty and violence and fear of British rule, where we had lost so much for this opportunity to finally, maybe, gain.

"Independence," I said aloud to the empty air, tasting the feel of this word in our newborn land. That perfect word, that ringing bell.

And the city echoed back, *Independence*.

AUTHOR'S NOTE

Rebellion and revolution have always been dear to my heart. For as long as I can remember, I have been hearing stories about those of my family who fought for India's independence and been taught that freedom was an incredible achievement, a triumph over the evil of empire. So it is perhaps no surprise that I have always been obsessed with rebellion stories, from *Lagaan* and *Star Wars* to *Anandamath* and *Les Misérables*. This book was the first I ever tried to write, nearly seven years ago, but it wasn't until I had others under my belt and years of research that I was ready to share this novel with you.

The end of British colonialism in India is not a distant historical event—my grandparents were born in British India. India won independence in August 1947 after a hard-fought battle, filled with sacrifice and pain. Freedom brought with it Partition, one of the largest forced migration events in history, which ended with more than a million dead and tens of millions displaced. The Indian independence movement is credited with being a nonviolent, inclusive movement—and it largely was. But there were also many freedom fighters who undertook violent operations, and their successes in terrorizing the British helped pave the way for the nonviolent movement's victories. And there were great rifts in the movement, on religious, caste, and geographic lines.

The British Empire learned lessons in their failures on the Indian subcontinent and used "improved" tactics to fight anti-colonial movements in their other colonies from cutting off entire cities to punitive camps to long-term curfews. *Ten Incarnations of Rebellion* is an alternate history that asks what might have been had the British used those tactics to prevent Indian independence. The book's timeline branches from real history in the 1910s, with more violent crackdowns on political parties, freedom of speech, and protest movements, and by the 1930s in this world, the major figureheads of independence and their followers have been killed. Over the next decades, this alternate-history India is subjected to militarized rule, constant surveillance, language erasure, and cultural suppression. The main events of the novel take place in a fundamentally altered version of the 1960s, in a city robbed of its young men, where a group of young women take up the torch of rebellion. Many readers will recognize that the book takes place in an alternate version of Mumbai that has been burned down, rebuilt, and renamed Kingston, an incredibly common name used by the British in colonial times.

Every change to the timeline, every act of brutality, every traitor and martyr, every despicable person's good deed and good person's despicable deed, is inspired by real-life events that took place either in India or elsewhere. To explain every real-world equivalent would take almost as much space as the book itself, and so I have included a long list of further reading that I found helpful in my research process, which contains documentation of all the parallels found in these pages and more. I do not endorse the viewpoint of every source, but they all have something interesting and productive to say about colonialism, rebellion, and oppression. While the events of the book are fictional, the actions of the British are not. From India to Ireland and everywhere in between, they have left a trail of genocide, famine, engineered sectarian violence, cultural repression, and theft. And through programs like Operation Legacy, they have put records of their crimes into literal bonfires, hiding the truth from the light of day.

The fights of freedom movements and the legacies of colonialism are not confined to history. Even today, millions live under physical and economic colonialism, and billions continue to be affected by the laws and actions of their former colonial masters. And the aforesaid colonizers refuse to apologize, make amends, or even return stolen items. On the hundredth anniversary of the Jallianwala Bagh massacre of 1919, during which British forces deliberately penned in thousands of Indians arrayed in peaceful protest and fired into the crowd until they ran out of ammunition, many people of Indian heritage expected an apology from the UK. Said the UK's minister of state for Asia and the Pacific: "I feel a little reluctant to make apologies for things that have happened in the past. Obviously, any Government Department has concerns about making any apology, given that there may well be financial implications to doing so. I also worry a little bit that we debase the currency of apologies if we make them in relation to many, many events." Attempts at mealymouthed historical revisionism can be seen everywhere—one need only look as far as the hallowed halls of Oxford or Cambridge to find respected professors declaiming the virtues of the empire for bringing science to the unwashed native masses. Some of these individuals are paraphrased and quoted in the British voices in this text.

Ten Incarnations of Rebellion is not interested in proving that the British Empire was a project of violence and terror. It accepts that as a historical fact. Instead, it is interested in examining the sacrifices and strength necessary to achieve independence, the selfishness and selflessness that go hand in hand in revolution, and the necessity of building coalitions across differences and dismantling indigenous forms of oppression. The main character of the story—and, indeed, every character—is defined by this struggle, her thoughts and actions flawed and imperfect but always in service of her higher cause. *Ten Incarnations of Rebellion* is a love letter to those who fought and an exhortation to keep fighting. The struggle is never over.

FURTHER READING

BOOKS

INDIAN HISTORY

Ambedkar, B. R. *Annihilation of Caste: The Annotated Critical Edition*. New York: Verso, 2014. First published 1936.

Asif, Manan Ahmed. *The Loss of Hindustan: The Invention of India*. Cambridge, Mass.: Harvard University Press, 2020.

Azad, Maulana Abul Kalam. *India Wins Freedom: The Complete Version*. Hyderabad, India: Orient Longman, 2003. First published 1959.

Butalia, Urvashi. *The Other Side of Silence: Voices from the Partition of India*. Durham, N.C.: Duke University Press, 2000.

Chandra, Bipan, et al. *India's Struggle for Independence*. Gurgaon, India: Penguin Random House India, 2017. First published 1988.

Dalrymple, William. *The Anarchy: The Relentless Rise of the East India Company*. New York: Bloomsbury, 2019.

Ghosh, Durba. *Gentlemanly Terrorists: Political Violence and the Colonial State in India, 1919–1947*. Cambridge, England: Cambridge University Press, 2017.

Guha, Ramachandra. *Rebels Against the Raj: Western Fighters for India's Freedom*. New York: Knopf, 2022.

Guha, Ranajit. *Elementary Aspects of Peasant Insurgency in Colonial India*. Durham, N.C.: Duke University Press, 1999.

Hajari, Nisid. *Midnight's Furies: The Deadly Legacy of India's Partition*. Boston: Houghton Mifflin Harcourt, 2015.

Karnad, Raghu. *Farthest Field: An Indian Story of the Second World War*. New York: W. W. Norton, 2015.

Khan, Yasmin. *The Raj at War: A People's History of India's Second World War*. London: Vintage, 2015.

Kolsky, Elizabeth. *Colonial Justice in British India: White Violence and the Rule of Law*. New York: Cambridge University Press, 2010.

Kuber, Girish. *Renaissance State: The Unwritten Story of the Making of Maharashtra*. Gurugram, India: HarperCollins India, 2021.

Liddle, Joanna, and Rama Joshi. *Daughters of Independence: Gender, Caste and Class in India*. New Brunswick, N.J.: Rutgers University Press, 1989.

Malhotra, Aanchal. *Remnants of Partition: 21 Objects from a Continent Divided*. London: Hurst, 2019.

Morton-Jack, George. *Army of Empire: The Untold Story of the Indian Army in World War I*. New York: Basic Books, 2018.

Mukerjee, Madhusree. *Churchill's Secret War: The British Empire and the Ravaging of India During World War II*. New York: Basic Books, 2010.

Palat, Raghu, and Pushpa Palat. *The Case That Shook the Empire: One Man's Fight for the Truth About the Jallianwala Bagh Massacre*. New Delhi: Bloomsbury India, 2019.

Pillai, Manu S. *False Allies: India's Maharajahs in the Age of Ravi Varma*. New Delhi: Juggernaut, 2021.

Pinto, Jerry, and Naresh Fernandes, eds. *Bombay, Meri Jaan: Writings on Mumbai.* New Delhi: Penguin Books India, 2003.

Sarkar, Tanika. *Rebels, Wives, Saints: Designing Selves and Nations in Colonial Times.* London: Seagull, 2009.

Sen, Amartya. *The Argumentative Indian: Writings on Indian History, Culture and Identity.* New York: Farrar, Straus and Giroux, 2005.

Tharoor, Shashi. *Inglorious Empire: What the British Did to India.* London: Hurst, 2017.

Wahab, Ghazala. *Born a Muslim: Some Truths About Islam in India.* New Delhi: Aleph Book Company, 2021.

Wolpert, Stanley. *Shameful Flight: The Last Years of the British Empire in India.* New York: Oxford University Press, 2006.

GLOBAL IMPERIALISM

Chakrabarty, Dipesh. *Provincializing Europe: Postcolonial Thought and Historical Difference.* Princeton, N.J.: Princeton University Press, 2007. First published 2000.

Elkins, Caroline. *Imperial Reckoning: The Untold Story of Britain's Gulag in Kenya.* New York: Henry Holt, 2005.

Elkins, Caroline. *Legacy of Violence: A History of the British Empire.* New York: Knopf, 2022.

Fanon, Frantz. *The Wretched of the Earth.* Translated by Richard Philcox. New York: Grove, 2005. First published 1961.

Gopal, Priyamvada. *Insurgent Empire: Anticolonial Resistance and British Dissent.* New York: Verso, 2019.

Harlow, Barbara, and Mia Carter, eds. *Archives of Empire: Volume I. From The East India Company to the Suez Canal.* Durham, N.C.: Duke University Press, 2003.

James, C.L.R. *The Black Jacobins: Toussaint L'Ouverture and the San Domingo Revolution.* New York: Vintage, 2023. First published 1938.

Jasanoff, Maya. *Liberty's Exiles: American Loyalists in the Revolutionary World.* New York: Knopf, 2011.

Mamdani, Mahmood. *Citizen and Subject: Contemporary Africa and the Legacy of Late Colonialism.* Princeton, N.J.: Princeton University Press, 2018. First published 1996.

Raza Kolb, Anjuli Fatima. *Epidemic Empire: Colonialism, Contagion, and Terror, 1817–2020.* Chicago: University of Chicago Press, 2021.

Sanghera, Sathnam. *Empireland: How Imperialism Has Shaped Modern Britain.* New York: Pantheon, 2023.

Thompson, Leonard. *The Political Mythology of Apartheid.* New Haven, Conn.: Yale University Press, 1986.

Wilkerson, Isabel. *Caste: The Origins of Our Discontents.* New York: Random House, 2020.

WORKS OF FICTION

Chatterji, Bankimcandra. *Ānandamaṭh, or The Sacred Brotherhood.* Translated by Julius J. Lipner. New York: Oxford University Press, 2005. First published 1882.

Singh, Khushwant. *Train to Pakistan.* New York: Grove, 1981. First published 1956.

Tagore, Rabindranath. *Gora.* New Delhi: Diamond Pocket Books, 2020. First published 1910.

ARTICLES

Bhuwania, Anuj. " 'Very Wicked Children': 'Indian Torture' and the Madras Torture Commission Report of 1855." *Sur—International Journal on Human Rights* 6, no. 10 (2009): 7–27.

Corradi, Anna. "The Linguistic Colonialism of English." *Brown Political Review,* April 25, 2017. https://brownpoliticalreview.org/2017/04/linguistic-colonialism-english/.

Ganneri, Namrata R. "The Hindu Mahasabha in Bombay (1923–1947)." *Proceedings of the Indian History Congress* 75 (2014): 771–82.

Kumar, Narender. "Dalit and Shudra Politics and Anti-Brahmin Movement." *Economic and Political Weekly* 35, no. 45 (2000): 3977–79.

Lanzillo, Amanda, and Arun Kumar. "The Invisible Women of Colonial India's Textile Industry." *The Wire,* November 9, 2021. https://thewire.in/history/the-invisible-women-of-colonial-indias-textile-industry.

Omvedt, Gail. "Non-Brahmans and Communists in Bombay." *Economic and Political Weekly* 8, no. 16 (1973): 749–59.

Pathak, Sushmita. "How Bubonic Plague Reshaped the Streets of Mumbai." NPR, March 7, 2021. https://www.npr.org/sections/goatsandsoda/2021/03/07/968856331/how-bubonic-plague-reshaped-the-streets-of-mumbai.

Rege, Sharmila. "Education as 'Trutiya Ratna': Towards Phule–Ambedkarite Feminist Pedagogical Practice." *Economic and Political Weekly* 45, no. 44/45 (2010): 88–98.

Sen, Samita. "Gender and Class: Women in Indian Industry, 1890–1990." *Modern Asian Studies* 42, no. 1 (2008): 75–116.

Spivak, Gayatri Chakravorty. "How the Heritage of Postcolonial Studies Thinks Colonialism Today." *Janus Unbound* 1, no. 1 (2021): 19–29.

Verma, Vidhu. "Colonialism and Liberation: Ambedkar's Quest for Distributive Justice." *Economic and Political Weekly* 34, no. 39 (1999): 2804–10.

Vicziany, Marika, and Jayant Bapat. "Mumbādevī and the Other Mother Goddesses in Mumbai." *Modern Asian Studies* 43, no. 2 (2009): 511–41.

ACKNOWLEDGMENTS

To my wonderful agent, Lucienne Diver, thank you for your unwavering support and belief in this book. I am grateful to have you and the Knight Agency in my corner. To my editor, Natalie Hallak, I am so privileged to have worked with you on this book. You have been a true partner, and *Ten Incarnations of Rebellion* is the book of my dreams because of your wisdom. Thank you. Thank you also to Ivanka Perez for your adept support, and to Aarushi Menon for the perfect cover for this book. Thank you to the entire team at Ballantine and my sensitivity readers for your incredible work on this book.

I am lucky to be so loved that the number of people who have helped me get where I am are innumerable. Thank you to Rebecca for being so generous with your brilliance and joy through the good times and the bad. Thank you to Ehi for your constancy and humor. Thank you to Rucha for telling me, "People don't eat mangoes like that." Thank you to Sione A. for believing in this book from the beginning. Thank you also to Ava, Sarah, Roshani, Emily, and Kate for your support in this crazy industry, to my Pitch Wars cohort, and to Sani, Juvy, Nina, Alex, Hannah, Jamie, Dan, and all my friends who have the patience of saints. Thank you to Judge R. and Judge H. for showing me what it means to embody justice.

To my family all across the world, thank you for your unwavering encouragement. To Aai, thank you for always being there for me, day and night, and for answering all of my questions, no matter how stupid. Your hatred of British colonialism is a continuing inspiration. To my father, thank you for being a cheerleader, paparazzo, and discerning reader all in one. To James, thank you for keeping the house afloat so I can write, and for your enthusiasm and optimism. To Ananya, thank you for the brilliant suggestions, and for being this book's biggest fan.

And finally, thank you to my great grandfather, the first lawyer in the family and a lifelong freedom fighter. Your sacrifices are cherished beyond measure.

CREDITS

BALLANTINE BOOKS

ART AND DESIGN

Rachel Ake
Aarushi Menon
Caroline Cunningham

PRODUCTION

Robert Siek
Katie Zilberman

MANAGING EDITORIAL

Pam Alders
Paul Gilbert

COPYEDITING

Hasan Altaf

PROOFREADING

Liz Carbonell
Susan Gutentag

EDITORIAL AND
PUBLISHER'S OFFICE

Natalie Hallak
Jennifer Hershey
Kara Welsh
Kim Hovey
Ivanka Perez

PUBLICITY

Chelsea Woodward
Jennifer Garza

MARKETING

Kathleen Quinlan
Amy Jackson

SUBRIGHTS

Denise Cronin
Toby Ernst
Rachel Kind

THE PRH SALES TEAM

THE KNIGHT AGENCY

Lucienne Diver
Elaine Spencer
Jamie Pritchett
Travis Pennington
Tyler Knight

ABOUT THE AUTHOR

VAISHNAVI PATEL is the *New York Times* bestselling author of *Kaikeyi* and *Goddess of the River*. She is a lawyer specializing in civil rights litigation, including issues of gender and racial justice. *Ten Incarnations of Rebellion* is her third novel.

vaishnavipatel.com

Instagram: @VaishnaWrites

ABOUT THE TYPE

This book was set in Sabon, a typeface designed by the well-known German typographer Jan Tschichold (1902–74). Sabon's design is based upon the original letterforms of sixteenth-century French type designer Claude Garamond and was created specifically to be used for three sources: foundry type for hand composition, Linotype, and Monotype. Tschichold named his typeface for the famous Frankfurt typefounder Jacques Sabon (c. 1520–80).